The Year of New Beginnings

The Year of New Beginnings

Book Four of The School of Dreams Series

Julia Sutton

Other Books by the Author

The Lake of Lilies

The School of Dreams Series:

Acknowledgements

A big thank you to Miika Hannila and everyone at Next Chapter Publishing, for giving me the opportunity to publish The School of Dreams series.

Thank you to Marilyn Wagner for editing my novel.

Thank you to the awesome readers who have invested their time in this series and have waited patiently for each book to be published.

Thank you to my friends and family for your encouragement, support and kindness.

I have loved creating this series and I hope that you enjoy this final instalment.

☺ Happy reading.

Dedication

For my lovely niece Grace xx

Chapter One

The sun rose steadily in the cerulean blue sky and over the land, tendrils of mist curled and danced. Rain had fallen late last night, leaving the ground damp and dotted with beads of silver dew, and the air smelt fresh, fragrant with the scent of summer flowers: heady lilac and sweet mock orange, the musky undertones of sweet pea mixed with the spicy rhododendron. Blossom fell from the gently swaying trees, lining the street in a cloak of pinks and creams. It was quiet enough to hear a thrush singing from a roof top and then the tranquillity was broken by a chugging sound, a bus turning up the street, fumes erupting from its exhaust pipe.

Evelyn was leaning out of her bedroom window, struck by the beauty of the world around her. Blue tits perched on the nearby telegraph pole in a neat line, swinging and whistling. Their dawn chorus filled her heart with joy, and as she stretched further out, she could see the neighbour's cats rolling in dew dipped grass; bundles of grey fur that made her feel so warm and emotional she felt like a Disney character on the precipice of falling into an eternal void of cliched joyous happiness.

A sudden gust of wind blew back her netting and lifted the leaves out of the gutter, twisting them high into the air. Evelyn shivered, drew her dressing gown tighter around her and turned away. Where to start first on this beautiful summer morning? Breakfast.

At the table she sat, stirring her hot porridge, sipping the sweet tea, enjoying the peace, the solitude, the stillness. Her head felt in a daze, a happy daze of wonder, excitement and a little bit of apprehension. Her stomach somersaulted with the prospect of what was to come, what the day would bring, and a tear sprang to her eye as she considered her dear departed Mam. What would she make of what was about to happen?

Life was full of surprises. Who would have thought after all these years alone she would find love, she would find Jacob. Evelyn stretched out her hand and gazed down at her sparkling ring, a symbol of ardour and attachment and her mind was full of him. The way his eyes crinkled when he laughed, his gentle kindness and the warmth that exuded from him. Her love for him had grown sure and steady. The days she spent with him had fixed the resolution in her. That he was noble and decent were one of the many reasons why she cared for him. Her heart was full of tenderness for him and today was her chance to declare it.

From upstairs she heard a door bang, the patter of feet running across the landing, the flush of the lavatory, the sound of laughter. Sophie stood in the doorway, a pretty vision in her pink pyjamas.

"Good morning," she hugged Evelyn, "it's your wedding day!"

By mid-morning the romantic hue had abated somewhat and the house was in chaos. Josh and Jake were tearing around, zapping each other with Nerf guns. Sophie shooed them outside, warning them to keep their smart wedding attire clean. The dogs were pacing, ears pricked with intuition that something big was occurring. They howled along to the music Sophie played, while she curled Evelyn's hair.

"What time is it dear?"

"It's almost eleven," Sophie replied, "we have plenty of time, so don't you worry." The curling tongs hissed with agreement. "How are you feeling Evelyn?"

"Nervous," Evelyn admitted, "but happy."

"It's such a glorious day for a wedding," Sophie glanced through the window at the brightness, "perfect."

The flowers arrived a short while later. Peony posies fragrant and sweet, buttonholes for the boys and a note from Flora wishing them luck. Evelyn stepped into her cream dress; her hands trembled slightly as she pulled up her zip. Into her ears she slid a pair of pearl earrings and a matching necklace clipped loosely around her throat. Sophie squirted her with a blast of fragrance, "it's Beauty by Calvin Klein," she fussed around her, "Evelyn you're stunning. Look." Sophie pulled her to the full-length mirror.

Evelyn blinked at her reflection, "my," she said, "is that really me?"

"Here," Sophie passed her a pair of ivory shoes, then someone was knocking on the door again. Sophie scurried out of the room, down the stairs. Jake was tugging on the door handle and the dogs were scraping their nails on the floor in excitement.

"It's only me," Jon Stokes poked his head through the gap, "I'm not too early, am I?"

"No," Sophie beckoned him in, "wait in the lounge, she's almost ready."

"I have a surprise for you," Sophie said to Evelyn who was standing at the top of the stairs, "well not just me, from us all. The university gang."

"What is it?" Evelyn's heart was racing with excitement.

"Come downstairs and all will be revealed. Be careful now in those shoes," Sophie and her twin boys were at the foot of the stairs, staring up at her with incredulous faces, "you look sick," Josh said.

"That's a compliment," Sophie said with a laugh.

"Hello," Jon walked into the hallway, "Evelyn you look very beautiful."

"Jon! What are you doing here?"

He lifted a camera, "I'm your photographer for the day."

"You are?"

Sophie giggled, "he's got one of those zoom in and out thingies. Very professional."

"I'm an amateur," Jon cut in, "it's a very enjoyable pastime. I'm going to make you an album, as a gift from us all."

"Oh. That's so kind," Evelyn dabbed at her dampening eyes.

"Your mascara!" Sophie screeched, "no Evelyn. No!"

They stood outside on the garden patio as Jon snapped away, "turn to your left, lift your flowers up, Sophie get the blasted dogs out of the way."

Evelyn's cheeks were feeling strained from smiling so much.

"Almost finished," said Jon, looking around, "just a few more over there on that swing." Obediently, Evelyn trooped over and sat down while the camera clicked, zooming in at different angles.

"I think that's enough," Jon said, smoothly slotting the camera into its case.

"One more surprise Evelyn," Sophie pulled her across the grass, "you have a lift to the registry office. We won't be needing a taxi."

They clattered through the house, Sophie yelled at the boys to come off their computer and to get their shoes on.

"Is Jon taking us?"

"Sure is," replied Sophie, "don't forget your flowers Evelyn."

The car sparkled and gleamed in the morning sunshine. It was so squeaky clean that even the wheel trims were shining.

"I had it valeted, from top to bottom," Jon said, patting the bonnet, "Ann insisted on the ribbon."

"It looks lovely," Evelyn gushed, "shall we get in Sophie?"

Jon pulled the door open, "madams."

Evelyn slid in, followed by Sophie and the boys, "Josh please stop swinging your feet, and Jake – stop picking your nose!"

Jon turned the key and the engine erupted to life, "hold on tight ladies, we're on our way."

* * *

Juliette was peering up the street with an excited Molly hanging onto her hand. Harry was kicking pebbles into the gutter and pulling at his tie.

"Is Evelyn wearing a princess dress?"

Juliette looked down at her daughter and smiled, "I don't know sweetheart, we'll have to wait and see."

A car pulled up a few feet away and Will staggered out, "cheers Mum." Hema followed him out, looking pretty in a lilac sundress.

"Have a lovely day," Flora papped her horn and drove away.

"So, where's the bride?" Will popped a stick of gum in his mouth.

"Not here yet, but Jacob's inside," Juliette smiled, "he's very nervous. How is Esme?"

"Crawling," Hema replied, "and into everything."

"I loved that age. Molly took her first steps at ten months, she was really forward for her age. Harry was a lazybones though, the complete opposite. Oh here's Ann."

"Hey, how you doing?" Will smiled at Ann who was being pushed along the pavement by her mum.

"I'm good thanks. I've bought confetti," she passed the boxes round.

"Have you had a nice summer Ann?" Juliette asked.

"Wonderful. A week by the sea was just what I needed. Bracing sea air, trips down the promenade and fish and chips on Brighton pier. What have you been up to?"

"I've been to Scotland with Ben, and the kids of course."

Ann grinned, "is he coming today?"

Juliette nodded, "he's on his way."

"Is she here yet?" Jacob was hovering in the doorway, peering up the street. A horn tooted in the distance and Jon's car slowly rolled down the road, ribbon fluttering in the wind.

"Get inside Jacob, get inside!" Juliette shooed him into the registry office.

They waited for Jon to pull up and open the back door. Sophie was the first one out, she smoothed down her satin dress before helping Josh and Jake out.

"Aw, Sophie's dress is pretty Mum," Molly twirled her handbag.

"Yes, she looks beautiful."

There was a round of applause as Jon helped Evelyn out.

"I'm so nervous," Evelyn clutched her throat, "is he here?"

"Yes," Juliette fussed around her, "you look amazing."

"Shall we go inside?" Sophie took Josh and Jake by the hand as they followed the others up the winding stone steps. They pushed the heavy oak doors open and entered the foyer. It smelt fresh; lavender polish and scent from tubs of freesias lingered in the air. Their voices echoed around them as they exchanged pleasantries. Then there was a sudden cheer which emanated from the upper floor.

Evelyn gazed up the marble staircase, watching as a young couple surged towards the steps. Their hands were clasped and they were laughing uproariously. A large group of people followed them down, wearing posh attire; voluminous dresses and extravagant hats that wouldn't have looked out of place at Royal Ascot day. Juliette and Sophie were swept along with the noisy crowd.

"Oh look," a young lady with striking cheekbones squealed with excitement, "she's going to throw her bouquet."

"I'll just move out of the way," Juliette scooted along, squeezed through a gap then yelped as an over excited boy literally jumped on top of her feet.

"Ouch!" Pain shot up her lower leg and instinctively she bent over to rub her throbbing toes, then looked up to see an object flying towards her. Instinctively she lifted her hands upwards, palms open as a dainty stem of roses and ribbons landed into them. The girl with the high cheekbones stared at her with slanted eyes, "who are you? They should rightly be mine. I've been with my fella ten years and he still ain't proposed."

Juliette thrust them towards her, "here have them."

"Nah I'm kidding! Looks like you need them more than me," the woman cocked her head to one side, "is that your fella over there?"

Juliette gazed over, her face lighting up at the sight of him. Ben was leaning casually against a stone pillar, his arms folded, a smile playing on his lips. He looked as scrummy as usual.

"Yes. That's him."

"Cor, he's dishy, have you been together long?"

"What?" Juliette tore her gaze away, "no, erm, I mean not long at all."

The crowd slowly dispersed, leaving Juliette room to drift over to him.

"Hi," she smiled up at him.

Ben pulled her into his arms, kissing her lips longingly, "I've missed you."

"It's only been two days since I saw you!"

"I know. I must be smitten."

Juliette's stomach twirled around like a slowly spinning washing machine.

"You look gorgeous," he mumbled huskily, "and you smell divine."

She jumped as his lips touched the curve of her neck.

"And you look very smart. Is this new?" She fiddled with his navy tie which was covered in silver stars.

"It was a gift from my niece," he replied, "you caught the bride's bouquet?"

"Oh yes!" Juliette laughed, "I'm not superstitious in the slightest though, so don't worry."

"Shame," Ben smoothed away a curl that had flopped across her forehead and Juliette gazed up at him, wondering what he was thinking.

"Ben!" Molly tore in between them like a mini whirlwind and flung herself into his arms, "Evelyn's getting married."

Ben lifted her up, "Shall we go get a front row seat?"

"Yes," Molly nodded, her eyes wide with excitement, "where's your beard gone?"

"Your mum made me shave it off."

"I did no such thing," Juliette scoffed.

"Come on," Ben said with a laugh, as they followed the others up the grand staircase.

Sophie and Evelyn waited as the guests filed into the ceremony room, then made their way slowly up the stairs.

"Are you okay?" Sophie whispered, smoothing Evelyn's dress and patting her lacquered covered hair.

"Very nervous," Evelyn admitted, "I can't quite believe what I'm about to do."

Sophie's heart strings were tugged at the look of shock registered on her friend's face, "you're so lovely Evelyn. This *is* happening. Now, come on, let's get you officially wed," Sophie paused, "shall I go in first?"

"Yes please," Evelyn nodded, "oh and Sophie dear, have you got the rings?"

"Tucked safely in here," she lifted a cute drawstring handbag, "I think the music's started, we need to get a shift on." Sophie tugged the door and tripping over the hem of her dress, stumbled forwards. All eyes turned to stare her way and she froze, like a rabbit caught in a pair of headlights.

The first beats of 'stand by me' swooned around the room. Sophie noticed the registrar nodding towards her and her feet moved automatically forward, towards Jacob. He was clearing his throat and mopping at his perspiring forehead.

"Is she here?" His voice had a strained plaintive tone to it.

"She's right behind me," Sophie whispered, sliding into place at the side of him.

The registrar, who was a jolly looking, middle aged woman coughed, "where is the bride?"

Sophie spun round, "she was right behind ..." the aisle was empty and there was no sign of Evelyn.

"Have I been jilted?" Jacob looked heartbroken.

"No!" Sophie was aghast, "just a minor hiccup ... a slight delay that's all. I'll just go hurry proceedings along." She moved away, grinning manically while Josh tugged on her skirt, enquiring when he'd get his chicken nuggets.

"Everything okay?" Ann asked, as Sophie sidled past.

"Just fine and dandy," Sophie's high pitch resounded in the quiet room.

"Evelyn!" Sophie hurried back out, praying that she hadn't run away.

Evelyn was leaning over the balustrade, with her back to her.

"Whatever's the matter?" Sophie beseeched, "this isn't time to day-dream about your novel Evelyn!"

Evelyn slowly turned, her cheeks and throat were stained a deep pink colour. "I-I ..."

"Are you having second thoughts?" Sophie's tongue clacked between her upper teeth.

"No! Maybe?" Evelyn looked as if she were in pain.

"That's normal," Sophie insisted, "I felt the same about Ryan ..." she stopped as she remembered she had just filed for a divorce from her estranged husband, "I mean ... it's okay to be nervous, but Jacob is nothing like Ryan .... Ryan's a rat and Jacob, well he's lo ..."

"What if our marriage is a disaster?" Evelyn's tone was calm, and the resignation in it scared Sophie, "what if Jacob has a change of heart? What if he wants a divorce after twelve months? What will I do then?"

"That ain't going to happen," Sophie held onto her friend's hands, "you know how much he adores you."

Evelyn bit her lip, stared down at her feet.

"Do you love him?"

Evelyn's head snapped up, "of course. Very much."

"Then there's absolutely no reason why you shouldn't be dancing down that aisle," Sophie tutted, "Evelyn, you are going to worry yourself into an early grave, this should be the happiest day of your life."

Evelyn emitted a shaky breath.

"Come on lady, get in there and let Jacob know how much you love him. You need to show him Evelyn, you need to show him."

"Yes." Evelyn nodded, a determined glint in her eye. Sophie gulped with relief then linked her arm through her friends. Together they trooped into the prettily laid out room.

"Start up the music again," Sophie said, brightly, "the brides on her way."

Evelyn's eyes searched for him. His back was ramrod straight, but as the music began, he turned to look and Evelyn was overwhelmed with an acute feeling of love and tenderness. She let go of Sophie and almost ran up the aisle towards him – dear Jacob, her husband-to-be.

* * *

After a short ceremony they slipped rings on and made vows to each other. The women all cried as they sealed their marriage with a kiss, then Jon was organising the newlyweds into position. Click, click went the camera lens. Then they were ushered outside for more group photographs. Aunt Gertrude, sporting a feather topped hat, passed Evelyn a quilted horseshoe.

"It's homemade," she rasped, her asthma made worse by the humid heat, "I know it's an old-fashioned gift to give at these modern weddings, but it will bring you luck and happiness Evelyn."

"Thank you," Evelyn hooked the pretty accessory over her arm, "I'm so glad you could make it. You're the only family I have left."

"Wouldn't have missed it for the world," Gertrude sniffed, "You look stunning by the way."

"It's Sophie," Evelyn pointed to her friend who was being pulled in a circle by Molly, "she's so good at make-up and hair."

Gertrude nodded her approval, "your friends are lovely, and you met them at university?"

"I did, but I feel like I've known them all forever."

"University has been good for you Evelyn. I didn't think you'd like it, but I was wrong. I think it's been the making of you. And your novel – wow! When will it be out?"

Evelyn beamed under the unexpected praise, "not for a while. It's being edited. There's no rush."

Gertrude changed tack, "are you sure it's okay for me to stay at yours for a few nights? You seem inundated at your house."

Evelyn smiled, "of course it's okay, I love having people there. That house has been empty and quiet for far too long," she paused, "and Mam would have loved it too."

"Evelyn!" Jacob was beckoning her towards him, "more photographs."

They left in a fleet of cars and taxis heading for the Golden Goose Pub & Restaurant. Evelyn gasped when she entered the room they had reserved. Heart shaped balloons bobbed around the large conservatory and the tables were decorated with salmon pink linen, candles and confetti. Romantic music played softly in the background and a line of paper hearts swayed lazily from ceiling hooks.

"Do you like it?" Jacob asked.

"It looks wonderful," Evelyn gushed, happiness radiating from her in waves.

They took their seats and raised their glasses as a bustling grey-haired lady toasted the happy couple.

* * *

After a delicious meal of medley of salmon and beef wellington, Sophie tapped her knife on the rim of her crystal goblet to acknowledge the commencement of the speeches.

"Sorry I'm nervous," she began, hands trembling slightly, "you all know how much I hate public speaking," she cleared her throat, took a deep steadying breath, "the first time I met Evelyn was on the enrolment day at university. We were there to study the same course and we sat together and got talking. My first impressions of Evelyn were that she was really nice and friendly too … then I saw more of her, got to know her better and I realised what a truly wonderful person she is. Evelyn is kind and caring and a loyal friend."

Sophie paused as a chorus of 'here, here' rang around the room. Sophie felt her confidence growing and smiled broadly, "one of the many traits I love about Evelyn is how humble she is. Not just in the way she sees herself, but most of all with her writing. I've been fortunate enough to read some of her work and the way she weaves words to create a story is ingenious. Evelyn is a fantastic writer, and with her combination of talent and enthusiasm, I am certain that she has a great future within the literary world." There was a round of applause.

Sophie spoke a little longer about Evelyn and Jacob and how happy they made each other. Then she raised her glass to toast the happy couple.

Jacob was the next one to stand up and talk about his wife and how he had loved her since he had first seen her, more than twenty years ago. In honour of Evelyn he had written a poem about love and happiness. Evelyn was wiping away the tears as he came to the end of his poetic recital. She squeezed Jacob's hand as she got to her feet to make her own speech. A speech which moved the guests with its passion for her husband and their future life together. Glasses were refilled with more champagne and the final toast of the evening was made. Then the waitresses busied themselves moving the tables while the guests chatted. Music blared from wall speakers and the children were the first on the dancefloor. The double doors of the conservatory were flung open to allow the summer breeze to waft into the warm room. The guests mingled, laughing and shouting above the sounds of the disco beat.

They celebrated until late in the evening, when Evelyn and Jacob left to spend their wedding night at a nearby five-star hotel. It had been a gift from aunt Gertrude, along with one of her famous Lancashire Hotpots.

Evelyn waved from the back of her car and settled with Jacob, clasping his hands while he nuzzled her neck.

"This is the first day of the rest of our lives together, I love you Evelyn."

"Forever?" She asked, eyes twinkling in the darkness.

"Forever."

Chapter Two

Four weeks later...

Will glanced at his watch. He was already half an hour late and the traffic going into the city was at a complete standstill.

"Bloody roadworks," he thumped the dashboard, "come on!"

Next to him, Flora shook her head and tutted, "you are just like your father – no patience."

"Sorry Mum," Will replied with a sheepish look at Flora, "I just hate being late."

"I'll have you there in no time," Flora pulled out of the line of traffic, slammed her foot on the accelerator and sped up the bus lane.

"Woah! You little rebel." He grinned, as his mum nervously checked her mirrors.

"Just hope there's no police about," she slowed down, slotting her car into a space at the top of the lights, "can you hop out here love?

As a reply Will unbuckled his seatbelt and sprang from the car, "ta-ra!" he dashed onto the pavement, waving at Flora, who was soon swallowed up behind a vast haulage truck.

Will weaved around the pedestrians making their way into the city centre. Then out of nowhere he heard his name being shouted and turned to see his mate Jimmy, hanging out the passenger side of a white van. He jogged back down the street, noting the sign on the work van now read Mitchell & Son.

"Alright?" Will gasped, pointing to the lettering, "I'm impressed."

"You're looking at a fully trained plumber mate. None of this university bollocks for me, I'm earning Will, mega bucks."

"I'm just off to work myself," Will said with a grimace.

"Oh yes," Jimmy chuckled, "you still working in a wine bar?"

"It's the student union bar actually," Will corrected.

"How's it going?" Jimmy pulled a cigarette out of its pack and tapped the edge of it, "haven't seen much of you over the summer."

"I've been busy with Esme."

"You been away?" Jimmy lit the cigarette, taking a deep drag, "me and Sadie went to Ibiza. It was rocking, non-stop partying. Hey maybe next year you and Hema could come?"

Will baulked at the thought of his reserved girlfriend living it large in Ibiza, "nah, we've got Esme to think of now. Somehow I don't think she'd enjoy the foam parties and the beach raves."

"Suppose not," Jimmy grinned, "I still can't believe that my best mate is all settled down. You're not even twenty man."

"Well I *am* settled down and a fully functioning mature adult, so you better accept it."

"Just kidding," Jimmy slapped Will's upper arm, "how much longer you got left at uni then?"

"Last year," Will replied, kicking at a ketchup-smeared chip wrapper which was trying to wind itself around his ankles.

"So what will you do? When you've finally graduated and grown up?"

"Journalism."

Jimmy coughed, "as in working for a newspaper?"

"Yep."

"That would be cool, especially if you covered sports news. Does your dad know?"

"Not yet," Will replied.

"Are you sure about journalism?" Jimmy frowned, "Dad would give you a job tomorrow as an apprentice if you wanted it Will."

"I'm sure," Will said with determination, "I've been thinking about it all summer. Thanks anyway, but I'm not wasting my degree on something completely unrelated. Plumbing's not for me."

Jimmy nodded, a look of respect flickering over his features, "you were always different, even at school. I knew you'd do something awesome with your life. Maybe I should go to uni, huh?"

"Why not?" Will replied, "it's not too late mate. You're going to be working for the rest of your life – do something you love Jimmy, don't settle, don't just exist."

"What could I do?" Jimmy laughed, "I'm a manual worker Will, it runs in the family, it's what I'm used to."

"You wanted to join the police," Will reminded him with his eyebrows arched, "can't you remember when we were little, playing cops and robbers, and you always had to be the big powerful detective."

Jimmy threw back his head and guffawed, "it wasn't real Will. It was just a dream."

"Then why don't you make your dreams come true for a change," Will shrugged, "just saying."

There elapsed a moment of silence between them, which was broken by the thundering of a motorbike whizzing past.

"I really have to go," Will backed away, "but Esme's one today, we're having a party, nothing fancy, just a little celebration, come and see her, bring Sadie too."

Jimmy lifted up his hand, "we'll be there buddy, see you later?"

"You betcha!"

Will ran the rest of the way. Past the row of banks and trendy wine bars, through the church grounds until he finally reached the university. There were a lot of people milling about, come to visit on one of the universities many open days. A plastic sheet declaring welcome flapped high above the entrance. Will slowed to a quick gait, nodding at the staff he had come to recognise over the last two years of being here. One of the librarians accosted him; asking him to help push a crate full of books to the learning centre.

"Thank you," she said gratefully, tucking behind a damp tendril of hair which had escaped from its high bun, "erm … what was your name?"

"Will," he grinned, "do you need me to put these on some of the shelves?"

"Oh no. They have to be checked in, logged onto the system, coded and sorted into topics," she blushed, "but thank you for the offer."

"No probs," Will was off again, down a steep flight of stairs into the student union bar.

Gladys the cleaner was sprawled across the bar, gazing at the manager's derriere with a lascivious gleam in her eye. Will crept up behind her and grabbed hold of her waist, "caught ya!"

Up went her tin of polish and duster as she yelled out in surprise. The tin of polish landed on Will's head.

"Serves ya right," she blustered, "you coulda' given me a coronary."

"Ah Gladys, but Mick would have given you the kiss of life," Will laughed, ducking away from her.

"Eh! You daft bugger."

Mick stretched up to his full height of six foot four, "alright our Will? How's your summer been?"

"Great ta," Will replied, looking around the deserted room, "where is everyone?"

Mick shrugged with an air of resigned nonchalance, "seems like the prospective students don't want Mum and Dad knowing about this place."

"This is the hub of the university," Will declared, "don't worry, this bar will soon be buzzing, especially when news gets around what brilliant cocktail makers the bar staff are."

"Let's hope so," Mick said sourly, "or you'll be outta a job. Now Gladys, stop fawning all over my clean bar, go and clean out the lavs or someut."

"I don't have to put with that kind of chat," Gladys threw Mick a stern look, "there's rules about bullying in the workplace." She ambled off, chuntering under her breath.

"Are you sure you need me in today?" Will glanced around.

"Yep," Mick emitted a huge sigh, "we had a delivery late last night that still needs organising, the stockroom looks like a bomb's exploded in it and I've got that much paperwork I feel like I'm the one doing an English degree, not you!"

Will picked up a crate, "I'll start with the alco-pops then shall I?"

* * *

Later that afternoon, Will walked into the city centre, heading for the toy stores. Hema had already spent a fortune on birthday presents, but Will had some extra cash burning a hole in his pocket, so maybe one or two more gifts added to the pile wouldn't hurt. Will caught the bus back with his hands full of carriers; a giant teddy for Esme to clamber all over, a complex looking bath toy which promised to provide hours of fun, and an electronic book for parent and child to read together.

'Where are you?' Hema's text pinged into his message box.

'**Coming babe**,' Will's succinct reply seemed to appease his girlfriend as he heard no more from her. He settled back with his iPod blaring popular indie music and hopped off twenty minutes later. Will was strolling casually down the street, when Ruby the family border collie shot towards him, tail wagging frantically.

"Who let you out?" Will grabbed hold of her collar and watched bemused as Hema hurried towards him, clad in her furry slippers and a cotton playsuit which revealed a considerable amount of thigh.

"What took you so long?" Hema berated, looking hot and frazzled.

"What's up?"

"Our mothers are what's up!" Hema puffed her cheeks out theatrically, "they're taking over Will, butting in and bossing."

"My mum?" Will was surprised to hear Hema talking negatively of Flora; they were usually so close. Shivani on the other hand...

"Yes even Flora! It's like it's a competition; see who can organise the most elaborate first birthday party ever," Hema sighed, "Mum seems to think that Indian food is going to be more popular than Flora's jam sandwiches and tea-cakes. I just had to get out of there."

"Where's Dad?"

"He's sloped off to the pool again, leaving me to deal with them. Oh and guess what? Uncle Evan is on his way."

"That's all we need," Will mumbled, "hey, I saw Jimmy. I've invited him and Sadie." Will paused as Hema's mouth turned into a sulky pout, "that is okay isn't it?"

"I suppose so!" Hema's tone was lifting higher and higher, "but I hope you told them there's no alcohol Will. That's all those two seem to think about now-a-days."

"They're young and have no responsibilities," Will shrugged, "we'd be the same."

"Would we?" Hema looked sceptical, "do we really want Esme seeing their drunken behaviour? They're not good role models Will, fawning over each other, swigging from bottles of vodka, smoking wacky backy!"

"So you won't be coming to Ibiza then?"

"What?!"

Will pulled her into his arms, "just joking. Leave it to me, I'll sort out the interfering Grannies."

"Good," Hema sniffed, "what have you got there?"

"More awesome presents!"

"Will, our daughter is going to be so spoilt."

"It's her first birthday – we're allowed to spoil her, it's not like we splash out on toys all year round."

"I suppose so," Hema replied with a sniff, "my hay fever has been horrendous today, I feel ill."

"Take a tablet," Will advised, "go and have a lie down and I'll finish off the arrangements."

Hema looked like the weight of the world had been removed from her shoulders, "thank you," she said, her voice back to being girly and breathless, "love you."

"Love you too."

* * *

"This book is so romantic," Juliette relaxed back on the swinging sun lounger with a dreamy sigh.

"Is it on the university's year three reading list?" Ben was standing at the other end of the garden, hosepipe in hand, regarding her with amused eyes.

"Erm, are Mills and Boon indicative reading for an English degree now-a-days?"

Ben laughed, "what's it about?"

"Well basically a devoted caring nurse falls for a gorgeous powerful doctor. There are lots of obstacles in their way; an irate ex, a vicious mother-in-law, the poor / rich scenario which *always* causes problems. But…"

"Yes?" Ben squirted his bedding plants.

"Of course, true love prevails."

"Soppy fairy-tale ending?"

"Bound to be," Juliette sucked her ice lolly, aware that Ben's attention was firmly on her mouth.

"Any sex?" He asked, casually.

"Dr Rivers really!" Juliette gave him a disapproving glance.

"So there's none then?" Ben looked disappointed.

"Just a little," Juliette smiled widely, "in fact I'm getting to a rather saucy scene. Boy this doctor is hot…arghhh," Juliette screamed as a jet of freezing cold water drenched her, almost tipping her from her seat.

"Oops sorry, thought you needed cooling down."

"Right!" Juliette sprang up, dashing into the utility she picked up a bowl of water and ran towards Ben, ejecting it in a wave over him. It covered his head and torso, dripped from his stubbly chin.

"Oh you are a bad, bad girl, Juliette," Ben was chuckling as he waved the streaming hosepipe in his hand, "I think you need punishing."

"Who do you think you are?" Juliette taunted, "Christian Gray?"

She was cut off by a stream of water which hit her face and neck, "okay sorry," she spluttered, "you are way nicer than him,"

"Better looking?" Ben aimed the nozzle at her bare thighs.

"YES!!!" She screamed, "sexy as…"

"I don't believe you Juliette," Ben directed the water at her blouse, making it stick to her skin provocatively, "you're going to have to show me."

"Stop! Stop! Please stop," Juliette danced as the water hit her feet, "I'll do anything you want."

"Anything?" Ben chucked the hosepipe down. In two strides he had reached her, lifting her into his arms, he carried her into the house.

"Ben your carpet," Juliette clung onto him, burying his face into his neck.

"It will dry."

"You really want to do this now?"

"Now Juliette!" He bounded up the stairs with her in his arms, into the bathroom where he set her down and banged the door shut.

"You're covered in grass," Ben chuckled, pulling off her sopping wet t-shirt.

"I wonder why," Juliette's hands went underneath his t-shirt, curling into the hair on his chest. She stepped out of her shorts and underwear, shivering at the wanton lust evident on his face. He pushed her back into the shower cubicle, opening her lips with his own, "I love you," he said urgently, lifting her arms up so her erect nipples squashed against his bare skin.

"Oh," Juliette gasped as a stream of warm water covered them both.

"Do you love me?" He rasped.

"So much," Juliette nodded fervently, "I love you so much."

Then she wrapped herself around him, clinging to him as he nipped at her throat and made passionate love to her, steaming the mirrors with their heat and their chemistry, until they both found their release and, sated, sank down onto the floor of the shower, wrapped in each other's arms.

"Ben," Juliette said sleepily, "I think you left the hosepipe on."

* * *

Three weeks prior to her first birthday Esme Bentley decided she had spent far too much time on her hands and knees crawling, so on a warm Sunday afternoon, when the entire family were lolling in armchairs snoozing, she grabbed hold of the chair leg and with all her might pulled herself into a standing position. This elicited a happy cry from Esme and made Will open one sleepy eye. He watched fascinated as she let go of the armchair and took a total of ten wobbly steps before falling back on her padded behind.

"Jesus!" He sprang to his feet, searching frantically for his phone, which had become wedged down the side of the cushion.

Flora stretched her tingling toes, gazed at her son and was just about to chastise him for taking the Lord's name in vain when Esme grabbed hold of her leg and pulled herself to her feet again. This time she managed to cross the entire sitting room floor on shaky ballerina tiptoes. At the other end she clung onto the coffee table and chuckled at her new found sense of freedom. Then everyone was wide awake and a plethora of camera clicking ensued.

"You clever, clever girl," Hema called to her daughter with exaggerated pride. Esme blew a raspberry in return and was off again, trotting to the fireplace, which had been covered with a metal fireguard which she clung onto. That's when the fun for Esme really started and the worry for all the adults in the house intensified.

So, on her first birthday, Hema had spent most of the day running around after her energetic daughter. Flora had been vacuuming and polishing in preparation for the tea party. Then Shivani and Daljeet arrived an hour early, carrying foil trays laden with Indian delicacies.

"Are those *jam* sandwiches, Flora?" Shivani asked with evident disbelief in her voice.

"Yes," Flora smiled brightly, "I've made strawberry and damson jelly, Esme loves them."

"But what are there for the adults?" Shivani wrapped her gossamer scarlet shawl across her shoulder, casting a critical eye over the table of food.

"Oh we all love them too," Flora replied, "especially Max."

Shivani's eyebrows shot up, "a headteacher eats jam sandwiches?"

"Yes," Flora was perplexed by the ridicule emanating from Shivani, "but I've also made banana butties too, so people have a choice."

"Banana," Shivani shook her head, "well maybe it's good that I thought to make some bhajis and samosas, so the guests will have some *adult* variety."

Flora's bottom lip trembled and Hema jumped to her defence, "Will and I wanted a traditional tea party, Flora's done a grand job and I've even made fairy cakes."

"You used to prefer sultana cake," Shivani stared at her pointedly. Then Hema disappeared in a desperate attempt to find Will, before things became a little too heated in Flora's kitchen.

Will sauntered in with Esme in his arms, hair sticking up and an air of chilled out ambience surrounding him.

"My granddaughter is walking!" Shivani clapped her hands, "and what smart shoes she has on. They are Clarks?"

"Of course," Will replied smoothly, "only the best for princess." He omitted the fact that Hema had purchased them from a local car boot sale, never been worn, box included. 'Probably nicked' had been Will's satisfied verdict at the time.

He passed his daughter into Shivani's outstretched arms and ambled over to Flora, who was stirring jelly into small ramekin pots, "you okay?" He whispered. Flora bit her lip, gave a small nod.

"Stay sweet," Will advised, "leave the monster-in-law to me. Shivani," he turned with a bright smile, "is Daljeet not here?"

"Yes," Shivani looked surprised, "he's sitting in the garden I think."

"He is," Flora confirmed, peering above the half netting, "Will, take Daljeet a beer. There are cool ones in the chiller box."

Will grabbed two, snapping the caps off, "would you like wine Shivani? And maybe we can sit outside too, leave Mum to organise everything."

Shivani looked around doubtfully, "well I suppose so, if Flora's sure she's okay?"

Flora wiped her hands on her pinafore and beamed at her guest, "you go with Will Shivani, I'm almost finished up here and I'm sure Esme will want to show her nanna how she can toddle around the garden."

Shivani followed Will outside, with a keenness to explore Esme wriggling in her arms.

"Ah Will, you are looking well!" Daljeet rose to his feet as Will set the bottles down on the glass garden table.

"And my *poti* - she is on the move!" Daljeet laughed heartily at the sight of Shivani tripping over her sari as she scurried after Esme.

"Yes. Now the fun begins."

The conversation turned to football. As they were debating Chattlesbury Football Club's chance in the Premiership, Max joined them on the patio, looking relaxed and ultra-cool in a pair of expensive designer sunglasses. He shook hands with Daljeet before reclining on top of Flora's cushioned sun lounger.

"You okay there, Dad?"

"Never better," Max replied, leaning back with his arms raised above his head.

"I hear that you have resigned! Is that true?" Daljeet surveyed Max with a look of horror and shock.

"It is," Max flicked back his wet hair and smiled, showing pearly white straight teeth.

"But why?!" Daljeet looked aghast with what he perceived to be Max's impulsive and irresponsible behaviour.

"To live Daljeet, to be happy."

"But ... but," Daljeet's lips were flapping wildly, "how on earth are you going to cope?"

"My sentiments exactly," Uncle Evan boomed, plodding towards them, "the daft bugger must be going through the male menopause. He'll be dying his hair and taking up golf next!"

Will sniggered, casting a look at his dad who looked completely unperturbed by this attack on his character.

Uncle Evan's rant continued, "how the devil will you cope financially, old boy? And further still, how is my poor sister going to cope with you moping about the house day and night? She told Grace you've informed the governors of St Mary's that there's no chance that you'll be returning in September? Utterly preposterous behaviour!"

Daljeet nodded in agreement, then Shivani piped up, "a man's place is to be the breadwinner. No wonder Flora is stressed, what with her job and a house to run. If you're not careful Max, your wife will be ill."

"Here, here," Evan clapped along boisterously.

Max popped a stick of gum in his mouth and chewed it thoughtfully, "Flora's right – I'm done with the world of education and I'm never setting foot in a school again!"

Up went Evan's hands, "now you sound like Will! I expect that kind of tantrum talk off my almost grown nephew."

Will stopped laughing, "now hang on." His eyes narrowed, as he regarded his red-faced uncle.

"Leave Max alone," Flora tutted, as she surveyed them all from the kitchen doorway, "I can hear you upstairs – what must the neighbours think?"

"Well it's damned irresponsible," Evan blustered, "you shouldn't have to bear the financial brunt of Max's mid-life crisis, Flora."

"Max is going to get a part time job and, in the meantime,, we have enough savings to live off comfortably for quite a fair bit, so everybody needs to stop...worrying."

"My sister...the eternal optimist," Evan countered, drily.

"Let's not forget," Flora continued, throwing her brother a stern look, "this is Esme's first birthday, I really can't understand why you're all so preoccupied with mine and Max's affairs. So why don't we all go on inside and watch her open her presents, before the friends and neighbours arrive."

As they all trooped back into the house, Max pulled Flora aside, sliding one arm around her waist, "thank you for your support love. Thank you."

Behind them, Will pulled a party popper, "let this party officially commence."

Chapter Three

Ann was sitting at her kitchen table, smearing two slices of toast with thick strawberry jam and watching the finger on the wall clock tick slowly around. It was only eight in the morning but she had been awake for hours. A mixture of excitement, fear and trepidation was swishing her stomach into knots and she shivered slightly, drawing the edges of her cardigan closer together. These September mornings were chilly compared to the heat of last months and the days were cloudier. The stifling heat of the sun was weakening; altering in preparation for Autumn – the season of leaf dropping. Jon strode through the open door, wearing only a towel tucked around his muscular waist. Beads of water trickled down his smooth chest and dripped from his shoulder length hair. Hair that had been grown in homage to his favourite rock star, the name slipped Ann's memory, but she recalled that he was the front man of Meatloaf.

Jon had glorious hair; dark and flowing, shiny and smooth. He was regularly ribbed by his bald colleagues and accused of being vain, but he wasn't in the slightest. Jon was solid, dependable, down-to-earth and strong and he wasn't afraid to get his hands dirty either which Ann had decided was the mark of a true man. She watched him as he passed her, heading towards the fridge. He pulled a carton of juice out and took a long gulp, "did you sleep well?" He managed.

"Better," Ann replied, "now that it's cooler."

"I wasn't referring to the weather," his mouth slanted slightly, "you can admit you're scared Ann, I'm nervous as hell."

"Has he texted you?"

"Nope." Jon pulled out a chair and slumped down, "imagine how he's feeling though, this is huge."

"I hope he's okay," Ann chewed her lip, "what time is Rose bringing him again?"

"Early afternoon," Jon replied, "but we're all sorted aren't we?"

"Yes we're ready. I've opened the windows to give the room a good airing and the bedding's all fresh and clean." Ann swiped at a fly that was buzzing over her toast, "I thought we could have spaghetti tonight... only thing is I'm feeling a bit sick at the moment... don't know if I can stomach cooking garlic and onion."

Jon pressed his hand over hers, it was damp with perspiration, "let's go out, to the new fish restaurant."

"Does he like fish?" Ann wondered aloud. Jon shrugged.

They both started talking at once, "you first," Jon said, with a chuckle.

Ann blew out her cheeks, "I was just going to say we need to be relaxed, confident, we're the adults here aren't we?"

"Is that a question or a statement," Jon grinned.

"Jon... I'm petrified."

"Hey," he leant over to caress her face, "you have absolutely nothing to worry about Ann. Sam likes you; he thinks you're awesome – remember?"

"He was talking about you too," Ann replied, entwining her fingers through his.

"Yes but *you've* built a bond with him Ann, he looks up to you."

"The pressure," Ann pulled a face, "Jon, he's going to be here twenty-four seven, permanently."

Jon let go of her hand, "Ann," he sighed, "I hope you're not having second thoughts. Not after all the meetings, the checks, the reports, the intrusion into our personal life."

"Woah," Ann replied, "I'm not having second thoughts! I'm absolutely certain that adopting a child is the right thing to do. But Samuel, he's just a boy, how will he cope living with a bad-tempered paraplegic?"

Jon rolled his eyes, "you're not bad tempered! Hormonal sometimes yes ... didn't I tell you how much you've mellowed since you've been at uni?"

Ann sniffed, "I suppose I have, must be the students I've been mixing with."

"Your friends are lovely and have been a very good influence on you," Jon picked up a piece of toast, the edges of which had started to curl, "how was Evelyn's honeymoon by the way?"

"Magical according to Sophie," Ann replied, "the way she was talking, you would think that Evelyn had jetted off to the moon instead of Jersey."

"Ah," Jon chuckled, "Sophie is sweet." He pointed his toast at her, "admit that you like her."

"I do," Ann smiled, "of course I've grown very fond of Sophie, of all of them in fact." Her mouth turned down slightly, "I can't believe this is the final year. Where has the time gone?"

"You *can* keep in touch with them," Jon said, "it doesn't mean your friendship has to end just because uni is going to."

Ann picked up her phone, "yes. I suppose there are some positives to Facebook after all."

"There you go. So, about Samuel?"

Ann beamed, "let's do this mister ... but first, maybe you should go put some clothes on? You're awfully distracting."

* * *

For the rest of the morning Ann and Jon cleaned the house. Jon tugged the hoover upstairs while Ann dusted downstairs. The upended shoes were placed neatly back on their rack. The scattered newspapers were dumped in the recycling bin. The kitchen sink was scrubbed until it gleamed, and the windows were polished until they sparkled. By midday they were both famished, Jon left to go to the local sandwich shop, leaving Ann alone to arrange cupcakes on a posh china stand that had been given to them as a wedding present and had never been used.

"Grubs up!" He burst back in, with a bundle under his arm. The delicious smell of fat fried sausages followed him into the room. Ann was almost salivating as he opened them out. She grabbed two plates, passing one over to Jon.

"I'll mop in here after dinner and then we can relax," Jon took a hearty bite, "those cakes look nice. Do you think Rose will stop for a while?"

"I should think so," Ann wiped a blob of ketchup from her lower lip, "for a cup of tea at least."

"Are Anton and Lulu coming?"

"I presume so, Lulu messaged me last night to say she'd see us today. It must be hard for them Jon ... saying goodbye like they do."

"They can come visit whenever they want."

"Sam would like that," Ann replied with an emphatic nod.

25

After lunch, Ann sat out in the garden sipping lemonade and skimming the local newspaper. She could hear Jon humming along to the radio as he swished over the linoleum floor with a mop. A car door slamming pierced the air. Ann held her breath in anticipation and sat up straighter, but it was the next-door neighbours' grandchildren, screeching hello. Ann could envision them charging through the house and out onto the back garden, gambolling across the soft, springy lawn, swinging from the apple tree, the boughs of which hung partly over Jon and Ann's fence. She tried to remember how old they were and if Sam would want to be friends with them. But she could tell from their chatter that they were quite a bit younger. Sam was almost a teenager, he would have his own circle of friends already established, she reminded herself.

Ann glanced down at the newspaper. It was all doom and gloom; a house fire started by a faulty tumble drier, a nasty dog biting incident involving a post man and an Alsatian. Then splayed across the centre was a heart-breaking photograph of a poor elderly man, whose face was bruised and swollen; another victim of mugging in the city centre side streets. Quickly she turned the pages, passing the TV guide with little interest, flicking over a health and wellbeing article on lowering your cholesterol naturally, Ann paused at the travel section. There was a lovely beach shot of a resort on the Balearic island of Majorca. The sea looked stunning and the restaurants and bars sounded ideal for a family holiday. Maybe they could go next summer she pondered. Next to it was a smaller article featuring the Jones' break in Blackpool. Blackpool! Ann's heart raced, Sam's never been to the seaside.

"Jon," she called with excitement. He popped his head out of the kitchen doorway. "Let's take Sam to Blackpool."

He scratched his head, "now?"

"No not now! I mean soon, before the weather turns too cold?"

"Yes. Blackpool's an excellent idea, loads of fun and will give us chance to bond."

"Next weekend then?"

He gave her a thumbs up, then the doorbell chimed and they both stared at each other, frozen like a pair of statues.

"Jon," Ann swallowed, "that must be him. Go get the door."

He raked his hand through his hair, "I'll ... be right back."

Ann folded the newspaper and reversed her wheelchair away from the table. She smoothed her hair, pulled the cuffs on her cardigan down, fixed a beaming smile to her face and then waited.

Rose was struggling with the sliding patio door, Ann could hear Jon chuntering that it needed oiling as he pulled it open. The curtain flapped outwards, caught in a gust of wind.

"Here's Ann," Jon sounded relieved.

"Hello," Rose stumbled out, carrying a tupperware tub, "I bought cakes."

"You did?" Ann exclaimed, "excellent."

"They're Sam's favourite; chocolate butterfly buns with extra cream."

Ann nodded, "is he? ... "

A headful of golden curls peeped from the doorway. He was dressed in casual jeans and a stripy shirt, and he looked nervous as hell.

"Hi," Ann beamed, beckoning to him, "come and sit down."

There was a moment of silence as Sam hung back, chewing his lip. Then he took a deep breath and scurried over to her.

"So," Jon clapped his hands, "I'll go make drinks."

Sam swung the rucksack off his back, unzipped it and pulled out a box which was tied with a fancy ribbon.

"These are for you," he mumbled, scuffing his feet on the edge of the loose slabs.

"For me?" Ann's mouth hung open as he thrust them towards her, "thank you."

Her fingers were clumsy as they tugged at the paper, "wow chocolates!"

"They're Belgian," Rose's tone was full of pride, "Sam chose them himself."

Ann stared down at the nut and praline luxury selection, "they look delicious. Thank you ... again."

"S'alright," He squatted down to stroke Snowy the cat.

Watching him with the animal reminded Ann of his eccentric foster parents and their menagerie of exotic pets, "Where are Lulu and Anton?" She glanced at Rose.

"On the way," Rose sank onto one of the garden chairs, kicking off her shoes, "there was a break-in at the homeless shelter last night again. The office equipment has been stolen; the computer, the printer, they even took a swivel chair. Pulled out all the drawers probably looking for cash, made a real mess of the place. Anton went out there at five this morning to help, he must be shattered, poor darling."

Ann shook her head, "did they catch them?"

"Nope. Everyone was tucked up in bed, no one heard a thing. They have them on camera of course, but they're faces are covered, so the police don't hold out much hope of detaining them."

"My real dad was a thief," Sam's forehead was wrinkled into tense lines, "a low life thief and a druggie. Everyone hates him, even his own family."

"Sam!" Rose remonstrated, "who on earth told you that?"

"Some lads from school," his hands balled into fists, "they said the apple don't fall far from the tree either. What does that mean?"

"Nothing," Rose replied firmly, "it means nothing."

Ann frowned, opened her mouth to speak when a ball came flying over the fence, bouncing onto the table in front of them. Sam jumped up, chasing across the lawn as it rolled away.

"Is he okay?" Ann whispered.

"It's a big day for him," Rose answered, "what Sam needs is love and patience."

"Of course, I understand."

They watched as he swung his leg back and kicked the ball high into the sky.

"A ball Ann, we forgot to get a ball," Jon placed the teapot and a bottle of Vimto onto the table.

"You still like your tea?" Rose chuckled.

"Still addicted," Ann confirmed, "we have a surprise for Sam and it's better than a ball."

Rose pushed her spectacles up her glistening nose, "did you hear that Sam? Jon and Ann have something for you."

Samuel's interest was piqued. He jogged over, gazing at them expectantly.

"We've been busy over the summer," Jon slung his arm across Ann's shoulder.

"Super busy," Ann confirmed with a happy smile.

"What have you guys been up to?" Rose cocked her head to one side.

Jon scratched his chin, "it's only something little."

"Nothing elaborate," Ann added.

"Wh-what is it?" dimples appeared in Sam's cheeks.

"Shall we show him?" Jon asked Ann.

"Yup, maybe we should."

They made their way back into the house. Ann stopped beside the stair lift which would take her up to the first floor. But before she had chance to heave herself over, Jon had her in his arms.

"Let's go the quick way," he bounded up the stairs.

Ann looked back at Rose and Sam, rolling her eyes, "he's always doing this."

"How heroic," Rose gushed.

Ann bristled, "of course he forgets this isn't a fairy-tale and I'm not a damsel in distress."

"And sometimes you forget you're disabled and need extra help," Jon replied, sharply.

"Sorry," Ann mumbled, "we're going to convert the downstairs lounge into a bedroom eventually. It will be so much easier."

John stopped on the landing, waiting for Sam to catch up. He nodded at a closed door, "this is all yours mate."

"Mine?" Sam stared at the door.

"Go on," Ann urged, "take a look inside."

Slowly Sam pushed the door open and stepped forward.

He gasped, "is this my bedroom?"

"Yes," Ann beamed, "it's your own personal space. Do you like it?"

Samuel stared wide-eyed at the freshly painted navy walls, the beanbag propped in the corner, the comfy looking bed and the drawn back velvet curtains. His feet sank into a soft, luxurious carpet as he walked over to the window. From it he had a glorious view of the garden; the shrubs and the fruit trees that stretched all the way down to a greenhouse at the end.

"Wow," was all he could muster.

"This is fantastic," Rose said, "just perfect for a teenage boy."

"We thought so too," Ann replied, "although we weren't too sure on the colour."

"Blue's my favourite colour," Sam's lower lip was trembling, "is that a PC?" He nodded towards the desk, where a black laptop rested next to an assortment of pens and a trendy looking lamp that intermittently changed colour.

"It sure is," Jon replied, plonking Ann on the bed so he could flick the switch on.

"We thought it would come in handy with your homework," Ann leant forward to watch Sam, "it seems it's all done via computers now-a-days."

Rose laughed, "aren't the youth of today lucky? I remember proper cartridge pens that stained your fingers and spending hours on a Sunday evening handwriting essays." She frowned, "schools were horrid places in those days – power crazy teachers who doled out corporal punishment on a daily basis, even to the wee babies in primary school. Thank the Lord education has progressed and kindness and understanding are encouraged now instead of belittlement and isolation." Rose sniffed, "sorry I'm digressing. So, what do you think Sam?"

Slowly Sam's lips lifted into a wide smile. He touched the lamp and it created a white spot of his palm "It's awesome – it's freakin' awesome!"

* * *

After Jon had given Sam a basic rundown of the computer, Ann passed him a brightly wrapped package. He tore into it with gusto, gasping at the contents.

"What is it?" Rose enquired, squinting over the rim of her glasses.

"A duvet set. A Chattlesbury FC duvet set!"

"New for this season," Ann was deeply touched by the happiness emanating from him, "there's a poster for you too, next to the wardrobe."

Sam dashed over and unravelled a large colour photograph of a striker heading a ball towards a goal.

"Can I put this by my bed?" His eyes were wide with excitement.

"You can put it wherever you want!" Jon proclaimed, just as the doorbell pinged.

"Ah," said Rose, "that should be Anton and Lulu."

Rose was right, Lulu glided into the house, wafting scents of jasmine and honeysuckle. When Ann asked what perfume she was wearing, she disclosed that she was experimenting with flowers from her own garden.

"I'm hoping to bottle it eventually and sell it at one of my craft fairs," she beamed, pulling Sam into a tight embrace.

Anton plodded up the drive behind her, carrying a large odd-shaped earthenware pot.

"This is for you," he said, thrusting it towards Ann, "hand made by Lulu."

"Oh," Ann stared down at the brightly covered piece of pottery, "it's beautiful."

"It will bring you luck," Lulu explained, "I based it on an African design, an amulet to give peace and protection."

Ann ran her fingers over it, before passing it to Jon who placed it on the mantlepiece.

"We can't stop long," Lulu sing-songed in her sweet voice, "there's a demonstration going on in the city today. Anton here is determined to protest."

"It's an objection against the new teaching pay structure," he elaborated, "the unions have organised it."

"The stress in teaching is becoming intolerable," Lulu said, with a shake of her head, "some nights Anton is up into the early hours, marking work."

"Then there's the behavioural issues I have to contend with," Anton added, "some of the students act like rabid animals."

"It's true of most of the public services," Rose said stiffly, "the nurses are grossly underpaid, the poor firemen risk their lives for a pittance and the police are attacked and criticised by the very people they are trying to protect!" Rose huffed with outrage, "and social work can be soul destroying."

Sam was watching them with wide, wary eyes.

"Anyway," Ann interjected, looking at him, "how about we give you a tour of the house? It won't take long."

"I must be going," Rose said in a crisp tone, "I need to complete my paperwork, but I'll pop and see you next week."

They all trooped back down the stairs. The social worker hugged Samuel, smoothing down his wild curls, "you are going to be very happy here, Sam." She shook hands with Jon and Ann, "please call me for anything ... night or day."

"We will." Ann and Jon chorused.

Then she was gone.

"We should be going too," Lulu's eyes were brimming with tears, "sorry I'm being silly and emotional."

"You're welcome anytime," Ann insisted, "I'll message you."

"Will you?" Lulu sniffed.

"Of course," Ann clutched her hand, "you're friends and we want to keep in touch."

Anton was patting Sam on the shoulder, "bye for now." Samuel rushed forward, burying his face into Lulu's skirt, she hugged him fiercely, "you can message me every day," her voice was choked with emotion, "I want to hear how you're getting on. Okay?"

Sam nodded and backed towards Jon, who placed an arm across his shoulders.

"Bye Sammy," Lulu and Anton were waving as they crossed the open door. Jon waited until they had disappeared out of sight then closed the door softly. "So," he said brightly, "how about that tour and then we go get some food?"

Chapter Four

Sam decided he did fancy fish and chips for tea, so they hopped in the car and drove through the city to McDougall's – the quality Scottish fryer.

"It's busy," Ann was surprised to see a queue of customers trailing out of the door.

Jon pulled up the handbrake with a crunch, "that's because they sell the best chips in the city. Shall we eat in?"

There was a small annexe attached to the chip shop where patrons could sit at plastic tables and be deafened by the overhead television which blared out a constant stream of MTV. Jon ordered three pieces of cod, a large bag of chips and a pot of mushy peas. They ate them out of the wrapper, soaked in vinegar, watching people pass by the window.

"These are good," Jon said, as he chomped on chunks of fish.

"What?" Ann was distracted by the loud music and the whirring of a wall fan.

"I said ... oh forget it," he leaned back in his seat.

"Is that a Dalmatian?" Samuel pointed across the street, where a lady in a murky brown trench coat was struggling to control a bouncy spotty dog. Each time a vehicle whizzed past, the dog barked and surged after it.

"It is," Ann replied, "you don't see many of those about. Isn't he or she gorgeous?"

"It's a she," the manager squirted a blob of antiseptic gel on the table in front of them and revolved his cleaning cloth in slow circles. "That dog is well known in the area for her bad temper – just like its owner. The pair of them need muzzling."

Jon chuckled, "upset you has she, Angus?"

Angus smacked his lips together, "don't you know Beryl Chambers lad? She's known as the local nutter – mad as a box of frogs, she is. Tried to stop my chip shop from opening – reckoned it was going to be an eyesore."

"Glad she wasn't successful," Jon scooped a mound of peas onto his plate.

"Of course, she wasn't successful. Although she tried her damned hardest to ruin it for me. Set up a petition, tried to stir up the local residents against me. Little did she know my best mate is a councillor. He managed to get her objection thrown out with all the other trash complaints. Busybody Beryl's held a grudge ever since."

"We love your chips mate," Jon sat back and patted his stomach, "the best in Chattlesbury I reckon."

Angus smiled broadly, "ere' have these on me then."

Ann stared down at the fizzy drinks placed in front of her. Images of rotten teeth popped into her mind. Sam's teeth were important, in fact his whole physical health was. He was now her responsibility and she was determined to take good care of him. When he excused himself to use the bathroom she said to Jon, "now I'm starting to understand how a first time Mum feels." Quickly she shoved the offensive, sugar riddled pop into her bag. "maybe we need to rethink our diet. Make sure he's getting all the right nutrients."

Jon scratched his head, "don't teenage boys live on pizza?"

A look of horror flitted across Ann's features, "in moderation Jon! I'm making a roast tomorrow, with all the trimmings."

"On a Monday?"

"Yes, on a Monday." They stopped talking as Samuel ambled back towards them.

Jon curled an arm around the back of the plastic chair, "well Sam, what do you want to do for the rest of the day?"

Sam blinked, "I'd really like to chill in my room, if that's alright."

"Of course you can," Ann slipped into her cardigan, "I have prep work to do before the semester starts anyway and you," she stared pointedly at her husband, "can mow the lawn."

Samuel carefully screwed his chip wrapper into a ball, "shall we go … home?" He mumbled.

"Home," Jon echoed with a wide grin.

* * *

The start of year three was a damp one. By mid-September the weather had turned nasty; howling winds and four days of continuous rain caused floods in the city centre which stretched to the grounds of the university. The entire ground floor carpets were ruined by a deluge of brown putrid water, the lifts were out of action and the electricity supply had been temporarily cut off. Subsequently, the English classes were temporarily reallocated to the business school, with its hilltop location. While the Dean supervised an army of contract cleaners in the main city campus, the nervous year three students attended their first lectures.

Sophie and Juliette stood at the entrance to the business school, gazing up at the chrome structure with its contemporary twisted façade and shiny silver peaks.

"This must be a new building," Sophie observed.

"I guess so," Juliette replied, "I kinda prefer the old-fashioned architecture."

"Me too."

The foyer was full of disorientated students, peering at the wall maps and new timetables. Juliette spotted Will, heads above many of the others. From the back of him he just looked gangly, with a headful of hair that sprouted in all directions. It was only when he turned around that you could appreciate how good looking he was. She caught his eye and waved.

"Ready for American Humour?" He queried.

Sophie pulled a face, "the House of Mirth? Not exactly fun reading."

"That's a different module. Are you enrolled for American Literature? This morning's module is American Humour – Portnoy's Complaint? Catcher in the Rye?"

"I'm definitely enrolled for American Humour," Sophie slapped her own forehead, "which means I've read the wrong book."

Will chuckled, "oh well you *could* mention it as a comparison in your essay I suppose. Don't stress though, there are only two books on the primary reading list and they're short."

"Thank God for that," Sophie rubbed her temple, "I didn't fancy writing about the House of Mirth anyway."

"I studied that at A level and actually enjoyed it," Juliette countered, "female repression and objectification? Themes which I intend on exploring in my dissertation."

"Sounds hard," Will unwrapped his cereal bar, "I'm exploring the ideology of what it means to be evil. Comparing Dracula and Frankenstein and critiquing evil acts within the two texts. What you doing Soph'?"

"Nothing quite so profound," Sophie replied, "my theme is friendship. I'm comparing the genuine characters with the superficial and looking at how people aren't always what you think they are. Exploring psyche and behaviours. I've chosen a contemporary author though, I find anything pre twentieth century too much hard work."

"That sounds excellent," Juliette was impressed.

A beeping noise ensued and all three foraged for their phones.

"It's me," Juliette held her phone aloft and looked down.

'I can see you.' Ben.

Juliette smiled, stretched on her tiptoes and scanned the room for him.

'Where are you?'

'I'm looking straight at you.'

Juliette was puzzled. All she could see in front of her was a row of tall plants. Then in between the foliage she caught a glimpse of movement; a shock of dark hair, a flashing of white teeth. What was he doing? She bit her lip, stifling a laugh.

'Are you stalking me?'

'Yes.'

Quickly her fingers flew over the screen, **'try and be professional Dr Rivers.'**

He appeared then in full view, looking so handsome that a lump formed at the back of her throat. He was grinning as he messaged again.

'Will you have lunch with me?'

'Here?'

'Why not?'

'Professional boundaries, that's why not.'

'I can help with your dissertation?'

Yeah right, Juliette thought to herself with a roll of her eyes.

'Okay then. Literary conversations only.'

'Absolutely. 1pm sharp.' He snapped his phone shut and sauntered off, not looking her way. Juliette couldn't help herself.

'I love you.'

That stopped him. For a moment he stood there, then another message came pinging in.

'Remember those boundaries Juliette.' She couldn't tell if he was, but she guessed he was smiling. Then he carried on walking and Juliette was distracted by Sophie's chatter about her new job.

* * *

"Welcome to year three," Doctor Samuel Brown stood at the front of the classroom smiling at the expectant faces focussed on him. Evelyn thought he looked like an old-fashioned gentleman. One of those pre-war aristocratic types with his tweed suit, gold pocket watch and posh accent.

"Don't look so scared," he continued, "I'm nice!"

He chuckled softly as he distributed the handouts.

"Have you had a good summer?" He was speaking to everyone but gazing directly at Sophie.

"Yes thank you," she replied, as the other students murmured politely.

"You." He pointed at Evelyn, "how did you spend your summer?"

Evelyn sat up straighter, "I ... erm, I got married."

"Married? How wonderful. Class, give this brave lady a clap."

There was a round of applause which made Evelyn blush.

"So, before we begin. I just need to tell you about the interview workshop which we run for our final year graduates. It's organised by the career's advisors. They're a friendly bunch and you can find them ..." he glanced at his notes, "at the Student Gateway Service, which is located within the registry block."

Blank faces gazed at him, "where you give in your essays – remember? That is one university building which luckily hasn't been flooded."

The students scribbled down the details.

"Ah, light dawns on Marblehead," Dr Brown said, "now where is that quote from? Is it a poem?"

"It's from a movie," a man sitting at the back shouted, "Cocktail!"

"A great film, anyway, I digress. I do recommend you attend; it is a very informative workshop which gives great advice on performing well at interviews. You will also get the opportunity to have a one-to-one chat with the lovely staff who will provide you with the guidance to enable you to make choices about any further education, training or work." Dr Brown cleared his throat and glanced down at his ream of handwritten notes, "so back to this module. We shall be studying a variety of media such as fiction, film, verse, political speeches etcetera with a view to making informed critical judgements about American Humour. This week we're going to look at the work of three writers in particular: Dorothy Parker, Ring Lardner and J Thurber," Dr Brown began fiddling with his laptop, "I spent the weekend preparing a spectacular slideshow which no longer appears to be there. Drat." He scratched his head, "sorry about this, folks. Talk among yourselves while I attempt to fix it."

The students began talking in hushed tones as Doctor Brown checked cables and wall sockets. After more computer tinkering, he emitted a loud sigh, typed something into his phone and sat behind his desk, clutching his tea.

Ten minutes later the door swung open and Ben Rivers strode in. His appearance elicited sighs. At her front row desk, Juliette smiled and sat up a little straighter.

"Ah Ben," Dr Brown was back on his feet, "I appear to find myself in a quandary."

"Again?" Ben's fingers flew over the keyboard. Boom! The whiteboard crackled then lit up, "you're back online. Will you be okay?"

"Yes, yes. Thank you. Dr Rivers saves the day again."

Juliette noticed two blond students at the adjacent table literally swooning. Another lady on the same table was practically drooling with desire and the man next to her was gazing at Ben with unbridled lust. Juliette's thoughts wandered and she found herself back in his bedroom, gazing into his eyes. She took a swig of water and averted her gaze to Ann who was talking about her plans for the weekend.

Then Dr Rivers left the room and Juliette felt her spirits deflating. How long was it until lunchtime? How long until she could touch him?

Chapter Five

"Right then," Ann wheeled herself towards the door, "let's do lunch."

The business school's refectory was significantly smaller than the main campus's but after complaining about disabled rights access to a security guard, Ann managed to bag them prime seats next to the jacket potato station. A group of students chuntered as they waited for the man at the kiosk to load their potatoes with beans. "Bloody airy-fairy English students taking over."

Juliette was hovering with her tray of spaghetti bolognese.

"Are you going to sit down dear?" Evelyn pulled out the last empty chair.

"I-I'm having lunch with someone … sorry."

Ben appeared in the doorway, looking for her. Juliette wandered off, as the others exchanged glances.

"Is it my imagination or are things between those two getting serious?" Ann bit into her apple, watching as Ben hooked his arm around Juliette's waist.

"She adores him," Sophie's face had taken on a dreamy sheen, "it's just like that film love story."

"The heroine dies in that," Ann said curtly.

"Oh." Sophie blinked, "well I think it's romantic anyway."

"Have you noticed the envious looks Juliette's getting," Ann nodded to a group of females who were pointing at them and whispering.

"I don't think she cares," Evelyn smiled at the way she was gazing up at him, "I just hope it continues after the course has finished."

"Yes, let's hope so," Ann swirled her tea, "because if Dr Rivers breaks her heart, he'll have *me* to answer to."

* * *

"Please sit down," Brian Hodges pulled out a chair and wiggled his eyebrows, making Juliette laugh.

"Thank you," she placed her food down and perched on the seat.

Ben was just about to slide into the empty seat next to her when Brian ducked forward and beat him to it.

"Stop monopolising the lady."

Ben had to take the only remaining seat, right at the other end of the table.

"So Juliette … tell me about your family."

She told him about Harry and Molly. Her protective older sister and her salt of the earth parents, "I also have five brothers," she concluded.

"My word! So there's seven of you?" Brian said, "how on earth did your mother cope? I'm one of two and we've caused mine nothing but grey hairs, so she says."

Juliette smiled as she thought of her own mother Violet; her fierce maternal love and indomitable spirit. "My mum's a strong character."

"A matriarch?" Brian queried.

"Something like that."

"So," Brian leant closer, "do you take after her?"

"I'm more like my dad," Juliette answered, "laid back and gentle."

"And does your Father have red hair too?"

Juliette laughed, "No. I've inherited it from my Granny."

"I thought red-heads were supposed to be fiery?"

"She can be," Ben shouted, "believe me."

Brian chuckled, "eat your lunch Juliette and I'll tell you all about my illustrious past."

Sometime later, her plate was empty and she had heard all about Brian's early life in Chippenham. Juliette stole a glance at Ben, who was deep in conversation with Doctor Brown, but whose eyes were planted firmly on her.

"How are you coping with my heartthrob friend?" Brian whispered.

"Fine, fine," Juliette grinned, "I mean it's certainly no hardship."

"I hope he's looking after you …"

Juliette's reply was instant, "he is … I mean, he makes me very happy."

"I can see that!" Brian blustered, "and I have to say, I've never seen Ben so sickeningly happy either. He seems to have lost *all* interest in his academic research."

Juliette's back gave an involuntary lift, "I hope I'm not distracting him?"

Brian winked, "you sure are, but in a good way. Take no notice of me and my obsession with work. Ben was worse than me you know, some nights he would be here until gone nine. Now he's out of the door before the students." They both laughed, "no really it's great. The whole English department think you've been a marvellous influence on him."

Juliette blushed and her toes tingled with happiness.

"But what about the Dean? I know teacher student relationships are frowned upon, even if I am mature. I worry his career will be ruined because of me."

Brian waved away her concerns, "don't worry about the Dean. He's more bothered about fine dining with corporate businessmen. Anyway, we've all got Ben's back and if there's any trouble or repercussions, we'll revolt like the true romantic rebels we are."

Juliette looked round the table, at the group of wonderfully quirky and gloriously bohemian lecturers.

"Besides," Brian looked with distaste at the entrance, "it's rumoured that Patrick Sullivan over there has had a lot of student-teacher affairs. Doesn't seem to have stopped him progressing through the ranks."

Juliette looked across at the notoriously smarmy lecturer, "I've heard that too. How is that allowed to happen?"

Brian exhaled angrily, "probably because he's managements favourite. Plus his father is a rich politician, which seems to have a lot of influence. They seem happy to turn a blind eye to his shenanigans, on the premise that everyone at university is a vote viable adult." Brian shook his head, "it is wrong of course but maybe I'm just envious."

"Are you married?" Juliette asked.

"Divorced," he replied with a frown, "twice. I cheated on the first one and the second one cheated on me. That's karma on me – huh?"

"Don't say that," Juliette protested, "maybe you haven't found your soul mate."

Brian's face lit up, "oh now I can see why Ben has fallen so hard for you: beautiful, kind and extremely lovely – perfect!"

Juliette fiddled with the butterfly clip twisted into her hair, "I'm *not* perfect."

"Yes, you are." She looked up at Ben who was leaning on the back of her chair.

"Excuse me Doctor Rivers," Brian huffed, "we were having a *private* conversation."

"Yes, too private and, from the looks of it, you were trying to steal her away from me. I think it's time we changed seats."

"Just when things were getting interesting," Brian grumbled, "it was lovely to speak to you, Juliette."

"Bye," Juliette gave him a little wave.

"Was he bothering you?" Ben tucked a loose curl behind her ear.

"No! He's actually very nice," her stomach flipped as she looked into Ben's dark, stormy eyes.

"He's a good friend," Ben acknowledged, "but I think he's attracted to you, hmm?"

"Ben hush, this is your place of work!"

"So?" He grinned, "I need to be alone with you. I need to speak with you somewhere more private."

Juliette felt heat stirring between her thighs and cleared her throat, "we can talk later. I should get going, I have a dissertation meeting."

"Play truant. Just this once."

"No!" A line of perspiration clung to her top lip, "aren't you teaching?"

Slowly he shook his head.

Juliette looked away from his lips and blurted out, "I like your tie."

Abruptly, Ben pushed back his chair and said in a loud, husky voice, "yes Miss Harris, I would be happy to show you the new computer suite."

"Please excuse me," Juliette waved to the other lecturers.

"Bye Juliette," Wilomena called, as she hurried out of the room after Ben.

"Can you come to mine? Just for a few hours?"

"Ben," Juliette touched his arm, "slow down. Of course I'll come with you; you know I will."

He grinned at her, pulling her close to him, "I knew you couldn't resist."

Ben was drumming his fingers impatiently on the steering wheel and frowning at the build-up of traffic in front of him. He seemed so tense today.

"Is your sister okay?" Juliette asked, resting her hand lightly on his thigh.

"Much better physically. Psychologically she's still very fragile," he glanced at her, "can you come with me? To see her?"

"Yes," she murmured, moving her fingers in gentle circles. He cleared his throat and she increased the pressure.

"You look smart today," she continued. Her internal, no filter monologue also added – 'you are so hot.' Juliette shifted across the seat, pulled by the giddy smell of his aftershave. Softly she pressed her lips against his cheek, moving upwards to flick her tongue against his ear. She heard the infinitesimal change in his breath, and the tensing of his muscles as he gripped the gear stick.

"Are you concentrating?" She teased, following his line of vision. "Ben." She frowned at the looming figure in front of them, "that bus is stationary. Ben!"

He slammed on the brakes and the car screeched to a halt, flinging them forward.

"Sorry!" She said breathlessly.

He started the car again and they moved forwards.

"Let's talk uni!" Juliette smiled, brightly.

"How was your romanticism essay?" He asked, tersely.

"Hard. It was very hard," Juliette closed her eyes, pushing away spontaneous thoughts of lovemaking. "Erm … what I mean to say is, it was challenging, but in a good way."

"You're clever. I'm sure you can cope. Finally!" Ben pulled off the main A road and sped down a junction that led to a series of twisty country lanes. Juliette stared out of the side window, mulling over what his plans would be for Christmas. She desperately wanted him to come to hers, for the whole day if he could, but she didn't want to pressure him, and his sister was still so poorly – he should be there with her.

"Your garden looks nice," Juliette waited for him to stop the engine, before sliding out.

"It looks even better from my bedroom," he grinned boyishly at her, slotted the key in the door and together they ran up the stairs laughing.

* * *

"What are you doing for Christmas?" Juliette asked sleepily, warm and cosy in Ben's arms and cocooned in a fluffy winter duvet.

"The question isn't what I'm doing – it's what you're doing."

"What?" She nuzzled his chest, hair tickling her nose.

"I've a surprise for you: for Harry and Molls too. So if *you've* made plans, better unmake them now."

Juliette gazed at him with suspicious eyes, "what have you done?"

He pulled himself upright, "we're going on a little trip for Christmas; the four of us."

"We are? Where to?"

"I'll give you a clue Juliette. Where does Father Christmas live?"

Juliette squinted, "the North Pole? You're taking us to the North Pole?"

Ben rolled his eyes, "jeez, you don't know much about Santa do you? Lapland Juliette, Lapland."

"Lapland? Oh my god, are you serious?"

"So serious it's all fully booked; flight, hotel, itinerary."

Juliette bounced up in the bed, eyes shining with excitement, "oh Ben thank you. Harry and Molly will *love* it. No cooking for me, no washing up, no peeling veg in cold water until my hands are red raw. No stressful food shop. This is going to be *heaven*." She grasped his head in her hands, rained kisses over his face, "thank you lovely man, thank you."

* * *

When the dissertation meeting had finished, Sophie packed up her belongings and headed off to the call centre. It was her third week at Hanley's and she had settled in well. Her colleagues were warm and friendly and had made her feel welcome right from the offset, apart from the receptionist, who appeared to be snooty with everybody. Sophie pulled onto the car park, splashing a pool of murky rain water high into the air. A lady who worked in accounts was struggling out of a car next to her.

"Where's the blasted sun gone?" The woman cast a critical eye over the storm clouds rolling overhead.

Sophie shrugged, hitching her bag onto her shoulder.

"Sophie? Is that your name? You're the new girl, aren't you? Andy's been touting you as his next great sales prodigy."

Sophie smiled at the mention of the Head of HR – an exuberant American with a dazzling smile who wore well-cut suits and glitzy watches.

"I'm enjoying it very much. I love chatting to the customers."

"I noticed your desk is the most colourful in the office."

They climbed up a flight of steps.

"Oh, they're paintings by my children and plants from my friend. I just wanted to brighten things up."

"You certainly do that."

Together they walked into the foyer, passing the longest standing member of Hanley & Hanley's. Henry, the white-haired cleaner was scrubbing at a tea stain on a mosaic table. He smiled as they walked past.

"Just one moment," an icy cold woman's voice called. Sophie and Sharon turned to look at the receptionist who was pulling off her ear piece.

"There's a meeting this evening. All staff must attend."

"Great," Sharon sighed, "Just what I need on a Friday evening."

They carried on to a lift which whizzed them up to the sales floor.

A low-level hum of noise greeted them. Staff on phones, talking to customers and the whirring of the photocopiers and the beeping fax machine. Sophie noticed Andy half perched on a desk, talking into his mobile. When he saw them he waved then beckoned them over.

"Ladies," he said brightly, cutting his call, "drinks tonight after the staff meeting?"

Sharon was immediately nodding. Sophie however was dithering.

"Is it your kids?" Andy asked, "bring them along, the wine bar has a great beer garden."

"They're having a sleep over at friends," Sophie explained.

"Even better," Sharon grasped her arm with excitement, "that means we can party all night."

Sophie laughed, "I'll have to check if my friend can get them organised first."

"You do that," Sharon nodded, then turned her attention to Andy, "so what does this staff meeting entail? As you can probably tell, I'm a very conscientious employee…"

Sophie had been chatting for three hours and twenty minutes. During that time, she had notched up twenty new hoover sales, seven extended warranty subscriptions, calmed a handful of dissatisfied customers and logged five repairs into the system. Currently she was listening to Ms Cuthbert. A sweet octogenarian who was telling her all about her army corporal sweetheart.

"He had the most gorgeous green eyes and a big quiff in his hair like a proper teddy boy. He used to write me love poems, very passionate they were."

"Sounds so romantic," Sophie sighed, "did you marry?"

There was a chuckle on the other end of the line, "bit of a problem there – being as though he were already married."

Sophie gasped, "Ms Cuthbert! Were you his mistress?"

"Yep. I never wanted to be the little wife at home baking in a flowery pinafore. I wanted to be free and independent, so being a scarlet woman with the occasional toy boy lover suited me just fine. My life's been full of adventures. Did you know I jumped out of a plane last week?"

"Wow!" Sophie ducked down as Sheila from the typing pool strode past, "so your lover – do you still meet?"

"Unfortunately not. He died, my Freddy. Got knocked down by a bus at Piccadilly Circus," Ms Cuthbert sniffed, "I couldn't go to his funeral of course but I planted a rose tree in my garden. A red floribunda – called it Corporal Freddy. The most beautiful flower in my entire garden. I must have hardy soil – don't you think?"

"Absolutely," Sophie cleared her throat, "well Ms Cuthbert, your hoover is all ordered, complete with accessories and an instruction DVD. It should be with you within seven days. Thank you very much and it's been lovely talking to you."

"You're a nice girl," Ms Cuthbert said, "goodbye and I hope you find your Freddy too."

"I …" Sophie stared at the buzzing phone.

"Awkward customer?" Andy was twiddling a pen, smiling at her.

"No. Actually, she was very nice." Sophie pushed back her chair, "would you like a coffee?"

"Please," he followed her through the large open plan office, into the staffroom, "so this evening, can you make it?"

"I can," Sophie emptied spoons of coffee into two mugs, "I won't be staying late though. Hangovers and two boisterous children are *not* a good combination."

"I wouldn't know," Andy held up his hands, "I have no responsibilities."

"Not even a cat?" Sophie said, with a smirk.

"How did you know?" Andy passed her a bottle of chilled milk, "I love kids though, how many do you have?"

"Just the two," Sophie replied, "twin boys."

"And you're not married?" Andy pointed at her ring finger.

"Separated," she stirred her drink, "are you?"

"Hell no," he threw back his head and laughed, "you could say I'm in-between girlfriends at the moment."

Uh-oh Sophie thought, player alert.

"Well I'll get back to work then," Sophie turned away.

"Sophie," Andy called, "You're doing real well. The management are pleased with you."

Sophie paused, "thank you. I'm enjoying it very much here."

The door swung shut softly behind her as she hurried back to her flashing phone.

Chapter Six

At 6.30pm precisely, the phones were redirected to the answer machines and the entire staff body trooped into the staffroom.

A few of the girls were huddled close to the T.V, watching a re-run of Loose Women. Others milled about, chatting in groups, making drinks, staring wistfully out of the window. Sophie spotted Sharon from accounts bent over, with her head stuck in the fridge.

"Oh hi Sophie," she glanced sideways at her, "fancy a slice of gateaux?"

"Go on then."

She pulled out a silver platter, on which rested an oozing chocolate cake.

"Well doesn't this look delicious." Sophie watched as she sliced two pieces and covered them with blobs of squirty cream, "it might help soak up the beer later."

Sharon nudged her and winked playfully.

"It's been a while since I've been on a girl's night out," Sophie thought fleetingly of Amber and wondered how she was doing. The last she had heard via Facebook, she had checked into one of Bulgaria's top hotels on a spa and ski week. Some of the photos had shown her in rather incriminating poses with a guy in clogs and her husband Martin had even liked it. Sophie made herself a mental reminder to drop her a message next week. Amber could be loud and gaudy but, underneath all the façade, she was a nice person. "Where are we going anyway?" Sophie enquired, licking a mound of chocolate off her index finger.

"A pub crawl of course, then a curry if you're up for it."

"Sounds fun." They made a dash for the last seats, as Andy and the other managers burst in with highlighters and wall charts.

When the evening out began, there were about twenty staff, hell-bent on having a drink and a laugh. But as the night wore on, the numbers dwindled, people tapered off into taxis leaving just six stumbling up the high street, towards the curry house. The strong breeze buffeted Sophie's face, bringing tears to her eyes. Behind her, Sharon was singing 'I Will Survive' in a high pitch, eliciting amused looks from passing commuters.

"She always does this on a night out," Hannah from the sales office whispered, "messy divorce."

Sophie nodded sympathetically, "how long have you worked at Hanley's?"

"This will be my fourth year," Molly replied, "it pays the bills I suppose," she cocked her head to one side, "I hear that you're a student?"

"Yes final year."

"I've always wanted to go to uni. I love anything to do with art: drawing, painting, design. I have a summerhouse where I escape reality. It's where I can lose myself in my art."

"You should go … to uni I mean. It's changed my outlook on life completely."

"I'm forty-three," Hannah sighed.

"So?" Sophie replied, "my friend is older and she's loving it. Seriously, age is no barrier to learning. And there's so much diversity at university," her eyes grew wide, "no one cares about gender or race or sexual preferences or how old you are. It's kind of like a dream world, that promises you can be whatever / whoever you want to be."

"Like a utopia?"

"Yes." Sophie nodded emphatically, "at least from my experience it is."

"Meanwhile in the real world, people are still being murdered in the name of religion. People are still being marginalised according to their gender and their sexuality and free speech is fine as long as it suits the politically correct brigade. You're right Sophie, university is a dream world because it's not based in reality. This is reality," Andy nodded to a man propped in a doorway, huddled beneath a duvet, "where the vulnerable and the sick and the poor are forsaken – what about their dreams Sophie? In my opinion, academia equates to idealism and theory and are these so called intelligent academics really as open minded and independently thinking as they like society to think they are. I think not. The down to earth, working class are society's true warriors. The proper hard workers, the grafters, the war heroes. If you want to experience real life, Sophie, learn it from them."

Sophie protested, "my friend is dating a very nice lecturer."

"How exciting," Hannah pulled the restaurant door open and whispered in her ear, "I think Andy has a soft spot for you."

Sophie blushed and decided to ignore that comment. She shrugged out of her coat as a smiling waiter danced towards them, grabbed their hands and pulled them into a clumsy pirouette.

Sophie ordered a biryani. The same that she always ordered whenever she dined in an Asian restaurant. This one however was spicier than was she was normally used to, and a jug of water was rapidly drunk, in-between mouthfuls of rice and chicken. Their table was right next to a draughty door and a ceiling fan that revolved rapidly above them, making goose bumps appear on the backs of her bare arms. The three guys in their party were seated at the right side of the table, talking football and cars. Sophie and the other two women; Hannah and Charlotte were discussing what was occurring in the T.V soaps. Akbul, their waiter for the evening, shimmied over to them and topped their glasses up with sparkling wine. From behind his back he produced two generous sized nan breads that were complimentary from the chef.

Hannah was the first to dig in. She tore off a chunk, dipping it into her bowl of bhuna, "so," she beckoned Sophie closer, "what do you think of our Andy?"

Sophie rolled her eyes, "he seems a nice friendly guy."

"Uh-huh," Hannah's voice had taken on a teasing tone, "what about his looks?"

Sophie glanced over, "he's handsome," she replied, grudgingly.

Charlotte from admin giggled, "I think he's as hot as hell."

"Did you know that his grandfather is a self-made millionaire?" Hannah stared at Sophie, "born into extreme poverty in the Irish slums."

Sophie tensed, "money doesn't impress me."

"Really?" Hannah and Charlotte said in surprised unison.

"I'm surprised," Hannah said, "you look as if you have money."

"I did," Sophie sighed, "I'm recently separated from Ryan O'Neill."

Charlotte gasped, "*the* Ryan O'Neill? The mega wealthy Chattlesbury foot-baller?"

"He's no longer playing for them," Sophie explained, "I don't think he's doing much of anything at the moment."

"But why are you working at Hanley's, Sophie?"

"Let's just say it's a case of having to." Sophie took a long sip of her wine and the subject was changed to the less risqué topic of holiday destinations.

"Madam your coat," Andy held her nutmeg coloured parka out for her to slide her arms into, "you smell nice, like flowers, like summer ..."

Sophie smiled, "it's lavender," she looked up at him, "thank you for buying dinner."

"No problem sweet cheeks," his American drawl was loud and pronounced in the empty restaurant, "you work hard, you deserve it."

Sophie turned to catch up with the others, but the sound of her name halted her.

"Sophie. Would you like to, I mean if you want to? Jeez this is difficult," He ran his hand through his fair hair, "do you wanna go for dinner, just the two of us?"

"Dinner?" Sophie echoed, "as in a date?"

"As in two friends who would like to get to know each other better?"

"I'm not ready for ... I don't want a relationship. Not now. I need to be on my own," Sophie was almost shrieking, "I just want to be alone for a while – just me and my kids."

"Hey sorry," Andy looked mortified, "I didn't mean to upset you. Heck me and my big mouth. Sorry Sophie. Forget I said anything, okay?"

Sophie nodded fervently, "I should go now. Bye Andy." She hurried away from him, out into the cold night air where she almost jumped in front of an empty taxi cab that was trundling up the leaf-strewn road.

* * *

"It's that one there," Sophie steered the taxi driver to a stop outside Evelyn's brightly lit house.

"Bit early for Christmas ain't it?" The taxi driver remarked. They both paused to gaze at the towering fir tree in the garden that had twinkling lights twined throughout its branches.

"It's like that all year round," Sophie replied with a smile, "how much do I owe you?"

After she had paid, Sophie rummaged in her bag and slotted her key in the front door. The warmth from the long hallway rushed towards her, enveloping her and drawing her in its warm embrace.

"I'm back," she called, slipping out of her shoes and unfurling her long scarf.

"Hello dear," Evelyn stood in the kitchen doorway. A tiny grey-haired figure holding a large bowl and wearing a pinafore over her trousers and blouse. She was smiling and words sprang to Sophie's mind: contentment, stability and home. Evelyn embodied the solid, dependable mother figure that Sophie had always craved. She rushed to embrace her, burying herself in her warmth. Evelyn balanced the bowl on one hip, "have you had a nice evening?"

"Oh it was okay," Sophie ducked her head towards the floor, "a man came onto me, or in your case Evelyn, I was propositioned."

Evelyn laughed, a lovely tinkling sound, "is that a bad thing?" When there was no reply she continued, "who was he?"

"One of the senior company managers," mortification resounded in Sophie's tone, "Andy from America."

"America? Well that does sound exciting, does he have a nice accent?"

Sophie snorted, "annoying would be the most fitting adjective."

"But he's nice?"

Sophie softened slightly, "he's gregarious I suppose."

Evelyn's eyes twinkled merrily.

"Are you teasing me?" Sophie felt her anxiety slipping away, "I'm not interested in *any* male relationship at the moment. What are you baking now?" She followed Evelyn into the kitchen, "it smells divine in here. Oh," her gaze flitted over the messy table, the pots and pans stacked in the sink, the overturned cookery books and the fine sheen of flour that was floating in the air.

"I've made, for the first time ever, a banana loaf. Plus a batch of chocolate fairy cakes *and* a Victoria sponge."

"You *have* been busy," Sophie commented, "but where's Jacob?"

"I sent him down the local for a tipple. He's back now, watching Mastermind."

Sophie squirted washing up liquid into a bowl of hot water, "I should take the dogs out."

"They've been," said Evelyn, happily, "we took them after the boys had been collected. Went for a lovely walk along the canal side. They've been lying in front of the fire since we got back. Exhausted I should think."

Evelyn tipped the last of the mixture into a greased loaf tin, "you've had mail Sophie."

"More bills!" Sophie scrubbed forcefully at a food encrusted palette knife, "how is married life, Evelyn?"

"Wonderful … perfect … okay maybe not perfect. Jacob is untidy and he snores," Evelyn tutted, "that was disloyal of me. What I meant to say was he makes me extremely happy and I'm very proud to be his wife." She wiped her fingers on her pinafore before popping the tin into the warm oven.

"I shouldn't be here," Sophie shook her head, staring down at the bubbly water, "you're newlyweds and you should have your own space. I'm a burden, aren't I?"

"Don't be ridiculous," Evelyn scoffed, "we're hardly love's young dream now. *Both of us* love having you and the boys here."

"Even the crazy dogs?"

Evelyn laughed, "especially the crazy dogs."

"Fair enough," Sophie grinned, "but it is only a temporary measure, I promise."

Evelyn chucked her underneath her chin, "this is your home for as long as you need it."

"Shall we have a nightcap before bed, Evelyn?"

"Absolutely dear. Let's get all cleaned up and then we can relax."

They busied themselves tidying the kitchen. As Sophie was hanging up the damp tea towel to dry, she asked Evelyn about the progress of her book.

"It's in editing," Evelyn replied, "but I've been assured it will be out in time for Christmas. Can you imagine Sophie? My novel will be on the shelves in bookstores."

"*Very* exciting," Sophie splashed sherry into three crystal goblets, picked up her pile of mail and padded barefoot into the lounge.

Jacob was snoring softly, the remote control rested on his stomach and his glasses had slipped down the bridge of his nose and were balancing precariously. They stifled gulps of laughter, while tiptoeing past him and sinking down onto the two-seater sofa.

"There's a wildlife programme on at ten," Evelyn whispered, "David Attenborough, my favourite."

Sophie relaxed back, drawing her knees up. She opened a thick brown envelope which turned out to be overdue council tax arrears from her old property. The next was a magazine subscription renewal, promising two editions and a lipstick free if she responded within two weeks. Sophie ripped it into neat little squares.

"More junk?" Evelyn queried.

"Yep."

She glanced at the last letter which had a red London postmark emblazoned across it. The paper looked posh and felt thick between her fingers. Sophie tore it open and pulled out a single sheet of paper. There was no address, but at the very top, underneath yesterday's date, was a mobile number. The letter began with Dear Sophie...

You do not know me but I am a friend of your father's - Anthony. I have news and need to speak to you Sophie.

This may come as a great shock to you, and I hope I haven't alarmed you, but your father is alive and wishes to make contact with you.

Please contact me on the supplied mobile number so we can talk further.

Hope to hear from you soon. Awaiting your reply.

The signature was swirly and fancy and undecipherable to Sophie's wide eyes.

"Whatever is the matter, Sophie?" Evelyn was staring at her with consternation.

The colour had drained from her cheeks and her forehead had grown clammy. She drew in a lungful of air, as the clock chimed ten o'clock and the letter slipped in a slow-motion dance from her hands, fluttering to the floor.

Chapter Seven

"Have you heard from Sophie?" Juliette asked Ann, as they entered the open elevator.

"Nope. Is she not coming today?" Ann sounded surprised.

"I thought she was," Juliette replied, "I've messaged her twice over the weekend. No reply."

"Maybe she's been at that hoover place," Ann clicked her fingers, trying to remember.

"Hanley's," Juliette supplied, "yes you're probably right, she must be busy."

"The business school really needs to upgrade their lifts," Ann cast a critical glance round the confined space. It was shabby and the back wall was covered with graffiti. There was an odd stench in the air that reminded Ann of stale clothes and cigarette smoke. It creaked ominously as it moved slowly up the floors. Juliette wrinkled her nose and nodded in agreement.

Finally, it juddered to a stop. The doors slid open and Will stood a few feet in front of them, peering at a map.

"Hi," he glanced up then back down again, "do you guys know where we should be heading?"

Ann shrugged, "all I know is that it's on the third floor."

"We'll find it. Come on." Juliette led the way down a pleasantly decorated corridor that had pictures of the city hanging from its walls. At the very end stood an odd-looking statue – a mismatch of metal, clumped together in odd shapes that bent and curved almost to the ceiling.

"*What is that?*"

Ann gazed at the accompanying plaque. "Distress. By Chattlesbury University's art students."

Will took a picture of it on his mobile, "maybe I'll make one myself out of baked bean tins."

"Samuel could have done a better job," Ann decided, "are those marbles?"

Juliette chuckled, "philistines. This is modern art ... I think," she cocked her head sideways to observe it from a different angle, "I wonder what the meaning of it is?"

"Maybe it doesn't have one. *Maybe* a bunch of students decided to clump together a load of old metal just for the fun of it. A let's point fun at a society that has to analyse and define everything."

"It *must* have a meaning," Juliette said.

"Here's a random one for you," Ann's voice rose a few octaves in a mockery of a posh accent, "this particular work of art conveys the angst of a modern, technologically obsessed society. Aren't I clever, aren't I super," she popped her gum in defiance.

"I say Ann, what a wonderful interpretation" Will rubbed his chin, "you're terribly wrong of course. This is a work of art that conveys a symbiotic world devoid of love and compassion."

"Jolly well defined, old boy," Ann pursed her lips together in an attempt to stifle laughter.

"You're both wrong. It's obvious that this masterpiece conveys an apocalyptic society, broken by mankind's greed," Juliette waved her hands in front of her face as they broke into loud peals of laughter.

"Actually, you're *all* wrong." An unfamiliar voice from behind added, "it was commissioned for Mental Health Awareness week. It signifies the broken mind."

"Wow," Juliette gulped back laughter and smiled at Leon Broome, head of the Student Union, "that is deep."

"Isn't it?" He patted a metal curve, "oops, not supposed to touch it."

"Why not?" Ann questioned, "isn't art supposed to be about using the senses? Touch creates emotion, feelings, understanding – am I right?"

Leon cleared his throat, "the Dean has a tendency to disagree. But he is a science graduate, which means the right hemisphere of his brain that controls creativity is under developed and isn't used enough. That's one theory anyway," he looked around quickly, making sure no one had overhead.

"Or maybe he prefers traditional art," Ann countered, "the type that has to be admired from afar. The type that has ropes around it. The type we can only look at."

"I love the Pre-Raphaelite paintings," Juliette said, "so romantic and striking."

"Ah yes," Leon agreed, "Dante Gabriel Rossetti. Very talented. The Walker Art Gallery in Liverpool has one of the most impressive collections of Pre-Raphaelite Art in the world. You should go. In fact, maybe I could organise a trip for the English department. Did they write literature too?"

"They wrote poetry," Ann nodded.

Leon clapped his hands, "excellent." He wandered off, muttering about coach companies and head counts.

Ann backed away from the sculpture, "we're late. Let's go find this work-shop."

* * *

"You do *not* need a cigarette." Evelyn admonished Sophie as they climbed the grassy hill.

"I need something," Sophie sniffed, "my hands are trembling. Look." She held ten trembling fingers towards the sky.

"It's shock," Evelyn's breath curled out in the chilly morning air. They silently watched the dogs bounding playfully, skidding over the frost-hardened mud. A hawk cawed above them, gliding across the misty sky. They were the only people up here, probably because the temperature had dropped dramatically. It was so cold, even for November.

"What will you do?" Evelyn mumbled.

"I have no idea. This is surreal. Is this really happening?" Sophie shook her head, trying to clear the racing, confused thoughts, "what shall I do Evelyn?"

"I think." Evelyn paused to clear her throat, "you should hear what this man has to say."

"You think I should contact him?" Sophie's voice had turned squeaky.

"Yes. I do."

"But … but, it could be a scam."

"And it could also be completely legit," Evelyn picked up a stick and lobbed it high into the air, "all I'm advising is to hear what he has to say."

"Dad … Anthony … he abandoned me. I was a child, Evelyn. I adored him and he abandoned me," Sophie's eyes filled with tears.

"I know," Evelyn soothed, placing a comforting arm around her shoulders, "it's your decision Sophie. Follow your heart. If it doesn't feel right then don't respond."

"Tear the letter up?"

"Tear it up," Evelyn nodded decisively. "Now, what shall we have for lunch? Homemade vegetable soup or poached eggs?"

Jacob was waiting for them at the bottom of the path as they turned into their street. He ambled towards them, his face twisted into a frown.

"Your mother's here."

"What?" Sophie glanced at Evelyn, "surely she doesn't know?"

"Of course she doesn't," Evelyn replied, "she probably wants to see the boys."

"They're at school!" Sophie hurried through the open door, almost colliding with Yvonne's bent-over frame, "Mum?"

"Darling," Yvonne straightened, "I was just admiring your shoe collection. It's a lot smaller than it used to be."

Sophie swallowed, "I've downsized. Would you like a drink?"

"As long as it's herbal, or ... do you have decaf?"

"We have both!" Evelyn unbuttoned her coat and smiled at Yvonne, "hello Mrs Fletcher."

"Hello," Yvonne stopped, "I'm sorry I've forgotten your name."

"Evelyn, and this is my husband Jacob."

Yvonne nodded at them both then said to Sophie, "can we talk?"

"In here." Sophie ushered her mother into the kitchen, "how are you?"

Yvonne collapsed onto a wooden stool, sighing theatrically, "to be truthful Sophie, I'm exhausted."

"Oh?" Sophie clicked on the kettle, "is Derek keeping you awake?"

"It's not Derek! Please don't poke fun," Yvonne picked at the edge of the table, "I don't think I can cope any longer with your husband."

Sophie tensed, "he's not *my* husband."

"He is in name!" Yvonne rubbed her eyes, "sorry darling I've accepted your decision to divorce him. He's becoming a burden. Derek and I are at our wits end."

"What exactly has Ryan been doing?" Sophie's eyes slanted suspiciously.

"Late night brawling. Drinking too much. Constantly moping about. The grocery bill has rocketed since he's moved in. He's lazy, Sophie, and he's a bad influence on Derek."

Sophie crossed her arms, "he was like that before. But then Derek didn't mind when he was raking in the thousands and riding the crest of popularity."

"Don't be so cynical Sophie. Derek ... he ... cares for Ryan very much, but even he's at the end of his tether."

"So. Let me guess. You're going to kick him out?" Sophie shook her head, "what true, compassionate friends you are."

Yvonne's mouth flapped open, "I thought you hated him! Remember what he did to you, Sophie?"

"He's on a massive downer," Sophie snapped, "and in my book, you don't kick someone when they're already down."

"Okay." Yvonne smirked, "I didn't want to tell you this but he's seeing another woman."

Sophie blinked, "I actually don't care."

"Your hairdresser Sophie. He's seeing that floozy hairdresser with the bleached blond hair and stilettoes, who looks like some weird 80s reject!" Yvonne was screeching now. The dogs whimpered and scurried underneath the table.

Sophie shrugged, "Good luck to them. We are separated, Ryan can do whatever he wants. And so can I." She banged the cups down and fruity water sloshed over the rim.

Yvonne sat up straighter, "are you seeing someone new?"

Sophie rubbed her temple, "Mother why are you telling me all this? What do you expect me to do?"

Yvonne cleared her throat, "I thought ... Derek and I thought maybe you could talk to him? Tell him to sort himself out. We've tried, but it's fallen on deaf ears."

"No." Sophie tapped her foot on the linoleum floor, as a muscle twitched in her jaw.

Yvonne jumped to her feet. Two red dots stained her cheeks. "You've never been supportive of me! You're just like your ... "

"My what? My father?" Sophie felt a pang of pain rock her body.

Yvonne stared, "sorry."

Then Evelyn burst through the door, carrying a try of empty cups, asking Sophie if she was alright.

"Mum was just leaving." Tears clouded her vision.

Yvonne pulled the belt on her coat tighter, "I'll be in touch." With that she was gone, slamming the front door so hard, the windows rattled.

Sophie turned to Evelyn, hurriedly wiping the tears away, "the letter."

"It's on the mantlepiece," Evelyn soothed, "what are you going to do?"

"I'm going to contact him." Sophie nodded. "I need my dad Evelyn; I need my dad."

* * *

There were about twenty people in the interview preparation session. That included a boisterous group of mature psychology students and a small group of PhD science graduates. A jolly looking lady came bustling in, carrying a half-eaten sandwich and a bumper bag of Doritos.

"Hey guys," she set her condiments down and waved, "great to see you all. My name's Maxine and I'm going to be helping you today."

The door squeaked open and Leon Broome poked his head around the architrave, "Before you begin Mrs Connor, can I have a quick word?"

"Go ahead."

He clapped his hands, "I just wanted to tell you about our recently organised debating team. We meet once a week to erm … debate."

One of the psychology students piped up, "debate what?"

"Anything," Leon shrugged, "topical issues, politics, the environment, religion, what's going on in education. Anybody care to join?"

There was silence. "You," he pointed at Ann, "sorry, madam. You seemed very articulate and opinionated when we were discussing art earlier."

Ann coughed, "am I?"

Leon nodded, "can I put your name down?"

"When is it?" She pulled out her personal organiser.

"Wednesday evenings in The Learning Centre. It's only a small group but we have tea and biscuits!"

"Then I'll come," Ann smiled, "Sophie loves chatting. Maybe she could join me."

"The more the merrier," he glanced at Juliette.

"Oh no," she held her hands up, "I work evenings, have two young children, plus uni work to cope with. I can't take on anymore. Sorry."

"Leon, maybe you could leave the form with me and any other students can sign up when they've had a think about it." Mrs Connor took the paper from his hands and Leon left the room with a nod.

"Now then," Mrs Connor began, "The most important thing we tell our prospective job hunting students is, to fail to prepare is to prepare to fail. Preparation is the key word folks. Without it you're unlikely to get the job and you will also not learn anything from the experience either. So what kind of things do you need to consider prior to the interview?" She picked up her pen.

"Dress?" A lady shouted from the back.

"Yes." Mrs Connor scribbled it down, "casual dress is a big no-no. You should always err on the conservative side; neat and smart always sends a message that you are taking the vacancy seriously. Anything else?"

"Punctuality," Juliette said, with a raise of her hand.

"Of course," Mrs Connor replied, "and arriving early makes an excellent first impression. Which means that you should plan your travel arrangements beforehand, for example, knowing where the interview is and allowing sufficient time to get there."

The conversation turned to possible interview questions as outside the window, storm clouds gathered and swirled.

* * *

"Jesus, look at the sky." It was breaktime and Ann and Juliette were grabbing food and drinks from the refectory. They stared out at the dark greyness that almost seemed to be touching the ground. The boughs of the trees were bending in the wind and litter was being tossed around the courtyard. A lady walking outside clung desperately onto her hat and the hem of her skirt as it flapped upwards.

"Jon will run you home," Ann decided, "It's looking scary out there."

"Looks like more blasted flooding," the lady at the jacket potato kiosk followed their gaze, "I'll be glad when the humanities building is open again, won't you?" She turned her attention to Juliette, giving her a cross look as she adjusted her hair net, "do you want butter?"

"Yes. If that's okay."

"Sorry love," the catering assistants tone turned contrite, "we're not used to catering for this many students. Just look at it." She nodded at the line of people stretching all the way back, through the entrance doors, "how on earth are we supposed to clear everything and still finish for two thirty?" She dumped the cheese down forcefully, "You didn't want any sides, did you?"

"Erm … no," Juliette picked up her tray and, with a longing look at the nearby salad selection, followed Ann to the till. The canteen was now full, but after complaining loudly about disability rights, Ann and Juliette were ushered over to a comfortable looking seating area. As the assistant stuffed the discarded wrappers into a black bag and swiped at the table with a dishcloth that reeked of lemon disinfectant, Juliette fell back onto a squashy leather chair, her legs swinging upwards.

"This is nice."

"Is it?" Ann bit into her Belgian bun, "I prefer the main campus. What the hell are they doing over there anyway? How long does it take to suck out a pool of water?"

Juliette's attention was distracted by the pinging of her phone. It was a message from Will, asking her to grab him a hot chocolate. She quickly ate her food, listening to Ann talk about the boy who had come to live with them. Then she cleared away their trays and hurried over to the self-service drinks machine.

As steaming water bubbled into the cup, she heard the sound of her name and turned to see Helena Mulberry with her back to her, scooping pasta into a plastic tub.

"Yes, she's called Juliette," she was talking to a short lady who was attacking the potato salad tray with relish.

"Juliette? How archaic."

"How ridiculously sickening. *What* were her parents thinking?"

Short lady tutted with agreement, "and she's his student? How unprofessional! Maybe the Dean should hear about this."

"He knows," cried Helena, "the pair of them have been flouncing about the university with a total disregard for discretion. Of course, I've tried to warn Ben."

"Did you have one of your little chats?"

"Yes. But you know how obstinate he can be. I think he enjoys rebelling against the hierarchy in this place and he refuses to listen to sense. If anything, it's making him more determined to carry on with this hair-brained relationship."

"Oh dear. I suppose the poor deluded girl believes that he loves her?"

Juliette winced as Helena snorted derisively, "AS IF. Ben Rivers does *not do* commitment. It's obviously some weird, menopausal fling on his behalf and we all know he has a weakness for redheads."

Short lady hummed knowingly.

"As for her, I can certainly see the attraction, who doesn't fancy him? But what will she do when she finds out that Ben is ultimately a long-term relationship phobic? I feel pity for her, I really do."

"Sounds doomed to me."

"Quite."

They wandered off, blissfully ignorant that their entire conversation had been overheard. Juliette gulped in huge lungsful of air, redness flamed her neck and cheeks and her body literally shook with rage. She stood for a few moments, trying to compose herself. But then Ann was beckoning her over, jabbing at her wrist watch and Juliette was consumed with anger for her, why does she always have such an attitude? She gritted her teeth and made her way back over.

On the way back to the classroom, Ann asked if she had made any plans for the weekend.

"No." Juliette snapped, "I have no idea what I'm doing!"

"Okay." Ann's eyebrows shot up with surprise.

"Sorry," Juliette rubbed her forehead, "I'm just a bit stressed."

Ann laughed, "it's fine. Everyone deserves a bad-tempered day. I should know, I have more than anybody."

Despite her inner turmoil, Juliette chuckled and as she did, the tension slowly drained away. I'm not doing this again she silently vowed, I'm not letting others come between us again.

"Here you go," with a bright smile she passed Will his pen and prepared herself for a debate on how to cope with psychometric tests.

Chapter Eight

Will was reading through the examples of verbal reasoning tests, when the guy sitting next to him struck up a conversation. He was called Boyd. He had messy hair that curled past his shoulders and silver studs in both nostrils and above his eyebrows. He was wearing a Pixies t-shirt and had anarchy tattooed across his left knuckle. He smelt odd; biker leather mixed with incense oil and the overpowering stench of weed. When he spoke, Will could see chipped yellow teeth and indentations around his mouth that looked like chicken pox scars. Will almost fell off his chair with surprise when he heard that Boyd studied accountancy, with ambitions to set up his own chartered firm.

"Don't let this grungy façade fool you," Boyd guffawed, spittle flying onto Will's blank paper, "this is my student slash weekend look. In my wardrobe I have five suits in varying degrees of blue, a briefcase and a state-of-the-art personal organiser. Oops," he dabbed at the spilt coffee which was staining his already grubby top. "I know what you're thinking ..."

Will looked away from his face, down at Boyd's grimy fingers which were now flipping a biro.

"I am the opposite of the archetypal, nerdy, financial whizz-kid. The anti-hero in a world of traditional corporate business men." He leant closer to whisper, "believe *this*. I know a lot about money; how to make it, how to shake it, how to move it about, how to double... no treble it. I can make you rich sonny."

Will flipped his sheet over to data sufficiency examples, "I can do that myself, through hard work, drive and determination."

"I like it," Boyd pushed against the table, tipping his chair onto two legs, "ambition. A man after my own heart."

Will glanced at him suspiciously, was this dude coming onto him? "My girlfriend thinks so," he quickly replied. Boyd's crestfallen face was evidence enough.

Boyd cleared his throat, "so. What degree are you studying? Wait, let me guess, Sports science?"

"English."

"Wow! I never would have … you like books then?"

Will shrugged, "yep."

"But what will you do … I mean what career entails loving books? Are you an author?"

"No. I'm not, but I know a lady who is. Actually," Will pushed away the sheet of stapled papers, "I'm seriously considering journalism as a career option."

Boyd nodded his approval.

"Journalism?" Mrs Connor stopped in front of their table, "sorry, I couldn't help but overhear. If it's a career in media you're interested in, one of the career advisors will be able to advise you," she glanced at her watch, "they should be here anytime now." She moved along, "and what are your career aspirations dear?"

"Teaching," Juliette replied.

"Excellent choice."

Mrs Connor pulled up a seat and began advising Juliette on the different routes into primary education.

* * *

An hour later Will turned into Great Bricklyn Street, which was just on the outskirts of the main shopping precinct. It was a long road, peppered with law firms, dentists and veterinary surgeries. At the very end, stood the headquarters of News Express, a two-storey structure of marble, old brickwork and stone pillars. He jogged up the steps, slipping on a pool of rainwater at the very top. He was soaked through, caught in a tumultuous shower of heavy rain that made his clothes stick to his skin and his teeth chatter. He flicked back his wet hair and dug in his pockets for the scrap of paper the careers advisor had given him. The ink had spread across the wetness and was now indecipherable.

"Are you going in?" A lady shaking an umbrella peered at him over designer pink frames.

"Oh yes," Will pushed the wooden door. Surprisingly it sprang forward with ease and the weight of him stumbled into a quiet foyer. A reception desk was to the left of him, where a security guard stood, staring at the flashing telephone system with bewilderment.

"She left you in charge again, George?" The lady with the umbrella walked past Will and pressed the lift button, "ignore them. They'll call back if it's important."

The guard stared down at the flashing switchboard, a flummoxed look on his ruddy face.

"What do I do now?" He removed his cap to scratch the itch on the top of his bald head, "oh bugger it. They'll have to ring back," he leant over the counter and Will caught the whiff of whisky, "she's powdering her nose *again*, trying to impress the governor."

Will looked at him blankly, *what was he on about?*

"You know the big boss, the man in charge, the Godfather of this fine newspaper."

"Oh," Will nodded, "actually, I'm here to see him too," he thought for a moment, his brow wrinkled in concentration as he tried to recall the name he'd been given, "a Mr Nielson? No, Mr Nelson."

The guard chuckled, "he ain't the boss mate. He's part of the editorial team yes, but he definitely ain't in charge."

"I've been given his name by a careers advisor from the uni," Will explained.

The guard stuck his hand out, "I'm Bob. So you want to be a journalist?"

Will shook it firmly, "I guess so."

"Well then lad. You better leave your morals right there on that mat."

"What are you up to, our Bob?" Clacking heels permeated the air, "I hope you're not trying to scare the poor lad off."

Gloria the receptionist had indeed been powdering her nose. As she walked closer, Will could see a clump of it dangling from her chin, and there were minute particles resting on the shoulder pads of her navy trouser suit. Her hair was platinum blonde; big curls that had been carefully backcombed and lacquered. She reminded Will of the women in that American eighties soap that Flora watched on the Gold channel. Dynasty, that was the one.

"My, you're nice looking," she appraised Will with lascivious eyes, "you're a babee though, young enough to be my son I reckon."

Will coughed, his sense of smell overpowered by the strong perfume that surrounded her, "I'm almost twenty-one."

"Are you now?" She leant over the desk, her cleavage straining against the buttons on her blouse.

"Is Mr Nelson free then?" Will was beginning to lose his patience.

Gloria sighed, "just a minute."

He turned away to gaze at the front-page news spreads that were hanging on the walls in frames. A visit from a member of the royal family. The opening of the city's new art gallery. A celebration of when Chattlesbury Football Club had been promoted to the premiership. Will felt his skin prickle with excitement.

"Okay sweetie," Will smiled at Gloria, "you can go on up; second floor, meeting room. Will you be a darling and take him up a coffee on the way?"

"Sure." He ambled over to the coffee machine, thinking of ways he could make a good first impression.

* * *

Ben pulled onto the car park of the Pear Tree Pub Restaurant & Ball Pit, scanning the grounds for a space.

"It's very busy," he put the gear into first and crawled forward.

"It always is," Juliette popped a peppermint into his mouth, "look, there's one." Swiftly he swung his vehicle between the white lines, pulling up the handbrake with a crunch. In the back seat, Molly was bouncing up and down with excitement and Harry was engrossed in his computer game.

"We're leaving the car now Harry," Juliette said, unclipping her seatbelt and pushing the door open, "turn off the game."

"I can't turn it off Mum," he flicked pause with irritation, "I'm on the tenth level, I've never got this far before."

"You're an addict," Molly sing-songed.

"No I ain't," Harry pulled a face at his younger sister.

"You are so," Molly folded her arms, "I heard Mum telling aunty Maz you are."

"Well all you care about is stupid Disney. Cinderella this, Snow White that," Harry mimicked, "aren't I pretty in my silly dresses."

Molly's bottom lip wobbled, "Muuuummmmm."

"Stop it, both of you. If you can't behave then we'll head back home for a roast dinner instead."

The threat of steamed vegetables quietened them instantly. Juliette shooed them in front of her and slid a glance at Ben, "kids are just so much fun huh?"

Ben slipped an arm across her shoulder, "*you* are a terrific Mum."

"Some days I'm not so sure," she replied, sounding weary, "I try though. I feel that's all I'm doing; trying my best to raise two stable individuals, trying to make their lives happy."

"Don't be so hard on yourself," Ben squeezed her gently, "my mum never knew where me and sister were half the time. Who wants to be super Mum anyway?"

"Not me." She smiled up at him, "Thank you."

Inside, the restaurant was, as predicted, packed full.

"Twenty minutes wait," a smiling lady wearing a black pinafore informed them.

Juliette hovered uncertainly in the doorway, "shall we go to McDonalds?"

"Nooooooooo," wailed Molly, "I want to play in the Pirates Den," she tugged at the hem of Juliette's coat, trying to pull her further inside.

"I'm too old for ball pits," Harry grumbled, "can't we go to Pizza Express?"

"Let's stay here," Ben decided, "they sell pizza, burgers too, so everyone's happy."

Harry, looking mutinous, scuffed his trainers on the carpet.

"Look ice cream," Juliette pointed to a section of the pub that had been sectioned off and aptly named the sweet store.

"Oh my," Molly gasped with excitement, "they have sprinkles and marshmallows."

"Are those real cakes?" Harry stared in wonder at the giant gateaux encased in the glass compartment. His face cracked into a wide smile as Molly pulled him with her to investigate.

Juliette sighed with relief, "I love the power of unhealthy food."

Ben ordered drinks from the bar and they perched on high stools, waiting for a table.

Juliette sipped at her blue frothy cocktail, "this is good."

"So, do you bring the kids here often?"

"Hardly ever," she replied, "we tend to eat at home. This is a real treat. Although I did come to a karaoke night with Maz and Dave once."

Ben sat back and crossed his arms, "with your friend?"

"Yes with Clive," she paused, "we should go out with my sister, the four of us. They're good fun … that's if you want to."

"Hmm. This is a first for me."

Juliette looked at him quizzically.

"Ball pit," he replied, grinning.

"Oh I'm an expert at sniffing out a play pub. But you … you're a ball pit virgin," she laughed.

A frazzled looking mother began pacing in front of them with a baby that was red faced and hollering, a group of children whizzed past, weaving around the chairs and tables.

"Bloody nuisance," a white-haired man, with skin like crumpled leather, shook his walking stick at them.

"I've never seen so many little people," Ben remarked.

"You don't mind?"

"What?" He stared at her with his gorgeous, mesmerising eyes.

She ducked her head, "the family thing … because me and my children … well we're a package."

There was an awkward pause. *Damn,* thought Juliette, *why did that sound so aggressive?*

He lifted her chin with his fingers, "you know I love being with your children."

"Sorry," she whispered.

"What's up?"

"Nothing," she shifted in her seat.

"Uh-oh," Ben grinned, "did you just blatantly lie to me Juliette?"

The sound of her name was like a caress, lifting the hairs on her arms, "I don't want you to feel tied to me," she blurted out, "not if you don't want to … if you just want a light-hearted, no-strings attached romance, that's fine."

Briefly she closed her eyes. *No it's not fine, it's not fine at all.*

His mouth set in a line as he pushed a hand through his hair, "is that what *you* want?"

No, she wanted to scream, *what I want is you – constantly, permanently, forever,* and that realisation scared her to death. She was consumed with the sudden fear that she was going to lose him. She slid off her chair, wrapped her arms around his neck, hugging him tightly.

"I love you," she whispered in his ear, "I'll always love you, no matter what happens."

"Listen," he murmured, taking her face in his hands, "I am completely, totally, sincerely, serious about you. You can't break up with me again. You just can't."

"No, no. You've got this all wrong," Juliette was gabbling now.

He put a finger over her lips, "I wouldn't care if you had ten children. I want you and I know you feel the same way. So why don't we stop worrying about the future and just enjoy loving each other."

She gasped as he lifted her back onto the stool. Her eyes flickered wantonly over his torso, the outline of his well-defined tricep muscles, to come to rest on his strong stubble darkened jawline.

"I know how strongly you feel about me."

"You do?" Juliette cleared her throat, pushing away images of lying naked in his arms.

"That's not arrogance," he continued, "I can see it in your eyes when you look at me and your hands when they touch me … Christ," he lowered his tone, "I meant what I said before – I'm playing for keeps."

Juliette's spirits soared, "happy to hear it."

"You better believe it," he pulled two menus from the stand and passed her one, "now stop looking at me in that seductive, teasing manner. You're damn distracting and there are minors nearby."

"Sorry," she studied the menu, "yes, do make sure you chose something hearty, something energising, something that will give you stamina."

"Oh?" His eyes brightened at her words.

"Didn't I mention Harry and Molls are having sleepovers tonight? You're welcome to stay in the spare room … that's if you want to," she fluttered her lashes provocatively.

Ben chuckled, "The spare room? Just looking at the meat section right now."

"One more thing Ben," Juliette scanned the menu, running the tip of her tongue over her top lip, knowing full well how that made him feel. "My name. Does it sound ridiculous to you?"

"I love your name! It's beautiful and suits you perfectly. Don't you dare shorten it to Julie. Jules is okay I suppose. Why?"

"Just checking. I love it too," Juliette grinned, "pick your steak, he-man."

Chapter Nine

"Where the bloody hell is Gloria? And who the hell are you?" Si Nelson had been pacing the room, dictating to his long-suffering secretary, when Will walked in with his usual confident swagger, "haven't you heard of knocking?" They both turned to stare at Will, who was immediately on the defensive, because of being bawled at by a stranger.

"The door was open," his tone was prickly, some might even say it had attitude. Si Nelson's eyes narrowed as he surveyed the floppy-haired youth in front of him.

"Are you trying to be funny? My door is always open. Now put the blasted coffee down."

Will sauntered to the desk and placed it next to the secretary's notepad. She gave him a small smile and a look of sympathy, a look which said, *someone get me outta here.*

Si Nelson turned away, stared out of the window and resumed his dictation. With a sigh, his secretary picked up her pen and began scribbling. Will thrust his hands in his jeans pocket and waited. Eventually Mr Nelson noticed that he was still standing there and whipped round to face him with a growl.

"The welcome room for advertisers is that way," he pointed across the office. Will shrugged, "I'm not an advertiser. Actually, I'm here to see you."

"Busy," Si snapped, "come back another time."

He grimaced at Will, his brow furrowed and his cheeks puffed out in anger.

Will regarded him with cool detachment; first impression was that this guy was a dick and a bully who looked a mess. His creased trousers had been teamed with an off-white shirt that looked as if it had been placed mistakenly in a coloured wash. It hung out of the waistband of his trousers and trailed down stumpy legs. Small, thought Will, with tall man inflected superiority.

"This won't take long," Will persisted.

His secretary put down her pen again and gazed at Will with surprise.

"Sorry. Who are you?" His sneering façade matched the sarcasm in his voice.

"I'm an English graduate. Third year. Interested in journalism as a career. Hoping to do voluntary work here. Available weekends and some weekdays. Hard working and eager to learn." Will paused his staccato speech to take a breath, "that's about it in a nutshell."

The room fell completely silent. Mr Nelson's face had flickered from annoyance to suspicious shock.

"How old are you?"

"Almost twenty-one."

Si nodded, "you've got balls. Sign him up Veronica."

* * *

A few hours later an excited Will was eating dinner with his family, relaying the conversation.

"I'm so proud of you," Hema gazed across at him, her face shining with love and admiration.

"This is the beginning," he replied, "this is the start of something big; something good." Esme wriggled in his arms, patting the top of his head with affection.

"My son the journalist," Flora shook her head, "it's the perfect career for you Will. I don't know why none of us considered it before." She sliced her lamb into neat little squares, "and speaking of new careers, Max has something to share with you."

"Down," Esme suddenly shouted, pointing to her push-along trolley.

"Fetch Nana some shopping," Will kissed his daughter's ruffled hair and let her go. She walked, wobbled, tumbled, then got straight up again, "so what's going on Dad?"

"I've found a job," Max replied, brightly, "just a few hours per day. Nothing exciting."

Flora tutted and waved her forkful of potato in the air, "stop being so modest Max. Tell them how excited you *really* are about it."

Max cleared his throat, "I suppose I am."

"It's in a furniture shop," Flora cut in, eyes twinkling, "and not one of those Scandinavian, mass produced ones either. It's an antique store in the city centre. Max is officially the new sales assistant."

"I'm more of a rep really Flora," Max said with a smile, "yes I'll be based in the shop, but I'm also going to be travelling; searching for the unique furniture, the stuff of character, the handcrafted. None of this machine churned out rubbish that you find in thousands of high street stores."

"Excellent Dad, well done."

"You haven't heard the best bit," Flora's face beamed with pride.

"I'm going to be making pieces for the store. Carpentry was always a big hobby of mine before teaching sank its teeth into me." His face was luminous underneath the soft lamplight. Will thought how long it had been since his father had looked so relaxed and happy.

"I had no idea," he exchanged a surprised glance with Hema, "so as well as being a fantastic swimmer, you can also make stuff?"

"Your father is very talented," Flora patted his hand, "he made a rocking chair for me, when I was pregnant with you. And when you were born, I would sit in the window and feed you. That was until you bit me of course."

"Ouch," Hema winced, "I don't miss those breastfeeding days."

Memories nudged their way into Max's mind; Flora in a blue frilly smock, fast asleep in the rocking chair, her hands resting lightly on her bump. Will climbing onto his lap for story time, rocking him to sleep in his arms.

"Have you still got it?" Hema asked.

"It must be in the loft," Flora replied, "we must get it down love. Show off your handiwork. Do you know he made the bench on the patio too?"

"The tree house," Will murmured.

"Ah yes, my masterpiece. You loved it up there, your mother could never get you down for tea."

Will's mind had wandered; to warm afternoons spent lying on planks of hard, scratchy wood, staring up at the sky and counting the birds and the clouds. Bruised knees from bending over, playing marbles. Sore hands from sliding down to the ground via hardy rope. Hiding behind the ladder, waiting for an unsuspecting Flora to come out with a basket full of wet washing, then soaking her with water guns. Long hot summers of happiness and fun. That was how the tree house made him feel.

"Why did you stop Dad?"

Max sighed, "life stopped me. The daily grind. The weight of responsibility. The constant pressure to succeed, to make money, to accumulate possessions, to compete with everyone else," he looked at Flora, "when did I stop loving life? Why didn't I pursue my true dreams?"

"You were a brilliant teacher," Flora replied, firmly, "that's a dream for many, and then you became an even better headteacher, an inspirational leader. You devoted years of your life to education, to guiding others. The children Max, remember the children."

Max stared mutely down at his lukewarm dinner. The atmosphere in the room nosedived to one of melancholy and regret.

"Hey Dad," Will grinned, "wasn't Jesus a carpenter? Good career choice. Some holy vibes going on there."

Flora chuckled and touched her crucifix, "speaking of all things holy, we have more exciting news. Holiday news."

"You're going on a cruise, right?" Hema said, "Flora, this lamb is delicious, so tender."

"We're not going on a cruise," Flora clapped her hands together, "we've booked to go to the holy land."

"The holy land?" Will echoed, "as in Rome?"

Flora rolled her eyes, "the *real* holy land."

"Do you mean?... The Middle East?"

Flora nodded, "Nazareth, the Dead Sea, Jerusalem," her eyes twinkled, "Bethlehem."

Hema's mouth fell open, "I thought Bethlehem was made up. Is it a real place?"

The table erupted into laughter.

"What?" Hema turned indignant and Will became uneasy.

"It's really dangerous out there."

"Suicide bombings," Hema continued, "death and hatred. How can that be holy?"

"Because religion is synonymous with war, always has been. And this is why I'm an atheist," Will dropped his cutlery down with a clatter, "not a good idea Mum."

"It's a guided tour," Flora argued, "we won't be wandering off anywhere on our own. I need to go, I need to see it." Her cheeks were flushed by the passion of her words.

"It's been on your mother's bucket list forever," Max revealed, "this is her dream, Will. This is her passion."

"Fair enough," Will said, with a resigned shrug, "just make sure you come back though Mum, okay?"

* * *

"Can you smell the sea, Sam?" Ann slid the car window down and hitched over. She heard Sam draw in a lungful of air. "it smells of salt," he said, "it smells fresh and it's cold."

"Blackpool is *always* cold," Jon chuckled, as he manoeuvred the car around the island, joining the main road leading into the centre.

They passed derelict boarded up buildings, tarnished with graffiti and high steel fences that surrounded half demolished factories, mountains of rubble and iron piping. Blackpool Tower stood majestic against a grey skyline. Jon regaled them with a brief history of its timeline.

"1891?" Sam echoed, "how do you know that?"

"Oh, Jon remembers all sorts of facts," Ann said, breezily, "he is a walking encyclopaedia." They turned in front of a multi storey car park, when suddenly a young girl darted out onto the road. Jon slammed on the brakes, clutching the steering wheel as the car skidded to a halt.

"What the . . . " he stared at the small pigtailed figure, clad in a bright yellow rain mac. She was holding a stick of pink candyfloss and a balloon that bobbed above her.

"Hannah!" Her mother scooped her up, mouthing an apology. Then they vanished, lost in a crowd of revellers, a stag and hen do that had merged into one raucous group that staggered up the street, spilling off the pavement. One of the men tugged off his t-shirt and took position in the middle of the road, head flung back and arms stretched open. A couple of his friends whooped with excitement and sprayed him with shaken-up cans of lager. A raven-haired woman ran towards him, cackling with hysterical laughter. Then she froze, her stiletto caught in a manhole. She waved her stick of rock around while screeching for a prince to come rescue her, while a furious shopkeeper bellowed at them all to behave and the distant sound of a police siren filled the air.

Jon, Ann and Samuel stared at the commotion unfurling in front of them.

"Welcome to Blackpool," Jon mumbled, as Ann slowly slid the windows back up.

They cruised down the main road, passing brightly lit amusement arcades, pubs with open doors that boomed funky music and tourist shops full of unapologetic tack. On the left-hand side, burger vans lined the pavement, wafting a heady combination of grease and onions, competing with the fish and chip outlets and the confectionary sellers. Food was everywhere. Sam pressed his face against the window, smearing the glass as he grinned at the sight of the inky grey sea. Then it was gone, hidden behind a tram that had followed them up the street and which advertised a set of sparkling teeth and a pantomime on the North Pier.

"What street is it again?" Jon craned his neck, looking for a turning.

"I will just check my electronic guide," Ann stared down at Google Maps, "according to this, we are literally minutes away. There." She pointed to a side street and Jon flicked his indicator right.

The sign to the Blue Bay Guest House swayed gently in the breeze.

"Apt name," Ann said, noting the blue pillars and matching door. The downstairs bay window was covered in a frilly lace netting and a neon sign, which flashed vacancies, greeted them.

"This is so seventies," Jon chuckled, hopping out to open the boot, "do you think we'll have kippers for breakfast?"

Samuel glanced up from his Gameboy, "what are kippers?"

"They're fish Sam," Ann replied patiently, "they were a popular breakfast dish, in the er … seventies."

"Cool," Sam's attention was back on Marvin The Monkey.

As Ann settled herself in her wheelchair, Jon pulled two weekender bags up the path and rang the bell. Samuel pushed Ann forwards and the three of them stood waiting on the step.

A few moments later, the door swung open and a lady with her hair in large rollers beamed at them. "You must be Jon and Ann?"

"Hello," Ann smiled, "and this is Sam."

"Perfect. Come on in," the petite lady led them up a wide, brightly lit hallway to a desk with a signing in book and an old-fashioned quill pen.

"Oh, that's just for show," the lady laughed, "now-a-days I tend to use this," she pulled a laptop from underneath the desk, "aren't computers great? It's certainly made my life a lot easier. So I get to spend more time on the laundry – lucky me huh? Excuse me, where are my manners? My names Audrey by the way." She patted her head, "tonight is my night off. Bingo with the girls."

Ann nodded, distracted by the garish bright orange wallpaper and the heavy brown drapes. Pictures lined the walls, stretching up the staircase. Her eyes lingered on one in particular, "is that Frank Bruno?"

"Yes," Audrey answered without looking up, "he spent a weekend here two summers ago. A true gent he was and that laugh," she chuckled, "he loved my sausages. I slipped him two extra when the other guests weren't looking, the chunky ones cooked in proper fat. None of this grilled rubbish in *our* guest house."

Jon's eyes brightened at the mention of food, "what time is breakfast?"

"Eight a.m. to ten a.m. sharp. Because after that I have a daily date with my hoover."

Her fingers flew nimbly over the keyboard, "now then, you're all signed in," she placed two card keys on the desk, "you're in room four, ground floor. I'll take you through, but first, let me show you the dining room." They followed her into a rectangle shaped room which was set out neatly with tables and chairs, "as I mentioned, breakfast is between eight and ten. If you want kippers, can you let me know in advance?"

"An English breakfast will be fine," Ann replied, with a smirk at Jon.

"Good enough," Audrey pressed her hands together, "so, we have guide maps, we have tourist information leaflets. We have discount vouchers. I can recommend restaurants, shows – there are a couple of really good ones running on the piers," she thrust a handful of leaflets towards Ann, "let me show you your room." She led them down the hallway, "do you prefer Indian or Chinese? There are quite a few dotted about and if Italian's your thing then I can recommend an excellent a la carte one. Here it is!"

She stood back to allow Jon access to fumble with the door. It opened into a pretty room of pink. The window netting was blowing up in a wide arc, "oops, forgot to close the window," she hurried over and slammed it shut, "I'll turn the heating up, it will soon be warm and toasty in here."

"This is our best room," Audrey pointed to the four-poster bed, "and there's a nice comfy single one over there for your son."

Jon dropped the bags down, "do we have a disabled access en-suite?"

"Of course," Audrey nodded, "I noted your requirements and I think you'll find it spacious enough. Now then, the bar is open until midnight, you will be very welcome for a drink with my husband and I, so enjoy yourself and have fun."

She backed out of the room, leaving a trail of perfume.

"Right then," Jon clapped his hands, "where to first, Sam? The beach or the funfair?"

"The beach!" Sam said, punching the sky.

"Just leave me here, I'll be fine," the wind was whipping Ann's hair across her face, and the noise of the sea meant she had to yell.

"Whoopee!" Sam tugged off his shoes and socks, throwing them in a heap, before running in circles with his arms stretched wide.

"He shoots, he scores!" Jon kicked the just bought beach ball high into the sky. They ran towards the sea, passing it between them. She settled back, clicking on her camera, zooming in on a group of donkeys and an adolescent couple, struggling to control their union jack kite. Her phone pinged in her gloved hand and Ann glanced down at a flashing Facebook notification symbol. Wasn't it mad how a social media app could inform her that Sophie and Evelyn were shopping in Chester, Juliette was watching Gone with the Wind and Will was feeling 'bleh' after a night of child free partying with Hema? They were so far away and yet so close that Ann could touch them. But was it possible to truly know anyone through a phone screen? How could a selfie or a status really convey a persona? Ann flicked through Juliette's profile, her public photos were all of her and her family, but recently in private, she'd uploaded a picture of Ben; a side angle of his face, he was holding a bottle of beer and had a football scarf wound around his neck. Ann zoomed in on him a little closer, he really was lovely looking, she thought with appreciation, and it seems that over one hundred people agreed with her. 'Hot' 'hunk' 'fittie' were just some of the adjectives used to describe him, but predictably, Jules was playing it very cool. Mysteriously answering the cries for who is he? With a few teasing question marks of her own. Ann wiped away a line of unladylike spittle and looked around for something to take an interesting shot to upload on *her* timeline. Why the sand, of course, it looked like a readymade art canvas with its swirly indentations and embedded razor shells. She began merrily snapping away, switching between portrait and landscape.

"Can I sneak past?" A lady's voice asked.

Ann looked up at a warm, rosy cheeked face, framed by a silk head scarf. She was holding a poodle back, the lead wrapped tightly around her wrist.

"Of course," Ann replied, "I'm sorry."

The lady glanced over her, "would you like me to take a few shots of you? Maybe with the tower in the background?"

"Oh no," Ann shook her head emphatically, "I mean, I don't really like photos of myself on social media."

"Me neither," the lady smiled, ruefully, "this society has gone selfie crazy, but maybe I'm old fashioned. I'm Moana by the way, and this is little Archie."

Ann bent to ruffle his ears, "he's gorg! Are you from Liverpool?"

Moana laughed, "how did you guess?"

"I've heard a lot of Liverpool accents about," Ann waved at Sam, who was bravely dipping his toes in the North Sea.

"Don't you know it's Liverpool-by-the-sea?" Moana pulled the belt of her trench coat tighter, "I come here every year, mainly for the bingo on the North Pier – the jackpots are HUGE, and the shows are pretty good too – especially the drag artists and strippers; groups of drunken women, with baby oil and feather boas, let loose from their controlling husbands for the weekend."

Ann's nose wrinkled, "not my scene. Also, I have an impressionable adolescent to take care of."

"You should check out the magic shows. The Sea Life Centre is good, and have you been to the Pleasure Beach?"

"That's on our to-do list."

Moana glanced at the darkening skyline, "looks like the Big One's closed. Far too windy." Ann could see the flags flapping like crazy in the distance.

"Well I suppose I'll be on my way. Archie here hates the cold and I have a rendezvous with a hot chocolate and a T.V set. Enjoy your stay."

Ann waved as she headed towards the embankment, then her phone was ringing and her mother was telling her all about her father locking himself in his potting shed, and the chicken stew she had burnt yesterday evening in the slow cooker.

As she was ending the call, Sam came racing back towards her and flung himself down onto the sand at her feet. She watched the rise and fall of his chest, the way he flung one arm across his face to hide the exhilaration of finally being at the beach.

"What did you think of the sea?"

"Freezing," Samuel replied, his teeth chattering slightly, "dirty, smelly, but amazing too."

"The sea down south is much nicer," Jon said, as he squatted next to Ann, "Are you warm enough?"

"Absolutely," she replied, as Samuel's stomach rumbled loudly, "I think that means it's time for lunch."

"How long is it until the spelling gala?" Jon bit into his big mac, spilling lettuce onto the table.

"January," Samuel replied, "I kinda wish I wasn't that good at spelling though."

"Why?" Ann cried, "you should be proud of your talent Sam," her eyes slanted, "is anyone at school teasing you?"

"No. Well maybe a little bit, but nothing I can't handle," Sam swallowed a chicken nugget, "it's just not cool is it? I wish I was good at maths or science instead."

"Words are cool," Ann replied, "don't put yourself down and never listen to the negativity of others – that usually stems from low self-esteem and jealousy – okay!"

"Okay," Sam nodded, a small smile lifted the corners of his mouth.

"It's raining," Jon gazed out of the window, "what will we do now?"

"How about the tower? How about the arcades?" Ann rattled her purse, "I have loads of change for the machines and maybe we could have a game of bingo?"

"Sounds good to me, what do you think Sam?"

"Cool! Let's go." He scrambled for the door and stood with his beaming face turned up to the rain.

"Is he really ours?" Ann asked, breathless with happiness.

"He's ours," Jon replied, with a proud, wide smile.

Chapter Ten

The following week began with disappointment for the English students. Doctor Rivers was absent from his Realism and the Novel lecture and was instead replaced with Wilomena Smythe, who complained bitterly of being the university stand-in for any absent lecturers.

"Is Dr Rivers okay?" Evelyn asked Juliette, as they prepared for a lecture on the imperfection of marriage through the literature of Middlemarch.

"He's on a course," Juliette replied, "spending a week at a university up North." *And I'm missing him already,* she added silently.

After the discombobulated lecture had ended, the students were given the seminar as a free study period. Will, Ann, Juliette, Sophie and Evelyn managed to bag themselves a table on the second floor of the Learning Centre. Many of the English students had followed them over and the library was packed and growing increasingly rowdy. Beatrice, the longest serving librarian, flitted around trying to hush everyone. There were signs blu-tacked to the walls, banning the use of mobile phones, but that was another rule which was being flagrantly ignored. Will was bent over, surreptitiously chomping on a ham and cheese baguette, when Beatrice placed a hand on his shoulder and pointed with pursed lips to a no food or drink notice.

"Jeez I thought universities were supposed to be battalions of revolution and rebellion," Will grimaced at Beatrice's back, "how risqué to be eating bread in a public area." He took a large bite, before stuffing it inside his rucksack, "what do you think Soph? Soph?"

Sophie's far-away gaze slowly refocussed back on her friends, "what?"

"Are you okay?" Ann looked up from her notepad, "you look awfully pale."

Sophie jumped to her feet, "I'm fine, but I erm ... I need to be somewhere."

"But what about American Humour? We were going to work on it together." Ann frowned, "the essay is due in a few weeks, we can help each other." She was aghast at her own words – *me! Actually instigating bonding group work.*

Will and Ann stared at Sophie, waiting for a response, but in her peripheral vision she saw Evelyn pointing towards the exit and frantically nodding.

"Sorry. I can't stay … I have an appointment," she pulled on her fake fur jacket, zipping it right underneath her chin. "I'll see you later in the week. Bye."

She hurried towards the stairs, leaving a bemused Ann shaking her head, "is it my imagination, but do Jules and Sophie seem a tad spaced out today? Are they having man trouble?"

"Hey," Will cut in, "leave us men alone."

Evelyn patted Ann's hand, "they're probably just stressed. So let's talk American Humour, and then we can all head off home."

* * *

She had arranged to meet Barry Coben at one o'clock. Already, Sophie was five minutes late and she still had to dodge across the tricky town centre, eight road split junction. She waited for the pedestrian sign to change to green and walked briskly across, her mind considering turning left out of town, towards the bus station instead of right towards the department store and the coffee shop where they had arranged to meet.

"Which way, which way?" Sophie hummed the Wizard of Oz tune and decided in this case, to follow the slate grey slabs which would take her back to her childhood and her own private Kansas and her father.

She followed a family of five down the winding street, watching the man lift the youngest child up onto his shoulders. *He used to do that to me,* Sophie longed to yell, *I adored my dad too.* The young girl was chuckling with delight, and Sophie felt tears sting her eyes. *I'm a wreck* she thought, *and I haven't even spoken about him yet. Oh Lord, what if he wants to meet me?* A sob escaped her lips and her shoulders were shaking with pent up emotion. Then Barry Coben was texting her; asking if she was still coming and Sophie picked up her walking pace, passing the happy family and a pair of loved-up teenagers.

When she arrived at the department store, Sophie decided to stall for time by spinning inside the revolving doors for a total of five times, before a security guard grew suspicious and came over to see what was occurring. As a dizzy consequence, when Sophie let go of the door, she careered in a diagonal line straight into a nude mannequin and they both fell in a heap on the floor.

"Have you been drinking Miss?" The giant of a guard helped her to her feet.

"No, absolutely not," Sophie swiped the dust from her skirt, giving him her brightest smile, "would you like to breathalyse me?"

"That won't be necessary love, just be careful now." His kind tone had Sophie's eyes brimming again.

"Can you show me the way to the coffee shop?" She asked, in a quiet, warbly voice.

"Let me take you love," he caught her by the arm, "are you feeling okay? You look as white as a sheet."

Sophie swallowed, "just family issues. I've arranged to meet someone and I'm late."

"Come on then, it's just up those stairs."

The kind guard chatted away as they walked, distracting Sophie with information about his family.

"I've bought the lad a computer for Christmas," he told her, "game mad he is. Have you any children lass?"

"Twin boys," she gave him a brief description of Josh and Jake.

"Well here we are then," he let go of her arm, "are you going to be okay?"

Sophie looked up at him gratefully, feeling much calmer and in control.

"I'll be right over there. Women's lingerie," he pointed a finger and chuckled, "just wave if you need me."

"Thank you." Sophie squared her shoulders and walked with confidence into the coffee shop.

To her surprise, Mr Coben looked relatively young. Sophie guessed he was probably in his mid-twenties - which had been a surprise to her – as from his impeccably mannered letter and text messages, she had expected an elderly gentleman. In his sixties at least. He asked if she wanted cake and pulled out a chair for her. Sophie sat opposite him, staring at his black bushy beard and matching eyebrows. Hairy she thought, noticing it sprouting from his nostrils and ears too. He asked if she was okay and she replied a little too quickly. A little too squeaky. A waitress bought them a tray of coffee and shortbread fingers. Sophie turned the spoon, watching the swirl of the froth and the different hues of mingling brown.

Mr Coben cleared his throat, "thank you for meeting me. Sugar?" He passed her the pot and she tipped some in.

"Mr Coben, do you have children?"

"Yes I have a daughter. Poppy's almost three."

"Poppy's a nice name." Sophie swallowed, "but would you abandon her?"

There was a lengthy pause before Mr Coben spoke again, "there were reasons Sophie. Will you let me explain?"

"I love this time of year don't you?" Sophie sipped her coffee, "when it's cold and dark but you get to stay indoors warm and safe with your family. I've recently separated from my husband, did you know that Mr Coben? I've had to sell my house, uproot my children. I'm in financial ruin. I hardly sleep and my doctor has got me on a course of strong anti-anxiety medication, that makes me feel like a zombie."

"I'm sorry to hear …" Sophie stilled him with a show of her palm.

"I have no family to support me. My mother is a mess. My grandparents are dead. There are no siblings to share the burden with. Life is pretty bleak at the moment." Sophie placed both hands down on the table and leant forward, "but no matter how hard things get, I would never abandon my children."

Mr Coben's mouth set in a firm line, "who was it that said that women are far more superior to men? There's a quote," he clicked his fingers, "someone famous." He flicked through the apps on his phone, "ah here it is; so William Golding reckons that women are foolish to pretend they are equal to men. According to him they are far superior and always have been."

"Is that his excuse?" Sophie hissed, "there is no excuse – EVER!" She slammed back her chair, rising on shaky legs, "this was a mistake. I should go."

"Sophie please. Please just listen," Mr Coben rose too, his eyes pleading, "this isn't about making excuses. This is about telling you why. You've only heard one side of the story, Sophie. Please listen."

"Why should I? Why do I have to listen? Just because Anthony decides he's had enough of hiding away and wants to salve his conscience."

"Your *dad* has never stopped loving and thinking about you. Did you receive the letters he's sent you each month, Sophie? Every month he wrote to you without fail. Until you were twenty-one, Sophie. With no response. Until your twenty first birthday Sophie – can you remember that cheque he sent which *you* cashed? And then a week later you sent him the cruellest letter imaginable, full of hatred and bitterness, telling him to do one, telling him you despised him and wanted NOTHING to do with him."

"What?!" Sophie's mouth hung open.

Mr Coben's eyes flashed with anger, "you have no idea what your father has been through, Sophie. You have no idea."

Sophie sank back onto her chair, gripping the table as her head swam with confusion, "I never received *any* letters. I thought he didn't care. I thought ..."

"You are telling me your mother never passed any correspondence on?" Mr Coben thumped the table, rattling the cups, "she never gave you your rightful inheritance? I knew it!"

"My inheritance? What do you mean? Dad, I mean Anthony, was bankrupt. He left us with nothing."

Slowly Mr Coben shook his head, "no Sophie. Your father is a very wealthy man. He owns a construction company in Hong Kong. That's where he lives, Sophie. He is a millionaire. And I'm your brother Sophie. You're Poppy's aunty."

* * *

"What did *you* think of Catcher in the Rye?" Ann's question was directed at Will, who had in fact been thinking about buying and devouring a handful of dime bars to quell his still rumbling stomach.

"Little." He replied, flipping the pages of the thin book in front of him, "I enjoyed it. I like the idea of alienation and dissatisfaction with American life. The main character, Holden. He's pretty cool."

Ann sniffed, "yes, alienation is a key theme in this novel, and it is definitely a critique on an America corrupted by distorted values."

Evelyn looked up from her scribbling, "what kind of distorted values?

"Consumerism for one, and the phoniness of Hollywood," Ann replied, "I like the character Holden too, Will – he stands apart from the crowd and has a simple, innocent outlook on life."

"It's similar to Huckleberry Finn, don't you think?" Juliette suggested, "both written in first person, through the eyes of a young boy. You could definitely argue there are similar themes of alienation and an unsophisticated understanding of the world."

"Yes!" Ann pointed her pen, "both narratives are naïve *and* humorous. Excellent comparison Juliette."

Evelyn glanced at the wall clock. It had been an hour since Sophie had left, and half an hour since she had sent her two texts. No reply, and now she was growing increasingly concerned.

"I just need to pop outside for a phone call," down the stairs she hurried, pausing at the edge of the first-floor flight of steps to catch her breath, and rub the base of her aching spine.

"Sophie," she yelled, after finally connecting, "are you okay?"

Sophie informed her she was fine and there was really no need to shout.

"Sorry," Evelyn said, in a quieter tone, "it's noisy here and I was worried. So, everything's really okay?"

Sophie was nothing like her chatty self and very mysteriously refused to give much away, just promising to speak to her later, before cutting the call. Evelyn stared at the buzzing phone in her hand, 'looks like it's back to Catcher in the Rye then.'

When she arrived back upstairs, Will was gathering his belongings together and explaining about his first voluntary stint at News Express.

"How on earth did you manage to get in there?" Ann asked, with genuine bewilderment, "I've heard they don't like graduates, and prefer the more practically experienced, been through the mill, hardnosed as employees."

Will shrugged, "I'm not technically an employee. This is all voluntary – remember, and anyway, I can do hard."

"Yes you can," Juliette's mind flickered to the stabbing incident and how brave Will had been.

"Right then I'll be off," he swung his rucksack onto his back.

"Don't forget our dissertation meeting next week," Ann called, "same place."

"I gotcha," he squeezed past Beatrice, who was sorting books into neat piles on her trolley. The librarian watched him bouncing energetically towards the steps and sighed, wishing for the freshness of youth for herself again.

As he was coming out of the Learning Centre, the Facetime cursor on his phone beeped. He clicked on it and a hazy image of Hema holding Esme appeared on the screen. His daughter was smiling at the camera and waving hands that were covered in chocolate goo.

"We've been making Rice Krispie cakes," Hema confessed.

"Save me some?"

"Daddy, Daddy save some," Esme sang.

"I've saved you twelve," Hema blew a kiss, "good luck at the newspaper. Thinking of you. Love you."

"Love you too," Will veered across the pavement, stumbling into the gutter, "what's for tea?"

Hema gave a significant eye roll, "some sort of Hungarian stew. Your mum's been watching twenty-four-hour European cooking again."

Will winced, "looks like we might need a kebab for supper then. Call you later, baby."

When Will arrived at News Express, he was surprised to see a brass band playing heartily in front of the entrance.

"It's the Salvation Army," the receptionist informed him, "raising money for their upcoming Christmas campaign."

Argh, Christmas, Will thought, *more expense.*

"You look smart. Different from before."

Will fiddled with the tie he had borrowed from his dad. A designer affair with red stripes that made him look like a proper grown up, and had Hema this morning in lusty raptures. Seems women loved a man in a tie, and Gloria was no exception. She was leaning a little too close for comfort; her perfume smelt sickly sweet and the unpleasant aroma of cigarettes clung to her breath.

"Before you go up, just sign here," she shoved a book and pen towards him, playing with her curls in a flirtatious manner, as he scribbled his signature, "see you later, William."

Will bypassed the lift, jogged up the stairs and burst exuberantly into the main open plan office of News Express. The place was teeming with people; hurrying to and fro; shouting into phones, feeding paper into copiers and tapping merrily onto keyboards. A sense of busy excitement pervaded the atmosphere, and the strong smell of coffee heightened the mania.

Nobody looked up as Will strode across to Si Nelson's glass-fronted office. The door was slightly ajar and as he neared, Will could hear shouting. Seems like Mr Nelson was being bawled at by his boss. Jeez, no wonder he was so antsy. It was clear to Will that attitude and bad temper came direct from the top and worked its way down at this place. The door swung open and a furious looking man came charging out, almost careering straight into Will.

"Sorry!" He yelled, "Gloria – where's my coffee?"

"Oh it's you," Si Nelson stopped pacing and pointed at one of the squashy leather armchairs.

Will sat down, looking at Mr Nelson warily. His face was bright red; sweat trickled from his forehead and his chest was heaving rapidly.

"Come back for more punishment?" He let out a bitter laugh and grabbed a stress ball from his desk, "I've devoted my life to this newspaper and I still get treated like a junior." He rubbed his temple with one hand and fervently pumped the stress ball with the other. "Remind me why you're here?"

"We spoke last week about me doing voluntary. I'm interested in journalism … as a career?"

Si stopped pacing, "oh yes. The gobby one. The ballsy one and dare I venture the must-be-crazy-for-wanting-to-work-here one?"

Will's polite laugh sounded strained, but Si Nelson hadn't noticed and continued talking. "My very efficient secretary has arranged this." He stuck his head out of the office and bellowed for Veronica.

"Have you organised the volunteer?" He snapped, when she appeared in the doorway.

Veronica gave him a cross look and a dismissive flick of her hair, "Mr Nelson. I arranged it all last week. Will's going out with the senior photographer."

"Not with Randy Rogers?" Mr Nelson blustered, "the man's a clown - he'll put him off journalism for life!"

"There was no one else free," Gloria bit back through clenched teeth, "and whatever we all think of Randy personally, he's a damned good photographer."

"I suppose he is," Si Nelson gave Will a thumbs up, "good luck lad." When Will remained seated, Si Nelson bellowed, "that was your cue to go!"

Chapter Eleven

"I think I need a sugar fix. In fact, I'm absolutely certain I need chocolate or something sweet," Sophie's hands were shaking, and her head felt fuzzy. Mr Coben jumped to his feet, waving his arms for service, "are you a diabetic?"

"No!" Sophie cried, "I'm just in shock."

"Everything okay sir?" A smiling waitress appeared at the side of their table.

Mr Coben sank back down, "two chocolate fudge cakes please, with extra whipped cream." When the young girl had gone, he leant towards Sophie, "are you okay?"

Sophie squinted at him, "are you sure you're my *brother*?"

"Yes. I'm your half-brother, Sophie."

"But ... Mr Coben, you don't look anything like me. I'm pale with blond hair and you're dark with a fantastic tan."

"My mother is from Hong Kong, she has a fantastic tan too, and please, stop calling me Mr Coben. I'm Barry – your brother, pleased to meet you," he stretched his hand across the table.

"This is surreal," Sophie mumbled, as she slipped her much smaller palm inside his. His grasp was gentle and warm, comforting somehow. For a long moment they were both silent, staring at each other.

"What happens now?" Sophie squeaked.

"Well," Barry cleared his throat, "I'd like to get to know you Sophie. I'd like you to meet Poppy and my wife Ariel."

"Ariel?" Sophie echoed, "isn't that a Disney princess?"

Barry Coben's face broke into a wide smile, "it's the name of the Little Mermaid, but it's also a popular girls' name in Hong Kong. If it pleases you Sophie, I'd like to meet your children."

Sophie's mouth flopped open, "if it pleases me?"

"Do you have boys or girls, or wait, you have one of each huh?"

"Twin boys. I have ten-year-old twin b-boys." Sophie stuttered.

"Twins!" Barry clapped his hands with excitement, "excellent. Dad will be so proud to have not one, but two grandsons."

"Dad? You mean you're going to tell Anthony?" The blood was suddenly pulsing quicker through her veins.

"Of course," Barry gazed at her and she was struck by a sudden resemblance he held to someone she knew: Josh! He had her son's crooked nose. Sophie curled her fist and drew in a shaky lungful of air.

Barry Coben was talking again, his voice full of emotion, "Dad wants to see you Sophie. He's on his way to England. He's coming for you Sophie – for you!"

* * *

Randy Rogers was a fine specimen of a man. Unblemished coffee-coloured skin, a high afro which glistened with some sort of oily lubricant, a dazzling smile and dark, dark eyes that looked almost black when they rested on you. His introduction to Will was a firm pat on the shoulder followed by a moonwalk across the marble reception floor that had Gloria in raptures.

"Man, I just love Michael Jackson," he cried, pointing to the ceiling, "can you feel it, can you feel it, can you feel it." His little ditty was then accompanied by a twirl on the spot and a crotch grab. Will decided at that moment Randy Rogers was a pretty cool guy.

"Do you like his music, Will?"

"Erm … I prefer Janet," came Will's diplomatic reply. Truthfully, he disliked pop and soul. He preferred guitar thrashing indie.

"Janet's good," Randy acknowledged, "hot dancer, but anyway, work; we should get going. We were due at the first job …" he consulted his watch, "half an hour ago."

Will waited outside News Express while Randy went to get his car from the nearby multi storey. He pulled up in a svelte, new design mini. Windows open and blaring Motown era Michael Jackson, "Hop in," he shouted and then screeched away while Will was still fumbling with the seatbelt. Randy darted across the city centre regaling Will about his family life. Apparently, his dad had been born in Jamaica, came over to England to work for the NHS, met and fell in love with a hairdresser named Sandra and the rest was history.

"I got two sisters," Randy said, holding up a couple of digits, "one's a dancer; lives down in London, absolutely gorgeous she is. The other sister's a teacher; secondary school, History; the family brainbox."

"No brothers?" Will enquired, wincing at the sight of a police car in the mirror, that appeared to be tailing them.

"Yep, but we don't talk about 'im," Randy slid a sideways look at Will, "he's in prison, likes the drugs too much."

"Sorry," Will's embarrassment led to him opening up, "I'm an only child. My dad was up until recently the head teacher of St Mary's primary."

"You're a catholic boy?"

"How did you know?"

"I been to that school a few times, covering fetes, shows, that sort of stuff." Randy let out a slow whistle, "looks like I better watch my manners then."

"I'm lapsed," Will confessed, "have been for a long time now."

"Phew," Randy mopped his brow, "only I don't wanna corrupt you in anyway."

"I'm beyond redemption, got a child outta wedlock," they grinned at each other and Randy held up his hand for a high five.

They arrived at Oaklands Residential Home ten minutes later. Thankfully the police car had been distracted by a group of rowdy workmen in a white van who weren't wearing seatbelts. Randy's erratic driving had been overlooked this once.

"Why are we here then?" Will shouted across the car bonnet.

"Fiftieth wedding anniversary. Miracle ain't it?"

They walked quickly through the gardens, arriving at a double-glazed, locked porch with a camera intercom. Randy pressed the buzzer.

"What do you want me to do?" Will asked.

"Here, you can start by holding this," Randy shoved a large Nikon camera into his hands and pulled a notepad and pen from his satchel, "can I trust you to jot down the details? You know dates, names, interesting facts?"

"Sure!"

A care assistant peered at them through the glass, "who are you?" She mouthed.

Randy flashed his press badge, "hey, we're the good guys, honey."

"You can never be sure now-a-days," she pulled open the door, "wipe your feet on that there mat 'afore you come in."

They followed her down a hallway into a sunlight-filled lounge, where elderly people sat snoozing in high backed chairs and a gameshow host chattered from a TV screen.

"Sylvia and Eddie are in the other room, with their family. We arranged a little tea party for them. If you wait here, I'll go see if they're ready for you. And being as though you're over forty minutes late, I'm sure you won't be complaining if they keep *you* waiting for a bit." She stalked off, sniffing with disapproval.

Randy rolled his eyes, helped himself to a handful of peanuts and flopped down onto one of the vacant arm chairs, "one thing you're going to learn real quick, Will ... everyone past their twenties hates the press."

* * *

Sophie stood shivering in the porch. The temperature had significantly dropped from a mild morning to a freezing afternoon. And the sun was drooping in a sky dulled by mist and cloud. Soon it would be dark and Evelyn was still at uni and she'd forgotten her key and Jacob might not be in and her dad, what was she going to do about her dad?

Jacob pulled the door open, his eyes crinkled from smiling and Sophie was struck by warmth for him as a lovely person and for how happy he made Evelyn.

"Hello lass. I was just doing a spot of DIY and I saw your shadow. Forgotten your key again, have you?"

"I'm hopeless. Just hopeless," with that she burst into tears.

"Hey, hey," Jacob ushered her down the hallway, one arm around her, "shall I make us a brew?"

Sophie rummaged in her bag for a tissue, "sorry. I've had a shock."

"Is it your dad?" Jacob asked, with a knowing nod, "Evelyn told me. She's been so worried about you." He clicked on the kettle, "you look half froze to death and as white as that sheet on the line. Will you tell me what's happened, wench?"

Sophie kicked off her shoes, curled onto the rocking chair and told him everything.

By the time Evelyn arrived home, Sophie's mind was feeling a lot clearer and she had calmed down enough to laugh at Jacob's jokes about their neighbour Ted and his overbearing wife.

"Sophie!" Evelyn rushed into the kitchen, pulling her into a fierce hug. "Are you okay?"

"She has a brother," Jacob announced, boiling the kettle again.

"A br ... " Evelyn appraised her with incredulous eyes.

"Sorry," Jacob cast Sophie an apologetic look, "I think you ladies should have a good old natter. I'll fetch us fish and chips for tea and can I pick up Josh and Jake from school for you?"

"That's so kind," Sophie could feel herself welling up with tears again, "you're both so kind."

"Come on now," Evelyn pulled a drawer open and passed over one of her best lace hankies, "We're friends, aren't we? And we'll sort this out together, Sophie."

* * *

After being invited to stop for a champagne toast and a talk to Sylvia and Eddie's relatives, Randy was eventually able to set up his camera and snap the happy couple. Will watched them holding hands, smiling for the camera and was reminded of his parents and their solid, dependable love for each other. Is this what it was like when you had been with one person for so long? There was an easy affection evident between the golden couple, but then Sylvia spoke about their turbulent life together through poverty, sickness and grief and Will reckoned this was true love: the everlasting kind. Oh sure, he fancied Hema, he really did, but his love for her had changed since Esme had been born. Now he felt an overwhelming protection towards them both. Heck, he'd almost died for her! And he wanted to take care of her, he wanted to cherish her. She was his girl and, as far as he was concerned, she would be forever.

"Here," Sandra, the care assistant, cast a halt to Will's ruminations by offering them both a piece of cake, "now make sure you do them a good write up."

"We sure will," Randy replied, stuffing vanilla sponge into his mouth, "so we'll just take some particulars and then we'll be going."

The particulars included a merry jig with some of the regulars to the tune of a greatest war classics CD. A lady called Mae had latched onto Will, said he reminded her of her poor deceased Tommy from the East End.

"I'm a hundred next month," she disclosed, as he ever so carefully twirled her around, "will you come back and tek my picture?"

"I'm sure that could be arranged," he replied, with a cheeky grin.

"Eh! Isn't he handsome?" Mae said to the row of elderly women singing along, "just like my Tommy." They nodded with approval and more tea and buns were consumed before Randy explained to the happy crowd that they must be on their way.

On the way out he told Will he was impressed, "you definitely have a knack with the general public, looks to me like there's a few people at News Express better watch themselves, 'cause you boy are a journalist in the making."

They spent the rest of the afternoon and the early evening whizzing across the city on various jobs; a book fair at a village hall, a charity fete at a local primary school and a demonstration against welfare cuts outside the main council offices. Randy dropped him back home at seven thirty, "you did good," he informed a yawning Will, "same time next week?"

"Yep," Will unclipped his seatbelt, "my handwriting's pretty neat, but if you're stuck on anything, text me."

"Will do." Randy sped off up the road, papping, and giving Will a thumbs up sign in his mirror.

Hema was standing in the open doorway, light bathing around her like a halo, making her features glow and sparkling her hair. She looked like an angel in her white furry onesie, Will sucked in his breath, slung one arm across her shoulders and dropped a kiss on her forehead.

"Did it go well?" She asked, gazing up at him.

"It went great. What have you been up to?"

"Cakes with Esme – remember? And we went to see Mum and Dad."

Will's eyebrow shot up, "I hope they were nice to you."

"They were," Hema smiled, touched the lapel on his jacket, "in fact there's a family wedding after Christmas and we're invited – all of us: your mum and dad too."

"Oh?" Will shrugged his coat off, "won't that be awkward?"

"They won't be there," she replied, "Dad's brother and his children have been banned. Please don't worry Will," her hand slipped inside his, "no one's going to hurt us."

"Okay," he smiled down at her, "so is tea ready? I'm starving and can't wait to sample my daughter's first attempt at cooking. Let's hope it's not like her nana's eh?" They walked up the hallway laughing together.

"There you are!" Flora pushed the sliding kitchen door open, allowing the aroma of wholesome food to waft towards them, "My Hungarian stew has been simmering for hours. We were all beginning to worry about you Will." She placed two hands on her hips as she berated her son.

"Sorry. I've been so busy, I forgot to text you."

"Never mind then," Flora stepped to one side so he could pass, "you're home now."

"Where is s ... " Will trailed off at the sight of Esme fast asleep in his father's arms.

"We've had a busy afternoon," Max Bentley announced, "playdough, stickle bricks and Peppa Pig." He shifted slightly.

Will raised an eyebrow, "no work?"

"Day off, and tomorrow I'm on the road, travelling the Midlands, scouting for furniture items for the shop."

Will sank down opposite his dad, thinking how happy he looked, how calm, how chilled, the opposite of the brow beaten, stressed out Headteacher Max of last year.

"You look tired," Max appraised his son.

"Yeah I'm worn out, but it was worth it," his face lit up, "I think I'm going to enjoy this voluntary."

Flora was watching him, as she carefully draped the damp washing over the airer,

"Will you be able to cope, love? This is your last year at uni and you're working at the Student Union Bar too, as well as caring for little Esme. You'll be wearing yourself out."

"I'll be fine, Mum. I'm cutting down the hours at the bar and I've kept on top of all the essays so far."

"What about your dissertation?" Hema asked, as she ladled the stew onto china plates.

Will frowned, "I admit I haven't had chance to work on it much, but I've started it and got it all planned out," he stood and went to help her, "so let's sit down for dinner and then I'll bath Esme, read her a story, put her to bed and then how about you and me watch a horror on Netflix and make plans for the weekend?"

Hema paused to gaze at him lovingly, "sounds perfect."

"Sounds heavenly," Flora added, smiling at her handsome son.

Chapter Twelve

"Are you missing him?" The question had been deployed in a teasing, light-hearted manner, but Juliette felt an actual twist in her gut at the mention of him.

"Yes, I'm missing him," she carried on scribbling notes in her A4 pad, quelling the urge to check her phone yet again.

Ben hadn't texted her yet today, but he had messaged her yesterday to tell her he was participating in a team bonding exercise. A day when grown men got to run around with plastic guns, firing paint at their opponents. She explained this to her sister Marie, who chortled, "sounds fun to me."

It was Sunday evening, Molly was watching a film with her brother in his room and Juliette and Marie were sharing a bottle of wine and had just consumed a takeaway. It was quiet and peaceful, until Marie decided to grill Juliette about her love life.

"When are you guys moving in together?"

"What? Can you really see Ben moving in here with me?!"

"I didn't mean here, you know that." There was a pause, "would you like to live with him?"

The thought of sharing Ben's bed every evening made Juliette grin, "hell yes. But I'm not going to suggest it, no way! I'll scare him off and I do *not* want to do that so please, no more talk of us moving in together, Maz."

Marie pulled a face, "I can't understand it. You're a pair of mature, life experienced adults who love each other. Surely living together is the next natural step?"

"I don't think too much about what should be happening in the future," Juliette replied, crisply, "I'm too busy enjoying the present, where I have this perfectly lovely, independent relationship with Dr Rivers. And really Marie, we haven't been together that long." She topped up their wine glasses, eager to change the subject, "how is my wee nephew anyway? And when can I munch him again?"

Marie's face brightened, "James is absolutely perfect and enjoying a bonding night with his daddy, who as you know, is completely besotted with him, and Jules you know that you are welcome to come and see him whenever you want to. In fact, how about next weekend? You can bring your 'friend with benefits' too."

Juliette laughed, "sorry I've made plans for next weekend."

"Oh? Anything exciting I should be jealous about?"

Juliette almost bounced on top of the sofa, "I'm going to see Ben play in his band."

"Oh wow! I forgot all about him playing in a band." Marie replied, "what instrument does he play?"

"The saxophone, and before you ask, he's good – real good."

"Not that you're biased," Marie cleared her throat, "so how's uni going? Are you coping with the workload or is the gorgeous Dr Rivers too much of a distraction?"

"Year three is hard," Juliette admitted, "tons of reading, lots of essays, and to top it all off, a twelve-thousand-word dissertation. I've been working every evening since the semester started, and Ben is a very nice welcome distraction, thank you."

"I can't believe you've almost finished your degree," Marie shook her head, "my sister the brain box. Will you have letters after your name?"

"I suppose so," Juliette shrugged, "I haven't given it much thought; besides I have to pass it first."

"You will, I just know it, and then we can plan your next move on the delectable Doctor Rivers."

"My *teaching career* will be what I'm planning next," Juliette answered.

"Oh yes, class be silent for Miss Harris or will that be Mrs Rivers? Has such a sweet ring to it doesn't it: Juliette Rivers?"

"Maz!" Juliette threw the nearest cushion, it bounced off the edge of the settee and sent an ornament flying off the mantlepiece, shattering it into tiny pieces on the marble fireplace. They both stared at the mess in silence, and then Molly wandered into the room in her Disney Princess nightie, her hair was sticking up and she was clutching a teddy tightly to her chest, "Mummy, I wanna go to bed now."

Juliette hurried over to scoop her up, pushing away bothersome images of herself in a white flouncy dress, smiling as she introduced herself formally as Mrs Rivers.

* * *

The start of a new week began with glorious sunshine and a crisp, white frost which adorned the trees and pavements. Evelyn was up early, pottering about in her dressing gown, braving the outside elements to scatter bird seed over the frozen lawn. When she went back into the kitchen, Sophie was sitting at the table, staring into space and looking as if she'd had no sleep again.

"Morning dear," Evelyn wiped her cold fingers on the warm hand towel, "would you like scrambled eggs? I've put some on for me and Jacob, but there should be enough for you as well."

There was no reply, just the beeping of the cooker that signified the eggs were cooked.

"Sophie?" Evelyn touched her shoulder, shaking her gently, "are you okay?"

Sophie blinked, ran a shaky hand through her knotted tresses, "I don't know what to do about Mum. What shall I do, Evelyn?"

"Well," Evelyn moved to the stove, taking the pan off the hob, "I think you should tell her."

"Everything? It will make her ill. The shock of ... of Anthony and Barry ... my brother, Evelyn, I still can't believe I have a brother."

Evelyn spooned the eggs onto three pieces of cooked bread, "then wait. Meet your brother again and his family and your dad Sophie, maybe you should meet your dad before you tell any of this to your mother."

Sophie nodded, "you're right. So the plan is meet Barry again, speak to d ... Anthony," she exhaled shakily, "see how things go and then speak to Mum."

"Sounds a good plan to me," Evelyn passed her the pepper pot, "now eat up, and then we can take the boys to school and head off to uni. That's if ... you feel up to it Sophie?"

Sophie sliced into the bread, "it will take my mind off all these personal issues – all the time, personal problems, weighing me down. And in the final year Evelyn, when the grades really count! Why can't my life just be simple?"

Evelyn chuckled, "at least it's interesting. Boy it's interesting living with you, you make me feel young and alive again, Sophie."

"And you make me feel happy and safe, Evelyn," Sophie chewed her breakfast thoughtfully, "have you heard from your publishers?"

"Yes."

Sophie put down her cutlery, "why didn't you tell me? Is it ready?"

"Almost," Evelyn's cheeks were rosy as she replied, "I'm just checking over the final edits and then yes. It should be out for Christmas!"

Sophie squealed, then she jumped up and jigged around the kitchen, pulling Evelyn with her. They were still hugging and whooping with excitement when Jacob popped his head round the door a few minutes later and asked in neutral tones if his eggs were done.

* * *

"Breakfast's ready," Ann hollered as she turned the spitting bacon rashers. The smoke alarm began beeping and Jon rushed into the kitchen, wafting his hands about.

"Everything alright in here?" He asked, watching Ann as she transferred the cooked bacon onto thickly sliced crusty bread.

"Yep. Open that window, would you love?"

"We're having bacon on a Monday?" Jon remarked, as he propped the window open and a blast of icy air hit his face, "that's usually a weekend treat."

"Yes well. Lulu texted me last night and told me that bacon sarnies are Sam's favourite breakfast. So I thought it would be a good start to his week. I've also made him lunch, do you think there's enough?" She nodded her head at an open plastic tub.

Jon went to investigate the contents: a chicken salad wrap, a pot of cheese dunkers, crisps, two pieces of fruit and a wedge of homemade banana loaf. Then he glanced at his own smaller packed lunch and his mouth turned down, "Sam's looks great, not too sure about mine though."

"Oh Jon," Ann said with a roll of her eyes, "he's a teenage boy. It's a well-known fact they need more calories per day. Besides, I've cut you a bigger piece of cake."

A mollified Jon smiled at her.

"Can you shout him again, love?" Ann asked, wiping a loose tendril of hair away from her eyes.

"No need," Jon pointed at the doorway where Samuel stood, looking neat and tidy in his school uniform.

"Morning," he smiled, "that bacon smells good."

"Help yourself," Ann wheeled back from the table, "there's sauce if you want it."

Sam nodded, made his way over and squirted ketchup onto his sandwich. They sat at the table, passing round the juice carton, munching their breakfasts.

"So what lessons do you have today?" Ann asked.

"Double French to start," Sam grimaced, "then English in the afternoon. Are you at uni?"

Ann nodded, wiped a blob of sauce from her chin, "dissertation meeting and then realism and the novel."

"What's it like?" Sam asked, "uni I mean."

"It's great," Ann replied, "from my experience anyway – the course is fantastic – really informative and enjoyable."

"Do you think you'd like to go to uni, Sam?" Jon asked.

"I guess so, I mean I'm not sure yet. There are school trips next year to a couple of the Midland universities."

"What subject interests you the most?" Jon persisted.

"English is cool. I like PE too." Samuel gulped down his orange, "I kinda like the idea of being a fireman or a policeman though, helping and saving people."

"My brother was a fireman," Jon shook his head, "saw a lot of bad stuff, but he was brave, real brave. He'd be the first one in a burning building, always risking his life for others."

"How come he never comes over?"

Jon glanced at Sam, "he died four years ago. Fell off a ladder at home – can you believe that? Clearing the guttering himself, broke the cardinal rule of ladder climbing – no one was holding the bottom steady for him and he fell onto a concrete wall."

"Sorry," Sam winced.

"It's okay Sam. It's a long time ago now, but in here," he tapped the side of his head, "he's still alive, he's still my big, brave brother. Those memories never fade."

"So," Ann clapped her hands, endeavouring to lighten the atmosphere, "let's get cleaned up and then we can drop you off at school."

"Actually," Sam replied, "I'm meeting Beth at the bus stop. We're catching the bus to school and I thought maybe she could come over for tea one of the evenings if that's alright?"

"Of course," Ann replied, "she's welcome any evening. Apart from Wednesday," she looked at Jon, "I forgot to mention, I've joined the debating team at uni. They meet weekly just for a few hours."

"What for?" Jon looked nonplussed.

Ann laughed, "to debate of course. I was trying to talk Sophie into coming with me, you know how she likes to chat, but she's been acting a bit odd just lately, I think she has personal problems again, so I didn't want her to feel pressured."

"So, you're going on your own?"

"Yes, I'm going alone. It sounds interesting and will look good on my resume – don't you think?"

"I suppose so," Jon let out a hefty sigh and turned to look at Sam, "let's get the student radical to uni then eh?"

* * *

The table in the Learning Centre was cluttered with books and pens and reams of paper full of notes. In amongst the chaos lay a bouquet of flowers – a beautiful composition of roses and carnations, wrapped tightly in peach cellophane with a trailing bow. Juliette was wearing a birthday badge clipped to her new brushed cotton dress – both of which had been from her sister, Marie. She was also wearing a pair of new knee-length boots, an extravagant present from her mum and dad. Her hair was piled high, fastened with a pretty diamante clip, which was a gift from Harry and Molly. She *was* a walking birthday present.

Sophie and Will had wandered away from the group searching for books to help them with their dissertation. Evelyn and Ann were bent over, their foreheads lined with concentration as they scribbled in their notepads. Only Juliette was distracted, thinking about *him*; his gorgeous face and mesmerising eyes, his sexy physique, his warmth and his kindness. The week without him had dragged interminably slowly, she had really missed him and it surprised even herself how much. *Hurry up*, she thought, glancing at the clock, willing the time fingers to move quicker.

"Have you made plans this evening?" Ann asked, "you smell divine by the way."

"Oh thank you," Juliette smiled, "I haven't made any plans, probably just a movie at home with the kids."

Ann looked up, "is Doctor Rivers back from his trip?"

"I think so," Juliette bit her lip, "I mean, I haven't heard from him this morning, but I presume we have him for this afternoon's lecture. How is your dissertation going?"

"Wonderful," Ann replied, "I've decided to compare and contrast Angela Carter's work with Leonora Carrington's."

There was no reply as Juliette stared off into space.

"And when I finish it, I'm going to wheel myself naked around the university shouting hooray!"

Still no reply. Evelyn had stopped working and was chuckling at Ann.

"What?" Juliette said, "well that sounds great Ann." Her phone was beeping and she reached down to tug it out of her bag.

'Can you come to my office?'

Juliette's stomach flipped over. She pushed back her chair, smoothing the wrinkles from her skirt.

"I have to go – sorry! I'm just popping out … for sweets."

"But what about your dissertation?" Ann smirked at the dreamy look which had flitted across her friend's face, "never mind. We'll see you in Realism and the Novel then?"

"Yes," Juliette waved, as she wandered towards the exit stairwell.

"Was it something I said, Evelyn?"

"I doubt it dear. I think Juliette has someone else on her mind."

They exchanged a knowing glance as Sophie and Will dumped a pile of books on the table.

"Where's Jules?" Sophie asked.

"Gone to fetch us all sweets apparently," Ann replied.

"Sweets? She never eats sweets," she gripped Ann's arm, "maybe it's a craving, maybe she's preg …"

"Don't be so naïve," Ann cut in, lowering her tone, "she's off to see Ben Rivers, and for goodness sake don't start a rumour about babies. There are enough people gossiping about them as it is."

Evelyn sighed, "it's so romantic, don't you think? In fact, I'm thinking of basing a couple of characters in my next novel on them."

"Why don't you write some erotica Evelyn," Will leaned back on his chair, pen wedged firmly behind his ear, "you could be a millionaire."

"I want to be taken seriously as a writer, Will," Evelyn's neck was turning red, "besides, I – erm, don't think I could do the subject justice."

"I could," Sophie nodded enthusiastically, "reclusive billionaire with deep trauma issues falls for his beautiful therapist. He would live on a ranch of course, in the Canadian mountains and he'd wear a cowboy hat, tight fitting jeans and boots with those spur thingies on. His shirt would always be slightly open to reveal dark hair and a solid gold St Christopher and really firm muscles," Sophie cleared her throat, "anyway, he would fall uncontrollably, madly in love with her and they would frolic in fields of golden corn and swim naked in swirling blue whirlpools, erm ... " she trailed off, noticing the others staring silently at her, "so anyway, what is this week's lecture going to be about?"

She could see him waiting outside the entrance to the Humanities building, arms crossed, pacing the floor.

"Hi," she said, feeling suddenly shy.

"Hi," he replied, eyes flashing.

"So, Dr Rivers," she followed him into the building, "did you have a good trip?"

"It was excellent, thank you, Miss Harris," he stepped aside so she could enter the lift. An influx of rowdy students pushed them towards the back. Juliette could feel the cold structural edge of metal against her back. They stood silently as the doors slid closed and the lift made its slow descent to the fourth floor. She could feel his thigh pressing against hers and then the touch of his warm hand as it twined around her fingers. Heat rushed to her cheeks as she cast a sneaky glance at his full lips. A mouth that drove her to abandon all self-control, a mouth that lit her alight with desire.

"Is Doctor Hodges in?" She whispered.

Slowly, he shook his head as a muscle flexed in his cheek.

The elevator seemed to take forever, stopping on each floor to let people out and let others in. Finally, it pinged onto the fourth floor and then Ben grabbed her hand firmly, pulling her through the crowd.

Once they had reached his office and shut the door she was in his arms and they were kissing passionately.

"Have you missed me?" He asked against her mouth.

"Yes," she murmured, twining her fingers through his thick hair.

He sank down onto his chair, pulling her with him onto his lap.

"Happy birthday," slowly, he kissed the curve of her neck, making her shiver, "have you made plans for this evening?"

"I erm ... no."

"Good, because I've booked for the four of us to dine at Chattlesbury Football Club's a la carte restaurant."

Juliette gasped, "you have?"

Ben nodded, "the table overlooks the pitch I've been told. It's posh, very posh. Plus I got you a little something." He opened his drawer to pull out a rectangular object, covered in shiny paper and a large metallic bow.

"Ben, this is too much. You're already taking us to Lapland next month!"

He shrugged, "you're worth every penny and I want to spoil you." He passed her the gift which she had to hold with two hands as it was quite heavy.

"What is it?" She tore off the paper and stared open mouthed at the laptop in front of her, "you got me a PC?"

"It's one of the newest currently on the market. That old computer of yours would never last another six months, and it's important you have a good PC to do your work on."

"Ben," she said quietly, "you're so good to me. Thank you."

"Welcome," he replied, grinning, his stomach flipping, heart racing grin.

"How was your course?" She asked, slipping her arms around his shoulders, hugging him tightly.

"Boring," he replied, "truth is I hated it, Juliette. I hated leaving you. I hated being apart from you. Continual Professional Development can do one."

Juliette gasped at the emotion she heard in his voice, "it's your job Ben, your career. Your livelihood. You must put it first."

"Before you? I don't think so."

Juliette drew back slightly, "what are you saying?"

"I'm saying I love you. I adore you. You mean the world to me." He held her face in his hands and stared into her eyes. "Do you feel the same?"

Juliette's legs trembled slightly as she replied, "yes I feel the same."

"Then marry me Juliette. Marry me."

The lecture passed by in a blur. Juliette was vaguely aware of them discussing Wuthering Heights during the seminar; Ben talking about the characters Cathy and Heathcliff and their overwhelming, irrational attraction towards each other. His smiled widened when he spoke about uncontrollable passion and deep emotional bonds that connect one person to another across time and space. Juliette gazed at his hands feeling star struck, watching his fingers lightly tapping his laptop. When she looked up, he was staring straight at her, making heat flood into her cheeks, and she had to tear her gaze away from him and look down at the blank sheet in front of her to compose herself. She had written nothing, for the past two and half hours her mind had been in a daydream, when she should have been concentrating on academic work, she had been fantasising about white dresses and church bells and wedding vows. Ben had noticed too. At the end of the seminar he drew her to one side and apologised for distracting her.

"You need to be thinking about your studies not me."

She had begun to protest but he stopped her.

"Give me your answer at the end of the year. I was carried away, I shouldn't have pressurised you like that. For now, concentrate on your studies."

"That could be difficult," Juliette replied, gazing up at him, "when the lecturer is so breathtakingly distracting."

Ben tutted, "don't think that kind of talk is going to get you an A, lady. I want extra hard work off you from now on, okay?"

"Okay?" Juliette grinned and then moved back, so another student could bombard the gorgeous Dr Rivers with literary questions.

Chapter Thirteen

On Wednesday evening, Jon, Ann and Samuel were parked in one of the disabled bays outside the university's main reception, waiting for Melanie to show. There was a full moon and the sky was dotted with stars and wispy clouds.

"Did you just hear that?" Jon said, gazing out at the frosty night.

Ann and Samuel looked at him, blankly.

"I'm sure I heard a wolf howling."

"A wolf?" Sam's eyes were big and round as he rubbed at the misted-up window.

"You mean a dog Jon," Ann said, with a derisory shake of her head, "Chattlesbury doesn't have a zoo and there are no wild wolves roaming about the middle of England."

"I think I heard an owl," Samuel pressed the button to slide his window down. They all listened keenly and then a wit-woo sounded, coming from the tall trees in front of them. The branches shook and a large bird flapped away. They watched it go; a dark silhouette against the moonlight.

"You wouldn't think there would be so much wildlife in the city centre," Jon remarked, leaning forward to turn up the heating a notch, "did you know Sam, they have foxes in the church grounds? And Chattlesbury Football Club is overrun with pigeons, they have to fly hawks and buzzards around the ground to frighten them off."

"Really?" Sam answered.

"Yep. We could have a walk round the church grounds while we're here if you want, grab a burger after, maybe walk down to the football ground, I've heard it's pretty impressive at night when it's all quiet and lit up."

"Actually," Sam began apologetically, "Beth's coming over. I said I'd help her with a maths test."

"Oh, okay no worries," Jon said, "looks like I get the T.V remote to myself this evening then."

Ann patted her husband's knee, "I'll only be gone a couple of hours. We could watch a film when we get back if you fancy it?"

"What about your uni work?"

"I *need* a break, I've been working nonstop. Time to take a night off."

Jon held up his hands, "no arguments off me. Here comes Melanie." He jumped sprightly from the car, headed to the boot and set up Ann's wheelchair, bringing it round to the passenger seat so she could slide over.

"Hi guys," Melanie called from across the street, "sorry I'm late, I got roped into showing a group of camera happy Japanese students around the Learning Centre. The debating team are waiting for you, Ann."

"Bring it on," Ann's smiled was wide in the darkness, "I'm ready!"

"Is that the debating team?" Ann was looking through the window at Leon Broome and the small group of people sitting with him.

"It sure is," Melanie replied, as she pushed her up the Learning Centre's accessible ramp, "do you want me to stay?"

"No it's fine," Ann replied, as they passed through the sliding doors, "I'll text you when I'm finished."

"Remember to have fun, Ann, debating doesn't have to be all doom and gloom," Melanie gave her a cheery wave and bounced off, pigtails flapping.

Ann wheeled towards them and when Leon noticed her, he jumped up, "Ann, so lovely to see you," he coughed, "I thought I may have put you off. I thought you may have changed your mind."

Ann smiled, "I'm very happy to be here."

"Excellent!" he ushered her forward, "come, come, settle yourself at our table."

"Our round table," a bespectacled man declared, "and we are the Arthurian Knights, endeavouring to right wrong-doings. Forging a path towards light with the spoken word."

"This is Randolph," Leon nodded, "he studies philosophy." Ann was amused by the tone in which he stated it, as if that was the reason for his imaginative comparison with British myth and folklore.

"Howdy," Ann smiled, her eyes already flickering to the person sitting next to him.

"I'm Shelly," the long-haired attractive lady waved, "first year dance and drama. I was roped into this club by Leon whom I've known for years."

"We went to primary school together," Leon explained, "this is Mary' he patted the shoulder of a grim looking woman with green hair, "she studies environmental science."

Ann's eyebrows shot up, "how interesting."

"Actually my name's Maree," she elongated the 'e' sound, "nice to meet you."

"I'm Calvin," the last person in the group stood up and took a bow, "education studies, third year."

"He aspires to be a secondary school teacher," Leon elaborated, "the poor fool."

"And now it's your turn," Randolph and the others looked expectantly at her.

"Well I'm Ann. I study English, I'm in my third year and I want to be a lecturer. Hopefully. I think. Maybe?"

Ann looked at the faces staring inquisitively at her.

"A budding lecturer, how wonderful!" Leon clapped his hands, "so let's open the biscuit tin and we can begin."

The biscuit tin consisted of a half-eaten packet of custard creams and an unopened supermarket savers garibaldi. Ann eyed them, vowing to bring chocolate fancier ones when she came next week. *If* she came back next week.

"I didn't think you could eat in here," she said aloud, thinking of the telling off Will had received from the librarian the other day.

"We shouldn't really, but I do clean up after us," Leon explained, "besides the librarian is my auntie. I suppose she's guilty of nepotism."

"Oh," Ann reached for a garibaldi, watching as Leon poured her a drink from a thermos flask, "so what kind of things will we be discussing this evening?"

Leon looked at Randolph who consulted his notes.

"Firstly," Randolph began, "what are we going to do about the trees on the ring road island? The council are determined to chop them down, irrespective of their age and beauty."

"I've started a petition," Maree chipped in, "all online of course. There are over one thousand signatures so far. Please encourage your friends and family to sign."

"What is their reason for wanting to cut them down?" Ann asked.

"They claim that the leaves are a nuisance and a danger to drivers when they blow down onto the road." Maree sipped her drink, "of course they could just cut them right back, but the council are on a money saving mission again."

"They think," Shelly said, "that it will be easier in the long term to completely get rid of them – even though they were the ones who planted them!"

"We need to fight this," Randolph pushed his glasses up his nose, "otherwise there will be no greenery left in the city centre."

"Agreed," Maree held her hand up, "if you leave me your email addresses, I'll send you further info and then we can start conversations on social media and here at the uni. Make other students and the general public aware."

"Yes," Leon nodded, "the council are a crafty lot, they'll try to push this through as quietly as possible. So, let's make some noise, people."

Ann felt a surge of excitement build within her, *this is what being a student is about* she thought; questioning authority, not just accepting.

"So next on the agenda; let's talk God." Randolph tapped the table with his pencil, "of course you're all aware, with the exception of Ann, that I am a firm believer."

"If there is a God then why is there so much death and destruction in the world?" Maree shook her head, "so much suffering."

"Basically, it boils down to man's free will," Randolph replied, "we each have a choice. A choice to act in a good way or a bad way."

"It hardly seems fair that innocent people suffer because of other people's bad choices," Leon scoffed.

"That's why we have laws Leon," Randolph countered, "punishment and retribution, heaven and hell. The ten commandments – to guide us."

"Well," Maree's eyes were glinting, "as a feminist I say the biggest myth ever perpetuated was Adam and Eve."

"The bible isn't a myth," Randolph snapped, "how else can we recognise and celebrate the beauty of the world around us."

"How about celebrating the simplicity of Mother Nature, who has always been and who will always be," Maree rubbed her temple, "why don't humans just accept instead of continually trying to question?"

Calvin was looking at Ann's down-turned face, "what about you Ann?" He asked, "are you a believer?"

"No," she replied with firm conviction, "my own opinion is that God as a heavenly almighty power does not exist."

"Please elaborate?" Randolph leant forward in his seat.

Ann took a deep breath, "where is this God? Where is this supreme being? Where is the God of the Old Testament; the true power, the almighty, the ferocious one. There are children in pain and suffering and dying," she looked upwards, "in your name God. In your name. You need to act. They don't have free will. They are exempt. Take your vengeance God," Ann slammed her fists down, "Take.Your.Vengeance."

"I say," Randolph's glasses slid to the end of his bulbous nose, "you certainly are a passionate lady."

"Religion is a subject I feel very strongly about," Ann answered.

"Ann," Leon Broome declared, "you are going to fit in very well with our debating team. I do hope you can make it each week."

Shelly was yawning, "why don't we debate soap operas? Is EastEnders a truer depiction of real life than Coronation Street?"

"How about we discuss that very worthy and current topic at the end of the session?" Leon suggested smoothly, "that way we can end on a lighter tone."

Calvin said to Ann, "we were debating contemporary feminism last week. It got a little heated."

"No Calvin, Randolph became agitated by my perfectly reasonable allusion to the Garden of Eden and my argument that, since then, women have been repressed, marginalised and subjugated by *men*," Maree spat out the last word as if it were a literal bad taste in her mouth.

"And it's still going on today," Shelly joined in, her voice tremulous with emotion, "why is it okay for Calvin here to sleep around and be praised? Yet because I do the same, I'm labelled a slut."

Calvin appraised her, "I know *I do*, but I wasn't aware you did! Why don't we discuss this further in erm ... private?"

"Calvin really!" Maree was appalled, "this is exactly what I'm referring to Ann – men and the judgmental patriarchal society, obsessed with one-sided sexual gratification."

Ann was just going to voice her agreement, when Leon slammed the lid back on the biscuit tin, "can we please try not to argue tonight? This is a group for intelligent adults to discuss issues in a friendly, neutral environment. Please refrain from making personal attacks towards others." He held his palms up, "we're all friends here after all."

An awkward silence ensued. Ann noticed Shelly casting mutinous looks towards Calvin and wondered if they were more than just friends.

"Okay," Leon said, decisively, "we'll move onto the next topic, which is …"

Randolph was leafing quickly through his notes, "erm … maybe we should leave sexuality and gender for another week?"

"We were going to discuss Delphinus and Cetacea," Maree stated with an eyeroll.

Randolph looked perplexed, "is that Latin?"

Shelly sighed and flicked her long mega straight hair, "she means her *favourite* topic: dolphins and whales."

"Oh of course," Randolph's frown morphed into a wide smile, "very cute creatures."

"Very hunted, threatened, *poor* creatures," Maree corrected, "*what* can we do to help them?"

"A demonstration here at the uni would be a good start," Shelly suggested, as she uncrossed her slim legs and wrapped them around the chair leg.

"Such wonderful creatures," Ann said, "although I'm ashamed to say I've only ever seen them in captivity."

"No!" Maree was horrified by Ann's confession, "those places are no better than goldfish bowls."

Ann felt her face flush and quickly countered, "From what I saw and read, they are highly intelligent."

"Indeed, they are," Maree replied, "scientists claim dolphins are second in intelligence after humans. They actually give themselves names which they recognise, and they only sleep with half of their brain!"

"Really?" The surprise was evident on Ann's face.

"Oh yes," Shelly cut in exuberantly, "they are also super friendly and caring too. I saw a programme once which showed how they look after their sick and old."

Maree fiddled with her phone and then flipped it onto its side, screen showing so everyone could see. They watched a pod of dolphins jumping through the bubbling surf churned up by a ship's hull.

"Just look how amazing they are," Maree swiped at her eyes, "it breaks my heart knowing how some countries kill them just for tradition or fun."

"Maybe you could organise a demonstration outside those countries embassies headquarters in London – take a petition with you."

Maree stared, "that's an amazing idea. Randolph jot it down!"

Randolph scribbled in his notebook.

"I may be playing the devil's advocate here," Calvin said, as he rolled his pen casually between thumb and forefinger, "but we could say the same about the elephants, the gorillas, the rhinos, the crocodiles – they're made into bags *poor* creatures. Why stop at dolphins?"

"Yes ladies," Randolph said in a deep baritone, "just because something looks cute it doesn't make it any worthier. What about the pigs?"

"What about the pigs, Randolph? I'm a vegan remember?" Maree pursed her lips.

"Do you eat pigs Ann?" Randolph regarded her with triumphant, already knowing eyes.

"I do love a bacon sandwich," Ann admitted, "but that doesn't mean I can't care about animal welfare."

"Of course, it doesn't," Maree agreed, "what's your point Randolph?"

"My point is an animal is being slaughtered for human consumption. Pigs and dolphins – they're the same!"

"And my point is," Maree replied between clenched teeth, "they are *not* the same. Pigs are livestock and are bred for food, their numbers can be controlled. Whales and dolphins are being hunted to extinction and for what? They are not edible because of their high levels of mercury, so why *are* they killed? For sport? For tradition? For scientific reasons? Whales and Dolphins are wild creatures that belong to the sea – not us. Humans cannot control the sea and therefore cannot control their population. They are gentle and intelligent creatures and it sickens me that, in this century, we still have their blood on our hands. Their slaughter is immoral and the same goes for the elephants and the rhinos and every other wild creature at jeopardy from trophy hunters and their ilk!"

"Hear, hear," Ann began a slow clap that spread around the table.

"Okay," Randolph said, grudgingly, "fair point. Leon pass the biscuits."

"Sorry," Leon's face was flushed as he shook the empty tin, "it seems like they have all been consumed."

"Maybe we should call it a night," Calvin said, with a pleading expression, "it's getting chilly and I have a long drive home."

"Maybe we should ask our newest member?" All eyes turned to Ann.

"That's fine with me," she replied, winding her scarf around her neck, "I'll text my husband, and next week the biscuits are on me."

Shelly laughed, "you're coming back?

"Yes, I've enjoyed our chat and it's a break from the books."

"Excellent." Leon patted her shoulder, "and feel free to suggest any topics for debate which you feel passionate about."

"Did you really enjoy it?" Shelly whispered, as they made their way to the exit doors. Maree stomped angrily ahead of them muttering about Randolph and the worldwide threat of misogyny.

"It was certainly different," she replied, watching Jon pull up in the disabled bay and jog towards her, "but that's good. Difference is what changes the world. Difference is what being a student is all about."

Chapter Fourteen

Sophie was having a meltdown in the work toilets. Her breathing was ragged, her face was hot and her hands were shaking. *I am having a panic attack,* she thought, scooping cold water over her cheeks in a desperate attempt to calm herself. Outside the door came the sound of laughter. As it swung open, she ducked into a vacant cubicle, locking the door and leaning against it. Breathing deeply, she managed to compose herself, and her wobbly knees. She pulled tissue from the lopsided holder and dabbed at her dripping nose. This morning she had woken with a sore throat, itchy eyes and a pain in her stomach which had more to do with the impending gut-wrenching prospect of seeing her *brother* again than any bodily influenza. Evelyn had declared her run down from stress and was, at this moment, cooking up a soup from bones of a chicken carcass. A remedy of great aunt Gertrude's, she had soothed Sophie.

She had been tempted to stay at home today, she felt ill and sick with worry. A day in bed had seemed heavenly in comparison with a morning at Hanley's. But it was warm here and it was distracting, and right now Sophie desperately needed to be thinking of anything else but her fugitive family from Hong Kong.

Sophie waited until the gaggle of giggling girls vacated the toilet before opening the door and resurfacing. She stared at her wide-eyed reflection and quickly dug out her make-up bag. Lipstick, blusher and mascara later she was ready to start work. She bolted across the sales office, scurrying to the haven of her high walled desk where she stared at the pictures of Josh and Jake. She hadn't told them yet; all week she had put off having to disclose that their runaway Granddad was alive and well and making millions on the other side of the world. She also hadn't yet mentioned that they had an uncle and a cousin and that they would be meeting them this very evening. Bottom line was that Sophie was frightened of unsettling them. With all the turmoil that had transpired in their lives just recently, she was consumed with the fear that divulging any further information on her delinquent family may seriously destabilise them. Evelyn had said children were resilient and strong, but still Sophie worried.

Her phone was flashing red; an impending sales call and it wasn't even nine a.m.

"Leave it," Sheila said, popping gum as she leant over Sophie's wall, "Jesus you look like death warmed up! Had a hard week?"

"Something like that," Sophie nodded.

"There's a few of us going out tonight. Andy's coming too," Sheila winked, "he was asking if you were coming."

"No!" Sophie said with some force, "I've made plans, important plans. And why would he be asking if I was coming?"

Sheila emitted a hearty sigh, "are you serious? He likes you Sophie."

"I like him too. He's very pleasant."

"Pleasant?" Sheila rolled the word out, "is that all you can say about him? I mean romantically, he fancies you. Haven't you noticed the way he looks and speaks to you."

Sophie reached for her ear piece, "I'm here to work," she replied stiffly, her stomach a flutter at the thought of Andy, the rather hot American highflyer, actually liking her *that way*. Surreptitiously she looked across the office where he was leaning against the water machine, talking to Angie, the flirty blonde bombshell from the despatch department. Hmm she thought, disbelief building inside of her.

"I think Andy likes everybody," she pointed out to Sheila, who frowned and slunk back down in her seat.

"Nine o'clock folks," the team leader whooped across the office, "let's get those sales in."

Three hours later Sophie's phone was flashing for what felt like the hundredth time. She pressed the connect button, pushing away thoughts of Barry Coben and Andy head of HR, determined to concentrate on her job.

"Good morning, Hanley's Hoovers, how may I help you?"

A bout of chesty coughing erupted from the other end.

Sophie waited politely for him to stop, "are you okay sir?" She queried, presuming that the deep bronchial tone belonged to a man.

"No, I'm not," a sour tone snapped. Cough, cough, "I'm bed bound with bronchitis and now the wife's hoover's packed up."

"Sorry to hear that sir," Sophie said with a distinct air of professional smoothness, "is it still under warranty?"

"Eh? Whadda' you mean? All I know is it's flipping packed up and we got a floor covered with dog hair," a long bout of angry coughing ensued. Sophie waited until it was quiet again.

"How long have you had your appliance sir?"

"Why you wanna know that?" His tone was now angry *and* suspicious. "Let me think ... I bought it for 'er indoors for our fortieth wedding anniversary."

"Really?" The word slipped out of Sophie's surprised mouth, "I mean ... how generous."

"She wasn't pleased with it," the man snapped.

I'm not surprised Sophie thought.

"Bloody ungrateful woman. Anyway, we're still married just about – forty three years now."

"So you've had it three years Sir?"

"Yup."

Sophie's fingers flew over her keyboard, "did you take out the extended warranty sir?"

"Eh? Course I didn't. Shouldn't have too. In *my* youth electrical appliances were built to last."

Sophie rubbed her throbbing temple, "sir I'm going to transfer you to our maintenance department." From the corner of her eye she could see Marjorie, head of repairs eyeballing her, whilst pointing at the argentite wall clock.

Yes, Sophie knew it was almost lunchtime; a time when the office emitted a collective sigh and the phones were redirected to somewhere else for an hour, but her patience had slowly dissipated over the morning. It seemed she had picked up every irate caller in the whole of England. Let Marjorie take the brunt, she decided. Mr chesty cough began to protest, but Sophie deftly cut him off and clicked him onto Marjorie's line whilst mouthing an apology.

"Someone's eager to leave today," Sheila, fellow sales operative commented.

"I'm not feeling too good," Sophie offered. She pressed her stomach, trying to dispel the tension. Her insides felt like a flattened spring ready to erupt, but fortunately her shift finished at midday. Maybe she could spend the afternoon curled up in bed, reading a trashy novel. No such luck, she was meeting Evelyn in half an hour.

"You look awfully pale," Sheila agreed, "ring in sick tomorrow, yeah?"

"It's my weekend off anyway," Sophie picked up the mugs she'd used today and walked to the staffroom. She pushed open the door with her hip and stepped inside, almost colliding with Andy. He was bent over the fridge, extracting milk, while the kettle bubbled away on the counter above.

"Oops almost," she skirted around him.

"Sophie," he smiled brightly, "your shift is over, right?"

"Yes," she replied, rinsing the mugs under hot water.

"Would you like to go for lunch? My treat, somewhere nice. Name the place."

"Sorry, I'm busy for the rest of the day," Sophie felt sincere regret. Over the months she had reached the conclusion that Andy was a really nice guy. Yes, he was brash at times but weren't all Americans? That was unfair she thought, gazing at him. He was gregarious – that was a fairer adjective to describe him.

"Oh damn!" He drawled in his strong American twang, "I wanted your advice – professionally of course."

Sophie's interest was piqued, "I have half an hour, we could talk here if that's any help."

She moved to the seating area and sat down.

Andy stirred his drink then joined her on the row of blue speckled chairs.

"It's Christmas in three weeks," he began, "I was thinking it might be nice to do something for charity."

"That's a lovely idea," Sophie smiled, "do you mean as in donating presents?"

"Yes! Maybe to a homeless shelter?"

Sophie nodded buoyed by his exuberance, "or possibly the children's hospital? Each staff member could purchase a small gift, wrap it and label it for a boy or girl."

"Wonderful idea." Andy jumped up, "Sophie you're an angel. I'll get my P.A to organise the finer details."

Sophie felt a warm flush of happiness bloom under his praise. She watched bemused as he backed towards the door, his eyes still firmly on her.

"Are you coming for drinks tonight."

"I can't sorry I have plans with … family," the word created a twist in her stomach.

"Hopefully another time. Bye sweet cheeks," he disappeared from the room with an ear-splitting grin and Sophie was left pondering how on earth he got away with calling staff members sweet cheeks in today's politically correct climate.

* * *

Evelyn was waiting for her outside the art gallery; a glorious piece of baroque architecture which was right in the middle of the city centre.

"Your hair looks nice," Sophie said, as she approached her.

"Thank you," Evelyn touched her freshly washed and curled head, "how was work?"

"Busy as usual," Sophie slipped her arm through the crook of Evelyn's, "shall we get Poppy's present and then coffee and cake?"

"Sounds heavenly."

They waited for the lights to change at the pedestrian crossing, "have you told the boys yet?" Evelyn queried.

"Nope."

Sophie skirted around an elderly lady who was pulling a tartan shopping trolley.

"I'm worried how they will react. I've always avoided the subject of their errant grandfather. How am I going to explain it all?"

"Tell them the truth," Evelyn advised, "I actually think Josh and Jake will be happy that they have other living family members. What about your mum dear? When will you tell her?"

"Not yet," Sophie's stomach gurgled as she spoke, "she's sort of settled and happy with Derek now, I'm afraid this might tip her over the edge. She hasn't drunk for months, but this, well it might drive her back to the bottle."

"She has a right to know, dear."

Sophie frowned, "she never passed on any of the letters that Anthony sent me. I could understand that maybe as a child she tried to protect me, but when I was older, she should have given them to me."

Evelyn nodded in agreement.

"And what happened to the money he sent me? I feel so mixed up about everything. Should I even have anything to do with these people. They are strangers to me."

"They're your flesh and blood," Evelyn said, "you've always told me you never stopped loving your father."

"Is it love? I love a memory Evelyn. It's no longer real. I'm messed up!" Sophie cried.

"Of course you're not," Evelyn soothed, "you're just a very emotional person who needs to sometimes try to control their feelings, and as for love - it's still real to you. In your heart it's real and that's all that matters. Only how you feel Sophie. You are allowed to love whomever you want." Evelyn patted her hand, "give him a chance love."

Sophie stopped walking, "where are we going Evelyn?"

"To buy Poppy a present?"

"Oh yes. What do you get a three-year-old girl now-a-days? I'm used to rough and tumble boys."

Evelyn pointed towards an alleyway, "there used to be a toy shop down there. Shall we go and investigate?"

"Okay," Sophie bit her lip, "thank you for meeting me today Evelyn and for all your advice and support. Jacob too."

"You don't need to thank me," Evelyn replied, "but a coffee and a slice of cake might be nice."

"You're on!" Sophie smiled as they marched towards Cuties toy shop.

After a lengthy perusal of the entire store Sophie eventually decided on a beautiful build-your-own enchanted fairy castle, complete with furniture and figurines. She also purchased a pretty fleece jacket, perfect for cold winter days.

"Is it enough?" Sophie fretted at the till.

"It's very generous," Evelyn replied.

They waited for the cashier to scan a roll of wrapping paper and a card through and pass Sophie her bagged purchases, then left the store.

"So, we need a coffee shop." Sophie glanced around, gauging where the nearest one would be.

"How about we go to the uni?" Evelyn checked her watch, "there's still a couple of hours before you have to fetch the boys and I need to look for a few more books."

Sophie nodded and they retraced their steps, crossed the main ring road and through the church gardens.

There was a large crowd of people outside the entrance to the uni. As they neared, it became clear from their uniforms that they were a group of secondary school children, there on a visit. A lady with tight, black curls, clutching a board, was shouting above the noisy chatter of the teenagers, endeavouring to organise them into lines. Sophie and Evelyn skirted round them, treading lightly up the steps to the sliding doors. The doors hissed open and they walked through to the entrance of the refectory. It was quiet, lunchtime was over and most of the students were back in lectures. A few of the catering staff had left their stations and were swiftly wiping tables down. Evelyn chose a seat, while Sophie grabbed a tray and filled it with drinks and two chocolate eclairs.

"No class today?" The till operative asked.

"No, a day off." Sophie smiled.

"But you couldn't keep away? That's commitment for you. Third year, are you?"

"Yes, English."

"Ooohh must be difficult all that reading. Here have these on me," she slipped two shortbread fingers onto Sophie's tray, "enjoy the rest of your day."

"Thank you," Sophie felt gratitude for the kindness of strangers – boy did she need it today, when she felt scared and vulnerable and unsure.

As she headed over to Evelyn, she noticed that her friend's face was luminous with happiness.

"Sit down Sophie," Evelyn whispered.

An intrigued Sophie slid onto the neighbouring chair.

"Dr Rivers just spoke to me."

"He did?" Sophie looked round and noticed the group of lecturers mingling outside the entrance.

"He asked me if I wanted to do a book signing here at the uni," Evelyn exhaled, shakily, "before Christmas if my books are ready for then."

"How wonderful," cried Sophie, "he is such a lovely man." They both turned to gaze his way.

"Yes. I'm so happy for Juliette. They make a beautiful couple," Evelyn stirred her tea.

Sophie sniffed, "Here's to true love."

They chinked mugs.

"And here's to your happiness, Sophie," Evelyn continued with a wide smile, "things are looking up for you, you just wait and see."

Chapter Fifteen

Juliette hopped off the bus, pushed her hands into warm, furry gloves and tightened the belt on her long scarlet coat. Her breath was curling into wispy clouds in front of her, and her nose and ears were turning icy cold from a dip in temperature and a strong buffeting wind. Her heels clacked along the cobbled street, passing the largest bank in the city and a row of shops and restaurants. The aroma of Indian and Chinese cuisine wafted by, making her stomach rumble and reminding her that she hadn't eaten since midday. Juliette turned down Hampton Street, a quick route which took her along the canal side.

It was early evening, the shops were now closed but the bars and restaurants were just waking up; preparing for a weekend of revelry and bustle.

She was looking for a particular club, named Jimmy's Tunes. She knew it was down there somewhere; amidst the fluorescent, bass thumping underworld. There were plenty of people about, so instead of guessing, she asked a young couple who directed her down a flight of glistening steps which weaved round in a horseshoe. Here she was: arrival at destination.

Jimmy Tunes was a long wall of black boards, with a door in the centre where a bouncer hopped on the spot and rubbed his hands to keep warm.

Juliette searched in her bag for her ticket.

"You're a bit early miss," the gruff voiced bouncer said.

"I'm here with the band," she replied, "Ben Rivers?"

"The bouncer looked over her with surprise.

"Ben? Lovely geezer. Come on through love." He untied one end of the rope, allowing her access to more steps and a door which opened into an electric blue corridor. Juliette stared up at the music memorabilia on the walls as she passed by. There were dozens of posters and pictures of bands that had played here over the years, autographs were pinned all over it too. Juliette squinted up, was that really Pink Floyd and the Rolling Stones amongst the many? Her eyes were distracted by an impressive fender guitar, which was attached to the wall on brackets.

"Wow," she managed, admiring the instrument.

"Impressive isn't it?" Juliette saw Ben's sister at the end of the corridor.

"You look beautiful," Alice said, as they gently embraced.

"And you look … like a glorious rock chick," Juliette grinned at Alice's leather trousers, long boots and goth style make-up.

"Do you like my wig?" Alice asked, pointing at the black spikes.

"Very authentic. How are you?"

Alice pulled her hand, "come get a drink and I'll enlighten you."

They sat at a round table, right next to the stage, sipping Bacardi and coke and talking about Alice's recovery from breast cancer.

"I still have to have follow up appointments, but I'm definitely on the mend and feeling so much better. After the op I was very tired, even picking up a kettle was exhausting. James and the kids have been brilliant though – they haven't let me do any housework and I've had flowers from them each week."

Juliette smiled, "I'm so glad to hear you're feeling better. Ben has been concerned about you."

Alice pulled a face, "oh big brothers can be such worry warts. I'm fine, honestly, and it's so nice to have a girly night out and to spend some time with the lovely lady who has captured my brother's heart."

Juliette felt her face flush and looked down at her drink, should she divulge Ben's wedding plans? No maybe not, even she couldn't believe he had meant it. He had been carried away on a spur of the moment madness. She would wait, she would concentrate on her studies and try to forget his tempestuous declaration. Even though the thought of becoming Mrs Rivers had her head spinning and her stomach in knots.

Sensing her discomfiture, Alice deftly changed the subject, "so have you seen my brother's band?"

"No but he's played for me. He's so good."

"He's always been the talented one of the family," Alice grumbled, "he can pick out a tune on the piano, even though he's never had lessons. He has magical hands and me, I'm tone deaf!"

Juliette laughed, "you have magical hands too or would that be green fingers? I've seen your handiwork in Ben's garden. The layout and the colours are wonderful."

"I do love gardening," Alice admitted, "it's my passion," she cocked her head to one side, "but what's your passion Juliette? Apart from falling for my decadent brother." They both chuckled.

"Education's my passion. Teaching children is all I've ever wanted to do," she sipped her drink, "I was distracted at school by a boy – fell pregnant, and I put my son before my career and then Molly came along and they had to come first. But my children are older, I feel now is the right time to pursue my dreams."

"And what do you make of university? I'm not academic at all, I think I would probably hate it." Alice stirred the lemon in her drink.

"University has changed my life," Juliette replied, "I didn't realise before, how much of a rut I was stuck in. Now my life is wonderful; I get to study books all day, made some truly amazing friends and I've met this man – this perfect man ..."

"Wait till you've lived together for a couple of months. He might not be so perfect when his socks are all over the floor and the toilet seat is continually up," Alice guffawed.

"I honestly won't care," Juliette said, with a dreamy look on her face.

"Oh my god, you have got it so bad," Alice's face turned serious, "does my brother know how much you *love him*?"

"He knows ... I mean ... yes, I think so," Juliette fiddled with the cuff on her sleeve, "do I look okay? I don't usually wear dresses. I just wanted to make an effort. It looks like everyone else is wearing jeans."

Alice briefly glanced round at the people streaming into the club, "you look beautiful. Ben will be knocked out, he loves all that girly romantic attire and your hair looks stunning."

Juliette touched her loose, red flowing curls, "thank you."

"Oh Jesus, look who's here," Alice's smile had turned into a grimace. Juliette followed her line of vision; Helena Mulberry was sitting on the other side of the room, looking striking in red lycra. Juliette felt her happiness deflating, *oh no*, she thought.

"Have you had the pleasure of meeting Ms Mulberry?" Alice muttered, through clenched teeth.

"Yes, she taught me in my first year," Juliette paused, "is she Ben's ex?"

Alice looked at her, opened her mouth to speak, when suddenly a loud drum roll reverberated around the room. The curtain on the stage twitched and a small bald man appeared, clutching a microphone in one hand, and a pint of beer in the other.

"Howdy folks."

There was a mismatched chorus of 'hello Jimmy.'

"Take your seat now, because we have a very special treat for you tonight." As folks settled at their tables, Jimmy crossed the stage to flick a few switches. The main lights in the club snapped off, but then a row of glitterballs lit up and at the floor of the stage, a dozen red and yellow lights began flashing and spinning. Juliette looked behind her; the room was almost full, the entire downstairs seating area was occupied and the upper tier balcony seats were rapidly filling up. She wondered briefly if Ben was nervous.

"I am pleased to announce the return of our very own Crimson Tide this evening." There was a fervent round of applause and whistling. "They haven't played together in a while – been in some sort of semi-retirement or so I've been told, but I am pleased to confirm they are back with a whole new playlist to get you moving and grooving." There was a swell in the noise of cheering and clapping.

"But before they play, the sultry Sarah Campbell is going to be singing a few songs to whet your appetite," he raised his hands, "ladies and gents, I give you Sarah," the curtain drew slowly back to reveal a lady in a sparkly dress and huge heels. Alice clapped her hand over her mouth and started sniggering.

"What's funny?" A swaying Juliette shouted over the opening bars of Dancing Queen, "she's good!"

"Can't you tell?" Alice yelled back, "Sarah's a he Juliette, he's a drag artist who is famous for picking on the audience, and we're sitting right on the front row!"

Juliette watched in horror as the flamboyant singer strutted across the stage, twirled on the spot and pointed straight at her. As she was beckoned on stage by a long scarlet nail, she was vaguely aware of Alice hooting with laughter beside her.

* * *

Juliette was made to sit on a chair in the middle of the stage, while the drag artist draped a feather boa around her. Then sultry Sarah whipped off her sparkly dress to reveal a tightly fitting body suit that showed off a washboard stomach and hard looking angular hips. Fishnet stockings completed the look, although the dark leg hair curling out of the lace top squashed any attempt at real womanly seductiveness. Hairy Sarah asked Juliette what her favourite song was. Cheeks burning, Juliette had mumbled the first thing that popped into her head. Sarah passed Juliette another microphone and they sang it together, well at least one of them did. Sarah actually sang Wonderwall by Oasis quite well, but Juliette screeched her way through her part, mortified to see most of the audience either sniggering or wincing. When they finally finished, Juliette was presented with a small bouquet of roses and thanked by the drag artist for being such a good sport. She noticed Ben watching from the stage side lines, belly laughing and flashing his perfect pearly whites. Juliette vowed that he would be the one lying in the cold spot later that night. Even acute devotion could be broken when siding with a highly embarrassing drag artist.

Sultry Sarah sang a few more songs; looking like a proper rock chic she / he twirled the microphone and shook her artificial mane to the thumping beat of Heart's 'how do I get you alone?' A man at the back of the room began jeering "in your dreams," in a loud northern accent that had Sarah's shackles rising. She jumped from the stage, ran towards the heckler and threw a pint of beer over his bald head. Then the bouncers got involved before it turned into a fist fight, lights snapped on and Juliette was mouthing, "what is this place?"

When the furore had abated and people were back in their seats, Jimmy came back onto the stage, mopping at his perspiring brow.

"Er yes, thank you Sarah. Now ladies and gents, it's that time you've all been waiting for." Jimmy held his hand high in the air, "make some noise for Crimson Tide," as he bought his hand down, the lights dimmed once again, the curtains whooshed open to reveal five men and their instruments. Juliette's eyes slid over a bored looking singer, a wild looking drummer who was banging a pair of sticks above his head, a curly haired guitarist who was almost doing the splits, a short man who was hidden behind a set of twin keyboards and Ben, smiling broadly with his saxophone hanging loosely around his neck. Alice started whistling and Juliette clapped along exuberantly as the band launched into Amy Winehouse's 'Valerie.'

"What do you think?" Alice bellowed.

"Fantastic. Utterly fantastic," Juliette's eyes slid over Ben, watching his fingers moving over the saxophone keys. He was wearing a white t-shirt that clung to his muscles and trendy ripped jeans. He looked extremely hot and Juliette licked her lips in appreciation. That was her man up there, a man who was uber talented, intelligent and sexy as hell. He looked directly at her and she bounced on her seat, waving like mad.

"I feel like a groupie," she yelled at Alice.

"I guess you'll be staying over tonight then?" Alice said with a cheeky wink.

"Oh yes!"

The singer belted out the last lyrics and the music stopped with a loud crash. The room erupted.

Half an hour later, Crimson Tide had stopped for an interval and had disappeared back stage. Their music was still ringing in Juliette's ears and she was buzzing with excitement.

"They are so good," she said to Alice, who was texting home.

"Told you," Alice looked up, "fancy another Bacardi?"

"I'll get them via the ladies," Juliette pulled her bag from underneath the table and stood up. She made her way across the room, weaving around the chairs until she reached the toilets. Of course, there was a line snaking outside the door. It seemed that all the females in the room had had the same idea. Juliette rang her mum's house while she waited. Violet Harris picked up on the tenth ring.

"Hello," she said, breathlessly.

"Hi Mum, I thought you'd gone out."

"I was playing let's dance on the Wii," Violet explained, "are you enjoying yourself, love?"

"Yes. Ben and his band are wonderful and I'm feeling a little tipsy."

"Good for you," Violet chuckled, "you deserve a break from studying."

"Are Harry and Molls okay?"

"Yes, wanna speak to them?"

"Sure, if they can drag themselves away from the T.V screen."

"HARRY. MOLLY." Violet's shriek almost deafened Juliette, she held the phone away from her ear for a moment and looked straight ahead into the cold eyes of Helena Mulberry. Juliette felt her euphoria at watching Ben deflate, drat! She thought she would be able to avoid the horrid woman, but here she was only two feet away. Juliette ducked her head and stared at her boots.

"Hello Mum," Harry's voice sounded warbly and far away.

"Hi honey, are you having fun?"

"Yep. Nan bought us popcorn and Maltesers."

Molly's voice burst through the earpiece, "we've made toffee apples too!"

Juliette winced at the thought of the sugar overload. Her children would be hyper. Then she had a vision of them both huddled close, clutching the phone and she softened, "well, have a great time and be good for Nan and Grandpops."

"We will," they sang.

"See you in the morning. Love you both."

"Hi Jules," Violet was back on the phone.

"Popcorn, Maltesers and toffee apples – Mum really?"

"Oh it's a treat," Violet scoffed, "don't be such a meany!"

Juliette laughed, "okay just this once. See you tomorrow."

"You need to have fun too love – enjoy yourself with that lovely Dr Rivers. Bye."

And her mother was gone.

Juliette stuffed her phone back in her bag and moved with the line into the toilets. The lighting was bright and the mirrors were smeared with handprints and make-up. A line of women leant forward applying lipstick and mascara, giggling with their friends. She noticed Helena Mulberry disappearing inside a cubicle and hoped that she would be gone by the time she had finished. No such luck, as Juliette unlocked the toilet door and rolled up her sleeves, she noticed her lingering by the hand drying machine. Juliette averted her gaze and rinsed her hands in the wash basin.

"Juliette?" The sound of her name had her looking in the mirror. Helena was smiling and Juliette felt herself prickle with annoyance as a memory flashed through her mind; Helena in the canteen ridiculing her name. She decided to ignore her and looked resolutely at her reflection. Her lipstick could do with reapplying, but other than that she looked fine …

"Don't you remember me?" Helena Mulberry had moved right next to her, their shoulders were almost touching, instinctively Juliette flinched away.

"Pardon?" Juliette just about mustered the good manners to answer.

"I'm the English Language specialist – Ben's friend."

Juliette bristled at the mention of her boyfriend, and spoken in such a soft seductive manner. *How dare she.*

"I know who you are," Juliette slowly twisted up her peach coloured lipstick, "I'd heard you were off sick at the moment."

She felt a moment of glee as Helena's perfectly made up face slid into a frown, "I've started back, on a staggered part time basis of course. Working full time at Chattlesbury University isn't in my foreseeable future anymore. Too many demanding students." The last two words hung in the air; tinged by bitchiness.

Juliette snapped the lid back on her lip crayon, "luckily, I get to leave at the end of the year."

"Oh yes, you're in your final year? How wonderful," Helena smiled, acidly, "I guess you'll be leaving all things university related behind then. Moving onto living in the *real world*."

"Not everything." Juliette's smile was saccharin sweet, "I'll still keep in touch with my friends and ... my lover of course. I think you know him? His name is Ben." With a toss of her hair, Juliette turned away.

"There's nothing worse than a foolish, deluded woman," Helena voiced, loudly. Juliette halted and the crowd of women in the toilet stopped talking to listen.

"What did you say?" Anger flamed in Juliette's stomach.

"It's not personal darling," Helena said, in a sarcastic monotone, "I've seen many women like you come and go. A cheap fling that's all you are. He'll soon be bored and then when he is, I'll be waiting, to give him a relationship of a higher, more fulfilling calibre."

Juliette was so shocked by the barbed comment, for a moment she stood dumbfounded. Then her shock turned to a seething rage.

"May I?" She motioned to a lady next to her who was clutching a glass of beer.

"Be my guest," the stranger was nodding fervently and offering her the glass. Juliette wrapped her hand around it, spun on her heel and splashed the entire contents over Helena's face and hair. There was a surge of titters and a few "go girl."

Helena was spluttering with shock, "you're mad, you're deranged."

Juliette leant right in her face, "this is a warning. Leave my boyfriend alone or I will come after you – understand?"

"Yes, I understand," Helena simpered, "I was only trying to warn you. I didn't want to see you with a broken heart, that's all. Us women have to stick together. It's all about honesty - women empowering women."

"This isn't one of your lectures," Juliette snapped, "and I'm not one of your facetious students. Don't you *ever* speak to me again."

She raised her head high and left the toilets, heart hammering, leaving behind a room full of people clapping, apart from one embarrassed, make-up smeared sodden one.

* * *

"I'm going over there," A seething Alice rose to her feet, ready to confront Helena Mulberry, "how dare she speak to you like that."

"Please don't," urged Juliette, "sit down. I dealt with it, maybe not in a traditionally intelligent academic way but never-the-less ..."

"You did great," Alice replied, sinking back down, "I would have slapped her."

Juliette shook her head, "violence is never the answer. I kind of feel sorry for her, she must be really desperate to throw herself at men the way she does."

"You and Ben are way too kind where Helena Nutter Mulberry is concerned."

"Did Ben have a relationship with her?" The question that had been bugging Juliette for ages was aired for a second time that evening.

Alice frowned, "did she tell you that?"

"She's sort of implied it," Juliette replied, "and Ben did tell me himself that he'd had a few relationships at uni."

"They were never serious," Alice explained, "as for her, she's a delusional, jealous mess."

"Oh," Juliette tried to look sympathetic, but inside she was cheering. "Looks like she's going anyway."

They watched Helena collect her belongings and head for the exit.

"Good riddance," Alice grinned, "are you ready for more Crimson Tide?"

"Yes please," Juliette picked up her drink as the lights dimmed and the second half commenced.

Crimson Tide belted out another six songs; an eclectic mix of classic and contemporary. The atmosphere in the club was electric; people were dancing in the aisles, standing on chairs and singing along. When Crimson Tide disappeared off stage they were enticed back on by thunderous applause, foot stamping, cheering and wolf whistles. They played an extra two songs before Jimmy hopped onto the stage to signify their closure. Juliette watched, enthralled, as Ben's fingers flew over his instrument. He was dripping with sweat and looked as if he were going to topple over from exhaustion. An ear-splitting crash and he held his saxophone aloft in the air, playing out the last note. Then they had finished.

Pandemonium broke loose in the room. Women clambered over each other in a race to reach the stage. Personal items were flung towards the band; a pair of stilettoes, a handbag, a cherry pink bra. The bouncers tried valiantly to hold the crowd back, but a few managed to break through. Juliette watched, with one hand clamped over her mouth, as two middle aged women heaved themselves up and charged at the band. One went straight for the singer, who was cowering behind the drum kit. The other veered off to the right, clasping Ben to her bosom, she rained kisses over his forehead, leaving a trail of lipstick marks. Juliette laughed at his look of panic.

"My boyfriend the rock god," she sighed.

"I think he needs us. Come on," Alice pulled Juliette's hand, shouted something at the bouncer who then moved away from the foot of the steps so they could pass.

After Ben had extricated himself from the exuberant fan's grip, Alice moved forward to embrace him. He grinned at Juliette over the top of his sister's head and beckoned her to him. Alice stood back, allowing him to take Juliette in his arms.

"What did you think?" He asked, breathlessly.

"You were wonderful," she replied, feeling star struck as she gazed up at him, "and hot. Literally."

She gulped as he pulled her against his firm torso, shaking his head so that droplets of sweat rained over her.

"Come backstage for a drink," he said, kissing her lips gently.

They shared champagne with the rest of the band and Ben introduced Juliette to all the other members. They were friendly, warm and put her at ease with their quips and banter. Alice sat on Pete the drummer's knee, flirting outrageously, while the lead singer, Rob, congratulated Ben on bagging himself such a gorgeous girlfriend. Ben held her close to him and asked her if she wanted to go for a curry and a few more drinks. Juliette agreed that it would be the perfect way to end a fantastic evening. They said their goodbyes and waited at the rear of the club, in an alleyway full of bins, for Alice's husband to pick her up.

"Have I told you lately what a great brother you are?" Alice's words were slurred and her steps wobbly, "in fact you," she pointed at Ben, "are the best brother in the world."

"I know," Ben said, with a deep chuckle, "you're not going to be sick, are you?"

"Uh-oh," she shook her head, "thanks for being there for me."

"What are big brothers for," he chucked her underneath her chin, "are you okay?"

"I will be," Alice swayed and Juliette held onto her. "Selfie time!" She clicked her camera button, capturing the three of them in a laughing head shot. Then James was zooming up the street, playing out a tune on his horn.

"Here's my lift," Alice waved at her waiting husband, "thank you for a lovely night," she hugged Juliette. "We need a night out with the four of us."

"Sounds good," Juliette replied, with a smile and a nod, she really liked Alice and was eager to spend more time getting to know her.

"See you soon bro'. Look after Jules," she stumbled off the pavement and into James's car.

Ben's brother-in-law gave them a cheery thumbs up before revving off up the lamplit street.

A clattering sound resonated in the darkness.

"What was that?" Juliette said nervously.

"Just a cat, look," Ben pointed up the alleyway, where a feline was hissing and arching it's back.

"I don't like it back here," she whispered, "it's spooky."

"Don't worry," Ben cuddled her close, "I'll protect you. What do you fancy to eat? Indian or Chinese?"

"Indian," Juliette replied, "I fancy a bit of spice."

"You do?" Ben laughed, "a bit of Fifty Shades?"

"Er no," Juliette smiled, "pain isn't my style."

"I know all about your style; fluffy onesie's and padded bed socks."

Juliette pushed him playfully, "it's cold!"

Ben's hand lingered on her buttocks. "You look sexy whatever you wear."

Juliette chuckled, "you are such a creep. I'm sleeping in the spare bedroom, especially after you encouraged the drag artist to pick on me."

"Fair enough," Ben nodded, "I could do with a good sleep anyway. Last time you slept over, you kept me up half the night with your snoring."

Juliette looked outraged, "I do not snore!"

"How do you know?"

"Now I'm embarrassed," Juliette huffed, pulling away from him.

"I'm teasing," he pulled her back towards him, "let's eat and then I can make it up to you."

They turned the corner onto the main city strip, where the bars and restaurants flashed neon in the darkness.

"Did you know there's over twenty Indian restaurants in the city centre?"

"No," Juliette was surprised, "that's a lot of curry."

"It's become the nation's favourite takeaway, even surpassing fish and chips."

"Well I only like the mild ones, I don't know how you can eat all those chillies."

"Madras is my favourite," Ben replied, "I had a Vindaloo in Birmingham once, never again, it gave me terrible hiccups and heartburn for days."

"Shall we try this one?" Juliette stopped to look at the menu attached to the wall outside, "they do cheese and garlic nans: heaven."

Ben pulled open the door, "after you madam."

* * *

After they had finished a delicious two course meal and consumed a bottle of wine, Ben called a taxi to take them home.

"That'll be eight pounds gov," the cheery cabbie said, as he pulled up outside Ben's abode.

While Ben paid, Juliette climbed clumsily out of the back. Her feet were aching so she slipped off her shoes and stood barefoot, gazing up at Ben's home.

"I love your house. This area is so pretty."

"It is nice, I've definitely lived in worse."

She looked at him sceptically.

"When I was a student," he elaborated, "I shared a house in a really slummy area that was rife for break-ins. The decent neighbours even had to chain down their bins and hanging baskets, it was that bad."

"Sounds like my area," Juliette said, drily.

They walked up the path, "yours isn't so bad," Ben said, "Chattlesbury is full of dodgier districts."

"Is it?" Juliette looked down at the floor.

"Hey," Ben lifted her chin with his fingers, "you could always move in with me."

The breath caught in her throat.

"Sorry," he held up his hands, "I know I shouldn't be pressurising you."

"It's okay," Juliette took the key from him and inserted it into the lock, "but thanks for the offer." She pushed open the door, placing her shoes neatly in the hallway, "has your cleaner been? It smells nice."

"Yep," Ben shrugged off his jacket, "I asked her to do an extra shift on account of my gorgeous girlfriend staying over."

Juliette touched his sleeve, "you are so lovely."

They stopped for a moment, gazing at each other.

"Do you want to watch a movie? It's still early."

"Sounds great to me," she followed him into the kitchen, hopping on a stool as he made them cups of tea. Then they carried them through into the lounge and both flopped onto the leather sofa. Juliette swung her legs up onto his lap, while he used the remote to flick on the television.

"So what do you fancy?" Ben looked at her expectantly.

"Erm actually," she moved her foot towards his crotch, "I'm not in the mood for T.V. Maybe we could make our own entertainment."

"Oh yeah," suddenly he pulled her by the arm onto his lap, "what do you want to do?"

He kissed her mouth, slowly sliding his tongue inside. Juliette's insides turned to liquid fire as desire coursed through her.

"I want to make love with you," she said, breathlessly.

Ben groaned against her mouth, "now?"

Fervently she nodded, "now Doctor Rivers. Now."

She tugged up his shirt, twining her fingers through his chest hair, kissing his neck. She felt him harden against her thigh and moved one hand down to tug open his zip. He flinched as her hand closed around him.

"Sorry," she whispered, flicking her tongue against his jawline. Hmm he smelt divine; aftershave combined with a raw manly scent. His fingers were pushing up her dress, stroking her thighs. Abruptly she got off him, stood in front of him swaying provocatively as she removed her clothing. He was watching her in the soft lamplight, his craving eyes raking over her naked frame.

Softly she spoke to him, "come to bed Ben," she held out her hand and led him to the foot of the stairs.

"It's chilly," she shivered, goose bumps appearing over her arms and legs.

"On the contrary I'm feeling extremely hot," Ben's hand ran possessively over her hips, then he was swinging her up into his arms and she was giggling as he puffed and panted to his bedroom.

* * *

Juliette woke with a sudden jolt. She had had a dream she was falling, through dense clouds, hurtling towards the ground. The room was deathly silent and she was alone in the king-size bed. She reached out her arm to touch his pillow. It was cold to the touch, telling her that Ben had been gone for some time.

She got out of bed, took one of his t-shirts from his drawer. It draped over her, skimming the top of her legs. She padded softly down the stairs, listening for movement. The house was deathly quiet. Ben's dog raised his head and regarded her with sleepy eyes as she passed him by, into the empty kitchen and the door which led to his study. It creaked open and he was there, sitting on his expensive leather chair, pen in hand, brow furrowed in concentration.

"Hello," she tiptoed into the room, avoiding the piles of books stacked on the floor, "can't you sleep?"

Ben raked one hand through his hair, "just incredibly busy." He smiled, beckoning her over. She snuggled onto his lap, burrowing her face into the warm arch of his neck.

"You look extremely appealing in this t-shirt," he pulled the hem up, but she tugged it back down.

"Concentrate on your work Mister," Juliette smirked, "what time is it anyway?"

"Five thirty. It's still dark outside."

Juliette yawned.

"Why don't you go back to bed? We don't both need to be up."

"But I miss you. It never bothered me before; sleeping alone, but now I hate it," she kissed his neck, "you're the last thing I think of before I go to sleep."

Ben shifted in his seat, running his hand underneath the t-shirt and cupping her bare breast, "and you're the first thing I think of in the morning."

Juliette moved back a little, "really? In the shower too?"

"Oh yes!" He chuckled.

Juliette gazed at the pile of paper on his desk, "are those essays?"

"Yep. First year poetry. I've marked twenty, have about another fifty to plough through."

"How do you do it?" Juliette crossed her ankles.

"What do you mean? The workload can be intense, but very pleasurable."

Juliette rolled her eyes, "I know you love your job. What I mean is how do you mark them? How do you work out what grades to give?"

"I follow specific criteria; assessing that a student has shown a good understanding of the modules learning objectives and outcomes. I also look for clear, well-structured argument, good referencing and acceptable knowledge of grammar and punctuation."

"Only acceptable?" Juliette slid her fingers into the back of his hair.

"You would be surprised how many students find basic punctuation and grammar difficult. It goes back to how they were taught at primary and secondary school, some have picked up bad habits from sloppy teachers."

"Did you have many girlfriends when you were at school?" She nibbled his ear and heard his sharp intake of breath.

"Oh yes I was a real heartthrob in infant school."

Juliette laughed, "I can believe it. What about secondary school?"

"Nope. Way too focussed on forging out an illustrious career."

"Do you aspire to be in university management? You would make a brilliant Dean or Vice Chancellor, whatever their titles are?"

"I like being with my students. One, in particular, constantly distracts me and stops me from working," he picked her up and sat her on his desk, "she's irresistible."

"Sorry," Juliette smiled up at him, "I just love being with you."

"You talk far too much, Juliette," he pushed the shirt over her breasts and took one nipple in his mouth.

Juliette gasped, arched her back as waves of pleasure washed over her.

"I love you so much," he whispered hotly in her ear.

Juliette gripped the table edge and wrapped herself around him, as beams of dawn sunlight bathed the room in a golden glow.

Chapter Sixteen

After all the worry and fuss, the dreaded talk with Josh and Jake had taken less than twenty minutes. For five minutes Sophie had skirted around the main issue by chatting about how well her boys were progressing at school. She then spent approximately seven minutes explaining what she had been like when *she* was a little girl.

"What's up Mum?" Josh had asked in his usual forthright manner.

Her very slightly older twin had always been perceptive, even as a toddler he was able to pick up on a tense atmosphere, whereas Josh was so laid back, he was almost horizontal, and the opposite in that life's tribulations seemed to just fly smoothly over his head, unnoticed.

"Nothing's up," Sophie squeaked, mind racing, "I've just had some news – family news."

Josh sighed, "what's Grandma Fletcher done now?"

"Nothing," Sophie's laugh bordered on hysteria, "for a change!"

"Is it Dad?" Jake was suddenly sitting up straighter, "is he okay?"

"Yes love, he's fine," Sophie rubbed his hand, "sorry. It's me, this is about my family," she sucked in a breath, "actually it's news about *my* dad."

"She means the grandad no one ever mentions," Jake eyerolled at his twin.

"I thought he was dead," Josh admitted.

"No!" Sophie said aghast, "did grandma ever tell you that?"

"Nope. But no one ever mentions him."

"You never even told us his name," Jake accused, with raised eyebrows.

Sophie's sigh was heavy and sad, "that's because I was very upset with him. Grandpa Fletcher has a new name now. His name is Anthony Coben and I'd guess he'd be in his sixties."

"Why don't you know how old he is?" Josh was staring at her with wide, innocent eyes. Time for the truth.

"When I was a little girl, younger than you guys. Grandpa was very ill, so ill that he ran away and I've never seen him since. And that's why I don't know much about him."

Josh and Jake looked at each other with excitement.

"Was he in trouble with the cops?"

"Was Grandpa a criminal?!"

"No. He was very poorly here," she tapped the side of her head, "and he was frightened and felt all alone. So he went to live in a different country until he felt better."

"Poor Granddad," Josh's lower lip trembled, "is he okay?"

Sophie nodded, tears brimming in her eyes, "Granddad slowly got better and he met a new lady and they had a baby and … and that baby's now all grown up and he's called Barry; he's your uncle and he's lovely."

"Uncle Barry?"

"Yes, uncle Barry – my brother, your uncle."

There was silence for a few moments while the boys digested this new information.

"Can we go see him?"

Sophie wiped the tears away, "even better," she said, smiling brightly, "uncle Barry is here. He's travelled all the way from Hong Kong."

"Is that in America?"

"No," Sophie chuckled, "but his wife is called Ariel, like the Disney character. Isn't that a pretty name?"

"Oh," Josh wrinkled his nose, "I guess."

Sophie rose to her feet and crossed over to their lit-up globe, slowly spinning it until she found Hong Kong, "uncle Barry's travelled all the way from here to Britain," she tapped the globe, "to see us and he wants to meet you boys … this evening."

Josh and Jake stared at each other in the ensuing silence and then both grinned.

"That's cool!" Josh whooped.

"Wicked!" Jake sprang onto his bed and began a series of jumps.

"You're okay with that?" Sophie was shocked that they had taken the news so well. She had expected a least a tiny sulk off one or both of them, but no, they were so relaxed.

"Are we going to his house?"

"We're meeting him at the ball pit restaurant."

"Uncle Barry wants to play in the ball pit," Josh said knowingly to his twin.

"Cool," Jake replied with a blasé shrug.

"No boys," Sophie began, "uncle Barry has a *daughter* who wants to play in the ball pit: a girl named Poppy, your cousin."

"Poppy?" Josh suddenly looked a little downcast that his one and only cousin was a girl.

"She's only three," Sophie continued, "so we all have to be super nice and super friendly to her, okay? Especially because it's her birthday today."

"Okay," Josh and Jake high fived each other and that was it: serious conversation over.

* * *

Jacob had made a very kind offer to drive them to the restaurant that night, when Sophie had protested that they could catch the bus, he had insisted. Evelyn hugged her tightly on the doorstep, making her promise to text that she was okay. She stood on the carpark, clutching her sons' hands, looking up at the brightly lit eatery, wondering what on earth she was doing here.

"Are we going in Mum?" Jake squinted up at her.

"Yes," Sophie forced her feet to move forwards, while her inner voice advised her to run away.

"How old is uncle Barry?" Josh chattered.

"In his twenties I think … younger than me at least."

"But Mum: you're ancient."

Josh and Jake sniggered, as Sophie pretended to box their ears. Feeling a little more relaxed, she pulled open the door and they stepped inside out of the cold.

The pub was quiet for a weekend, the threat of snow on the local weather channels seemed to have kept people at home. Sophie went straight to the bar and ordered herself a vodka and two cokes for the boys. She slugged the drink back, wincing as it burnt the back of her throat.

"I'm ready," she spoke to herself, in an attempt to quell the nervous fluttering in her stomach, "I can do this."

Sophie scanned the area around the ball pit. No sight of Barry Coben.

"I'm too old for ball pits," Josh grumbled.

"I'm not!" Jake struggled with the laces on his trainers which were tied in a double knot. He tugged at the heel and flung them besides the entrance, "whoopee," wham! He dived headfirst into a pile of multi coloured plastic balls.

"Be careful!" Sophie called.

"Mum!" Jake shook his head, "I'm not a baby."

Josh sat at the nearest table and pulled out his hand-held computer game.

Sophie looked longingly at the bar, "I'm just going to get another drink."

Neither boys reacted as she slunk off.

"Vodka please," she requested, "with coke and ice."

She watched the bar man fill the glass almost to the rim with ice, before he squirted a small amount of spirit in.

"Make that a double," Sophie decided. The ten pound note she was holding shook slightly as she pressed it on the bar. *Go away nerves* she told herself, *be brave.* From her handbag she pulled a compact mirror and inspected herself. As she was smoothing her honey blonde hair, a face appeared in the mirror. Sophie jumped in fright, flinging her compact up in the air. It clattered at her feet, the glass cracked and broken.

"Sophie are you alright?" It was Barry Coben aka her little brother.

"That's seven years bad luck," she gabbled, "I can't cope with anything else going wrong in my life."

Barry held her shaking hands, "on the contrary Sophie, I think your life is heading in the right direction."

"What do you mean?" She stared up at him; this stranger who was part of her flesh and blood.

"I mean, we're bringing you home Sophie, where you belong."

* * *

Barry's wife and daughter were absolutely beautiful. Sophie stared at the youthful looking, petite woman, whose long brown hair was parted in the middle and secured with two diamante clips. Ariel held out her hand and enveloped Sophie's in a gentle handshake.

"Hello," she said, in perfect English.

"Hello," Sophie squeaked, heart hammering, "it's so lovely to meet you."

"This is Poppy," the little girl was hiding behind Ariel, half her face peeking from behind a denim clad leg.

Sophie hunkered down, "hello Poppy," she said, softly, "happy birthday."

Poppy stayed where she was, gripping her mum's legs.

"How old are you?" Sophie asked, smiling warmly at the gorgeous little girl; she had never seen such a dainty child, Sophie thought she looked like she was made of the finest porcelain; flawless skin and long curly eyelashes. Poppy let go of her mum and began twirling her plaits.

"Speak up Poppy, don't be shy," Barry urged, gently.

Poppy held up three fingers, "I'm three."

"You are? Wow!" Sophie pointed at her sons who had stopped playing and were standing stock still, staring at this bizarre family reunion. "Josh and Jake are ten. Say hi guys."

The boys held up a hand and said "hello" in unison.

Barry stepped forward to swing Poppy into his arms, he came nearer to Sophie.

"This is your Aunty Sophie, she's my sister, Poppy."

Poppy reached out to touch Sophie's hair, "pretty hair."

Sophie's insides flooded with emotion, a huge grin spread over her face, "thank you. I love your trainers!" She touched the pristine white lace ups, with the soles made of flashing lights.

"They were from Oxford Street," Ariel said, proudly, "we landed in London and spent a few days sightseeing."

"London is wonderful, isn't it?" Sophie replied, "I should show you around Chattlesbury; there's a beautiful river here and a stunning new art gallery, theatres and breath-taking countryside. We have it all here." She paused, "that's if you are stopping?..."

Ariel looked at Barry who shifted and looked down at his feet, "we can only stay for a few weeks Sophie. But we'll be here for Christmas!"

Sophie's spirits plummeted, she'd only just found him and hadn't considered the possibility that he might be leaving again so soon, but not wanting to spoil the atmosphere she smiled and said, "that's wonderful."

"Josh, Jake," she called her sons over. Jake skidded across the carpet, Josh was more composed; casually strolling over.

"My word," Barry said, "I didn't realise your sons were identical. They look just like you, Sophie."

"Hi Uncle Barry, I think you need a shave."

"Jake! Don't be rude," Sophie was mortified.

But Barry wasn't bothered in the slightest. He threw back his head and laughed heartily, "You're probably right," he agreed. Then he clapped his hands and called a hovering waitress to show them to their table.

* * *

"Are noodles on this menu?" Ariel was scrutinising the list of food in front of her.

"Afraid not," Sophie replied, "they don't have a Chinese section yet."

"In Hong Kong it is considered good luck to eat noodles on a person's birthday, it is believed to boost long life and blessings."

Barry laughed, "darling we are not in Hong Kong. Let us sample the traditional English cuisine. I say we all order fish and chips!"

"Yes," Sophie said, with excitement, "and I recommend the crumble for dessert; made with traditional English apples and oodles of thick, creamy custard."

"Sounds heavenly," Barry closed his menu with a decisive snap, "now I want to talk to my nephews. Boys, tell me all about your lives."

Josh and Jake both begun speaking at once; jabbering away about school and their favourite computer games. Sophie smiled and turned to Ariel, who was seated next to her.

"How was your journey here? Was it a good flight?"

"It was eventful," Ariel replied, "there was much turbulence, many children crying and frightened. Barry and Poppy slept most of the way here, I could not settle. But when I saw the lights of the famous London, it did not matter."

"Tell me about Hong Kong, I've googled it and it sounds amazing."

"It is," Ariel agreed, "I am very proud of my country. Did you know the name translates to fragrance flower?"

"How beautiful. Please, tell me more."

"The city has the highest number of skyscrapers in the world and it is considered a bad omen to have apartment buildings that end at the fourth floor," Ariel cocked her head to one side, "are you superstitious Sophie?"

"I guess," Sophie replied, "a little. I mean I avoid walking under ladders and won't put new shoes on my table, I don't like killing spiders and, if I see a magpie, I try to find two for joy," she tittered, "my granny had some funny superstitions. The best one was that she believed it was bad luck to cut her toenails on a Sunday."

Ariel laughed, "that is one I have never heard."

"She was wonderfully eccentric," Sophie continued, "she didn't trust banks, thought capitalism was the ideology of the devil. When she died, we found hundreds of pounds stuffed at the back of the toilet."

"Excuse me ladies," Barry said, looking round, "shall we place our order?"

"Oh, it's not waitress service here," Sophie said, "I'll go up and order for us all."

"Here," Barry thrust a wad of twenty-pound notes at her, "I insist on paying."

"Okay, thank you," Sophie took the money and went to the bar. While she was waiting in the queue, a text message pinged into her phone. She swallowed when she saw it was from her mother.

'Hi Sophie, are you busy this evening? I could pop round with a bottle or two xx'

Sophie's panicked fingers flew over the keys, **'no – sorry I'm busy with uni work – maybe another time.'**

A few minutes later, her phone was beeping again, **'fine – see you whenever then.'**

Sophie could just picture her mum's sulky face. She felt guilty for lying to her, but there was no way she could divulge that she was eating a meal with her brother: a half sibling her mother knew nothing about.

"Can I help you?" The serving girl was smiling pleasantly at her. Sophie shook her head and focused on the menu.

The fish and chips were served in a basket, twenty minutes later. Before they ate, Barry raised his glass and proposed a toast to his new-found family and their good health. The main meal and dessert were consumed and, to Sophie's relief, enjoyed by all. After the waitress cleared their table, Sophie picked Poppy up, cuddling her onto her lap. Josh and Jake wandered off with 'aunty Ariel' in the direction of the ice cream parlour. Sophie watched them go, a wide smile on her face.

"Your wife is so pretty, Barry, and very lovely. How long have you been a couple?"

Barry leant back in his chair, pulling thoughtfully on his beard, "since school. The first time I saw her, I knew she was the girl I would marry."

Sophie sighed, "that's so romantic. What do you do Barry, for a living?"

"I work for Dad."

Sophie blinked, "how is Anthony?"

Barry pursued his lips, "Dad hasn't been well, Sophie."

"Oh," her fingers flew to her reddening throat, "nothing serious, I hope!"

"He had cancer of the bowel."

"What?!"

"It's okay," Barry soothed, "he made a full recovery. He's fine Sophie, really."

Sophie dabbed at her perspiring forehead with the back of a damp hand while Barry looked away at his phone.

"He was close to death though, Sophie," Barry spoke the words slowly.

Sophie stared at him with horror as he explained how Anthony had flatlined twice on the operating table.

"We thought we had lost him," Barry continued, "and then even after the operation, he was still so frail. The doctors didn't think he would cope with the chemotherapy, but he did."

Sophie released a held-in shaky breath, "poor d ... I mean, that's good to hear."

"Sophie," Barry suddenly clasped her hands, "when he first came round, after the op, he kept saying your name, over and over. So Ariel and I decided to try to track you down. We hired a private investigator, it wasn't hard to find you, Sophie ..."

"Because of Ryan," Sophie finished, she smiled at Barry, "my ex-husband has his uses. I'm glad you found me, I'm glad I have a brother."

Barry squeezed her hands.

"So," she cleared her throat, "now you can tell D ... Anthony I'm okay."

"I can't do that," Barry shook his head.

"Why not?" Sophie questioned, "I'm not an angry child anymore. I understand Barry ... really I do, and I don't bear any ill feeling towards him."

"I don't think you *do* understand," Barry stared unnervingly right into her eyes, "because he's here Sophie. Your dad is sitting right over there."

* * *

The colour drained from Sophie's face, "are you joking?" She whispered.

Barry slowly shook his head, "turn around Sophie."

"I ... I'm frightened," the confident, adult Sophie had been possessed by the vulnerable inner child of her youth.

"Oh Sophie," Barry sighed and pulled her into an embrace, "I'm so sorry you've been alone. I don't want to hurt you, Sophie. I want you to be complete, I want you to be happy. And Dad too – you need each other. He's never stopped loving you Sophie. Let him back in your life. Allow him the chance to make amends. Please, turn around."

Sophie squeezed her eyes tightly shut, she conjured an image of him in her mind; a handsome man who wore well cut suits and who swung her up in his arms when he came home, the musky smell of him and a rumbling laugh as he tickled her and lifted her upside down.

"Okay," Sophie nodded fervently, released Barry's hands and swivelled in her seat. Her gaze flitted over an elderly couple ordering at the bar, a family of six eating knickerbocker glory's, a fireman pushing buttons on the flashing bandit, a waitress rushing past with hot food. Then her gaze focused on a man sitting alone, he was reading a newspaper and over the top of the pages she could see a felt hat, the type that Bing Crosby wore in those old black and white movies. Slowly he rose and her breath caught in her throat. He put the paper down to reveal a smart suit and tie, shoes which were so shiny Sophie thought she might be able to see her reflection in them. Her gaze lifted to a clean-shaven face, lips curving into a smile and piercing blue eyes. The rest of the room dwindled away and her world froze into complete silence. "Dad," she whispered, as tears slid slowly down her cheeks.

She felt like she was floating across the room, being pulled by a magnet of incredible strength. How should she greet him, she wondered; a handshake, a chaste peck on the cheek, a smile, a wink, a nod? Instead she stood in front of him, gazing at this stranger who had created her, silent and still; like a statue. For years she had dreamt of this moment: the big reunion. In her fantasy, she had fallen into his arms and they had skipped off together into happy ever after land; father and daughter, back together forever. The reality was a little more awkward. She didn't know what to say, she had no clue how to act. She felt incredibly numb, emotionally exhausted and a little bit resentful. An image of herself as an abandoned young girl flashed through her mind; the disbelief, the pain, the tears, the rage. Standing at the window, a forlorn child, desperately awaiting his return. He had hurt her, oh God her father had scarred her emotionally. This was no fairy-tale, she had been abandoned and left dependent on an alcoholic mother who was a broken mess. A mother whose demons had robbed her of a carefree childhood. A mother who had weighed her down with loss and bitterness. A mother who still wasn't right. Anthony must have seen how she felt, her feelings were all over her face as she looked at him, like a book which had been forced open, all the secrets tumbling out. His smile slid down, his step faltered, he reached for a chair to rest against.

"Sophie," was the only word he could muster.

"No," she took a step back.

He held out his hands, his eyes pleading, "please."

"I need some air, I need a ... moment. I have to message Evelyn, I promised I would," her voice was rising in pitch, her breathing was becoming shallow, she felt sick and dizzy with a combination of nerves and adrenaline. The vodka she had guzzled earlier rose in the back of her throat. She moved away, "please wait."

"I'm not going anywhere," Anthony said, softly.

Wham, the door swung open against her flat palm and Sophie was inhaling deep lungsful of cold December air. With shaking hands, she called home. Evelyn answered after three rings. She soothed her, she listened, she made suggestions, she reassured her everything would be alright. She would be waiting up for her when she came home, with cocoa and a warm fire. The lamps would be on and her bed sheets would be turned back.

"Take it slowly," she advised. Wonderful, kind, loving Evelyn, with her magical hands and her huge heart.

Sophie snapped her phone shut and walked back inside. Her father was still there, grasping onto the chair. He looked unbearably sad and resigned and old and alone. Sophie was overcome by a sudden swell of emotion and she recognised it as love. This was her father, her flesh and blood and she loved him with all of her being and the realisation made her sag with relief and hope that, together, they could overcome their problems. She took his cold, frail, blue veined hands in hers and smiled, "it's time to talk. Dad."

Chapter Seventeen

"So, this is goodbye," Will stood in the street in his dressing gown and slippers, watching his Dad lift the suitcases into the boot of the car, "text me when you land okay?"

"Will do," Max turned to face him, "don't forget to feed and walk the dog."

Will yawned, "don't worry Dad, I'm on it. Besides, Mum has left me a list of to do's as long as my arm."

An early morning jogger ran towards them and Will stepped back to let him pass. "What time is it?"

"Just gone five," Max drew a wad of cash out of his pocket, "this is for emergencies, don't blow it all on takeaways."

"Thanks," Will took the money, just as his mother came bustling down the path.

"Right," Flora said, crisply, "the washing basket is empty, the ironing is folded and put away, I've hoovered from top to bottom and cleaned the bathroom, the bed sheets have all been changed, Oh I just know I've forgotten something."

Will put his arm around Flora's shoulders, "chill Mum, just go and enjoy yourself."

Flora bit her lip, "what will you do on Christmas day?"

Will grinned, "lie in bed?"

"We've discussed this," Max said with a sigh, "Flora, they will be fine."

"But we've never been away over Christmas before Max. It's not just Will and Esme to consider, Evan's come to us every year, I hope he'll be okay."

"Your brother is a grown man and more than capable of entertaining himself. Anyway, he has a girlfriend now to mollycoddle him."

"She's his lady friend," Flora corrected with a tut.

Will sniggered, "his lady friend with benefits you mean?"

Max held up his wrist watch, "we should go, the motorway could be busy and we don't want to miss our plane."

Flora hugged her son, tightly, "don't forget to water my plants and *please* take care of yourself and Hema and little Esme too. I'll ring you every night."

"Every night?" Will scratched his head, "a text will do Mum. Have a great time and make sure you come back, the Holy Land might want to keep you."

"Flora get in the car," Max ushered her into the passenger seat, then turned to Will, "bye son."

"Bye Dad," he waved as they pulled away and until they had turned the corner, then he looked down at the wad of cash in his hands and a huge grin spread over his face.

"Oh you're up! I was going to bring you breakfast in bed," Will smiled at the sight of Hema plodding about the kitchen in her fluffy onesie.

"I couldn't sleep," she replied, clicking on the kettle and filling two mugs with coffee, "why are you looking so happy this early in the morning?"

"Because we've got the house to ourselves for a change! Plus I've had an idea."

"Oh no, I know you and your ideas. What are you planning now?"

"This," Will waved the cash notes in the air, "is going to pay for a party."

Hema's eyes lit up, "here? Tonight? What about the neighbours?"

"Yes tonight. We'll invite them. They'll only stop for an hour tops – they're old. Don't over sixties go to bed about nine?"

"Probably," Hema agreed, "I'm not inviting my parents though, they will totally spoil the atmosphere. Imagine Mum dancing Bhangra to Dizzy Rascal," she shuddered with the possible embarrassment of it all.

"And uncle Evan drinking all the beer and boring everyone with his army anecdotes?"

They looked at each other, "erm … no!"

"So, friends only," Will decided.

"I'll compile a list," Hema began fumbling through drawers, looking for a pen and paper.

"What about food?" Will said, "I don't fancy having to cook a hundred sausage rolls."

"Takeaway pizza?"

Will pointed at her, "sorted, and no washing up – bonus. As soon as the shops open, we'll go get the beverages, ring round the guests and then relax for the rest of the day." He sank down onto the chair, pulling Hema with him, she wound her arms round his neck and they kissed as the kettle whistled merrily and upstairs, their daughter began screaming for attention.

* * *

"What is this soiree for, exactly?" Jon dipped his razor into a sink full of warm soapy water and glanced in the mirror at Ann, who was carefully applying sparkly eyeshadow.

"Hema called it a pre-Christmas party," Ann shrugged.

"Do his parents know?"

"I doubt it," Ann snorted, "from Will's description, his dad sounds severely straight-laced and his mother neurotic. They've gone on holiday, left Will home alone. He's probably celebrating having a bit of freedom for a few weeks."

"I suppose it has to be done."

"What?"

"The ubiquitous wild party while the olds are away." Jon smirked, "didn't you have one?"

"No, I didn't. My sister was far too sensible. Anyway, Will and Hema have a child Jon, I doubt that this evening will be wild."

"True. So who is going exactly?"

"Everyone according to Facebook. Will had tagged about fifty people. If it gets too rowdy though we can leave, Samuel might not enjoy it and there's a lecture tomorrow. Goodness knows why Will picked a Sunday evening."

Jon chuckled, "you have turned into such a … parent. Samuel will love it and you need to relax."

"I'll relax when my dissertation is complete and year three is officially over."

Jon wiped his face with a hand towel, "well I plan on enjoying myself anyway. Which means that this evening I'm ringing a taxi so I can have a proper drink."

Ann's face softened as she regarded her husband, "you deserve to have a good time, you work so hard at that hospital."

"It pays the bills, I suppose."

"It's more than just a job, Jon. I know how caring you are with your patients. Why do you think I fell in love with you?"

"Because of my rippling physique?" He kissed the tip of her nose.

"That too," Ann zipped up her make-up bag, "I'll go see if Sam is ready and we can head off."

Thirty minutes later, the three of them were squashed into the back of the taxi, with Ann's wheelchair wedged firmly in the boot.

"How do you spell embarrassing?" Ann said to Samuel.

"Easy," Sam replied, reeling the word off without hesitation.

"How about supercilious?" Jon added.

Samuel frowned, "what's the definition?"

"Snobbiness. Thinking you are better than others."

He spelt it correctly out. They gave him a round of applause.

"Here's one for ya," the taxi driver piped up, "spell automobile, you know as in a car."

Samuel spelt it correctly.

"Like spelling, do ya?" The taxi driver asked.

"He's in a competition," Ann explained proudly, "representing his school for the entire Midlands area."

"Well done. I liked physics myself. Could have gone to uni I was that good, but I liked driving more, meeting people. Now I'm self-employed and on a good day I can earn hundreds." He clicked on his indicator and turned off the main road, "I've learnt more through real life experiences than a classroom could ever teach me."

Ann nodded with agreement.

"So lad, what do you aspire to be? Am I looking at a future poet laureate or an expert in linguistics?"

Ann was impressed by the taxi driver's obvious intelligence.

Sam shrugged, "I guess I just want to be happy."

"Right answer," the taxi driver grinned in the mirror, "one of the biggest icons in the world had the same view. John Lennon said the same thing after his teacher asked him what he wanted to be when he grew up. According to school, being happy wasn't enough. They told him he didn't understand the assignment and his reply was they didn't understand life."

"You have plenty of time to decide what you want to do Sam," Ann smiled at him, "it's only recently I think I'm on the right track, professionally."

Sam's eyes shot up, "as a lecturer?"

"Yeah … I really think I could do it."

"Right-o folks looks like we're here," the taxi driver slotted his automobile into a space underneath a bowed oak tree, "that'll be a fiver please."

Samuel hopped from the cab, leaving Jon to rummage in his pockets for loose change. Once Ann was settled in her wheelchair, they passed through a creaking gate and up the edge of a bordered lawn. Will's house radiated light and a muffled music beat pulsed towards them. Before Jon had the chance to knock, the door swung open and Will greeted them.

"Come round the back," he said, leading them up a path which snaked round the edge of the house, "it's good to see you."

He tugged open the glass sliding patio door.

"Are we the first ones here?" Ann asked, as Jon lifted her through the opening.

"Yup."

"This is Sam," Jon patted his adopted son's shoulders.

"Is that a real record player?" Ann asked.

"Oh yes," Will rolled his eyes, "Dad's new hobby is collecting vinyl, now he's given up being a headteacher of course, come through to the kitchen, Hema's making cocktails."

They passed into a room partitioned off by a concertina door. Hema was leaning against a sink, balancing Esme on one hip and shaking a chrome cocktail mixer.

"Hi," she turned towards them with a grin, "grab yourself a glass."

Jon picked up two glasses for him and Ann, while Will poured Samuel a glass of squash.

"*This* is a margarita. I'm so excited!" She opened the shaker, tentatively sniffing it.

"Pour it out girl … I'll go get some cherries," Will stuck his head round the pantry door, "I know they're in here somewhere."

"Your daughter has grown," Ann commented, as Hema put her down, "she's beautiful."

Esme gazed up at her, let out a gurgle and then lunged across the floor, patting the lights dancing across the linoleum.

"Thank you," Hema passed them their drinks, "so cheers."

"Oh, this is good," Ann licked her lips, "we need more cocktails in our life, Jon."

"Sex on the beach?" He wiggled his eyebrows.

"Right-o," Will plopped cherries into their drinks, "let's get this party started."

* * *

An hour later the house was full and pulsing from the sound of a disco beat.

"Five hundred pounds man," Jimmy was telling Will, "was what I earnt last week."

Will could almost see the cash signs floating in front of Jimmy's eyes.

"We went to London. A major job in a textile factory. Dad put us up in this hotel where the waitresses were hot," he lowered his voice, "one slipped me her number."

"What about Sadie?" Will said, with a shake of his head.

"We're not married yet!" Jimmy slapped his shoulder, "just because you've found Mrs Perfect." He shrugged, "me? I'm keeping my options open. Will look at your daughter!"

Esme was bopping away, encouraged by a crowd of clapping onlookers.

"Takes after me," Will grinned, "natural rhythm. Another beer?"

He went into the kitchen, where Hema and Juliette were googling cocktail recipes.

"Ah here it is: vodka, cranberry juice, peach schnapps and orange juice."

"Delish," Juliette mixed the contents, giving them a thorough shake.

"Where's Soph?" Will asked, as he reached across to slice a lemon, "I texted her but no reply."

Juliette dropped her voice to a whisper, "it's her Dad – the one who abandoned her as a child? He's reappeared back in her life with her brother in tow."

"Wow!" Will hoisted himself onto the breakfast bar, "that's deep. So I presume Evelyn can't make it either?"

Juliette popped a cherry in her mouth, "she's looking out for her, you know how close they are. Now I'm going to find my gorgeous boyfriend and maybe he'll dance with me. Oh Will, do you have any eighties music?"

Will scratched his head, "Madonna?"

"Perfect," Juliette shimmied out of the kitchen.

"Where's Esme?" Hema asked Will.

"In the lounge I think."

"She's not even two Will – you can't just *leave her*. What if she grabs one of Flora's fireplace pokers?"

"She's fine, she was twirling around, flashing her nappy a few minutes ago."

"I'll go check on her," Hema tutted and left the room, with Will close behind her.

"Oh," Hema stopped abruptly, making Will bump into her, "that's so cute."

Ben was bouncing Esme in his arms. She had one hand on his cheek and was pulling his nose with the other one.

"So," Will nibbled at her ear, "now you know our daughter is safe, how about a dance?"

He pulled her into the centre of the room, "I'm looking forward to Christmas, just me, you and Esme."

"What about my parents?"

"What about them? You have other siblings, Hema. Can't they go visit your sister in Manchester?"

"You mean the golden child? She's expecting again and my brother's going on some retreat to India. No, they can go to the temple like they usually do, and I'll ring them after Christmas morning breakfast."

"What will we have? Mum usually chargrills eggs benedict."

"I'll cook us sausage butties with onions and tomato ketchup, Richmond of course, none of that Walls shit."

Will nodded with contentment, "this is going to be THE best Christmas. And I was thinking, when Esme's in bed maybe you could put on that white lacy basque and do a little dance for me?"

Hema chuckled, "depends what you get me."

"Whatever you want baby!"

Chapter Eighteen

"Oh Jacob I'm terrified," Evelyn bent over to tie the laces on her shiny new shoes, "do I look okay?"

"As beautiful as ever," Jacob was at the sink, scrubbing at an egg-encrusted pan, "will you have enough books do you think?"

"I'm sure forty will be enough, plus I have bookmarks and matching pens."

"And if you run out, you can direct them to the Amazon site," Jacob smiled, "I'm so proud of you darling. A fully fledged author."

"And I think it's marvellous," the door swung open and Sophie flounced inside, "You look perky dear," Evelyn said, as she straightened up.

"I slept well for the first time in months and I had *the* best dream."

"Oh?"

"Ant ... I mean Dad and I were in a hot air balloon floating over the plains of Africa."

Jacob turned to look at her, "you mean the Serengeti?"

"Uh-oh," Sophie balanced her chin on the palm of her hand and stared dreamily into space, "below us were hundreds of wildebeest and giraffes. We drank champagne and watched the sun set, and then a huge dust cloud took us to Egypt, over the pyramids and the Nile river, where we danced in a Bedouin tent and ... then I woke up."

Evelyn patted her hand, "that sounds a nice dream, but back to reality, how are things going between you and your father?"

Sophie's face lit up, "so good Evelyn. We talked for hours the other night. We still have a lot to discuss, but slowly we're getting there," she picked at her nails, "he's invited me to Hong Kong. Apparently, he has this huge house on stilts. Slap bang in a rainforest."

"Will you go?"

"I think I should. The boys would love it, and I'd like to see his home. Hong Kong sounds amazing," Sophie paused, "I've had an idea Evelyn … say no if you want to but I … wondered if he could come for Christmas lunch … Barry and his family too."

Evelyn smiled, "that will be fine. How many will there be?"

"Urm … just three more adults and one child. Will the table be big enough?"

"We'll make room," Evelyn replied, "it's so good to see you looking so happy."

Sophie sighed, "I am. I'm just dreading telling Mum. I keep putting it off, but know that I have too."

"Leave it until after Christmas," Evelyn said, crisply, "we'll have a marvellous time and all these problems can be sorted out in the New Year. In the meantime, will you help me with my book signing?"

"Of course! I can be an author's aide for the day."

"You can be her glamorous assistant," Jacob hung the dishcloth over the tap, "and when you both come home, I'll order us a Chinese to celebrate."

"Perfect."

* * *

When they arrived at the university, a crowd of people had gathered around a busker, who was strumming a guitar and warbling into a mouthpiece. Will was leaning against a lamppost, talking to Juliette. As they neared, Sophie heard the tail end of their conversation.

"I've written five thousand words so far," Juliette was telling him, "it's the secondary reading I'm finding time consuming, so many books to read."

"I'm finding the referencing a real pain in the arse," Will grumbled, "who cares if my footnotes are perfect?"

"You'll get marked down for bad referencing," Juliette advised, "I'm making mine perfect. I desperately want a high grade. A 'B' at least."

"Me too," Will rubbed his hands, "I'm on course for a 2.1 and nothing's getting in my way. Hi Soph," he paused to hug her.

"Can you help Evelyn?" Sophie asked, "she's weighed down with books."

Will went to take a pile out of her arms while Juliette hooked her arm through Sophie's.

"Are you okay?" She hugged her arm, "wanna talk?"

"I'm okay," Sophie replied, "and I'm looking forward to Christmas with … my Dad," Sophie was overwhelmed with emotion and burst into tears.

"Oh you're not okay," Juliette searched in her bag for a tissue, "here, your pretty mascara will be all streaky."

Sophie sniffed, "sorry. My emotions are all over the place at the moment. How's you? Are you still in love?"

"Erm is the grass green and getting greener each day?"

"That doctor is one lucky guy."

"*Too* lucky. I'm going into town later, Christmas shopping. I have no idea *what* to get him. Guys are so hard to buy for, aren't they? Will you come help me?"

Sophie blew her nose, "yeah sure."

She tugged the door open, "oh there's your doctor."

He was standing at the end of the corridor chatting to a group of students. When he saw her, he looked up and grinned and her stomach flipped over as he walked towards her.

"Hi," she smiled up at him, "are you okay?"

He seemed distracted, "I'm looking for something …"

"I'm standing right here and I've loved you forever."

"I meant my rucksack," he said with a laugh, "is Evelyn ready for her book signing?"

"Yep. Where will that be, exactly?"

"Just outside the Learning Centre. I'll go get some tables."

She watched him saunter off and took some books from Evelyn, "are you excited?"

Evelyn's eyes were shining as she replied, "I am. My very first book signing."

"Have you got a pen?" Juliette fussed.

Evelyn nodded, "Jacob leant me his best Papermate," she rummaged through her bag, "I've got water and tissues and sweets. Will I need anything else?"

"Just your perfect self. Will you save me a copy of your book? I'm going to start it this evening and I'm so excited to read it. So, will you be okay with Sophie, while Will and I work on our dissertations?"

"Yes dear, and thank you."

Juliette wandered off, with Will trailing behind her.

"Here come your first customers," Sophie said, with a nod towards a group of Japanese students who had stopped to stare at her precariously balanced book pile.

* * *

A few hours later, Evelyn had sold almost three quarters and was rubbing the side of her hand. Sophie was sorting the money into neat piles on the table.

"Evelyn you have made a small fortune!"

"This calls for a celebration," Evelyn decided, "I shall treat us all to drinks in the Student Union bar."

Sophie laughed, "on a lunchtime? You *are* getting rebellious."

"It's Christmas," Evelyn threw up her hands, "and the last day of term."

Quickly, they collected their belongings together and went into the Learning Centre, where Will was sprawled with his head in his hands.

"Are you alright?" Sophie asked, patting him on the shoulder.

"Analysing Dracula is giving me a headache. Have you read it, Soph? Got any tips?"

"I've seen the film" she replied, brightly, "I thought it was really erotic and I love Gary Oldman, he's such a great actor – don't you think?"

Will opened one eye, "I suppose so. Where is Ann by the way?"

"She's had a meeting at her adopted son's school, but she's on her way." Juliette stopped typing, "shall we have lunch now?"

"I'm treating you all to a celebratory Christmas drink in the Student Union bar."

"Sounds good to me," Juliette snapped her laptop shut, "erm … can I invite Ben too?"

"Of course," Evelyn replied, "the more the merrier."

* * *

"My, doesn't it look pretty in here?" Evelyn and the others stood in the centre of the bar, gazing at the sparkly decorations.

"What would you all like to drink?" She pulled a crisp twenty-pound note from her purse.

"How about wine?" Sophie suggested, "none of us are driving, let's get tipsy."

Evelyn ordered the drinks while the others found a table.

"So," Sophie lowered her voice to a whisper, "there's a rumour going around that Leon Broome is having an affair with one of the history lecturers."

"Really!" Juliette grinned, "so I'm not the only one?"

"You haven't heard the best," Sophie continued, "her husband who is Head of the school of Computing was caught soliciting and is in real big trouble with the Dean."

Will laughed, "share the love I say."

"Here we go," Evelyn came bustling over with the tray of drinks, "help yourselves." She settled back next to Sophie, on the squashy leather sofa. Will poured the drinks out.

"Will Ben want wine?"

"Yep," Juliette nodded, "he drinks anything. Oh, here he is." She patted the empty seat next to her and he sat down, hooking his arm around her waist.

Will raised his glass, "merry Christmas everybody!" Next to him, Evelyn detonated a party popper.

* * *

The next two weeks flew by, amidst the chaos of Christmas preparation. On Christmas Eve, Sophie went into Hanley's for her last shift. She had booked some holiday so she could spend time with her dad before he left for Hong Kong. She had planned a fun filled itinerary that involved whizzing him around the city on a sight-seeing tour; the new art gallery, the canal locks, the beautiful city park and gardens and the stunning woodland and lake.

As she was struggling through reception with a box of gifts for her work colleagues, Andy slid across the polished floor towards her.

"Howdy Miss Sophie!"

"Hi," she transferred the weight of the box onto the other hip.

"Look up!"

As she gazed up, he leant forward and pressed his lips to her cheek.

"I'm allowed – it's mistletoe."

"Merry Christmas," Sophie smirked, wondering how many other staff members he'd kissed.

"Todays the day," he bounced around her like a playful puppy.

She swallowed, "the day?"

"The children's hospital – remember?"

"Oh yes! Sharon's organised all the presents for you. They're in the staffroom I think."

"They're already in the boot of my car," Andy grinned, "you're having a day off."

"Me?" She gazed at him bemused.

"Yep! *You* are coming with me."

"What do you mean? Where?"

"The children's hospital of course. I want you as my assistant, or should I call you Mrs Santa."

"I possibly *can't*," Sophie blustered, "what about my sales? I won't hit my daily target and then I won't be eligible for the Christmas bonus. Then I have to tidy my desk, I'm off for two weeks – remember?"

Andy wafted his hands in front of her, "it's all sorted. You don't need to worry your pretty head about any of that stuff."

Sophie noticed the receptionist staring at the pair of them with raised eyebrows.

Sophie let out an exasperated sigh, "what do you want me to do?"

He took her hand, "we're dressing up!" Swiftly, he tugged her to the boardroom.

Rhondda, the cleaner, was bent over emptying the waste paper into a bin bag. As they entered, she shot upright.

"Mr Davies! What on *earth* was going on here last night? There were party poppers everywhere, glasses and bowls all over the staffroom, a pair of women's stilettoes in the men's toilets and the fridge in the staffroom had been left wide open, completely ruining the sherry trifle! I'm worn out!"

"Oh," Andy looked sheepish, "the management had a few after work drinks that's all. Sorry Rhondda. There's a hamper for you at reception to thank you for all your hard work over the year."

"Well okay then," a mollified Rhondda shook out her duster, "I'll just finish up here and be on my way. Is that yours?" She nodded at the red suits folded over the sofa.

"It sure is. Merry Christmas. What will you and Mr Rhondda be up to?"

"Oh we're going to my sister's, she's an amazing cook and she likes entertaining so it saves us the bother. Merry Christmas then," she pulled Andy close to her heaving bosom. Sophie smiled at their friendly banter and went over to inspect the suits.

"These look hot."

Andy scooped them up, "we won't be in them long. Are you ready?"

"Yes okay," she followed him out of the building towards the staff car park.

* * *

On the way to the hospital, Andy regaled her with tales of his family. His grandfather owned his own company, making locks, and lived on a sprawling ranch in Texas. His two elder sisters ran a perfumery and make-up chain in New York and his brother managed The Bouncing Bears Football team in Oklahoma.

"Wow," mumbled Sophie, "your family are diverse."

"Aren't they?" He popped a stick of gum into his mouth, "we're a close bunch. Christmases are great – a roaring log fire, a giant tree and turkey, and carols on the veranda.

"Do you miss them … living here?"

"Sometimes," he popped the gear stick into second, as he manoeuvred the roundabout, which would take them to the main hospital car park, "I'm flying out tomorrow. England is nice and all, but my heart is with my family at Christmas."

Sophie nodded, "family time is important."

"Where we live, the scenery is amazing," he glanced across at her, "could I send you some pictures? Do you have WhatsApp?"

Sophie looked down at her lap and smiled, "that would be nice. I'll give you my number. You can message me anytime," a flush stained her cheeks at the sound of her own words. Did that sound too forward? She wondered.

"Finally, I get your number!" Andy grinned, and pulled up the handbrake with a loud crunch.

They watched as an ambulance sped past and skidded to a halt outside the accident and emergency entrance. Doors were flung open and the paramedics hopped out, carrying a man lying prostrate on a stretcher.

Sophie clambered from the car and went around to the boot to help organise the presents into two different piles.

"I get the girls then?"

"Sure," Andy nodded, "I thought sparkles and bows were your thing?"

"They are," she looked up at him, "so shall we go get changed?"

* * *

After an energetic gait through the hospital grounds, they reached the children's ward. The corridor leading up to it was painted bright yellow, with sunflowers and butterflies dotted over the walls and ceiling. Sweet piped music wafted from overhead speakers and the doors were festooned with stars and stems of climbing ivy. They were considering which button to press, when a doctor pulled open the door and breezed past, with a group of harried looking students in tow.

Andy put his palm flat against the door and she snuck underneath. Heat immediately struck her. And the smell of fried potatoes and onions.

"It's so quiet," she whispered, "I thought children's wards would be noisy."

"Maybe they're all taking an afternoon nap?"

"Where are the staff?"

The corridor in front of them branched off two ways.

Andy grabbed her hand, "let's go this way."

At the reception, two nurses were organising painkillers into cups. The tallest of them glanced up as they leant on the counter.

"Howdy," Andy grinned, "we're Mr and Mrs Santa."

"You are?" Tall nurse frowned, "we haven't been told about this, have we Sarah?"

"No but I heard someone in admin saying they had organised a Christmas treat for the children."

"How lovely," Tall nurse beamed, "would you like to follow me, I'll take you round the ward."

"We need to change first," Sophie pointed at the suits Andy was holding, "is there a room we could use?..."

"We've only got the disabled toilet. It's pretty spacey though."

Andy nodded, "lead the way."

"This is cosy," Andy pulled off his tie and began opening his shirt buttons. Sophie averted her eyes, "I'll go behind the shower curtain."

She tugged the plastic sheet across and removed her trousers and blouse.

"Man this suit is heavy," she could hear him puffing and panting and envisioned him struggling into it.

"Um, mine is very short," Sophie held the costume up towards the light, "are you sure this isn't a child's?"

"Of course not! It was from the department store in the city centre."

Hmm, more like Ann Summers she thought.

She stepped into the fabric and pulled the zip up. Her hair fanned out around her shoulders and she gazed down at her bare legs which were growing pimply from the cold.

"Here's some tinsel," Andy's hand appeared over the metal frame.

Sophie tied it around her ponytail.

"Can you do mine for me?"

She tugged back the curtain and stood on tiptoe to twine it underneath his shirt collar. He smelt lovely: aftershave mingled with toothpaste and she'd never noticed before how blue his eyes were. Not a light sky blue, more of a stormy sea colour.

He was gazing at her mouth, "are you ready to play Mrs Santa. You're my wife for the next few hours."

"I suppose I can manage it," Sophie smiled, and followed him out of the toilet and back to the nurses station.

They were passed into the care of Sister Rosemary, a stern looking woman who strode in front of them with her hands clasped behind her back.

"This way!" She shouted, "the children are in the T.V room." She came to a sudden stop and berated a couple of young nurses who were making eyes at a passing doctor.

"Some of these young girls forget they're supposed to be here to care for the sick! In my day, nursing was a vocation for the genuinely caring, but I'm retiring in six months so it will be someone else's worry."

Sophie cast a sideways glance at Andy, who was pulling a scared face.

"Here we are," Sister Rosemary stopped outside a glass-fronted door, covered in handprints, "please do be aware there are some very sick and frail children." Gently, she pushed open the door, ushering them inside.

Twenty inquisitive faces turned to stare their way.

"Look who has come to see you!" Sister Rosemary stood back.

Andy clasped Sophie's hand and tugged her forwards.

"SANTA!" A tiny child with golden curls rolled towards them.

Andy squatted onto his knees, the little girl wobbled towards him, gazing in wonder. He held out his arms and she cuddled against his chest. It was right at that moment that Sophie's insides melted.

Chapter Nineteen

Will was bent over, gazing through the oven door, when Hema sashayed in, her arms full of Christmas dinner table accessories.

"Is it done yet?" She asked, placing the crackers and serviettes carefully around the plates.

"It looks brown on top, the legs are a bit pale though. How long has it been in?"

"Almost three hours," Hema held up her fingers, "maybe give it another half an hour?"

"I'm starving," Will grumbled.

"You always are!"

She hurried over to the cooker to take the bubbling bread sauce off the hob, "has your Mum texted?"

"Yep," Will chuckled, "apparently she and Dad are going on a camel ride, followed by an authentic massage and then having Christmas lunch in a posh tent in the desert."

"Sounds fun. Your poor Mum could do with some pampering. She works so hard taking care of everybody." Hema bit her lip, "Is it hot over there?"

"Warm apparently," Will leaned over and stuck his little finger in the thick sauce, "now this is nice!"

"It's only out of a packet," Hema gave him a friendly shove, "go watch our daughter, I'll be in as soon as I've finished organising the table."

Will ambled out of the room and into the lounge, where Esme sat surrounded by crumpled sheets of wrapping paper and sparkly bows. When she saw him, she gurgled happily and held up the toy she was holding.

"What have you got there?" He swiped at the discarded paper and flopped down onto his side next to her, "shall we open another present?"

Esme pulled herself into a standing position and wobbled over to a brightly wrapped sphere-shaped object.

"Open it then," Will urged, holding out his arms to gather her back close to him. He peered at the tag, "oh this is from uncle Evan and his lady friend."

Esme tugged off the paper with her chubby fingers. The present was a spinning top. She pressed down on it and watched transfixed as it whirled across the room, beams of light reflecting off it.

"How quaint," Hema watched from the doorway, "has she actually finished opening them all?"

"Yep, all apart from this one. The most important of them all." He picked up the present and passed it to a babbling Esme. Swiftly she tore off the paper, to reveal a giant fluffy bear with shiny eyes and a bright button nose.

"What shall we call him?" Will scratched his chin.

"How d'you know it's a he?" Hema called.

"It's a he, isn't it princess?" Will moved his arms and legs, "how about Benji?"

Esme gurgled happily and launched herself onto his soft furry body.

"I love this tie," Will pulled the tags off with a snap.

"I thought you could wear it when you're doing your journalism. You will look very smart," she gazed down at her hand, "and I love this ring. It's so sparkly."

"You're worth it," Will stepped over the paper and pulled her close, dropping a kiss on her head., "I'll go carve the turkey."

Hema shook out a black bag, "and I'll start clearing up this mess."

* * *

"Where shall I put uncle Barry?" Sophie was staring down at the table, name card in hand.

Josh looked up from his remote-control car, "next to me, next to me."

"Okay. And Grandad can go on my right and Ariel on my left. Jake, can I put Poppy next to you?"

"Yep," Josh replied, "does that mean I have to cut up her meat?"

"Yes. You'll probably have to help her, she's only tiny, isn't she?"

"She's kinda cute," he replied, "but she keeps hugging me, I'm not sure if I like that."

Sophie laughed, "she hugs you because she likes you, that's why. So, Evelyn and Jacob can sit together, that's the table sorted." Sophie clapped her hands, "boys, you need to go get changed."

"Why can't I stay in my pyjamas?" Josh grumbled.

"It's Christmas day!" Sophie said brightly, "and we're *all* dressing up."

"Even Jacob too?"

"Of course!" Sophie shooed them out of the room and up the stairs, into a bubble-filled bath that smelt of apples and cinnamon.

Downstairs, Evelyn was basting the potatoes and onions, before prodding the turkey with a fork to check the juices.

"How's it looking?" Jacob asked, busy with his task of folding bacon around the sausages.

"It's almost done," she replied, banging the oven door shut with one slipper clad foot, "have we enough champagne?"

"Four bottles in the fridge, chilling."

Evelyn nodded her approval and went to turn the radio up, Cliff Richard's 'Mistletoe and Wine' rang out, "have we enough food?" She wondered.

Jacob caught her by the waist, spinning her round, "I'm sure there will be plenty, and in the meantime, I just wanted to tell you that I'm so happy you're my wife. This is our first Christmas together."

Evelyn stood on tiptoes, winding her arms around his neck, "and it couldn't be more perfect. Thank you for my presents." The timer pinged loudly.

"Oh, that's my cauliflower cheese," gently she tugged at his burgundy dickie bow, "you look very handsome by the way, and Christmassy."

"You go get changed and I'll sort out the food."

Evelyn walked up the creaking stairs, running her hand along the tinsel blu-tacked to the handrail. At the top of the stairs, Josh and Jake grappled on the landing. She smiled at their boisterous closeness and their infectious vitality.

Sophie came out of the bedroom, showing off her new Christmas jumper; a sparkling reindeer which had been a present from Evelyn and Jacob, "I love it," she gave a little twirl, eyes merry, "do you like your writing set?"

"It's beautiful," Evelyn said, with a smile, "and the perfume and chocolates are exquisite. You're far too kind Sophie."

"You deserve spoiling. Now boys, go get changed."

They sat in the lounge watching Christmas Top of The Pops, drinking luke-warm bucks fizz out of polystyrene cups.

"This is yak," Josh pulled a face, "can I go get some coke?"

"Okay," a distracted Sophie glanced at the wall clock and drummed her fingers on the arm rest, "they're late."

Evelyn looked up from her knitting, "only by ten minutes dear." Bang went the door.

Sophie jumped up, smoothing her velour leggings, "I'll go."

Jacob flicked off the TV and exchanged an amused glance with Evelyn.

Sophie could see their silhouettes through the speckled glass of the front door, she hurried to open it.

"Merry Christmas!" They rang out, arms full of presents.

"Merry Christmas everyone," Sophie beamed and took her father's hands in her own, "merry Christmas Dad."

"My word this is delicious," Barry exclaimed, wiping his mouth on a festive napkin, "thank you Evelyn."

"Oh, I had lots of help," Evelyn replied, "and it looks as if little Poppy has enjoyed it too."

All eyes turned to the little girl, who was siphoning the remnants of her gravy up with determination.

Sophie turned to Ariel, "tell me about your family. Do they live in Hong Kong too?"

"Oh no," Ariel replied with vigour, "two of my sisters live in America. One is an actor and the other a cosmetic dentist. My parents still live in Hong Kong though, in a little village. They've lived there their whole life."

"Of course we've invited them to stay with us," Barry added, "dad's house is huge and plenty big enough, but they insist on remaining in their village."

"Wait." Sophie's eyes widened, "you all live together?"

"Yes Sophie, our house is huge. Three times as large as your, how can I phrase it, little English mansions."

"When can you stay with me?" Anthony asked, quietly.

"I'm not sure," Sophie swallowed a piece of turkey, "I have to finish uni and then I must save the air fare. And I have to organise it around the boys too ..."

Barry stared at her aghast, "you won't be paying Sophie. The air fare will be a treat from your little brother. And you won't be needing spending money either. This is going to be an all expenses paid trip."

"Thank you," Sophie beamed at her brother, "but I insist on contributing a little."

"We could go in the school holidays," Jake said, helpfully, "then Mrs Trotter won't be hating on us."

"Snort, snort," Josh quipped.

Sophie laughed, "her name's Mrs Tranter and she's a very lovely lady."

"So, you can come in the summer?" Anthony grasped her fingers.

"Hopefully," Sophie nodded, "I mean yes ... definitely. And I'm looking forward to meeting your wife."

"And she is eager to meet you too," Anthony cleared his throat, "how is your mother?"

"Mum?" Sophie swallowed, "oh she's fine. You know, the same effervescent Yvonne."

"Last week I heard you telling aunty Evelyn she was a royal pain in the arse," Josh accused.

"And then you said that her and uncle Del were a pair of pathetic losers." Jake added.

Sophie felt her cheeks redden, "that was just a joke," she let out a chuckle.

"Where is Nan Fletcher anyway? She usually comes to see us at Christmas. Shall I invite her over?"

"No!" Sophie shouted, her voice acutely high pitched in the deathly quiet room. "Nan Fletcher's busy." Sophie didn't let on that she had spun a yarn so long and complicated that Sophie couldn't even remember herself what she was actually supposed to be doing today.

"I hope I haven't made things awkward for you," Anthony said, "your mother and I ... well it was a long time ago and I bear no ill feeling towards her. How could I? She gave me you. The most precious gift in the world."

"How beautiful," Evelyn jumped up, "I've just had an idea for my new book. Excuse me a moment while I go find my pad and pen."

"She's author," Sophie disclosed to her family, "she's always having bolts of inspiration."

Poppy suddenly began banging her spoon with some force on the table.

"What's the matter?" Josh asked, in the most soothing voice he could muster. He leant closer so she could whisper in his ear, "oh she wants to know when the pudding's coming."

"Would you like to help me serve it up?" Sophie held out her hand, waiting while Poppy clambered off the chair and together they disappeared into the kitchen.

* * *

After the dessert and coffee had been consumed, and the dirty crockery had been washed and placed away, Jacob and Barry folded up the dinner table and helped the twins set up their ultra-modern, state of the art virtual reality headsets. Josh coerced Jacob into being his first opponent and the others watched as the pair of them ducked and dived, wafting their light sabres around.

Sophie sat with her father, shifting through baby photographs of the twins.

"This one," she said proudly, "is when they first learnt to ride a bike without stabilisers."

Anthony reached inside his suit jacket, "and this … is you."

He passed her half a dozen polaroid pictures, the edges slightly frayed and grown yellow with the passing of time. They felt like warm pieces of card in her hands and as she stared down at them, tears pooled in her eyes.

Anthony reached across and tapped a picture of her in his arms, "this was your fifth birthday."

"I remember!" Sophie cried, "you bought me a spotty Minnie Mouse dress complete with a set of ears."

"Can you remember this?" He nodded at a photograph of her sitting on rocks, looking windswept in a lady's arms, the sea a distant splash of colour.

"Is that Mum?" Sophie's voice was a tremulous warble.

Anthony nodded, "we were happy then. Before I …" she heard the catch in his voice, "before I messed everything up. It was all my fault Sophie. I should never have left you."

"Oh Dad," Sophie hugged him tightly, "it's okay. You were ill."

From the corner of her eye she could see Barry advancing on them, "it wasn't just that, was it Dad? Tell her."

Sophie drew back, "tell me what?"

But Anthony was shaking his head vigorously, "No!"

Barry squatted down in front of Sophie, "the thing is, Sophie. The real problem wasn't our Dad, Sophie. It was your mother."

Blood drained from Sophie's cheeks, "what do you mean?"

"She squandered his money Sophie. Pressurised him to earn more and more so she could indulge her lavish lifestyle. And then she had an affair, with his boss. Everyone in the company knew except for Dad, and then they made him a scapegoat, blackened his name and ousted him. Dad is the victim, Sophie. Your mother helped ruin our father's life."

* * *

A sudden bang on the front door made everyone in the room jump. Jacob pulled off his headset.

"I'll go," he said, frowning at an ashen-faced Sophie.

The ticking of the clock sounded magnified within the room, and the atmosphere was suddenly heavy and laced with expectation.

"Sophie. What's wrong?" Evelyn rose to her feet, "are you cold? You have goose pimples."

"I ... I ..."

"Here you are!" Her mother's girly high pitch floated ahead of her into the room, "We were just passing and saw the lights on. I thought you were going to Evelyn's aunts."

Slowly, Sophie turned around. Her mum was leaning against the architrave, swathed in a scarlet coat and boots that reached past her knees.

Yvonne looked around inquisitively, "who are all these people? Do introduce me to Evelyn's relatives."

Josh and Jake were up on their feet, running to hug their nan and then Derek popped his head around the door, singing Wizzard's 'I Wish It Could Be Christmas Everyday,' in an inebriated warble that had Poppy giggling and swinging her legs high into the air.

"What are you doing here?" Sophie mumbled, moving her body to shield her father.

Yvonne tossed back her hair, "well what a welcome! And on Christmas day too. I've missed you Sophie. We usually see each other. Derek and I were worried, we thought you might be ill."

"You can see I'm absolutely fine," Sophie glanced at her brother, whose face had turned thunderous. "Shall I see you out?" She jumped to her feet.

"Sophie!" Yvonne exclaimed.

"That's blooming rude that is," Derek cut in, "not even an offer of a drink. And I don't mean tea."

Sophie inhaled deeply, trying to compose her racing heart. "We can see each other tomorrow. I'll do us a boxing day buffet."

"Can't we stay for one drink?" Yvonne persisted, "I promise Derek will behave."

Evelyn rose to her feet and was hovering close to Sophie.

"Sophie's right," she began, "we were all just finishing up here any ... "

"Do you know who I am?" Now Barry was on his feet.

Yvonne peered at him over her designer glasses, "are you going to enlighten me?"

Sophie spun round to face him, shaking her hand, "no," she warned.

"It's her brother silly," Josh was struggling to remove his headgear, "he's uncle Barry."

There were a few moments of stunned silence, and then Yvonne laughed, an awful shrill, high-pitched sound, "your Mum's an only child Josh. How can she have a brother?"

Barry moved to Sophie's side. Yvonne stared at them both.

"Is this a joke?" She screeched.

Slowly, Barry shook his head, "far from it. I'm Sophie's brother. We both share the same father."

Yvonne slid down onto a vacant chair, "Anthony?"

Nobody spoke for what seemed like an agonisingly long time, even the twins stood silent.

"I'm here," Anthony stood up and turned to face Yvonne, whose hand flew to her mouth to cover her shock and disbelief.

"Is it really you?" She whispered, gazing at him, "you look so old."

"And you look as glamorous as ever."

"So this geezer is your first husband?" Derek was scratching his head, "I thought he'd snuffed it."

Yvonne pointed at Anthony, "*you* disappeared. *You* deserted me. *You* abandoned our daughter."

Barry advanced towards Yvonne, "*you* deceived him. *You* treated him appallingly. *You* drove him away."

Yvonne's mouth flapped open, her eyes darted towards Sophie, "don't listen to him."

"Oh, but I have listened, Mother," Sophie's eyes were cold and glinting, "and I believe them. *I* choose to side with my dad and my brother, so why don't you *just leave.*"

Yvonne let out a bellow and charged towards Anthony, fingers coiled and raised. Sophie moved quickly, placing herself in front of her father. Then Barry took hold of her arm and she screeched at him to let her go and Derek's fists were up, ready for a fight.

"Out of my house," Evelyn said, crisply, marching down the hall, swinging the front door open.

"You haven't heard the last of this," Yvonne warned, "and Sophie – you're a traitor!"

"Bye Mum," Sophie waved, "merry Christmas." Barry slammed the door shut and Sophie hurried back into warmth and light and her dad.

"Are you alright?" She whispered, taking his frail hands in hers, "how could she treat you like that, after you've been so poorly."

"It's okay. We knew it was going to happen, sooner or later. I've never liked confrontation though, especially now, when I feel so weak. Your brother on the other hand …"

A sudden loud bang reverberated round the room, rattling the windows and fireplace ornaments.

"What on earth …" Jacob pulled back the curtains, "your mother's boyfriend has just thrown a plant pot at the window!"

"Is the glass cracked?" Gasped Evelyn.

"I think it's alright," Jacob ran his finger down the pane, "they're up the street shouting."

"Shall I call the police?" Evelyn asked.

"No!" Sophie peered out of the window, "that could make matters a whole lot worse, she'll cool down when she's sobered up."

"I've caused trouble between you," Anthony shook his head, "sorry."

"Don't worry about them," Sophie continued, "I'm bothered about you." She squeezed his hands, gently kissed his cheek.

"And I'm bothered about you," he replied, as they smiled at each other.

Chapter Twenty

The New Year arrived, bringing snow showers and high winds. Max and Flora returned from their holiday, full of wondrous excitement, showing off hundreds of photographs and colourful narratives of their time in the Holy Land.

"Did you see the Turin Shroud?" Will asked, licking the sugar off an oozing jam doughnut.

"Wrong part of the world. That's in Italy," Max explained.

"We did see the Church of the Nativity in Bethlehem," Flora's eyes were shining, "which is alleged to have been built over the birthplace of Jesus. It was amazing."

Max opened the door to the pantry and gazed inside, "did you actually do any food shopping while we were away?"

"A little," he fidgeted on his seat, "we went to the Tesco One Stop, does that count?"

Flora jumped to Will's defence, "there's milk, eggs, potatoes and bread. All essentials of a staple diet. I'll rustle up chips and eggs for tea tonight and in the morning we'll go do a big shop."

"Don't forget dime bars," Will said, hooking his rucksack over his shoulder, "I'm off to uni now."

"Do you want a lift?" Max asked, "I'm not back at work until tomorrow. Oh, the joys of living a stress-free existence."

"If you don't mind, that'd be great. I'll just go say bye to Hema and Esme; they're still snoozing."

Max dropped Will off just outside the main reception.

"What you up to today?" Will asked, as he unclicked his seatbelt.

"I'm going into town to buy some toiletries," Max peered into the front mirror, "my skin's looking a bit dry these days. Then I'm going to take your mother for lunch and I think I'll finish off with a swim."

"Don't wear yourself out then, Dad," Will unfolded himself from the car with a cheeky wink, "see ya."

When Will arrived at the canteen, it was full of students, who were looking decidedly downbeat.

"Has some catastrophe happened?" Ann asked, looking around, "even the staff look glum."

"Probably just post-Christmas blues," Juliette replied, "I'm happy."

"You're always happy," Will flipped his seat onto two legs, an action which had one of the more mature students, a cleaner and a passing catering person, looking at him with disapproval.

"What is it with this university? It feels more like a military dictatorship, then a progressive, forward thinking establishment."

"Everyone's power crazy here," agreed Ann, "but anyway, Juliette why are you so happy?"

She shrugged, "I've had *the* best Christmas."

"Plus, she's madly in love," Sophie added.

"That too," Juliette agreed.

Ann looked at her fondly, "where was it you went – Sweden?"

"Lapland," she corrected, "Finnish Lapland to be correct."

"What was it like?" Ann asked, "I do love travelling."

"Amazing. Lots of hills and forests and Inarijärvi Lake is breath-taking. We stayed in Rovaniemi, which was a good base for lots of sightseeing."

"What kind of things did you do?" Asked Sophie.

"Heaps. We visited the museum, the church, the Santa Claus village which has its own Santa Claus Post Office and a reindeer enclosure. We even took them on a husky safari. The kids were blown away."

"Sounds heavenly," Sophie said, with a dreamy, glazed expression.

"How was your Christmas?" Juliette asked, gently.

"It was fantastic," Sophie exclaimed, "being with Dad again after all these years of being apart. It was kinda overwhelming."

"Is he still here?"

Sophie nodded, "he's due to go back mid-January. I've been trying to cram so much into these few weeks. It's a wonder the poor man isn't exhausted."

"How was your Christmas and New Year, Ann?" Juliette asked.

"Special. Having Samuel with us was the best present Jon and I could have wished for and New Year's Eve was great, we had a knees up at my sisters."

"Good to hear that everyone had a great time," Will said, "so what's going on today?"

"American Humour," Ann replied, "followed by another dissertation meeting."

"Any idea what this week's topic is about?" Sophie asked.

Will pulled a folded, battered handout from his jeans pocket, "post modernism and humour. Sounds deep."

Sophie pulled a face, "that sounds hard."

Will slung an arm around her shoulders, "come on, you can sit next to me and we can have no idea what it all means together."

* * *

The lecture wasn't as complex as they had anticipated. After a brief talk on postmodern irony, satire and cultural exhaustion, the lecturer played a video clip taken from the Simpsons and afterwards they discussed how moral issues are explored through the cartoon's playfulness. They examined this further in the seminar by looking at Pulp Fiction; a film which they analysed as being full of horrifying violence, but which is dealt with in a comic playful manner.

As they were collecting their belongings, Ben stuck his head around the door and beckoned to Juliette.

"Hello," she whispered, letting him take her hand and pull her up the corridor. She had given up trying to be discreet, especially when he was so determined to be open about their relationship. "what are you doing?"

He opened a classroom door and pushed her inside, "just checking that you're okay."

Juliette smiled, winding her arms around his neck, "I'm fine. You need to concentrate on your lectures."

Softly, he kissed the edge of her mouth, "are you free this evening? You never answered my text."

"Sorry I'm working," Juliette stroked his back, "don't you have essays to mark?"

"Tons," he replied, "tomorrow then? Movie and burger night?"

"Sounds lovely," she backed out of his arms, smoothing down her top which had risen up.

"Love you," he grinned, kissing her hand.

"Love you right back." She sighed, as he turned his back and strode off down the corridor.

* * *

"How's the big dis going?" Jon stood behind Ann, staring at the numerous books strewn across the table.

"I'm actually really enjoying writing it," she replied, "and it's exciting to look over Leonora Carrington's work. She was a surrealist artist you know, as well as being a great writer."

Jon looked over her shoulder, "the hearing trumpet?"

"Yep. Brilliant book. Is Sam okay?"

"He's revising and I think the nerves are kicking in."

"I can imagine," Ann closed her book firmly shut, "that's enough uni work for the day. Can you take me upstairs? I want to see if he's okay."

Samuel was lying stretched out on his bed, headphones on, feet tapping.

"Hi," Ann waved, as Jon carried her into his room and deposited her on the bed next to him.

He pulled off his headset and pushed himself up onto his elbows, "I would have come down, you should have shouted me."

"It's okay," Ann wrapped the edge of the duvet around her, "it's cold up here. Would you mind turning the heating up Jon?"

Jon laughed as he left the room, "is that my cue to go?"

"What's wrong?" Sam asked, his lower lip trembling.

"Nothing! Absolutely nothing." Ann smiled, "I just wanted to check you're alright. You've been up here hours, do you want a break? We could go to the park, have a kick around with Jon. Hot chocolate in the café?"

"Yeah okay. My head feels fuzzy, I didn't sleep too well last night."

"Right then," Ann said, decisively, "let's get outta here."

It was a chilly day, but the sun was shining, so they decided to wrap up warmly and walk to the park. When they arrived, it was busy. A brass band was playing, and the field was full of bouncy, inflatable fun.

"You want a go?" Jon pointed at a giant slide, where a group of horrified look-ing parents watched as their enthused, shoeless children bumped and thudded to a stop on the safety mats.

"Erm ... no!" Sam replied with an eye roll.

"Jon, he's in secondary school," Ann cut in, "far too grown up for slides."

"Come on then," Jon tackled the ball out of his arms, bouncing it along the turf.

"Just leave me here then," Ann yelled. At least she was under the shelter of a giant oak tree, along with an amorous teenage couple and a dozen or so roaming dogs. One was sniffing around her wheelchair, she shooed it away, dug in her coat pockets for her phone and a packet of dried up Murray mints and settled back to watch the mini match between Manchester United and Liverpool.

The following morning, Ann was up early, nerves tying her stomach into knots.

"I feel as if I'm the one taking the test," she admitted to Jon, who was resting on a feather pillow, reading the new Andy McNabb novel.

"I'm nervous too," Jon replied, sliding his kindle away from him.

"Shall we get ready?"

"It's only just gone six," he belched, "oh stuff it. Let's get up and get or-ganised."

An hour later, Ann was helping Samuel tie his posh silk tie into a Windsor knot. "You look so smart," she said, her face reflecting her proud sentiments.

"Hey Sam!" Jon ambled into the room, "do you want some aftershave? The ladies love it apparently."

Sam took the proffered bottle, "smells alright," he splashed a handful onto his cheeks.

"Put it on your neck Sam and your jaw," Jon gave him a demonstration.

"If you boys have stopped with the cologne battles, can we get in the car and *go*?"

On the way to the M6, Jon stopped to pick up Anton and Lulu.

"I'm so excited," Lulu tugged her long purple coat out of the gutter and then slammed the back door shut, "thank you for inviting us Sammy," she leant across to peck his cheek.

On the other side of Sam, Anton was wrestling with his seatbelt and mutter-ing about work, "I've been up most of the night marking, I'm exhausted."

Ann glanced round, "don't you teach music?"

"Yeeessss, but before you say it my students have to write about the theory side of it too. Admittedly, it's not as time consuming as an English teacher's marking, but I'm also a year mentor and the go-to person for any union slash workplace dilemma issues."

Lulu tutted, "oh Anton, do stop moaning. This is Sam's day to shine. We don't want it spoilt by your negativity."

"Sorry," Anton replied, drawing a paper bag from his coat pocket, "anyone care for a strawberry bonbon."

The spelling gala was held in a large function room just outside Manchester's city centre. After they had parked, they made their way to the entrance, bypassing a long line of spectators who were waiting outside a set of double doors.

"I think we need to go in this way," Anton pointed to a smaller door, where an affixed contestant's sign fluttered in the breeze.

A jolly looking, curly haired lady, holding a clipboard, ticked off their name and smiled brightly at Samuel, "come this way, dear." She led them down a corridor that reeked of lemon disinfectant.

"Most of the contestants have arrived now, they're just taking refreshments in the foyer. Would you like tea? Coffee? We have custard creams and chocolate digestives and pringles – if you like that kind of thing. I'm more of a savoury kind of gal myself."

"All food sounds good to me," said Jon, with a lick of his lips.

The foyer was full of school children and harassed looking teachers. Samuel spotted two of his class mates and Mrs Benson, who was trying valiantly to control the rowdy group.

"How many are in your team, Sammy?" Lulu enquired.

"Six of us. There's Maria, the maths genius. Charlie the award-winning gymnast and three lads from the footie team."

"And there's you," Ann said softly, chucking him underneath the chin, "the clever boy with a way with words."

Sam shrugged, "I'm okay I guess."

"You're far too modest," Lulu enthused, "have you written anymore poetry lately?"

Samuel looked down and shuffled his feet, "a little."

"You write poetry!" Ann exclaimed, "that's fantastic, I love it. I studied an Introduction to Poetry module in year one. We looked at the great classical poetry through to modern day. Do you like reading it too?"

"I like the war poetry and Maya Angelou. We've been studying them at school."

"Yes! Still I Rise is my personal favourite. She was one multi-talented lady."

"What kind of themes do you write about, Sam?" Ann continued.

"Family issues, mental health," a blush stained his cheeks as he spotted Bethany Miller waving at him, "everyday life."

Ann looked round, "I understand, and I'd love to read some of your work one day, that's if you *want* to show me."

"Cool," Sam said with a nod, "I mean yep."

Half an hour later, the spectators took their seats and the teams waited backstage to be called up. Mrs Benson berated Charlie to pull her skirt down to a respectable level and then confiscated chewing gum off everyone, including Sam.

"How will it look for our school's reputation, chewing like chevs on the stage."

Charlie and Maria giggled, their lips blowing outwards, "you mean chavs, Mrs Benson."

"Erm yes that's correct," Mrs Benson pursued her lips, "so remember team, keep a cool head, do *not* panic and if you think a word's too challenging, just have a go anyway." She paused to watch a group marching up the stairs, "those are the ones to beat: Marston Academy. They've won the trophy for the past five years running. Their headteacher is a very competitive man, so let's beat them peeps. Let's take the trophy home with us."

* * *

Ann passed along the sweets and whispered to Jon, "when is it Sam's team's turn?"

"According to the programme, they're up next." He moved his tongue over a hard piece of toffee which had become lodged in his back molars, "boy these words are *hard*. I don't think I could spell them myself."

Ann peered over her new spectacles, "you couldn't spell weird?"

"I keep forgetting the 'i' before 'e' rule," Jon twined his fingers through hers, "by the way, you look very erm … appealing in those new glasses. Like a sexy secretary."

Ann turned his cheek to the stage, "keep your focus on Samuel," she slid him a little smile, for his eyes only.

The compere bounced onto the stage, microphone in hand, full of enthusiasm.

"Now we have the last two teams to partake, and they are Marston Academy and Ormiston New Academy. Can you give them a big cheer and a warm welcome."

Jon jumped to his feet and Ann waved a good luck flag enthusiastically in Sam's direction.

The youthful group took their seats. When they were settled, the compere opened his mouth to begin, when a Mum from Ann's row jumped up, rushing over to the edge of the stage, throwing a teddy towards one of the girls in the group.

"Excuse me," she edged her way back along the row, stopping to tell Jon that it was a token to bring them good luck. Then the lights in the building were dimmed and the contest began.

The first word that Sam was challenged to spell was 'accommodate,' which he reeled out correctly.

Jon gave him a big thumbs up, "I'm impressed," he said to Anton, who was sitting on his left, "I always thought that that word had one 'm'."

After Sam it was Charlie's turn. Ann noticed Bethany staring at her with envious eyes and reckoned that she had a rival for his affections in the golden-haired Charlie.

The compere asked her to spell handkerchief, giving her an accompanying definition, but Charlie missed out the 'd' which bought them two below Marston Academy. Mrs Benson was biting her nails with trepidation.

The compere went along the row again, and Ormiston managed to draw level.

"It looks like we have a tie break," he shouted with excitement, "which means that each team has to choose a candidate to represent their school for the final knock out," he glanced at his watch, "but first we'll take a quick comfort break."

It seemed that the entire hall emitted a collective groan. The lights were snapped back on and people flooded out towards the toilets and the refreshment stand.

Sam came lolloping over and they surged forward to embrace him and pat him on the back. He gazed at Ann, sitting there beaming up at him, and knelt down to hug her.

"You can do it," she said, eyes shining, "keep calm, okay?"

"Okay," he nodded, "can I get a drink? My mouth's really dry."

"Of course," Jon wandered off, with his arm around his shoulders.

"I'm so proud of him," Lulu said with a sigh, "he's come on so well since he first came to us. He was so troubled back then. So hurt and lost. Now when I see him with you it's clear that he's happy and thriving," she patted Ann's hand, "you're wonderful with him. Both of you."

"Thank you," Ann said, "we've actually been so surprised that he's fit in so well with us. I was wondering if I should broach the subject of his mother. Maybe he could try contacting her again?"

Lulu shook her head firmly, "I would advise against it," she replied, "we tried and the foster parents before did too. She's just not a nice person. Probably best to leave the issue alone for now. Let *him* decide for himself when he's an adult."

"She doesn't deserve him anyway," Anton replied, with a tinge of bitterness, "Lulu and I have never been able to have children and yet the undeserving ones seem to pop them out like peas."

"Life *is* unfair," Lulu agreed.

"Yep." Ann nodded, looking down at her wheels, "look at what's happened to me. But you know what, it bought me to Jon, and he's worth all this crap and pain. We wouldn't have met if I wasn't disabled. I spent years feeling angry, but now? I focus on the positives not the negatives."

"Excellent outlook to possess, Ann," declared Anton, "oh look, here comes the celebrity."

After consuming a large lemonade and a packet of mini digestives, feeling buoyed up by praise, Samuel jogged onto the stage. The compere cleared his throat, "my glamorous assistant will flip this coin and whomever gets tails will be the first speller. Come out here now boys, come out here."

They pushed back their chairs and filed to the front of the stage. After a theatrical coin flip the compere announced, "the candidate from Marston Academy, please step forwards."

Samuel surreptitiously watched his competitor swallow and step underneath the spotlight.

"Oooookay. Spell the word embarrass for me please, Calvin. As in to make someone feel awkward or ashamed."

Calvin actually smirked, and glanced backwards over his shoulder at Sam, who was counting to ten in his head, to try to gain control of his nerves.

He spelt it correctly with clarity and confidence.

"Well done. Well done," there ensued an exuberant round of applause from his school mates and a polite smattering of claps from the competing school.

"Samuel please step forwards."

Ann's breath caught in her throat as she watched him, "his hands are shaking," she whispered to Jon, "and his forehead looks clammy. What if he passes out?"

"He'll be fine," Jon replied, "ask Lulu to chant or to send him cosmic good vibes or someut."

The compere consulted his list and then asked Sam to spell the word pharaoh.

"What the heck?" Jon blustered, "does that begin with an 'f'? That's *too* hard for a twelve-year-old."

"Shush," Ann replied, "it starts with a 'p' Jon. A silent 'p.' "

Stuttering slightly, Samuel slowly spelt out a p..followed by an h … followed by an a …" then he paused for a full ten seconds, and the last four letters came rushing out in a gabble.

"CORRECT!"

The entire Ormiston Academy went wild.

When the attendants had finally managed to calm the crowd, it was Calvin's turn again. There was complete silence as he began to spell out the word millennium. This time he wasn't so cocky. His tongue stumbled over the l's and then stuttered over the n's, until finally he reached the final letter. There was a pause.

"Sorry. That's incorrect. There are two n's in millennium."

Calvin's head went into his hands, "bollocks," Samuel heard him say.

"Samuel. Your word is arctic. As in the region around the North Pole."

"Oh God, oh God," Jon mumbled, "arctic roll Sammy. We had it last Sunday."

"Silent 'c' Sam, remember the silent 'c'."

Sam spelt out the a and then the r. Then he paused, mind whirring, *what came next* he thought, was it a 't' or a 'c', *which one was it?* He looked at the light in the ceiling, his brow furrowed in concentration, "C!" He shouted, "t …i … c"

"That is CORRECT!"

Sam's classmates ran to hug him, lifting him high into the air, tears of happiness blurred his vision as his eyes sought out Jon and Ann: his Mum and Dad.

Chapter Twenty-One

It was a Saturday full of sunshine and perfect for a wedding. Flora sat at her dressing table, gazing into the mirror.

"What do you think, Max? Peach or pink?"

"Hmm?" Max was standing in front of the full-length mirror, twirling his tie into a fancy knot.

"Lipstick Max, I mean lipstick," she turned to face him, the silver fascinator in her hair catching the light, "never mind."

Their bedroom door squeaked open and in rushed Esme, a mini whirlwind that leap-frogged over the floor rug, gambolled across the wooden flooring and skidded to a halt beside Flora.

"Don't you look beautiful," Exclaimed Flora, making room on the seat for her to clamber onto. Esme gazed into the mirror, twirling her hair around one finger and patting her reflection with the other hand. Hema had dressed her in white taffeta, dainty satin shoes and a pearl necklace and bracelet set on child-friendly springy elastic.

"Look *I* have pearls too," Flora pointed to her own darker coloured necklace.

"I think that yours are a tad more expensive," Max replied, drily, "where did you have them from?"

"You bought them for me," Flora responded, patting them, "and they weren't from Claire's Accessories either, not like this little munchkins," she slid her hands around her granddaughter's midriff, tickling her playfully.

"Claire's Accessories," Max shook his head, "isn't that a shop for teenagers?"

"It's Mummy's favourite shop isn't it, sweetie?" Flora dropped a kiss on Esme's upturned nose. "Would you like some powder on those beautiful cheeks?"

Esme nodded happily, fingers tiptoeing across the oak veneer.

"These are bronzing pearls," Flora explained, "and they make your skin look like a sun kissed angel." She swiped some across her forehead, nose and cheeks.

"And this is eyeshadow," she tipped the pot up towards the light, "it's shimmery." Gently she dabbed some over her lid.

"And finally, we have lipstick," Flora held two in her hand, "peach or pink darling?"

Esme pulled the top off the pink and flicked some across her lips.

"Oh careful!" Flora laughed, "you have to stay in the lip line Esme, like when you're colouring in with Daddy."

"How beautiful are you?" Max knelt down in front of Esme, "you'll be the centre of attention. And Flora," he cleared his throat, "you look very lovely too."

Flora beamed under this unexpected praise, "thank you," she bent to fasten her shoes and then scooped Esme up into her arms, "let's go find your daddy."

Will was in the kitchen, filling the changing bag with nappies, when Flora came waltzing through the door with a giggling Esme in her arms.

"Mum, you look … stunning," Will's mouth hung open slightly as he turned to appraise Flora.

"I've never worn such high heels before," she admitted, "and this dress was awfully expensive; a Jasper Conran."

"Don't we all look super smart," Hema added, taking a wriggling Esme into her arms, "have you got the presents, Flora?"

"Yes, all wrapped and tagged."

Will bent to wrap Esme inside her coat.

"It's cold out there," Flora said, reaching for her own warm shawl and gloves, "I do like a winter wedding though," she peered outside the window, "there's frost on the ground and robins in the bird bath. How lovely."

"I must say," Max said, as he strode into the kitchen, "I've attended a range of faith weddings: Catholic, Presbyterian, Jewish. But I must say, I have never been to a combined Hindu and Christian marriage."

"I'm not the only rebellious one in the family," Hema said, as she zipped up her jacket, "Arjun of course is allowed to act whichever way he desires, because of course he's a man. So for him, marrying a non-hindu would never be an issue."

Will shrugged, "I'm just looking forward to the samosas."

They gathered outside the church and waited for the bridal party to arrive. The bridesmaids arrived first, in a sleek limousine, with the mother of the bride who was sporting a red feather bow, saucer-style hat. The vicar stood in the church doorway, clutching his prayer book, the hem of his robes lifting upwards in the breeze. He smiled at Will, took his hand and welcomed him to St Bartholomew's, then moved to mingle with the other guests. Hema was struggling to control an overexcited Esme, who was swinging on the entrance gate. Ever the peacemaker, Flora took her by the hand and led her to some stepping stones to jump across. The church was built on a hill, with a winding lane that led down to a prettily laid out village. Flora could hear the vicar telling an elderly couple that it dated back to the fifteenth century and its exterior walls were made from archaic limestone and decorated with stunning stained-glass windows.

Next to arrive were the groom and his best man, who came roaring up the avenue in a gleaming sports car, complete with ribbon. The windows were wound down and music was blaring from a local radio station.

"As cool looking as ever," Hema reached up to peck her cousin's cheek, "are you nervous?"

"He's absolutely bricking it," his best man, Fernando, replied for him, "luckily I have an emergency supply of cigarettes and gum to tide us over."

They wandered over to chat with the vicar. Flora linked her arm through Hema's, "doesn't the bride's mother look striking?" She commented, "red is such a lovely colour for a winter wedding, don't you think?"

From behind them came the sound of loud papping. A black Rolls Royce slowly crept towards them and the guests rushed forwards, eager to cast an eye over the bride in her splendour and glory.

After the church ceremony had finished, the guests gathered on the grassy area under the wedding photographer's instructions. For the following hour they waited to be called up onto the embankment in specific groups. Finally, the last shot was taken; a landscape photograph of the entire wedding party, complete with still shots of air flung confetti.

Then they slowly dispersed back to their vehicles and a forty-minute drive, which would take them to a function room, decorated with hundreds of balloons, in the heart of the city centre. Outside the entrance, a group of drummers and a trio of female bhangra dancers welcomed the guests to the Hindu version of Arjun and Melissa's nuptials.

* * *

Juliette was crossing the main road which would take her to the main city centre shops. In her hands she held a carrier bag full of products that needed to be returned; a too-big onesie that completely dwarfed Molly, and an illuminating gun of Harry's whose lights flickered dimly instead of shone. There was also a pack of bed linen that needed to be returned – a present from Marie that was missing a pillowcase and had a valance sheet that looked bobbly and worn instead of smooth and fresh.

The January sales had reached their peak. The city centre was packed on a cold Saturday morning. Shoppers jostled round jacket potato kiosks and candyfloss stalls. The smell of burning hotdogs and roasting onions wafted upwards towards white drooping clouds. The expectation of snow had the ladies wrapped up warmly in long coats and matching scarf and hat sets and there were groups of men, hanging outside the pubs in their football fleeces, clutching pints of beer, waiting for the match to begin.

Juliette skirted around a group of children and crossed underneath the huge winter hanging baskets to pull open the door to the department store. She passed the lighting department, up the elevator and headed for customer services, but as she neared, she noticed a long line of people waiting and could hear their grumbles from the handbag section. A quick glance at the store plan informed her that on the floor above, she could find the coffee and cake café. Up the stairs she went, pushing open the metal bar with one hip, grabbing a tray and sliding it towards the fresh sandwiches.

"Would you like sugar with your tea?" A friendly looking cashier with a lopsided hair net asked.

"Two please," Juliette confirmed, "and a packet of shortbread too."

From her purse, she pulled a crumpled ten pounds note and waited for the change, before scanning the café for a free seat. It was busy, but she managed to find a small table wedged next to the disabled toilet.

"Happy New Year, love," a man on the next table looked up from his soup and winked her way.

"Happy New Year," she unclipped the belt of her coat, draped it over the chair and sat down, feeling the opposite.

As she stirred the sugar into her tea, she pulled her phone from her bag and scanned her inbox for messages. None. For two days she hadn't heard from him.

So instead she logged into Facebook, where Sophie was checking in around the city with her Dad, and Will and Hema were attending a wedding in the suburbs. She flicked back to her messages, her finger hovering over his number. Should she contact him? Or should she wait for him to contact her? What had happened two nights ago? Her mind scrambled to remember the exact details. She had been his guest at a staff function at the university. A proper posh affair it had been. He had worn a dickie bow and she had worn a long fancy dress. Marie had styled her hair and lent her a diamante necklace. They sat at a round table, covered in linen, so white it dazzled, and crystal cut goblets that reflected the light off the voluminous ceiling chandelier.

The food had been exquisite, the champagne had been delicious and so bubbly it tickled her nose and bought tears to her eyes. There had been awards given out: employee of the year, inspirational leader, recognition for student support, outstanding research methodology. They seemed to go on forever and, by the end of it, Juliette was more than tipsy and raring to dance on the polished wooden floor.

She remembered being spun round to Motown and hugged tight to Celine Dion, standing on tiptoe to twine her hands around his neck and throwing her head back with laughter when he nibbled her ear. Then they were dancing in a big circle with the other English lecturers and that's when the fun stopped. She had felt a shove on her back and a kick to her ankle and then she was tumbling to the floor and the music stopped, and the speaker she grasped onto fell with her with a crash. The entire room had gasped, the lights were snapped back on and people gawped as she unravelled her gown from her velour shoes and pulled herself onto her feet and turned around.

Ben was pulling *her,* tugging her away, sitting her on a chair and giving her glasses of water. Then she was left alone, feeling embarrassed and ridiculed.

"Are you okay?" Brian Hodges had whispered, holding out his hand.

For the first time in her life, Juliette literally saw red. She hitched up her dress, grabbed her shoes and ran in her stockinged feet over to the table, pushed the chair Helena Mulberry was sitting on with such force that it tipped upwards, wobbled for a few seconds and then crashed back down, splintering the wooden legs and bringing the entire tablecloth onto the floor with it.

"What the ...?" Ben gazed down at her and then at Juliette, "calm down," he warned.

"Calm down?" She had been so surprised by his words that she laughed, "me?"

"You. Yes you." He grabbed her hand, "let's go outside."

He slammed open the function entrance room door, "you've had far too much to drink!"

"She's the drunk!" Juliette blustered, "you said it yourself."

"She's ill," he replied, "and she clings onto me for support – that's all it is."

"Well maybeeeee," Juliette hiccupped, "she should *leave you alone*."

"And maybeeeee, you need to control your jealousy! We're friends, acquaintances, colleagues." He shrugged, "I'm kind to her, not many people are."

"You're way too *nice*. She kicked me and pushed me over. *She* attacked me!"

A muscle pulsed in his jaw, "and you threw a drink over her at my gig – did you think I wouldn't find out? So, what do you want me to do?"

Juliette backed away, "I shouldn't have to tell you. You should *already know*. And it's obvious that you're siding with *her!*"

"Don't be ridiculous. Where are you going?"

She hurried down the winding staircase, "home," she yelled back, "and you're not invited!"

He was still standing there, calling her name like he usually did, but this time she didn't look round, she didn't run back to him. Instead she held up her hand and shouted "goodbye!"

And that had been Thursday evening in a nutshell.

Since then, she had hardly slept and her appetite had dwindled. She felt nauseous when she thought of the way she had behaved and fretted over how his very intelligent, sensible colleagues would now perceive her. *I'll never be invited to a university awards evening again*, she thought, dunking her biscuits in the half drunk tea, *I am such a bitch.*

"Penny for 'em," the man on the next table piped up, smiling her way, "only you look lost ... in your thoughts I mean."

"Oh, I've just got a few things on my mind," Juliette replied, smoothing back a stray curl, "too much Christmas merriment."

The elderly man laughed, "I gave up the drink years ago, it changes you, alcohol, and sometimes not for the better. Now-a-days I'd rather have a cuppa. That way I get to keep my inhibitions and self-control."

"Yes you're right," Juliette finished her drink and slid her arms back into her warm coat.

"Off for more shopping are ya?"

"I like to call it retail therapy." She stole a peek at her last picture on her camera role; a selfie close up of her and Ben rocking it in Lapland, and the wrench in her stomach reminded her how much she adored him and wanted him and loved him. Right, she thought, no more feeling sick, she said goodbye to the kind old man and moved her feet forwards, down the stairs and into the perfumery department.

Aftershave, she thought. He loves it. Her boss had given her a Christmas bonus, she could afford it and he was worth spoiling and she wanted to make friends with him, she hated falling out with him. She wandered around the counters, sniffing the tester bottles. An immaculately made up lady helped her choose a small bottle that wasn't too expensive and smelt divine. She was thinking about kissing him, when the sales assistant relayed the price for the third time.

"Oh sorry," Juliette pulled out her bank card and watched as it was swiped through.

"Thank you, madam. Have a good day." A bag was thrust towards her and then she was on her way.

After the bed linen had been exchanged and Harry's toy and Molly's onesie had been refunded and exchanged for two new release children's books, Juliette left the store and treated herself to a warm, fresh, sugary doughnut. She sat on a bench and ate it while she people-watched. The world passed her by and she thought of her dissertation and the remaining five thousand words she had to write. According to her planning, it should be complete within the next month and then she had all the time in the world to focus on the final essays. The essays to end all essays. The end of the third year. The end of university life.

In between the flower stands and the tree foliage, she could see the number thirtythree bus trundling towards the stop. If she ran, she could possibly make it, but something told her to stay. She picked up her bags and walked towards the alleyway, where all the quaint shops were joined together. She ducked through the doorway of Romero's, an Italian boutique store and meandered past exquisite clothing and a stunning shoe collection. Juliette picked up a beige leather pair, turned it over and then gasped at the price. Two hundred pounds!

Erm no, that could feed her household for an entire month. The assistant asked if she needed any help, her hasty reply was that she was just looking, before she left the shop with the bell tinkling overhead.

After purchasing pens, paper and a handmade card for her mum's birthday from the tiny gift shop, she decided to head back home. There was a pile of washing and ironing to sort out, the beds needed changing and the whole flat could do with a good hoover. Her heels clicked on the cobbled stones as she retraced her steps. Outside the coffee shop, a group of rowdy teenagers jostled past her. Juliette stopped, huffing with annoyance she moved towards the window and gazed in. Her eyes scanned the heads of strangers, a harassed looking waitress and the shop manager, who was counting out rolls of bank notes. Then she saw them.

Ben had his back to her, but she recognised his dark hair, broad shoulders and tan jacket. He was lifting a cup in his right hand and the other was raking through his untidy hair. The cuff of his bright white shirt slid upwards to reveal his gold watch on his wrist, glinting in the dim light of the café. Opposite him, Helena Mulberry leant forwards; a little too close. She was twirling the spoon in her cup a little too slowly, she was looking at him a little too seductively. Juliette held her breath as she stretched out a set of red varnished fingers and touched his arm. Her hand rested there lightly for a moment. She waited for him to shrug her off and move away. Instead he seemed to gravitate towards her and she was touching his face lightly, trailing her fingers over a few days' worth of stubble and not just conversing with him, she was positively murmuring.

Juliette began backing away, her hand clapped over her open mouth. Anger flickered somewhere deep inside her; a fire that slowly ignited and coursed through the blood in her veins. *Well, now it all made sense* she thought, *what a fool am I? The rumours about him were all true – he was a commitment phobic, he was a player and definitely **not** the right one for her!* Her breathing had intensified to a level at which she thought she might have to take a puff on her inhaler and her legs felt strange; stiff and shaky. As she was about to turn and flee, away from this awful, heart-breaking scene, she locked eyes with that horrid woman and watched as her face registered shock and then fear. Juliette stood still, waiting for Ben to turn around and notice her standing there but he seemed completely embroiled with *her*. She felt the cold edge of the marble bench touch the back of her knees and willed herself to go, but she was sickeningly mesmerised by the smile on Helena Mulberry's face, which slowly intensified to one of smug satisfaction. *You can have him,* her mind raced as she pulled her phone out of her bag and quickly typed a succinct message: **you're dumped**.

Her chest was heaving and she felt sick to her stomach, but still she waited; waited for him to wake up and realise how manipulative Helena Mulberry was? Wait for him to realise how lucky he was, having her? She saw him look down and a look of bewilderment cross his handsome face. Then she decided to run; up the alleyway, scattering cans and detritus; past a grubby looking man, propped in a shop doorway, who looked at her with glazed uninterested eyes. As she rounded the corner onto the main high street, she bumped into a couple holding hands.

"So sorry," she sobbed, tears falling from her eyes. *The taxi rank, where was the damned taxi rank?* She looked around, eyes frantically searching. She could see the black cabs, waiting outside the cinema complex. They were more expensive, but they would have to do. She needed to get home. Now.

"Oi watch out, love!" A market trader leaning against a stack of banana boxes berated her, as her leg caught his tray of oranges, sending them rolling everywhere. She turned around to mouth a shaky apology, tears clouding her vision.

"It's only fruit love," he called, noticing her distress. As she hurried towards the busy crossing, people stopped to stare. *I must look like a madwoman,* she thought, *calm down, calm down.* Then she heard her name being called and her lower lip trembled involuntarily. *Don't turn around. Don't stop.*

"Ere that man's shouting you love," a tiny grey-haired lady with a tartan shopping trolley touched her arm, "can't you hear him?"

Politeness made Juliette stop. She glanced over her shoulder. He was apologising to the fruit seller, whose pears were now all over the floor.

"Stop." Ben yelled in her direction, "please wait." He was hopping in a diagonal line, in an effort to avoid the oranges which were still rolling with awry abandonment. Children had joined in the fun and were chasing the escaped fruit, while the parents stood and stared from her to Ben and back again.

"Go away!" She shouted, "I never want to see you again."

"Is that right?" He yelled, "dumping me *again*?"

"Too right," she hissed, whipping her head back round she ran towards the crossing, which was on green and full of quickly moving pedestrians. She immersed herself between them in an effort to hide away. She could hear him still calling her name, but by now she was back on the pavement, running towards the black cabs, fumbling in her bag for her purse. The taxi driver at the top of the line saw her coming and opened the door in preparation.

"Thank you," she said gratefully, flinging herself onto the leather seat. It was cold and slippery and she slid down, legs splayed in a most unladylike manner.

"Where to, darling?" He asked in a friendly northern accent, clipping his seatbelt into place and turning on his radio. The loud crackle made her jump.

"Forrester Court," she said, breathlessly, "please hurry."

He touched his cap, smiled widely at her in his mirror, "I'm on it."

As he pulled away, there was an almighty bang.

"What the?..." The taxi driver slammed on his brakes and craned his neck out of the open window.

"What is it? What's wrong?" Juliette gabbled.

"Looks like somebody's been knocked over, poor sod. I best get going 'cause the old bill will be here in no time and the whole ring road will be closed off. Nightmare it will be."

Juliette held up her hand, "wait!"

The taxi driver looked at her with a puzzled frown, "I thought you were in a hurry. Now missus, I hope you aren't wasting my time. I got other punters I could be driving about, you know."

"I know that," Juliette said with a nod, "I need to check that it's not him." She fumbled with her belt, "I need to make sure he's okay."

"Who? Where are you going?"

"Here," she thrust a ten-pound note at him, "I can get another taxi."

She pulled the handle but the door didn't budge.

"You've put the child locks on," the taxi driver said with a laugh, "here let me."

He leant over and pulled. The door swung open and she stumbled out onto the road, twisting her ankle in the process. It throbbed as she hopped in the direction she had already come. Down the street she limped. In the distance, she could hear sirens wailing and growing nearer.

"Ben?" Her voice was trembling with emotion, "Ben!"

A large circle had formed around the crossing.

"Who is it?" Her voice cracked as she pushed through the crowds, "who's been hurt?"

No one answered, just the whispering of people as they craned to see what was happening. Juliette was crying again as she moved towards the traffic lights, *please don't let it be him.*

"It's a middle-aged man by the looks of it," she heard one woman say, "it's a dangerous crossing. This'll be the third accident in six months."

"Excuse me," she waited for a lady at the front of the circle to let her pass through. Then she saw a figure, lying on the ground, and a small group of people squatting around him. Her breath caught in her throat as she stood on tiptoes to see who it was who was lying on the ground.

Then she saw his feet. They were green. Green trainers with funny swirls on the soles. Fitness gear. Running shoes. Ben hated running. It couldn't be him. It wasn't him! Briefly, Juliette thought of Flora and her unwavering belief in God and in her mind she thanked him over and over.

"Is … is he okay?" she asked the person standing next to her, who was actually a very tall man, who could see everything that was occurring.

"He's been knocked off his bike …" he replied, blithely, "but he looks okay. He's conscious so that's a good sign."

The ambulance came tearing around the corner, moving the crowd back and then a policeman started shouting and waving his arms and telling people to disperse.

"There's nothing to see here," he hollered.

"My boyfriend," Juliette implored, "I've lost my boyfriend."

"Go over there, Miss," the ruddy-faced copper replied, "my colleague will be arriving shortly. She's erm … a female like you and I'm sure she'll be able to help."

Juliette stared at her phone. *What a horrible message to send him,* she fretted. *She hadn't even given him the chance to explain. Maybe he'd gone home. Maybe this time he'd gone for good.*

Her fingers flew over her phone, *are you okay?* She enquired, *where are you?*

A minute later a reply pinged into her message folder, *I'm fine, I'm standing right here.*

She felt a tap on her shoulder and warm breath curling around the nape of her neck and she spun around and fell into his arms.

"It's okay," he mumbled, holding her face in his hands, "it's not me: it's not me."

"I was so worried," she held onto his arms, "I thought you were hurt. I thought it was you."

"As you can see, I'm fine," he smiled his stomach clenching, pulse racing grin "absolutely."

Juliette released his arms and looked down at her feet, *I'm supposed to be mad at you,* she berated herself.

"About that text," she began, "I was angry. Maybe I shouldn't have sent it."

Ben raised one eyebrow, "is that an apology?"

She gazed up, tapping her foot, "and I'm waiting for an explanation."

"For what exactly?" He thrust his hands into his trouser pockets, "we were talking."

"It looked more than that to me," she stuck her nose in the air, "she was fawning *all over you.*"

Ben scratched his head, "she was? I honestly didn't notice that but anyway, I was talking about you."

Feeling angry, insulted and growing more jealous by the second, Juliette moved back, "I don't appreciate you discussing me with one of your exes !"

"It wasn't like that," he quickly cut in, "let me explain."

"No. Bye." She picked her carriers out of the mud and leaves and turned to leave. But he pulled her back round to face him.

"You are the most infuriatingly stubborn woman I have ever met. I was telling her to leave us alone. To stop pestering me and to stop being bitchy to you."

"You were?" Juliette said doubtfully, she wanted to believe him, she really did.

"And as for her fawning all over me? That's just her way, she's like that with everybody. Theatrical is one way to describe her."

"Okay," she sniffed, her mouth lifting into a tiny smile, "did she get the message? Because if she ever ..." she wagged her finger, "crosses me again ..."

Ben grabbed her waist, pulling her closer, "she knows. I made it quite clear how perfect you are and how much I love you."

"You do?" Her arms circled around him as he kissed her mouth, and leant his forehead against hers.

"Every inch of you," he murmured.

Juliette gulped, "why aren't you in a lecture anyway?"

"I pulled a sickie."

"A sickie?" Juliette laughed, "isn't that what your students are supposed to do? What were your reasons, Dr Rivers?"

"Melancholy and heartbreak." His face turned serious.

"You didn't say that!" Juliette's mouth dropped open, "what will your colleagues *think*?"

"Only joking," he clasped her hand, pulling her back towards the city centre, "I told them I had a bad case of food poisoning, which I am now going to rectify with a pie and a pint in the nearest pub. Coming?"

Juliette hurried to catch up with him, "you betcha!"

Chapter Twenty-Two

"Ouch!" Will winced as Hema pressed the cold wet flannel to his upper cheek-bone and temple.

"Hurt does it?" She moved backwards to survey the reddish, purple bruise, "this is what happens when you insist on acting the hero."

"What did you expect me to do?" He grumbled, "when your family continually hate on us."

"Balvinder is harmless," she responded through gritted teeth, "he made a comment about problems within mixed culture marriages that's all. If you hadn't drunk too much vodka then you probably wouldn't have noticed what he said."

Will ducked away and rose to his feet, "and if your cousin hadn't stabbed me then maybe I wouldn't feel so on edge."

"He's in prison Will: seven years. I'm sorry, how many times do I have to apologise."

"It's not your fault," he pushed his hand through his floppy hair, "forget it."

Hema went to the sink and threw the dishcloth into the bowl of warm, soapy water, "your dad was funny though, telling the pujari he was a radical, or how did he phrase it, 'a man who was influencing young people against other cultures.'

"He was on his Catholic soapbox again," Will acquiesced, and they both sniggered.

"Living with you guys, I know all about the pros of Christianity, so can we forget it?" Hema asked, keen to go run a scented bath for herself and Esme, "I thought the wedding was fun; especially the dancing."

"Oh yes," Will ruffled her hair playfully, "I saw you on the floor doing all the right moves. What was the song again?"

"Oops upside your head – a classic. Are you off to uni today?"

"Nope. We have independent study – *again*. I'll pop into the library, grab a few books for the dissertation research, then I'm meeting Randy. We're going to cover an antique fair and then the mayor's granddaughter's christening." He kissed the crown of her head which smelt like toffee apples sprinkled with cinnamon, "what will you do today?"

"Nothing much, probably take Esme to the park," she peeped through the half open slats of the kitchen blinds, "it's sunny. Far too nice to be inside."

"I've some spare cash," he dug in his pockets, "go treat yourself, and that doesn't mean spend it all on Esme, she's spoilt enough."

"Thank you," she smiled up at him, "fancy a bacon and egg sarnie?"

* * *

"Whaddya fancy? Bigmac or quarter pounder?" An hour later, Will was in Randy Rogers' car at a McDonalds drive through, somewhere along the A48 heading out of Chattlesbury.

"Bigmac, all the way," Will unclipped his seatbelt and reached inside his denim jacket for loose change. His stomach was pleading for more food, even though it had not long digested a late breakfast sandwich.

The assistant leant out of her window, "you'll have to park up: in bay two," she held up two fingers, a surly look on her face.

"I thought it was supposed to be fast food," Will grumbled.

"I ordered a cheeseburger as well," Randy said, sheepishly, "I always get parked up for them."

"I can wait," Will relaxed back, his fingers crossed at the nape of his neck, "this antique fair. What will we be doing, exactly?"

"Mingling bro'," Randy slapped his thigh, "and don't forget to take notes or better still use the voice recorder on your phone, I'll pick out the good quotes later."

"Cool," Will nodded, "and the christening with the mayor?"

Randy zoomed across the car park into the vacant bay and pulled up the gearstick with a crunch.

"Now *that* should be good. There will be councillors there, or as I like to coin them; the gutter rats."

"Isn't that what they call the press?" Will queried.

"Yerp. We hate each other, the feeling's mutual." Randy turned off the engine and flicked onto the diary section of his phone. "Now. We shouldn't be too long at the antique fair, the christening however will probably drag on. I've been invited to the buffet afterwards, which means that as my guest, you get to come along too."

Will thought fleetingly of the anticipation of delicious finger food and licked his lips in anticipation.

"Oh here she comes," Randy could see the waitress, a petite framed youngster, in his wing mirror, advancing on them with a brown paper bag. He wound down the window, took the food from her and found another parking spot for them to eat their lunch.

"Throw it in the back," Randy advised when they had finished. Will looked round at the rubbish accumulating on the rear seat and placed his empty burger wrapper precariously on top of an empty four pack of energy cans and a half-eaten sandwich from Marks and Spencer. Randy swung them out of the drive-through, back onto the main road and twenty minutes later they were at the antiques fair.

"Looks busy," Will commented, after they had left the car on the edge of a grassy slope. He looked down at his feet and his white trainers, which had sunk into two days' worth of rain-soaked dirt, and were currently turning an off colour brown. His feet squelched as he followed Randy down an embankment and over a bramble covered style.

"Didn't know we had joined the rambling club," he smirked as he hopped over the wooden opening. Spread out in front of him were hundreds of cars, packed tightly together, "this is big. I thought antique fairs were quaint little affairs, so my mum tells me."

"It's *the* main Midlands event," Randy replied, swinging his camera across his chest, "come on, let's go mingle."

"What if I need to take photos?" Will asked out of the corner of his mouth. They were waiting in the line to enter the enormous function room.

"Hey. snap away bro'," Randy clapped him on his back, "use your phone camera – you can forward them to me and I'll upload the ones I like."

An elderly lady, holding a bucket, asked them for the entrance fee. After paying, Randy moonwalked through the door and across the polished floor, halting beside a matronly looking woman wearing a blue spotted gown and who looked at the photographer over purple steel framed spectacles.

"Mr Rogers! You're late."

"Sorry Miss Upton, bad traffic," Randy coughed into the collar of his jacket, "my assistant will be erm … assisting me today."

"Can you please ensure that the elderly gentleman with the grandfather clock will be in your paper. He's one hundred and one you know and is very well liked within the area." She moved a little closer and lowered her tone, "we've also organised a little bit of light entertainment for our patrons, which includes a group of very talented Morris dancers. Can you erm … give them some coverage?"

"Sure," Randy flicked his entrance stub between his forefinger and thumb, "anyone you know personally?"

Miss Upton beamed, "my nephew is the main dancer and he's very talented. I will of course allow free refreshments for you and your friend?"

"Sounds a good deal to me," Randy picked up his camera and took a snap at the surprised Miss Upton, "let's get to work, Will."

* * *

On Monday morning, Evelyn was up at five o'clock. During the night, she had heard Sophie crying again, for the third consecutive evening on the trot. She snuck out of bed and listened at her bedroom door and was just about to knock, when the sobs had abated. She tiptoed down the stairs, tying her velour dressing gown tightly around her midriff. After making a pot of breakfast tea and popping two sugar cubes in cups, she clicked on the central heating and went back up to Jacob, who was coming out of the ensuite wearing stripy pyjamas and a look of puzzlement as to why he was up so early. He took the tray from Evelyn and pulled back the duvet cover.

"Get back into bed dear, I'll pour the tea."

Evelyn hung her gown over the bottom of the iron bedpost, slid her feet out of her furry slippers and clambered onto the high, springy bed.

"This is early, Evelyn; even for you," Jacob poured out the tea and milk and passed her a cup.

"Sophie woke me," she replied.

"Was she upset again?"

"She was. I tried to speak to her about her mother yesterday, but she clammed up tighter than a crab."

"You mustn't force her," Jacob advised, "let her talk when she's ready. In the meantime, all we can do is be here for her."

"That's true," Evelyn sipped the warm, sweet tea, "am I interfering?"

Jacob patted her hand, "you are being kind and sweet and that's why I love you. Now, have you remembered today I'm off on a train excursion with my friend?"

"With Ronald?"

"Yes. That's if … do you want me to stay here with you?"

"No, no," Evelyn smiled, "you go and enjoy yourselves. I'm going to be busy in the garden, pruning the shrubs and having a general tidy up. Shall I make us cottage pie for supper?"

"Yes please, and on my way back I'll bring us some proper fish shop chips."

Evelyn placed her empty cup onto her side dresser and slid down under the duvet. "Turn the lamp off darling and we'll have a wee bit more sleep."

After an hour of tossing and turning, Evelyn rose to see Jacob off with a packed lunch and a peck on his cheek, she spent the morning out in the garden. It was a frosty day, but the sun was shining brightly in a beautiful blue, cloudless sky. Evelyn set to work with her secateurs, pruning the dead ends off a row of stunning evergreen bushes. The recent snow fall had killed her winter baskets, but there were snowdrops and violet heather growing hardily in the cold, stiff border soil.

"Evelyn," Sophie was calling her from the utility door. She looked up and watched her tiptoe across the lawn in her best winter boots.

"I'm off out," Sophie revealed, with a distinct air of mystery.

"And can I ask where you're off too today? Looking all spruced up." Evelyn pulled off her cloth gardening gloves and smiled.

"I'm taking Dad on a walk around Wexford Park and Gardens."

"Oh, how lovely, I haven't been there in years; maybe ten or so more," Evelyn sighed, "is the old country house still there?"

Sophie confirmed it was with a quick nod of her head, "apparently the staff dress up in proper Victorian attire and they've built a posh new restaurant in the courtyard. It says on their website that you can enjoy a fine dining experience while watching the horses in the adjacent paddock. They have lamb feeding in the spring of course, it's far too cold for that *now*, but they have goat and rabbit feeding – the boys would love it – and there are real p … p … peacocks."

Evelyn looked at her with a sharp eye, noting her growing distress, "he goes home tomorrow?" She asked softly and proffered a clean tissue from her pocket.

"Yes," Sophie replied, wiping her nose.

"Will Barry go too?"

"He doesn't want to, but he has no choice. Work commitments, Poppy's schooling," Sophie's lips wobbled into a smile, "they've grown to love England, both him and Ariel. They're making plans to visit twice a year; maybe three if they can."

"And you can go there too," Evelyn said, with empathic kindness, "Hong Kong sounds wildly exciting and glamorous! I've seen it on T.V., lit up with a thousand lights and so many cars … and skyscrapers that look as if they're touching the starry sky."

Sophie grinned at Evelyn and her colourful use of language, "it does look impressive, but Hong Kong is *so far away*. What will I do? I've only just found them and already they're leaving: my family, my family."

"Isn't your mother family too?"

"Sometimes I'm not so sure."

"I think she does mean well, Sophie," Evelyn swiped the dirt flakes off her knees, "and she tries her best."

"Oh she's very trying. Sorry that was unkind," Sophie sighed, wearily, "we've drifted apart, Mum and I. She blames university, but I … think it's saved me."

Evelyn gazed at her, overcome with emotion, "we never would have met. Who would have encouraged me to step out of the shadows? Who else would have encouraged me to write? And to take chances and to love life? You Sophie – YOU!"

They stepped towards each other, wound their arms around each other in a spontaneous hug. "Thank you for taking care of me," Sophie's words were muffled against Evelyn's hair, "thank you for looking out for me, when I was all alone and needed it the most. You've helped me too Evelyn, in so many ways. I've grown up since I started university. Since I met you."

Evelyn chuckled, "look at the soppy pair of us. Go on out with your Dad, cherish the time you spend with him, and Sophie, you're going to see him in the summer. When all of this … university, will be finished and you'll be starting a new chapter in your life. But will it include Andy, I wonder?"

"Andy?" Sophie drew back slightly.

"Yes. I don't think you realise you're doing it, but just lately you do seem to be speaking about him an awful lot."

Sophie laughed light heartedly, "Oh Andy? He's been WhatsApping me over the Christmas holidays. Sending me pictures of his family and some fantastic scenery of where they live."

"He sounds lovely. It's good you have friends where you work."

"Yes erm ... well I'll be off then," Sophie lifted her hand in a static wave, "can I bring Dad here for tea, Evelyn? I want to spend as much time as possible with him."

"Of course. I'll set an extra plate for him at the table and afterwards, we'll all relax, with some fine red wine."

"No sherry, Evelyn?" Sophie teased.

"Not tonight," Evelyn watched with a smile as Sophie clambered ungainly over the patio wall and back through the open door. She sank down onto her knee rest, picked up the discarded trowel and attacked the clay soil with vigour.

* * *

"How have you got on?" Randy was busy masticating the tail end of a jumbo hot dog, while Will was rubbing his aching jaw.

"I've never talked so much before," he divulged, "look at this." He flipped open his notebook, which was almost full of hastily scrawled notes, "and ninety-nine photos on my camera roll."

"You've been busy," Randy nodded his approval, "so let's go see the grandfather clock geezer and then we can leave."

"I'd like a hot dog too before we leave," Will was sure he could fit one in.

Randy pointed behind him, "the food van's thataway. I'll wait here and just erm ... text the missus."

"Are you married?"

"Yes but I don't wear a ring, neither does she. We don't even live together. Separate lives. Separate properties. It's a mutual thing."

"Oh," Will was just about to voice his opinion on marriage, when Miss Upton bustled towards them, enquiring exactly what Randy was going to be putting in that "rag of his."

Will went to stand in the queue and was breathing in the aroma of junk food fat when the lady in front of him turned and smiled brightly up at him.

"It's Will isn't it?" She asked.

"Yep. Sorry I ..."

"I'm a teacher at your old secondary school: MFL?"

Will looked blank.

"Modern foreign languages," she chuckled, "and they say the elderly have trouble with their memory."

"Oh *now* I remember," Will clicked his fingers, "Miss Brent, Brown, Buxom?"

His eyes travelled from the top of her smoky brown hair, down to the v-neck sweater which was showing an ample amount of bosom.

"I'm *Mrs* Davies," she replied, "the only Welsh teacher in the entire academy. How could you forget me?"

"You don't sound Welsh," Will shrugged, "plus it's been a while. I'm in the final year of an English degree, school seems a lifetime ago."

Mrs Davies nodded, "I heard you were doing well. And you have a baby ... with Hema Kumar?"

"Yep."

"I have two of my own," she patted her protruding stomach, "and another one on the way."

"Crikey," Will's gaze flickered over her face, "you don't look old enough to have two kids. It must be mega hard. How old are they?"

The conversation continued for another ten minutes until Will was at the top of the queue and almost salivating over the copious selection of food on offer.

"Enjoy your last year at uni Will, good luck for the future, and please remember me to Hema." She drifted off and then Randy appeared at his side, tapping his watch and telling him to get a shift on.

Chapter Twenty-Three

"Here it is," Randy emitted a low whistle, "impressive ain't it?"

Will stared up at the church towering in front of him. Archaic was the best way he could describe it. From the arched oak entrance door with its iron hinges and the stunning stained-glass windows, the turrets and the imposing steel cross, everything about it screamed 'old.'

"Are those gargoyles?" he pointed to the garrotted top, where grotesque figures scowled down at them.

"Looks like it," Randy shuddered, "this place reminds me of the 'Omen' – you seen that film Will? The coming of the anti-Christ?"

Will shook his head, "Is it better than the Exorcist?"

"Even scarier and the music – man, it kept me awake for a few nights," Randy began rifling through his glove department, finally extracting a bent Twix, "want a finger?"

"Er … no, but thanks," Will was flabbergasted he had actually met another person who ate more than he did.

"There's the family," Randy said, mid chomp, "Angela Dupont – a French bint who insisted on keeping her aristocratic family name. I heard she was too embarrassed to take the mayor's more common Jones surname. Doesn't mind spending his money though," Randy's face twisted into a scowl, followed by a mirthless laugh, "she's the one in charge, the boss, the matriarch, or as I like to call her: the dragon!"

Will twisted the air-conditioning up full blast and swiped at the condensation accumulating on the front windscreen. Angela Dupont was indeed striking, in a Hollywood Wives type manner. She was statuesque. A Marilyn Monroe style curvy blonde with plum blusher accentuated cheekbones, lips bloated by fillers and whose hair was piled up in a tight high bun that looked as if it was literally elevating off the top of her head. Her movements were exaggerated; sweeping arm movements, wide eyed sexiness and provocative head tossing galore. Will felt exhausted just watching her.

"Is she an actress?" He wondered aloud.

Randy guffawed, "you'd think so wouldn't you? But no, the woman has never worked a day in her entire life. She's old money Will; the bourgeoise, born with a silver spoon in her gob. She epitomises everything I detest about the upper class."

Will grimaced, "then let's get this job over."

The mayor arrived a short while later in a sleek limousine, with the city's flags attached to the roof and flapping in the wind. He was a chubby man, with a startling shock of charcoal coloured hair, wrinkled cheeks and forehead and a hooked nose which reminded Will of a bird of prey. He walked oddly; a combined slow down skip and a limp, aided by a walking stick on which his gout-riddled fingers rested.

"How old is this geezer?" Will asked.

Randy shrugged, "in his mid-sixties, although he looks way older. Time hasn't done him any favours and I reckon it's about time he retired."

Will nodded his agreement. "What's his name?"

"Mr Jones to you," Randy quipped, wiping the chocolate from his mouth with the back of a Primark receipt he'd found in his pocket. "His Christian name is Bartholomew, or Bart, as in the Simpsons?"

They watched the mayor be air kissed by his wife and a younger woman, who could easily pass as her twin.

"That's their daughter," Randy scowled, "Agnetha – the baby's Mummy, another money grabbing leech."

Will shook his head, "who wears fur coats now-a-days?"

Randy swung his camera over his shoulder, "she's a trophy hunter too. Her and her husband have spent thousands chasing lions all over Africa."

"Somehow I don't think I'm going to like this family," anger was evident in Will's tone, he could never understand how anyone could hurt animals for fun.

"This is real life, Will, where anything goes. Welcome to the underworld of journalism," Randy slapped his shoulder with a fond smile, "come on Catholic boy, say a few hail Marys for me."

Once the mayor spotted Randy, he was straight over, drawing him away to discuss photograph order, locations and the most flattering angles and lighting.

"Not that I'm trying to tell you how to do your job, Mr Rogers, but Agnetha has over twenty thousand followers on Instagram and is looking to go into modelling as a career. Her image is very important, as is the rest of the family's." He lowered his tone, "Angela has been approached to advertise skincare for the more mature lady and my son has just filmed an aftershave commercial in Hawaii. I have a beautiful family indeed."

"No problem, Mr Jones," Randy's tone was so squeaky he could have passed for Michael Jackson himself. "I'm a professional. Leave everything to me."

"And who is this ... boy?" Bartholomew Jones gave Will a derisory once over.

"Just my assistant."

Will was left alone, offended by Randy's brusque manner, he looked away, dug in his rucksack for his mobile telephone, notepad and pen, looking for someone interesting to interview.

The christening was a long drawn-out ceremony which had Will nodding off against a stone pillar. A young girl with wide blue eyes nudged him as the priest was asking for donations towards the church funds. Will yawned and looked around. The church was full. The last thing he could remember they were singing all things bright and beautiful along with a group of frilly-gowned choir boys. As the priest led the congregation outside, a woman sprang to her feet and began shaking a tambourine to her rendition of Sister Sledge's 'we are family.' Will leant against a gravestone as Randy organised immediate family for photographs. An adolescent member of the Jones' family had disclosed to Will that the mayor had paid the vicar a substantial amount to mention his illustrious career within the city. Will jotted the details down, biting back a laugh and allowed the girl a selfie with him.

"This is going on my Facebook wall," she said, "me, friendly with a journalist and a fit one too. My mates will be so jealous."

Will was about to correct her that he was in fact a full-time student with a steady girlfriend, but she disappeared, fiddling with her phone and leaving the aroma of Black Poison lingering in the air.

Once the church photographs were finished, it was off to the christening party, which was held at a nearby golf club.

"What shall I do?" Will asked Randy, who was rummaging in the boot of his car for his tripod.

"Mingle Will. Chat. Dazzle them with your scintillating smile and personality. Anything, as long as you get me a scoop! I need a promotion Will, I've been stuck in the same position at that damned newspaper forever."

"O-kay," Will drew the word out, "I'll try my best."

They made their way through a posh foyer full of trailing ivy that climbed up the walls and hung from the ceiling. A steward dressed in formal attire directed them into a lounge where the family were already mingling.

"Catch you later," Randy said, as the mayor beckoned him over, "have a drink Will. This." He moved his arm outwards, "is all paid for. May as well enjoy yourself."

"So yes, I'm a distant cousin of Agnetha's." Will was scribbling down the details of a life story which had been relayed to him over the last half hour.

"Thank you, it was nice to talk to you," Will edged away, taking a glass of champagne from a passing waitress with gratitude. He sank down onto a swirly covered chaise lounge, sinking his face into the palms of his hands. This was not going well. The whole afternoon had been more of a meet and greet, without a sniff of a decent story. Every single person he had met had been a narcissist. The irony was that none of them were interesting enough to write about. He flicked through his notes. Boring was the best adjective he could summon. *What kind of journalist in the making was he?* With a sigh he tucked away his jotter and pen and flicked through social media instead. A furtive perusal of the room told him that Randy was busy hobnobbing with people he apparently loathed. When Will caught his eye, Randy gave him a big thumbs up and an overly gratuitous grin. He was telling the people around him in a tone loud enough for Will to hear that he had his very own assistant and then began touting Will as his next protégé or project.

"My journalist in the making ..."

Will looked away at his rapidly moving Facebook feed; a consequence of having over eight hundred friends. He clicked onto Hema's wall, where even his mum was having more fun than he was. Flora had been tagged eating ice-cream at a nearby park. Underneath was the cutest picture of Esme in her stroller, wrapped up warmly with vanilla gloop around her mouth. Ice-cream in midwinter? Will shook his head, overcome with a sense of longing. *Oh, how he wished he was back home with them.*

"You look more depressed than me," a woman sank down next to him, holding out a cigarette, "want one?"

"I don't," Will declined, "but thanks."

She tossed her hair, shrugged and pulled out a throw-away lighter.

"Aren't there laws in place banning those things in public places now?" He looked around, yet the other guests and staff seemed indifferent to her anti-social habit.

"Who gives a ... " she stopped, "the mayor's my daddy, which means I can pretty much do whatever I want and have whatever I like."

Will stayed silent – he was in no mood for a debate and he had had his fill of spoilt spongers for one day. He was surprised by her appearance though; dyed black hair with purple stripes running through it, black kohled eyes and lipstick, black fishnet tights that tapered down to a pair of heavy duty doc martins and a pentagon symbol around her throat – she was obviously a goth and the complete opposite to her plastic looking Barbie sister.

"Who are *you* anyhow?" She asked, head cocked to one side, "got a girl-friend?"

"And a baby," he confirmed.

"Shame," she blew a plume of smoke towards him. Attitude, thought Will, hackles rising, instinctively he moved away.

"You never answered my question! *Who are you?*"

"I'm with the photographer from the newspaper. I have a burning ambition to be a journalist."

"Sounds like a cool dream," she smiled, showing even, white teeth, "what type of journalism?"

"Not sure yet," Will shrugged, "I'm on the bottom rung of the ladder, but eventually I'd love to be a war correspondent."

"Brave! You mean you don't want to chase celebrities? You don't want to be one of the paparazzi?"

"Nope," Will grinned, "what about you? What's your dream?"

"Famous artist? Children's illustrator? Designer? Heck, I have no idea. I'm Monica by the way, but you can call me Mo."

"I'm William, but please call me Will."

"Will do ... Will," she elbowed him playfully in the ribs.

"So what's it like, being the daughter of a mayor?"

"Shit," Monica pulled a retching face and they both erupted with laughter. "Do you want to hear some *real* gossip?"

He watched her flick ash into an empty champagne flute, "I'm all ears, but … only if you let me record it?"

"Sure," she flashed him a naughty smile, "as long as *you're* clear that this didn't come from me."

"I can do anonymous," he gave her a smile of encouragement.

"I'm serious Will … what I'm about to tell you," she swallowed, "let's just say is very sensitive, confidential information. If anyone finds out it came from me …" She trailed off, furtively looking around.

"I promise you'll remain anonymous," Will's eyes glinted, "go on."

"Okay," Monica smirked, "Agnetha. The baby's Mummy."

"Oh yes, your sister?"

Monica snorted, "got it all hasn't she? Rich banker husband, sprawling mansion in the country. Ten household staff. A fleet of uber-cool cars and chauffeurs because the dimwit can't drive. Art worth thousands. Jewellery worth millions."

Will gulped his drink, "lucky girl."

"I hate her," Monica drawled, "she's a total embarrassment and I'm the total opposite. I live in a bedsit; proper student digs, funding myself through art college in London and broke, like, *all the time.*"

Uh-oh thought Will, this was sounding more and more like a bitter vindictive grudge.

She stared at him.

"I know what you're thinking: I'm jealous right?"

Will looked away, shifted in his seat.

"You're wrong," she continued, "I like being poor. I loathe money, I always have. I would rather be skint and happy than rich and lonely like Agnetha. Of course Daddy doesn't see it that way," she emitted a sharp laugh, "she's his golden child always has been and yeah I probably am bitter, mainly because she's lazy – never worked a day in her damn life and she's nasty too Will; cruel to her staff and her animals. Cold and manipulative to her family, even to her own husband poor bloke. No wonder he's having an affair."

Will swallowed.

"Yes that's right. I caught them at it; him and the Swedish nanny. He's been grovelling and offering me bribes ever since."

"You could be rich," he whispered, "no more bedsit."

"I told you I'm not interested in money," Monica snapped, "I want revenge on the bitch."

"You sure you want me to put this in the newspaper?"

"Yes," she said with conviction, "I want to embarrass her like she's humiliated me all my life. She upstaged me on the night of a major acting role in a school play – threw a hissy fit, said she was seriously ill so Mummy and Daddy would stay home with her. The bitch only had a cold. She paid a hairdresser to ruin my hair on the evening of my prom. She stole my first boyfriend, just because she could. I adored him but she … she didn't even really like him. It was merely a game to her, the spiteful cow."

"She sounds vile," Will glanced over at Agnetha who was laughing girlishly with a man who wasn't her husband. "But what about your dad? And your mum? It will hurt them too if this comes out."

"There's no if Will," Monica stubbed out the cigarette on the bottom of her boot, "I want this on the front page – okay. As for my parents," her lip curled up, "Mum's a selfish alcoholic and Dad's a pompous fool. He doesn't even know Agnetha's not his …"

"What?" Will's eyes widened, "Agnetha's not … you're not her *sister*?"

"Half-sister," she corrected, "we share the same Mummy; lucky us."

Will checked his phone was still recording before asking, "who is her father then?"

Monica shrugged, "I can't say for definite, they're a few possibilities."

Will let out a low whistle.

"Mum was fooling around with a few men at the time of Agnetha's conception. Odds on it's the ex Chattlesbury football club manager."

Will's mind whirred, "Ron Fairfax?"

"Yep." Slowly Monica nodded, "what a whore eh?"

"Are you sure?" Will's finger hovered over the stop button.

"Mummy dearest made a full confession to me during a drunken row, two years ago," Monica replied, "like I was some sort of priest at confession. She probably can't remember, she was that plastered. Of course, Dad has no idea, but I reckon it's time he learnt a few hard home truths about his beloved wife and favourite daughter."

"In name only," Will shook the arm he'd been leaning on, which was tingling with pins and needles.

"Exactly. Ha."

An hour later, as Randy was packing away, Will sauntered over and passed him his phone.

"There's your scoop."

Chapter Twenty-Four

"I think that's enough gardening for one day," Evelyn tugged off her gloves and smiled down at Sophie's dog, who was gazing up at her with a large stick in his mouth.

"Drop!" She reached down to pick it up and threw it down the length of the garden. The Labrador went charging after it, skidding across the turf and rolling into a large bush. A few moments later he was back, tail wagging furiously. Evelyn absentmindedly patted him on the head, her mind on what chore she should be doing next. Her kitchen shelves could do with a sort out and the fridge could do with a clean. She went inside picked up a dishcloth and a bottle of lemon disinfectant and swiped the fridge door. Then her thoughts turned to Sophie and the divide between her and her mother. She wondered what she could do to help and an idea formed in her mind. She pushed the thoughts away, concentrated on her cleaning but they kept resurfacing: an image of Sophie crying, followed by a recollection of a hysterical Yvonne. No, thought Evelyn. No more chores today. Today she would try to make amends, today she would try to fix things. Evelyn walked sprightly up the stairs, quickly changed out of her mud-stained trousers into a clean skirt that smelt fresh: like summer. She picked up her keys off the cupboard and opened the front door. She would be back in time for tea and then she would explain to everybody.

Evelyn knew the name of the road but not the number. After alighting from the bus, she walked slowly along Rosemont Avenue, peering up each drive for a sign of a car she recognised. She knew Yvonne owned a white Hyundai, she had been to her house in it. Ah there it was, nestled underneath the bay window of a large detached. Evelyn opened the creaking gate, walked quickly up the path and pressed the bell. She rang it five times and was just about to leave when a shout from above startled her.

"Who is it?" The voice said.

Evelyn peered up, shielding her face from the glare of the strong afternoon sun.

Derek was leaning out of an open window, his face covered in droplets of what looked like paint.

"Hello," Evelyn raised her hand, "it's Sophie's friend – Evelyn."

"Oh hi," Derek grinned, "fancy helping me with a lick of emulsion?"

"Erm … I wanted to speak to Yvonne."

"Shopping," he eyerolled, "but she should be back soon – wanna wait?"

"Okay."

Evelyn heard him thudding down the stairs, the scrape of a metal lock.

"Come on in," he swept the door open.

Evelyn followed him into a spacious hall that was full of flowers, she counted six vases brimming with colour. There was also a glittering chandelier suspended from an elaborately plastered ceiling. Evelyn swallowed, the coving alone must have cost a fortune. Derek paused at the foot of a sweeping staircase that reminded Evelyn of a set from Gone With The Wind.

"Sit down in the sitting room," he grinned at his own wit, and pointed to an ice blue leather sofa which matched the walls and drapes. "Ryan's in the T.V room, watching Jeremy Kyle, I'll tell him to come say hi." He was gone before Evelyn could object.

She perched gingerly and looked around. In the corner stood a piano where more flowers rested and a sideboard with posh looking glass ornaments. There were portraits on the wall of Yvonne in various poses and a large heart-shaped, framed photograph of herself and Derek in an amorous clinch. Evelyn noted that there were none of Sophie or her grandchildren and wondered if they had been taken down. As she was peering behind, Ryan O'Neill came into the room.

"Hello Sophie's friend," his hair was sticking up and there was a considerable amount of dark stubble lining his jaw, "what's your name again?"

"Evelyn," she replied, smiling politely, "hello, how are you?"

"Pretty crap at the moment, sorry for swearing."

"That's okay," Evelyn said nervously, "this house is beautiful."

Ryan looked around, "it's okay I suppose. Yvonne doesn't keep it as nice as Sophie kept ours."

There ensued an awkward pause, "how is she? Good I hope?"

"She's fine, busy working at the call centre and … and uni."

"Oh yes. I heard she had a job," he sucked in a breath, "never thought that day would happen and she's stuck it out at uni? I gotta say, that's an even bigger surprise."

Evelyn felt a flicker of annoyance ignite inside her, "Sophie's working very hard," she said firmly, "and we're almost finished. She'll have letters after her name Mr O'Neill."

He didn't reply, just stared at the wall clock.

"What are you doing with yourself?" She ventured.

"Nuttink," he bit out, his Irish lilt reverberating in the cold room, "absolutely nuttink. The club still don't want to know me. All my footie friends are avoiding me. My own publicity team have dropped me. I'm a down and out!"

"You have Derek and Yvonne," Evelyn protested, "you have a home over your head and food in your stomach. Maybe you should count those as blessings?"

"Are you religious?" Ryan was almost sneering, "because no offence lady, but I stopped believing when I was eight." He raised his hands skywards mocking her.

Evelyn bristled with anger, when suddenly a door banged shut and Yvonne called, "coo-ee, I'm home."

Evelyn sat up straighter as Sophie's mother flounced into the room.

"Derek, I've bought you new underwear … Calvin Klein of course …" She stopped when she saw her uninvited guest, "*what* are you doing here?"

"Hello Mrs Fletcher."

"Don't you be all polite and nicey nice with me," Yvonne's tone was scathing, "from what I can remember the last time I saw *you*, your husband was threatening me with the police!"

"You did throw a plant pot at our window," Evelyn replied, calmly.

"I had received a huge shock! It's not every day your runaway rat of an ex turns up out of the blue."

"It's okay, I understand," Evelyn's cheeks burned. Truthfully, she could never comprehend the reasons why Yvonne was so unstable, her behaviour so erratic, but she was here for Sophie, so she kept her disapproving thoughts to herself. "I wanted to speak with you in private if possible, about Anthony."

Yvonne stared at her for a moment, "Ryan can you leave us please?"

"Why?" Ryan objected, "I am still Sophie's husband, maybe I could help," his eyes glinted with the opportunity to ingratiate himself with his estranged wife.

"Go and help Derek," Yvonne said, "he's working so hard on the decorating and it will do you good to keep busy honey, stop you dwelling on the past."

Ryan left the room chuntering and Yvonne flung herself down on the sofa next to Evelyn.

"I'm at the end of my tether with Ryan O'Neill," her voice rose higher, "it's like he's given up on life!"

"Maybe he should speak to a counsellor," Evelyn suggested, stiffly, "Sophie found it helped come to terms with everything she's been through."

"Oh, boys will be boys," Yvonne waved the idea of psychological help away, "what he needs is a job – a purpose, a reason to get up in the morning. And as for Sophie, she seems perfectly fine to me."

"Hardly," Evelyn said with a tut, "she's had no choice but to cope, Mrs Fletcher. What with her marriage separation and her father reappearing in her life … it's been a struggle for her."

Yvonne snorted, "she looked extremely cosy with Anthony on Christmas day, but then she always was a Daddy's girl," Yvonne's eyes narrowed, "as for her *brother* – I've never been so insulted in all my life. What an attitude!"

Evelyn opened her mouth to speak but Yvonne continued her rant, "everyone seems to have forgotten that *Anthony* abandoned his wife and daughter. I'm the true injured party here, not him."

"Are you?" Evelyn queried, feeling brave, "I heard you had an affair when he was at his most vulnerable. Sophie's dad was wrong for running away – yes, but he was extremely ill and felt like he had no other choice. He had no support from anyone, Mrs Fletcher, including his errant wife."

Yvonne's mouth flapped open, "so now you insult me in my own home."

"I apologise," Evelyn twined her fingers on her lap, "but sometimes the truth needs airing and the fact is that it was you that drove Anthony away. If you would have loved and cared for him, maybe he wouldn't have left."

"I don't have to listen to … "

"Sophie is the real victim here," Evelyn interrupted, "she was just a child who adored her father and suddenly he vanished. Can you not comprehend how heart wrenching it has been for her all these years?"

"Well I acknowledge it must have been difficult for Sophie … " Yvonne licked her lips, "why are you here Evelyn? I already feel terrible enough as it is."

"I want ... I thought you could make it right ... for Sophie," Evelyn smiled, "I hoped that you could find it in your heart to make peace with Anthony ... make friends, for Sophie's sake."

Yvonne's lips set in a firm, obstinate line, "no."

"Please Mrs Fletcher," Yvonne took hold of her hands, "be the compassionate, loving person I know you are. Be the bigger person, I guarantee it will bring you closure too."

"You don't give up do you?" Yvonne said with a resigned sigh, "would you like a drink? I'm afraid we only have herbal though. This is a caffeine-free household."

"No, but thank you," Evelyn replied.

"I suppose you have a plan?" Yvonne said with an eye roll, "I'm doing this for my daughter, Evelyn and my grandchildren, not him."

"Fair enough," Evelyn leaned closer with a smile, "this is what I thought you could do."

* * *

"That was delicious."

Sophie watched her father wipe away crumbs from his top lip.

"It's been too long since I've enjoyed afternoon tea and scones."

They were in Mrs Timms' Teashop, resting their feet after another busy day of sightseeing. They sat in a window seat, next to a frost encrusted glass.

"It's so cold today," Sophie said, her breath billowing out in front of her.

"I had forgotten how cold it can get in Britain," Anthony shivered. "I brought mainly light clothes."

"Oh Dad," Sophie sprang up, "here, have my jacket." She draped her woollen coat around his shoulders. "What would you like to do now? We could go watch a movie or look round the shops or ..."

Anthony placed his hands over Sophie's, "how about we go home?"

"To Evelyn's?" Sophie's voice lifted with surprise, "yes of course."

"I want to watch my daughter bake her famous shortbread I've heard so much about."

Sophie blushed at his tenderly spoken words and the actuality of being claimed as his flesh and blood.

"I'm nowhere near as good as Evelyn," her face was demure as she looked at him, "but I'll happily bake you some – for you all – Ariel and Barry, Poppy too and you … you can take some back to Hong Kong, to your wife," she trailed off.

He was staring at her with such love and pride she was overcome with emotion. Sophie clasped his hand and said silently *don't go, please don't go.*

As if reading her mind Anthony answered her, "I have to. Hong Kong is my home, Sophie. I feel like an alien here."

Slowly she moved her hand away, "I've only just found you again," she whispered, "I need more time …"

"Will you come to Hong Kong in July? It's not too long to wait and you can stay for a month, six weeks, two months – you decide Sophie."

"I will come," she promised, "of course I'll come."

"Then that's settled, and while we wait, I will Skype you each week, text you every morning."

"Really?" Her lip wobbled.

"Really," he leant across to peck her cheek, "you have grown into a fine woman Sophie: strong, kind, caring, capable. Your mother did not do too badly, hmm?"

"I suppose not," she said, grudgingly. "Dad. You won't disappear again?"

Anthony looked at her solemnly, tears pooling in his eyes, "no Sophie, I'll never leave you again."

They smiled at each other, while the rain pattered down on the weather-beaten window sill.

* * *

"So now *we* have reunited, is there no chance of a reconciliation with your husband?" Anthony set his cup down and signalled to the waitress that they were finished.

"Erm … no," Sophie had withheld the full gory details of Ryan's infidelities and his selfish behaviour, "no chance what-so-ever."

Anthony nodded, "you are a beautiful lady, I think that you will only be single for a short time."

"I actually like being single," she picked a piece of fluff off her skirt, "I can do what I want and please myself. Just me and the boys: it's perfect."

"You have done well, coping alone. You are strong, Sophie, stronger than you think."

"Thank you," Sophie said, quietly, "it *has* been hard and I'm exhausted all the time, but I actually think I'm going to be okay."

"Let me help alleviate some of the burden," he said, brightly, "I have something for you. Two things actually."

Anthony dug inside his blazer pocket and pulled out a burgundy box and a white envelope, "these are for you."

"For me," Sophie stared down at them, "what are they?"

"Open them," he smiled, his eyes twinkling.

Sophie ran her fingers over both of them, deciding to open the box first, she fumbled with the catch.

"Oh. Oh." Sophie gasped, tears clouding her vision.

"It's beautiful, isn't it?"

She gazed at the gold heart locket.

"It was your grandmothers. A family heirloom; cost a fortune when it was purchased. Before she married your grandfather, she had an affair with an American soldier, he was the love of her life apparently. He bought it for her as a gift for her birthday. They were all set to marry but he was killed in the trenches."

"That's so sad."

Anthony shook his head, "she never got over him. This locket meant everything to her. And she never removed it, even on her wedding day to another man."

Sophie carefully picked it off its blue cushion. It was heavy, with a long chain and an ornate clasp.

"When you were born, she gave it to me, told me I would know when the time was right to pass it on to you."

Sophie smiled, "can I open it?"

"Of course."

Her fingers felt clammy as they prised apart the locket. Sophie gasped at the contents; two pictures, cut perfectly round, to fit inside. Two faces – herself as a young girl and the other was a carefree, youthful looking Anthony.

"It's perfect," Sophie swallowed back a sob, "thank you. I will treasure it."

Anthony rose to his feet, "now I will always be close to you, in here Sophie," he pointed to his chest, "the miles will not separate us again." He stood behind her and waited patiently for her to lift her hair.

Gently he secured it around her neck, "it suits you," he stood back to admire her, "you look like her – your grandmother, she was breath-taking too. My daughter."

He patted her shoulder and she placed her hand over his.

"Open the envelope Sophie," his breath was warm on the nape of her neck.

"What is it?" she wondered aloud, running her fingers underneath the opening. Carefully, she pulled out a card which had a drawing of a cute mouse holding a flower. The line above it simply read, 'I Love You.'

Warmth coursed through her, with shaking fingers she opened the card, something fluttered out and fell onto the table, but her eyes were on the handwritten words inside:

'For my daughter, I will love you forever. Dad xxxx'

Tears ran freely down Sophie's cheeks as emotion overcame her.

"Look on the table Sophie. This is for you. This is my gift to you."

Sophie squinted down at the blank rectangle. Slowly she turned it over. Her breathing stalled, her stomach clenched as she surveyed the cheque made out to Sophie O'Neill, for the sum of five hundred thousand sterling pounds.

Chapter Twenty-Five

"I've finished!" Crowed Ann. Pushing away her computer, she flung her arms upwards. This started a Mexican wave around the kitchen; Samuel, who was working on his homework, lifted his hands up and then Jon, who was standing at the kitchen sink, raised his marigolds skywards.

"It's not due for another couple of months," Jon sounded impressed.

"I'm just too clever," Ann stretched her right arm behind her neck.

"And organised," Jon added.

"Seriously, the best decision I made was to do all my reading for it over last summer. Now I can concentrate on the remaining essays, and that's it, year three over. Undergraduate degree complete."

"And the start of your new life Mrs what-shall-we-call-you? BA Hons Stokes? What do you think, Sam?"

Sam grinned, "I think it's really cool."

"This calls for a celebration," Jon tipped the lukewarm soapy water out of the bowl, "tea this evening shall be on me. Name the restaurant, Ann."

Ann pondered for a moment, "how about the new Cantonese?"

"Which one's that?"

"The one in town Jon, the one we passed last week and stopped to look at the menu. I've heard some of the students rating it as delicious."

"Sounds like a plan," Jon went in search of his new razor, leaving Ann and Sam to chatter excitedly amongst themselves.

The House of Canton was positioned in the middle of the city, next to the offices of News Express and a barber's with a 'Half-price hair cut on a Tuesday' sign emblazoned in its window. Sam held the door open for Jon to wheel Ann into a scarlet painted room, full of Chinese lanterns. Soft piped music swooned around a dozen or so prettily laid out tables and velour chairs that one could sink comfortably into. As they were being seated by a handsome waiter, Ann noticed Juliette and Ben sitting at a corner table. They both smiled and waved.

"Those two still in love?" Jon picked up a menu and took his reading glasses out of their case.

"Oh yes," whispered Ann, "and its serious from what Sophie's disclosed. He's even asked her to move in."

"Gotta admit, those two look good together," Jon furtively glanced at them, then back down at the starter section, "they'll have gorgeous babies ... eye up she's coming over."

"Hi Ann, Jon and Sam?" Juliette bent to hug each of them.

"Have you had a nice weekend?" Ann asked.

"Yes, but far too much socialising. I haven't had a chance to complete any of my outstanding essays.

"Ann has finished her dissertation," Jon blew out his cheeks with pride.

"Brilliant!"

"I've finished it in draft form," she corrected, "it still needs editing and erm ... tweaking."

"I'm about half way through mine and still researching, but it's coming together," Juliette smiled and looked back at Ben, "we've been to see a horror movie, the new Stephen King remake."

"I'm still trying to talk Ann into watching that," Jon chuckled, "she prefers romance though."

"Romance?" Juliette's voice lifted with surprise, "I never would have thought that was your thing, Ann."

"It isn't," Ann replied, blushing, "I like suspense films with hidden meanings – a bit like my books, really."

"You told me your favourite film was Beauty and the Beast," Samuel teased.

"Oh, this gets better," Juliette laughed, "a closet Disney fan. Have you met my daughter?"

"Okay you guys," Ann shook her head, but her eyes were dancing with good humour, "I liked it when I was your age, Sam. Anyway, Juliette, did I tell you Sam won his spelling gala? He is now the proud owner of a trophy and one hundred pounds worth of book vouchers."

"Fantastic," Juliette enthused, "well done Sam." A waiter carrying two trays of sizzling beef stopped beside Ben, "so I'll see you at uni tomorrow?"

"Yep," Ann took a sip of the table water, "enjoy the rest of your evening."

Juliette went back to her seat and then the waiter was hovering next to Ann's table, ready to jot down their order.

Jon decided to ignore Ann protestations and ordered the second most expensive champagne on the drinks menu.

"Can I have some?" Sam asked, youthful hope etched across his face.

"Just a small glass," Ann replied, "otherwise Rose, Anton and Lulu will be telling me off!"

Jon poured out three glasses and Samuel snatched his up immediately, "it's fizzy," he pinched his nose, "it tastes good."

"Delicious," Ann agreed, taking a small sip.

"So, a toast," Jon held his glass in the air, waiting for the others to join him, "well done to Sam for being a word wizard."

"Here, here," they clinked glasses and Samuel looked suitably euphoric.

"And now," Jon's eyes rested on Ann, "to my wife. Congratulations on finishing your dissertation."

* * *

"I guess this is goodbye," Sophie's words were muffled against her brother Barry's shoulder.

"Goodbye for now, dear sister," Barry moved back, swiping Sophie's hair off her forehead, "you are everything and more I could have wished for. Thank you for your kind hospitality."

Sophie placed her hands on his shoulders and pecked his cheek, "and thank you for being my perfect little brother."

"Aunty Sophie," Poppy was at her feet, making a clenching sign with her chubby fists, "cuddles."

Sophie scooped her up, balancing her on one hip she rained kisses over her rosy cheeks, "goodbye sweet princess, be good for Mama and Dada."

Poppy squealed in response, tugged on her hair and then shimmied down her leg so she could watch two young children revolving on a fifty pence elephant ride machine.

"No Poppy, we haven't time," Ariel steered her towards Barry and then opened her arms to Sophie, "my turn," she pulled her into the fiercest embrace. *Boy Ariel was strong for someone so petite.*

By now the tears were flowing down Sophie's face, "safe journey home," she squeaked, "I'll write."

"Every week?" Ariel was crying too.

Sophie rubbed her nose with the back of her hand, "I promise."

Then she glanced at Anthony and everyone else in the airport dwindled away.

"Dad," her tone trembled with her knees, "I don't know what Mum said to you and I guess you're not going to tell me, but thank you for making peace with her. Thank you for being so kind, generous and … and … understanding. She's never been the easiest of people to like and get along with. You could so easily have told her where to go, to leave us all alone but," she clasped his hand, "you're better than that."

"We all have our demons," Anthony rubbed her thumb and forefinger gently, "everyone makes mistakes, especially me! I'm sorry I missed out on your younger years. With all of my heart I'm so sorry I left you, Sophie."

"S'alright," Sophie hiccupped, "I must look like a panda huh? Remind me to wear waterproof mascara next time I see you."

"Which will be soon, Sophie. Very soon."

She stared into his eyes: her father, her friend.

Without speaking, she thanked him again for the locket and the money. The cheque had been safely deposited in her bank account and would stay there until she decided what to do with it, and the locket was hanging around her neck, close to her heart. Sophie thought back to yesterday, the day in the café, when she had tried to refuse his monetary gift. She had pushed the cheque back across the table, but he just kept sliding it right back at her. Telling her repeatedly it was her rightful inheritance, it was given out of unconditional love for his one and only daughter. Her protestations had grown weaker, until she had finally accepted it with profuse thanks and tears of gratitude.

"Bye Dad," she was enveloped in the warmest of hugs that lasted minutes but felt like an eternity.

The Tannoy overhead informed them the gates to flight 356 to Hong Kong were now open for boarding.

"We should go," Barry's eyes were full of empathy, "we don't want to miss our flight."

With reluctance, Sophie pulled away to see a mirror image of herself, where tears ran silently.

"Bye," a strangled sob escaped as Sophie turned away, walked quickly from the departure gate. She held her head high and kept moving, refusing to look back in case … in case she completely broke down. Then she was moving through the exit doors, leaning against a bollard, gasping for air, while happy people milled around, tugging suitcases past her in the rush to escape the inclement weather of Great Britain.

* * *

"I have to admit I'm less than a quarter of the way through," Will shifted in his seat, glancing with guilty eyes at his personal tutor.

"Your proposal is good Will, but we're in February now – less than two months until the hand in date." Tarquin Haverstock rested his chin on steepled fingers, "how are you getting on with your other essays?"

Will winced; he could either be honest or lie. He opted for the truth. "Behind with them, too."

"Is there any reason why?" Dr Haverstock queried.

"Life?" Will pushed a hand over his head, forgetting that the length of his hair was now short and spiky as opposed to long and floppy. "A baby to care for, two jobs. Man, I'm never going to pass this degree."

"Of course you are," Dr Haverstock passed him a mint, "I understand Will, I've been in your position, minus the baby; that must be hard."

"She's an angel," Will jumped to Esme's defence, "my angel."

Tarquin Haverstock smiled, "all I'm saying is if you're struggling with deadlines, ask for an extension, ask for support from a student union rep. They love rebelling against us lecturers."

"Okay," Will laughed, "I'll work on it over the next few weeks and get a few more chapters to you."

"Email it to me, save your legs."

In the office next door, Juliette was chatting to Brian Hodges about the very same thing.

"Excellent so far," Dr Hodges poured tea from his flask, "want one?"

"Yes please," her mouth was dry and it dawned on her that she hadn't had chance to grab a hot drink yet this morning.

He began searching his desk for a cup or mug. She sat quietly until he had found one.

"Your proposal was great, no surprise there. But the first two chapters impressed me even more."

Juliette grinned, "I'm enjoying writing it."

"Good. Good. Just a suggestion, tighten up on your punctuation. Of course, *I'm* relaxed about it, but the second marker may not be. You don't want to drop a grade because of missing commas."

"Will do," Juliette sipped her tea, her gaze resting on Ben's empty desk. A second later, the door rattled open and he backed in, clutching a mountain of books, shirt hanging out the back of his trousers and his hair tousled.

"Morning," his face lit up at the sight of her.

"Morning," happy bubbles fizzed inside her stomach as they stared at each other for a lingering moment.

"Yes hello Ben. Lovely to see you," Brian was smirking at them both.

"Brian," Ben nodded, placed his books down, "I hope you're being professional with *my* student."

"Do you need to ask?" Brian blustered, "I'm professional with all of the students, whereas you ..."

He was cut off by the sound of rapping on the door. It swung open before either of them could speak, the Dean poked his head round the wooden frame and informed them of an email which he had sent out to the entire English department. "A meeting lunchtime with myself and the Vice Chancellor."

Juliette's spirits plummeted, *farewell to my lunch date.*

Ben glanced at her, "is it mandatory?"

The Dean cleared his throat, "it's important Dr Rivers, that's all I'm revealing." He pulled the door closed, disappearing from view.

"I should be going," Juliette stood up, swinging her bag onto her shoulder, "thank you for the chat and the feedback, Dr Hodges."

Brian cast a sneaky glance at Ben, "anytime Juliette and I mean *anytime.*"

Ben scowled and, as she passed, grabbed hold of her hand, "who's your favourite lecturer?"

Juliette rolled her eyes, "you guys are so immature."

"See you in your first lecture, Miss Harris," Ben called.

She could hear them laughing together as she firmly closed the door.

* * *

Sophie arrived at the lecture twenty minutes late.

"Sorry," she tiptoed past Dr Rivers, taking a seat in-between Juliette and Will.

"You okay?" Juliette whispered.

"An emotional wreck, but nothing changes there huh?"

Juliette was distracted by Ben, who was pointing his i-pad pen at her, "pardon?"

"Middlemarch Miss Harris, what did you think of it?"

Juliette's cheeks flamed with embarrassment; he knew she hadn't read it.

"Middlemarch is ... brilliant."

"Brilliant?" He frowned, "can anyone in the class help enlighten Miss Harris further?"

Hands shot up around the room and Juliette slumped down in the seat feeling annoyed. For the rest of the lecture she refused to look at Dr Rivers, even when he paced past her desk. *I am not going to be distracted,* she vowed, scribbling notes in her jotter. At eleven they paused for a comfort break. Sophie told the others about her father leaving. When she had finished, Juliette rose to her feet and stalked towards Ben.

"Did you deliberately set out to humiliate me?" She snapped, pretending to throw something in the bin next to where he was standing.

"You should do the reading Miss Harris," he quipped, "no favouritism here," he leant closer to whisper, "my office now."

"I need to pee," she retaliated hotly, "text me later."

She flounced out of the classroom but as she was marching down the quiet corridor, she could hear him clicking his pen as he followed her. He tugged at her hand, opened a door and pushed her through it into an empty classroom.

"Ben! What are you doing? What's wrong with you?"

"Sexual frustration," he cupped the nape of her neck, drawing her face close to his.

Juliette swallowed, "we can't ... not at uni."

"I know," he groaned, "I just find you irresistible, especially in those skinny jeans."

"I'm glad you like my jeans," she stepped away, "but you need to concentrate on Middlemarch."

Ben grabbed hold of her waist, pulling her against him. His mouth was so insistent against hers she immediately kissed him back, winding her arms around his back.

"I love you," she murmured, "but please don't tell me off again."

"Well I never. You two again!" The shocked words had them springing apart.

"Gladys." Ben and Juliette stared at the cleaner with relief.

"Are you okay?" Ben asked tersely, frustration evident in his voice.

"I'm okay," she coughed, "and I can see that you're well."

"Never better," Ben grinned, "and how's my favourite domestic goddess getting on?"

Gladys chuckled at the compliment, "underpaid, over-worked, the usual. I was going to give this room a quick polish, but if you're busy I can come back?"

"No need," Ben replied, "we were just leaving ... so see you around, Gladys."

"Hmm," Gladys observed them as they went with a shake of her head.

"Ben!" Juliette marched off in front of him, "try and be professional, and no more picking on me in class!"

* * *

Once the seminar was over, they enjoyed a leisurely lunch together in the refectory.

"It's good everyone is here," Ann commented, "seems like we've all been distracted by personal stuff lately – including me."

"I'm way behind on my dissertation," Will thumped the bottle of ketchup he was holding and smeared sauce over his chips, "I've been spending far too much time at News Express. Free of charge I might add."

"Are you enjoying it Will?" Evelyn asked, "it must be so exciting being a journalist."

"I am," Will replied, "but I need to put my uni work first. How many essays are due?"

"Four," Ann licked the sugar sprinkles from the doughnut she was holding, "plus your dissertation."

Will grimaced and told them about the possibility of applying for an extension.

"I could do with an extension too," Sophie said, when he'd finished speaking, "I'm way behind with *everything*. Do you think they'll let me if I explain about my turbulent personal life?"

"Of course they will," Juliette said with conviction, "you've really been through it just lately. I'm sure your personal tutor will understand. But you need to speak to them soon Sophie, don't forget or put it off."

Sophie nodded, "I'll pop and see her this afternoon."

"I reckon they get loads of extension requests," Ann said, "and here's Melanie to tell us all about it."

They turned to watch the bubbly notetaker skipping across the room, "hi guys. Nearly the end. How are you all getting on?"

Evelyn, Juliette and Ann replied "good" in unison, while Will gave a thumbs down and Sophie bit her lip.

Melanie frowned at the two of them, scraped back a chair and plonked herself down. "Tell me all about it, I'm sure I can help."

Chapter Twenty-Six

Will's mind was elsewhere. While Melanie rattled on about her time as a failing under-graduate student, he was thinking of Esme. Over the weekend she had developed a nasty cough, this morning she was hot and prickly – screaming the place down when Hema had attempted to bathe her. Max had told them in his 'been there, done that' superior attitude, that she was probably just teething, but Will wasn't convinced. Esme was usually so calm, so affable. It was out of character for her to wake once during the night, never mind four times. So, a trip to the doctor had been organised, and now Hema was texting to inform him that Esme had a chest infection. His poor little girl was on her first course of antibiotics.

"I have to go," he gave his apologies to them all and left the building, running all the way to the bus stop.

"I'm home," he yelled. The door slammed shut behind him, caught in a strong gust of wind. Hema came out of the lounge, a finger pressed to her lips.

"She's sleeping," she whispered, "dosed up on baby paracetamol and covered in menthol eucalyptus."

Will peeped his head round to see his daughter sprawled on the settee, clutching her favourite teddy while snoring softly. Hema beckoned him towards the kitchen. Flora was laying the table with cutlery, she looked up when he entered, and Max was at the stove, stirring something in one of the stainless-steel pots.

"Everyone's here," Will said with surprise.

"Hello to the worker," Flora wiped her hands on her pinafore and went in search of the salt and pepper pots.

"It's been a quiet morning, so they let me finish early," Max carried on turning the mixture, "imagine me doing *that* at St Mary's."

"Your dad is in a flap because they've organised an assembly for him. He's worried the governing body will try to persuade him to come back." Flora touched Max's shoulder lightly as she walked past.

"No chance," Max replied calmly, "I like my new stress-free existence too much. Shall I add herbs to this, darling? It tastes a little erm … bland."

"I forgot the herbs," Flora turned the herb rack, taking out a few small jars, "this should do it." She opened a drawer and tipped oregano and thyme and a few other spices onto a table spoon. Ruby suddenly shot out from underneath the table, ears pricked, tail wagging furiously. She began to growl and then emitted a series of low barks.

Will caught her by the collar, "ssh."

"It's only the paper boy," Flora pushed open the sliding door, allowing the dog access to shoot down the hall. A moment later she came rushing back, the evening newspaper hanging from her jowls.

"Good girl," Max took it from her and sat down on a breakfast stool.

Flora was sampling the bolognese sauce, "this is good," she offered Hema a mouthful.

"Hmm," Hema winced, "is it supposed to be spicy?"

"Oh, I thought I'd pep it up a bit by adding a few crushed chillies and garlic. Too much tomato can be rather bland, don't you agree Will?"

"Whatever you say, Mum."

"Well it's almost ready. Can you boil the kettle for the spaghetti love?"

Will flicked the switch and kissed Hema on the mouth as she went by with a tray of garlic bread.

"Boy that is strong," he coughed, "think we'll all be eating mints for breakfast tomorrow."

"Remind me to cancel the newspaper in the morning, Flora," Max was shaking his head with disapproval as he perused the front page.

"What's up?" Will peered over his father's shoulder and gulped when he read the main headline, 'Mayor's wife and daughter in wild love affairs shock.'

"But you love reading News Express," Flora crunched dry spaghetti into a pan, "whatever's the matter?"

"They're no better than the trashy tabloids," Max replied, "I'm really not interested in reading about the mayor's family sordid love lives."

Hema and Flora glanced at one another, "speak for yourself," Hema said, "I love reading about that kind of stuff."

"News Express is supposed to be an intellectual family paper. They'll be writing about UFOs and celebrities next."

Flora and Hema giggled, "did you know about this, son?"

"Er ... erm ..." Will was saved from answering by a loud rap on the back door.

"Who's that?" Max bit out, grumpily.

"Oh, Max it's only Brenda from next door."

"Can't she use the front door like normal people?" He mumbled.

Flora swiped at him with her tea towel, "we've been neighbours for decades. Be nice. Please."

Brenda came bustling through the door, clad in her dressing gown and curlers in her hair.

"Sorry for my attire," she began, "I've just got out of the shower, Gerald and I are dining out tonight."

"What can I do for you, Brenda?" Flora smiled, "would you like a drink?"

"No thank you I won't stay," she stared pointedly at Max, "I just had to speak to you, Flora."

"About what?" Flora lowered her tone, "would you like to go somewhere more private."

"It's not concerning me," Brenda replied, huffing, "although it is a delicate matter." She looked over at Max, whose attention was firmly back on the newspaper, "I see you've read the headlines?"

"Oh that!" Flora's eyes glinted, "Max was just about to tell us the juicy gossip."

"Pure filth!" Brenda snorted with disapproval.

"What do you mean?" Flora cocked her head to one side, "it's just a newspaper article Brenda – hardly pornography."

Will swallowed and sidled into the chair opposite his father.

"Can I remind you who the article is about, Flora? The mayor's wife Angela Dupont. I would call her a lady but after this revelation, well ... all I can say is I'm very disappointed in her behaviour. And she was due to make the opening speech at our annual church music concert!"

"Oh." Flora bit her lip, "is it that bad?"

"It's worse," Brenda threw her hands up in the air, "awful gossip splashed across the whole of Chattlesbury. Money bribes, affairs, there's even a rumour that the eldest daughter isn't even the mayor's own flesh and blood. This is awful Flora."

"But … but, that is their own personal business, surely we shouldn't be judging others."

"It's all over the paper, Flora," cried Brenda, her cheeks rosy with outrage, "*everyone* will be judging them, including our own priest. He will never allow her to stand up in front of his congregation and make a speech when, when she acts so abominably."

Max looked over his newspaper and uttered the words Flora thought she would never hear, "I agree with Brenda, this is a scandal. Maybe you should find someone else to open the music concert."

"It might not even be true," Flora replied, "you yourself are always preaching that a person shouldn't listen to idle gossip. Maybe you should make your own mind up, Max."

Will cleared his throat, "it's not idle gossip Mum. That article is all true and they're really not nice people, the mayor's lot. Dad's right; you should find someone else."

"Will! You've shocked me, you're usually so open minded. How do you know that it's true? It could be wild exaggeration."

"I know because I interviewed the source Mum. *I* got the scoop. I can't disclose where from, but it came from a very reliable person."

"This is down to you?" Brenda glared his way, "well thank you for spoiling our concert. Do you know young man that the flyers have already been distributed, now people will come purely for the scandal."

Will raised his hand, "sorry, but this would have come out anyway."

Flora looked at her son, her face registering cold shock and disappointment.

"Let me explain," Will began. "we pay to put these people in positions of power. They happily take the tax-payers money. They make these inspirational speeches; behave this way, do this, do that. Yet behind closed doors they're nothing but hypocrites. The mayor and his family are corrupt, Mum, and the public who *do* pay their wages have a right to be informed."

"A right to be publicly humiliated? A right to be hounded? It's wrong Will … it's unchristian."

Will blanched at Flora's words but was utterly surprised when Max jumped to his defence.

"Sometimes these people need to be ousted," Max's sonorous voice had everyone's attention. "Flora, not everyone in this world is as good as you are."

"I know," she interrupted, "you've told me a thousand times: I'm naïve, I'm soft."

"That was the old me," Max rose to his feet, "and it wasn't meant as a criticism." He placed a comforting hand across her shoulder, "you are lovely and kind."

Will sniffed, "you're an angel, Mum." Beside him, Hema nodded in agreement.

Brenda pulled the tie on her dressing gown tighter, "so that's settled then. No Angela Dupont. I will personally call her to tell her that her presence at the music concert will *not* be required."

"It seems I'm outnumbered," Flora mumbled.

Brenda moved towards the door, "I should go, but Flora, we need to arrange a meeting as soon as possible. The concert is only three weeks away and we need to decide who can take her place. Who is good at inspirational speeches I wonder?" She tapped her chin.

Flora's eyes lit up as an idea formed in her mind, "we need an outstanding pillar of the community. Someone driven, charismatic, attractive, who is verbose and excellent at rhetoric."

"You're not talking about Cliff Richard are you, Mum?" Will joked.

"Who Flora, who?" Brenda was agog with excitement.

Flora smiled brightly at her husband, "it's you darling Max. You will be perfect for the role."

Will laughed at the dawning look of horror crossing Max's face.

Flora continued with determination, "and your dear son Will shall be helping you write the speech."

* * *

The following morning, Will was woken by a gentle rap on the door. He glanced at the alarm clock next to his bed and was surprised to see that it was past nine o'clock.

"Come in," he struggled into a slouched position, rubbing the sleep from his eyes.

"It's for you," Flora held the telephone in her hand, "morning."

"Morning. Where's Hema?"

"Up early with Esme. They've gone for a walk to the shops." Flora bounced into the room, looking fresh and pretty in a daisy printed skirt and chiffon blouse, "I'm off to work so see you this evening." She placed the phone down on the duvet and went back out.

"H-hello," Will cleared his throat, waiting for a reply.

"Will? Sorry did I wake you?"

"It's okay. Who is this?"

"It's Gloria from News Express."

Will sat up a little straighter.

There was a silent pause, "are you still there?"

"Yes," Will fiddled with the edge of the duvet, *please don't ask me to work today.* He'd planned a family day with Hema and then this evening he was going to work on his dissertation.

"Si asked me to give you a call." Gloria sniffed, "is there any chance you could pop in to see him?"

"I'm kinda busy with uni work," Will replied, evenly, "what's it about?"

Gloria sighed, "I have no idea Will. But he's been in a fantastic mood for days. I don't think he's been as happy since the nineties."

Will laughed, "you've worked there that long?"

"Unfortunately, yes."

"Give me forty minutes, I'll be there."

"Brilliant. See you in a bit." She cut the call, leaving Will wondering what was in store for him.

"But you promised, Will," Hema was bent over the pushchair, unclipping Esme.

"Babe. I won't be long." Esme jumped from the pushchair like a coiled spring.

"I'll get you a Subway while I'm up there."

Hema's mouth lifted into a small smile, "well okay. But I want to go out, Will, we've been stuck in the house for days. The sun's shining, fresh air will do Esme good."

"Is she okay?" Will looked down at his daughter, who was wrapping herself around his lower legs.

"A lot better today. The antibiotics must have kicked in. And as long as she's wrapped up warmly, she'll be fine."

"Where d'you want to take her?" Will scooped Esme into his arms, she gurgled with delight and began patting his cheeks.

"I thought we could catch the bus into the city and do a bit of shopping, via the park of course. And I've bought popcorn. The three of us could watch a movie later."

"A matinee?"

"Yes," Hema put her arm round Will's back, leaned her head against his forehead.

"Sounds a perfect plan to me," he replied, kissing her chastely on the mouth, "let me pop to News Express, then I'm all yours."

When Will arrived at the headquarters of News Express, a large group of staff were gathered in the foyer.

"Will," Gloria beckoned him over with the hook of a scarlet fingernail.

"Everything alright?" He glanced at the journalists who were talking in hushed tones.

Gloria grimaced, "the mayor and his wife are here, threatening lawyers and court action."

"Where's Randy?" Will sounded calm, but his insides were twisting uncomfortably.

"He's over there," she pointed to a couch where the senior photographer sat, eating a sandwich.

"Hey bro'," Randy wiped egg from his chin as Will walked over.

"Are we in trouble?" Will squashed next to him.

"Nah man," Randy seemed unperturbed and rather gleeful, "There's never been so much excitement here since Chattlesbury won the FA cup. Si Nelson will sort it."

Will sighed, "did you get your promotion?"

"Oh that? Nope, but it's okay, I was due to retire soon anyway."

"So all this was for nothing?" Will chewed the skin around his thumb nail.

Randy slapped him lightly on the shoulder, "you got the truth out there. Serves the mayor right. It's about time someone knocked him from his council pedestal."

"And by doing that I've wrecked a few lives in the process." Will felt overcome with guilt.

"You need to stop this right now. That's if you're serious about becoming a journalist. Listen to uncle Randy and don't beat yourself up. It was a fantastic scoop!"

Will was still unconvinced, "maybe I'm not cut out to be a journalist."

"You *are* a journalist." He smiled, the filtered rays of sunlight beaming through the blinds lit up his face. "Just talk to Si, okay?"

Will stood up, "I suppose I should go on up there then."

Randy's attention was already back on his phone. "Better put on some protection gear first."

The first-floor office where news articles were written was eerily quiet and empty, except for an admin clerk who was struggling to pull paper out of a jammed printer. Will went to help, and while he was on his hands and knees peering into the bowels of the machine, she revealed the mayor had insisted all the reporters should leave while he spoke to Si Nelson 'in confidence.' The shrill ringing of unanswered calls ratcheted across the open plan floor. Will passed them by, scanning above desk walls, his eyes sought out Si Nelson's office. As he neared, he could hear raised voices and the sound of a woman sobbing. Behind frosted glass he could make out two figures standing and one seated. Si Nelson's door was firmly closed.

Will hoisted himself onto a nearby desk, swung his legs up off the floor and listened.

"Mr Jones, please calm down." Will had never heard Si Nelson so softly spoken.

"Calm down?" Came the menacing response. "You've ruined my wife's reputation. I'm going to sue you for defamation of character."

"Then we'll see you in court," Si Nelson's tone turned firm, "this newspaper is not going to retract or apologise. The story came from a very reliable source."

The door swung open to reveal Angela Dupont clutching a tissue, mascara streaked down her ashen face. The mayor was as red faced as his overcoat. He looked livid.

As he blustered Angela's innocence, Will noticed her blanch and hold out a tentative hand towards her husband, "maybe we should leave it. Surely the public will reject these allegations and it will all blow over, darling."

"Leave it? Angela, this filthy rag has used malicious gossip to attempt to blacken our family name. They *will* make a full apology."

"That wasn't our intention." Si Nelson stepped back, "we deal with facts and, as I previously stated, we will *not* apologise for airing the truth."

"You!" Mr Jones charged towards him; fists clenched.

Si was fast; positioning himself behind his desk. "Will. Call the police."

The threat of the law stopped the mayor. He glared from Si to Will, his breathing ragged.

"Bartholomew, stop." Angela shouted the words at her husband, "you'll have another coronary and then that will be on the front page. We mustn't involve the police for goodness sake!" She walked stiffly towards her husband and stroked his cheek, "you've been awfully brave darling but let our solicitor deal with this," if she were a cat, Will surmised, she would have purred, "and when he has, we'll make this rat and his paper grovel for eternity."

Satisfied that her threat had gained her the upper hand, Angela flung her fur scarf across her shoulders and made towards the door.

Mr Jones's face twisted into a sneer as he snarled at Si, "I wouldn't use your newspaper to wipe my arse. Take this as a warning – I'll be watching you."

Will ducked his head down as they stalked past towards the lifts, knocking pens from tables and kicking wastepaper bins over as they left.

"Are you coming in or not?" Si Nelson stretched his arms above his head and then reached for his stress ball. Will walked into his office, watching the assistant editor warily as he slumped down on his leather chair. "Have you brought me coffee?"

"Nope." Will was overcome with a sudden compulsion to explain, "this is my fault Mr Nelson. I should have stopped Monica; I shouldn't have recorded the conversation and I definitely shouldn't have given it to Randy."

"Ssh," Si put his finger to his lips, "don't mention the source unless we absolutely have too."

"You mean if it goes to court?"

"It won't get that far," Si's tone was brisk and self-assured, "did you see Angela Dupont's face. She's guilty alright, but she's a sly one and a damned good liar. The mayor needs to watch her, not us, eh?"

Will shifted uneasily on his feet.

Si Nelson squinted across at him, "you look like the world's about to end. Lighten up Will, this kind of stuff happens all the time, you did good."

Will opened his mouth to speak but Si carried on, "Randy told me how fantastic you are with the public. Did you know the newspaper's sales have doubled in one evening? The big boss was so elated, he promised everyone a pay rise."

"That's … good." Will was struggling to find a suitable adjective to convey how he felt.

Si's face briefly softened, "you Catholics do guilt so well. It will eat you up inside if you let it. *Don't worry.* We're all mega proud of you here. That's why I asked you to pop in."

"I can't do anymore voluntary, university is mad, final year essays looming."

"I remember it well," Si grinned, "only in my day it was free. Truth is, I ain't bothered about you doing voluntary."

"Oh?" Will stared at him, wondering if this was his cue to permanently leave.

Si spoke slowly, "I know you have to concentrate on your degree at the moment, but I have a proposition for you Will. You've impressed me, and not many people do. I'm offering you a job as a trainee *paid* reporter. I want you on my team here at News Express, when you've finished uni, when you start real life. What do you say Will?"

Chapter Twenty-Seven

The weeks rolled by and the icy grip of winter slowly melted away to herald spring with its rebirth and renewal. Buds began flowering on the trees and in borders as the temperature slowly rose and the nights became lighter. Amongst the third-year students there was relief and excitement as the end of the final term drew to a close. Lectures and seminars halted, allowing the students to use the last few weeks of independent study to finish dissertations and module essays. Ann was the first to hand in her completed work, closely followed by Evelyn and Juliette. Will and Sophie lagged behind and had no choice but to request extensions.

Sophie was sitting in the garden on a warm Sunday afternoon. Books and paper were strewn across the patio table. Her dinner plate was full of half eaten food. She was too stressed to eat, too stressed to contemplate anything other but her word count. Last night she had finally completed her dissertation and was now in the process of editing it. The grammar software installed on her PC was currently flashing an entire paragraph of work as grammatically incorrect. The spell check had picked up numerous mistakes and it seemed that she had loads of misplaced commas – everywhere. *Drat* thought Sophie, *this is going to take forever.* She was vaguely aware of a shadow falling across the glass table and looked up into Evelyn's kind face.

"You've finished it then?" Evelyn set down a tray of tea and biscuits.

"Not quite," Sophie took a sip of the sweet tea and reclined back onto her padded seat, "thank you, I needed that."

At the end of the garden, Jacob was kicking the ball between Josh and Jake. The dogs were barking and jumping around them. The scene bought a smile to both Sophie and Evelyn's face.

"He's a darling, isn't he?" Evelyn gazed at her husband with loving eyes, "I feel as if we've been married ten years instead of one."

"Jacob is lovely," Sophie agreed, "he's a wonderful role model. The boys adore him."

Evelyn straightened the books into a neat pile, "have they heard from their father?"

"Not for a few weeks … but I'm meeting Mum for lunch tomorrow so I'm sure I'll hear all the usual excuses."

Evelyn frowned, "are you sure you won't come on the art gallery trip, Sophie? You've almost finished your work and there are plenty of spaces left."

"I still have an essay to tie up as well as this dissertation," Sophie shook her head, "no, I can go there anytime. I want to do well, Evelyn. I'll be so thrilled if I pass this degree. Andy mentioned there could be better job prospects for me if I do."

"Did he?" Evelyn smiled, "I'd like to meet him."

Sophie's high-pitched laugh had the boys staring at her, "we're just friends," she countered.

"Hmm," Evelyn teased, "have you got a picture of him yet?"

Sophie rolled her eyes, "he's sent me tons of photos on WhatsApp," she fished in her bag for her phone, "I think this is my favourite though."

Evelyn took her phone and stared down at the picture of a handsome man dressed in climbing gear, with a snow-covered mountain as a backdrop.

"He looks very nice," Evelyn used her fingers to zoom in on his stubble-lined face.

"He is, I mean I wasn't sure about him when I first met him, but now I've got to know him I've realised he's good and sincere and he's kind."

"All the things Ryan's not," Evelyn cast her a rueful look.

Sophie sighed, "Ryan is … weak. That's always been his problem."

Evelyn patted her hand, "and you've always been strong. I just don't think you realised it."

* * *

The following morning, Sophie was at the Learning Centre by eight o'clock.

"You're keen," a librarian who was struggling with the door lock appraised her.

"Mad, more like," Will shouted, ambling towards them, "Hi Soph." He enveloped her in a warm hug then carried her books as they limboed underneath the metal barrier.

"Did you finish it?" Sophie swung her bag onto a vacant table and draped her cardigan over one of the seats.

"No. Still half a chapter to do."

"Will!" Sophie stared at him with wide eyes, "it's due in today. You won't be able to ask for an extension on the extension."

"I know," Will shrugged, "I was up half the night with Esme. She just didn't want to sleep and Hema was exhausted, so me and my princess made fairy cakes at two o'clock this morning. Want one?" He flopped a Tupperware box on the table.

Sophie took a cake out and took a hearty bite. "Oh, these are good."

"Here," Will slid another across the table, "Mum said you're to have two because you've been working so hard you've lost weight."

"Your mum?" Sophie was puzzled.

"She saw you at the supermarket, said you were racing around like someone demented."

"That sounds like me at the moment." Sophie agreed.

"Me too. So, Mum said you're welcome round ours any night for tea."

Sophie blinked, "your mum is an angel, Will."

Will nodded, "you have no idea."

Sophie pulled his arm, "so let's nip over to the canteen, get some caffeine and chocolate and smash these final essays."

"Not forgetting the dissertations." Will dumped his belongings and followed her out.

"Looks like that's the trip to the art gallery," Will pointed to a large group of people waiting outside the main reception. "There's Ann."

"Let's go say hello," Sophie tucked her purse inside her jeans pocket and waved at her group of friends.

"Hi guys," Melanie bounced towards them, pigtails flapping, "have you changed your minds?"

"Unfortunately not," Will responded, "still haven't finished."

"Speak for yourself," Sophie elbowed him playfully, "I'm almost done."

"You'd better get working then," Ann wheeled herself towards them, "no slacking off to the refectory."

"We're just going to get drinks," Sophie hugged her, "have a great time. Where's Jules?"

"Where d'you think?" Ann thumbed backwards where Juliette stood, her arms wrapped around Ben Rivers midriff.

"Those two are so cute, aren't they! So, Evelyn will you be back for tea?"

"I should think so dear, but Jacob suggested we have a takeaway."

Sophie nodded her agreement, "well, have a great time and please send me pictures." Will and Sophie waited for them to board the coach before making their way to refreshments.

As Sophie was waiting for the drinks machine to chug out her cappuccino, her phone beeped. It was a cryptic message from Andy, **'settled down at last.'** and then an image began downloading.

Sophie swallowed, *was he actually sending her a picture of a romantic interest?*

Why shouldn't he? A voice inside argued, *you're only friends anyway.*

She watched the flashing cursor manoeuvre in a three-hundred-and-sixty-degree circle, before an image of an adorable dog appeared on the screen. Then another message appeared, **'meet Bonnie, my Labrador puppy.'**

Quickly Sophie replied, **'she's gorgeous! Xx'**

Damn! She hadn't meant to put kisses. That could convey she had feelings for him. It was too late, the text was sent. Sophie stuffed her phone away out of sight and went to pay for her drink and confectionary. Then it was back to the Learning Centre to boot up their laptops and knuckle down to writing about literature.

Four hours and twenty minutes later, they were both finished.

"Are we done?" Will scratched his head in disbelief.

"We're done," Sophie beamed with delight and stamped her feet with happiness, "that's it; undergraduate degree complete!"

Sophie's finger hovered over the print button, "are you ready Will?"

"Yep. Let's do this." They pressed print in unison and watched the paper begin filtering out of the machine.

"Now you wait for your results," a passing librarian commented.

August seemed a lifetime away.

Will stretched his arms, rubbed his neck; sore from bending over for too long.

They sorted their papers chronologically, inserted them into tidy wallets and clipped them into place with their personal student details.

"Let's get outta here." Will swung his rucksack over his shoulder and with one last nostalgic look around the vast library, they made their way out into the glorious May sunshine.

* * *

"So, it's only two weeks until the prom," an excited Melanie sucked a mouthful of coca cola through a straw, "have you all figured out what you'll be wearing?"

Ann, Evelyn and Juliette exchanged blank looks.

"I've been too busy," Juliette admitted, "but I'm sure I can dig something out."

"Dig something out? You're not going to a funeral, Jules. You should all be thinking big flouncy dresses, sparkles and glitter. Tell me Sophie hasn't let me down?"

"I think she's forgotten about it too," admitted Evelyn, "we've all be snowed under with work."

Melanie reached across the table for the salt pot, "but now it's time to party. Your essay writing days are well and truly over."

"On the contrary," Ann bit into her burger, "mine has just begun."

"Oh yes, sorry Ann I keep forgetting you want to be a lecturer," her eyes widened with excitement, "when you're staff, you'll get to go to the prom every year."

Juliette's ears prickled, "the lecturers go too?"

"Of course," Melanie grinned, "and the notetakers. Didn't Ben tell you?"

"I just presumed that it was a student thing."

Melanie chuckled, "oh you are in for a treat. Talking of delectable treats ..." she trailed off as Ben walked towards them.

"Ladies," he smiled, "did you enjoy the gallery?"

"Excellent," Ann replied.

"The perfect way to end a term," Evelyn added.

Ben's eyes moved from Juliette to Evelyn, "how is your book faring now it's out in the big wide world?"

"Good so far. I received my first royalty cheque and the reviews have been coming in," Evelyn blushed with happiness, "I'm talking at the local library next week."

"Very good, Evelyn," Ben sounded impressed, "maybe one day I'll be analysing your novels on one of my modules."

Evelyn blushed even more.

"What are we doing for the next three hours?" Ann glanced at her watch.

"It's free time, whatever you want to do. As long as you're back at the coach for four o'clock."

"How about shopping?" Melanie suggested. Ann and Evelyn nodded their agreement.

Ben squatted next to Juliette, as the others began chatting amongst themselves.

"Are you okay?" He pushed a curl off her forehead.

Juliette gazed at him longingly, "I'm good. Especially now that you're here. What would you like to do for the rest of the day?"

"More sightseeing. There are some fantastic places to visit here. We could go on a boat trip. Alone?"

"You mean sneak off?" She whispered.

"Exactly that."

Juliette scraped back her chair, placed her small hand in his larger one, "see you later, ladies."

"Erm Jules," Melanie grinned at them both, "prom dress shopping Saturday. Women only. Put it in your busy diary, okay?"

Chapter Twenty-Eight

Sophie was meeting her mum at the new French restaurant at one o'clock. At twelve forty-five she was still waiting in the queue at the student registry, with her work clutched in her hand. On their walk across town, Will had told her about his scoop and subsequent job offer at News Express.

"This is so exciting," Sophie exclaimed, emitting a half yawn, half grin, "sorry, I'm exhausted."

Will yawned along with her, "me too."

"Next!" A bored looking admin clerk stared at them.

Sophie walked to the counter and passed over her final essays and precious dissertation.

"Have I filled everything in okay?" She chewed on her bottom lip.

The admin clerk sniffed, "everything seems to be in order. Sign here please."

Sophie scribbled her signature, waited for her receipt and then stood back for Will to be served.

She arrived at the restaurant five minutes late. Sophie had rushed across town, arriving at Nikkita's damp with perspiration. The waitress informed her that Ms Fletcher hadn't yet arrived. She gave Sophie a glass of sparkling water and directed her to a red velvet waiting area. Ping! Another message arrived in her inbox – it was Andy again, sending more puppy photos and then she received a message from Melanie, informing her of a girly prom dress shopping day planned for next weekend. Sophie's toes tingled with excitement as she tapped it into the diary section of her phone. The door pinged open and a lady backed into the restaurant pulling a pram. She was followed by another, similar looking, older woman. Sophie glanced surreptitiously at them. How odd to be wearing fur coats on such a warm spring day.

The head waiter hurried over and greeted them in an obsequious manner which had been lacking when Sophie had entered the restaurant.

"Ms Dupont," he crowed, "how wonderful to see you again, and may I say how beautiful you are looking this fine day."

The woman with the beehive hair simpered, "thank you Françoise," she offered him her hand and he swept her across to the best table in the room. The younger version whom it seemed was called Agnetha, was left to lift her child out of the pram and then squash the contraption into position right next to Sophie's feet. She applied the brake with a resounding click, almost flattening her toes in the process.

"Don't mind me," Sophie mumbled as she scrolled through Facebook.

Françoise was back, questioning how long the rest of her party was going to be. "We can't keep the table for any longer than twenty minutes," he was obviously unhappy with her reply that her mother was frequently late.

"Take me to the table and I'll order a bottle of wine," Sophie said, decisively.

Françoise raised his nose in a haughty salute and led her to a table laid with a lantern and fresh roses. He wedged her firmly underneath, ensuring no escape, at least not until the bill was settled, and then offered her a gold edged decorated drinks menu. Trust her mother to choose the most ostentatious restaurant in the whole of Chattlesbury. Sophie would have been happy with an Eddies Fast and Tasty Burger. She coughed as she glanced at the wine prices. She had heard there was a worldwide Prosecco shortage, but this was ridiculous. Twenty pounds for a bottle that she could buy in a supermarket for less than a tenner? *No thank you,* thought Sophie, opting instead for a nice sounding bottle of Chardonnay. The head waiter opened it with a flourish, poured a tiny amount into the glass before bowing theatrically and backing away to offer more sycophantic flattery to the two women and the baby at the next table.

Sophie immediately filled her glass with more wine and took a sip. The conversation from the next table floated over towards her and, feeling sublimely relaxed, Sophie sat back and eavesdropped.

Françoise sounded almost orgasmic as he described the hot smoked salmon and the mouth-watering seabass, not to mention the plump moist prawns. Sophie expected Ms Dupont to be throwing her head back and squealing with pleasure at his sensual sounding prolonged discourse. She eventually decided upon the succulent sole for her and her friend and a banana split for the young child. Francoise drifted away and the woman with the big hair began complaining of her morning.

"It's been utterly horrendous," she drawled, "News Express are determined to ruin our reputation. What can we do, darling?"

"I'd love to get my hands on whoever dug up this story."

Sophie sat up a little straighter. *Will,* she thought, an image of his angst-ridden face as he explained about his scoop and the subsequent fall out, floated in her thoughts.

"Your father must never find out the truth," Ms Dupont lowered her tone, "at the moment he believes it all to be lies. We have to tread very carefully."

"Me?" The younger woman's lip turned up into a sneer, "aren't you worried that he'll kick you out, Mother?"

"Aren't you worried he'll disinherit you?" Came the barbed reply.

"None of this is my fault, Mother. I didn't ask to be born. If you hadn't acted like such a harlot, I'd be rightfully his ..."

Sophie hid her gasp with her napkin.

Ms Dupont slammed her glass down, sloshing liquid onto the table. "I'm going to hire a private investigator and find out who leaked the story."

"It could be anyone!" Her daughter scowled, "how many people have you confided in over the years whilst drunk? Whom exactly have you told?"

Ms Dupont squinted, "I've told a few close friends of course. A couple of trustworthy household staff. And I think a few family members might know."

Sophie bit back a laugh, slid down her seat and reached for her phone.

"Christ! You may as well have written the article yourself," Agnetha balled her napkin in fury, "we need to approach this in a different manner."

"How darling? This is hopeless."

"By gaining public sympathy," her eyes lit up as ideas began forming, "a jealous possessive husband. A brute of a father. We could come out of this as the victims."

"What about Monica?"

Agnetha's eyes narrowed, "what about her? There is no way my half-sister is getting her hands on my inheritance. I have a plan, Mother ... this is what we'll do."

Sophie listened wide eyed as her fingers underneath the table typed out a quick message to Will.

'That expose you told me about? It's all true. You don't need to worry Will. You don't need to worry at all."

* * *

Almost half an hour had elapsed and Sophie had almost given up hope of her mother showing up. Feeling irked, she called Françoise over and asked for the bill.

"Madam will not be eating?" He eyed the half empty wine bottle.

"There must have been an emergency ..." she began to apologise, but the head waiter looked at her with such condescension her hackles rose and she stopped speaking abruptly.

"So *just* the wine for madam?"

Sophie pulled out a crisp ten-pound note, by way of a reply, "keep the change," her sweet smile mocked that there would only be a penny for smarmy Françoise.

As Sophie was slipping her arms into soft cotton sleeves and preparing to leave, her mother burst through the door. Yvonne rushed over, mouthing apologies and informing her in an emotional high pitch that Ryan and Derek had been involved in an automobile accident.

"Are they okay?" Sophie asked.

"The paramedics were called, but thankfully it wasn't serious and they didn't need medical treatment," Yvonne snatched off her sunglasses, throwing them down onto the table, "they were arguing over the radio station of all things. Went over a hill, straight into the back of a parked vehicle."

"No injuries?"

"Just a pair of bruised egos," Yvonne clicked her fingers for staff attention. Françoise scurried over, kissing Yvonne on both cheeks before passing them the food menus.

"Soup of the day is French onion," he declared.

Yvonne ordered another bottle of wine and then disappeared to the lavatories. She returned reeking of perfume and her make-up had been carefully reapplied. She glanced over her daughter as she sat back down.

"Since when did you stop wearing lipstick? And eye make-up too?"

Sophie took a bite of the complimentary bread, "for a while now. I've been so busy with uni and work it's just not been on my list of priorities."

Yvonne surprised Sophie by complimenting her, "you never needed that muck anyway. You've always been naturally pretty."

"Thank you," Sophie sipped the fruity wine, "how are things with Derek?"

Yvonne grinned widely, "Derek is a darling. We've been together almost a year now and I'm happy, Sophie," she fiddled with her rings, "I know I haven't had much luck with men but this feels different ... it feels right."

"I'm happy for you Mum," Sophie said with sincerity, "and how is Ryan?"

"Even better news. Ryan," Yvonne paused for effect, "has landed a job at a secondary school helping in the P.E. department."

"No way!" A spray of wine showered out of her mouth as she coughed.

"Steady on," Yvonne looked at her pointedly, "finally he's dragged himself out of his self-pity and depression. He's even started helping around the house."

"Ryan doing housework?" Sophie almost laughed.

"He's only washed up once," Yvonne conceded, "but it's a start."

"Well that's good ... I'm glad he's sorting himself out."

"And I'm glad Anthony's sorted himself out too." Yvonne unfolded her napkin, "there. We can both be charitable."

"Yes we can," Sophie agreed firmly, "all this bitterness and anger, it's no good, is it Mum? I think we both have learned to let go of the hurtful past and look forward to a positive future." Sophie reached across to take her hand, "and I do love you Mum, isn't that what life is all about?"

Yvonne nodded, "of course it is darling and I love you too. I've been unbelievably selfish and I'm sorry for that. I'm glad you've found your Dad again. I'm glad you're happy and I'm proud of you Sophie, you're not just a pretty face."

They chinked glasses, "here's to love and happiness and cleverness. Long may it continue."

Chapter Twenty-Nine

"Kids! Go get washed and dressed," Juliette scrubbed at the grill pan then placed it on the drainer, along with all the other utensils she had used to serve up breakfast. "Do we have to?" Harry plodded into the kitchen, a tiresome look on his face.

"Absolutely, you have to," she pointed at the wall clock, "you have exactly ten minutes before your dad will be here."

He hoisted himself onto a breakfast stool, pulling on the sleeves of his too large, plain blue top.

"Where are your Spiderman pyjamas?"

"I'm too *old* for Spiderman, Mum," he grumbled.

"Okay," she replied, "well maybe we can buy you some footie ones then."

There was no reply, just the sulky face of a pre-adolescent boy staring down at the floor.

"What's up?" Her tone was crisp, "don't you want to go to your dad's?"

"It's not Dad ..." he was cut off by the arrival of a whistling Molly.

"Look. I can whistle with two fingers now," she popped two digits in her mouth and emitted a piercing noise.

"Ah," Harry's hands were over his ears, "make her stop."

"And where did you learn that?" Juliette gazed down at her daughter when she had finally run out of breath.

"At school of course," Molly rolled her eyes as if it were obvious, "we've been practising in the playground."

"I bet the teachers just love you," Juliette mumbled, stroking her daughter's soft golden hair.

"Charlie's cutting my hair today," Molly beamed, "that's why Harry's miserable."

"Your hair? But you've always loved it long honey, are you sure?"

Molly's head bobbed quickly up and down, "I'm having a bob. They're in fashion now, Mum."

"Oh." Juliette touched her long red locks.

"Charlie said for Christmas she's gonna put highlights in, too."

"Maybe I should speak to Charlie first," Juliette thought briefly of Marty's new girlfriend; a bubbly cockney who was nice enough. "You guys are really growing up, huh?" She opened her arms and they both rushed forward to hug her.

"So Molly will have her hair cut," she said to Harry, "it won't take long and then you can ask Dad to do something that you like."

"I suppose so."

"Go and get ready," she shooed her children in the direction of the bathroom, dried her hands and then followed them down.

"What else have you got planned for this weekend then?" Juliette perched on the edge of the bathtub.

"We're going fishing." Molly lathered soap on her face and began a slow series of circular movements.

"Daddy's taken up fishing?" Juliette was surprised by this revelation.

"Yep. He caught a trout but then he put it back."

"No, he didn't, silly," Harry waved his toothbrush at his sister, "he just said that 'cause you were crying. He fried it in a pan really and then ate it with some chips."

"Harry," Juliette cast her son a warning look but Molly's thoughts were already racing ahead.

"Can we have a fish Mum? We don't have any pets and Lucy's got three dogs and a rabbit."

Juliette sighed, "that's because Lucy lives in a big house with a big garden. It wouldn't be fair to coop a dog up in a flat and a rabbit would be far too messy, Molly."

"But a fish would be okay, Mum?" She looked at her with wide innocent eyes.

"Maybe," Juliette conceded.

"Ben promised he'd take us to the Safari Park. They must have goldfish there."

"He did?" Juliette couldn't remember that conversation.

"Goldfish are silly," Harry splashed water over his face, "they just sit there in their bowl doing nothing. I want a big dog that I can play ball with."

"Ben's got a dog," Molly said, "and when we move in with him, we'll get to take Heathcliff walks and cuddle him."

Juliette froze, *woah,* she thought, *had her daughter overheard her talking about the subject with her sister?*

"We're not moving in Molly," Harry eyed his sister with disdain. "Mum's just his girlfriend. We're staying here forever."

"Do you like it here?" Juliette passed her son a hand towel.

"Nope," came Harry's reply, "the neighbours are loud and it smells funny."

"I want a garden," sighed Molly.

"Me too," Juliette said, firmly. "I'll let you in on a secret. We're not staying here forever because *I* am going to be a teacher and earn more money – remember? And then we can leave and live somewhere pretty like ... Evelyn and Sophie."

Harry punched the air with excitement.

"Will Ben come too?" Molly's eyes were wide with excitement.

Juliette felt a longing stir deep within her, *yes, yes,* she wanted to shout. Instead she winked and said "maybe."

"That means no," Harry retaliated.

"It means," she looked at them lovingly, "I want to be absolutely sure that you like him enough for us to live with him. Imagine it – he'll be there with us all the time!"

"That's okay," Molly shouted, "I think Ben's really nice. He reads me stories and he tells funny jokes and ... and he's the handsomest man in the whole world."

Juliette laughed, "I agree with the last bit Molls."

"Ugh," Harry shook his head.

"What about you, Harry?" Juliette regarded her son with serious eyes, "do you like Ben? Would you like to live with him?"

Harry thought for a moment, "yep. Ben's cool."

Juliette high-fived her children and then the doorbell rang and she hurried to answer it, beaming with happiness.

* * *

"Do I have to wear a dress?" Ann was sitting in the passenger seat of Melanie's car, watching the vehicles in front slow down at a set of red traffic lights.

Melanie pulled up the gear stick with a crunch and grinned at Ann, "hell yes!"

"But I prefer trousers," Ann grumbled, "I haven't shaved my legs since the winter."

"You wear trousers all the time," Melanie commented, with a shake of her head.

"I wear jeans," Ann corrected, "a trouser suit would be more modern – don't you think?"

"No Ann. I'm thinking sequins and tulle skirts and satin shoes, glitz and glamour – that's what prom is all about!"

"Maybe at secondary school," she mumbled.

"What was that?"

"Nothing. Look," Ann pointed to the green light and the empty road in front of them.

Melanie slammed her foot on the accelerator and they shot forward. "Is it the next right?"

"The second right and then the first left."

Melanie switched lanes and indicated, "I hope Jules is ready, we're late as it is."

"There she is," they peered through the windscreen, at a figure waiting at the corner of the street. Juliette jogged towards them, opened the back door and slid in with a cheery hello.

"Please tell me you're going to wear a dress." Melanie looked over her shoulder before pulling away and re-joining the traffic.

"Of course," Juliette clicked her seatbelt into place, "and my sister's warned me not to pick my usual black."

"I agree," Melanie said, "colour would look good on you, especially with your striking hair." She turned up the radio and they relaxed back, prepared for the hazardous journey to Birmingham.

An hour later, and two detours around the massive ring road, Melanie parked outside Celebrity's Bridal and Prom Wear. Evelyn and Sophie were already there, leaning on Jacob's car bonnet, drinking bottled water and fanning themselves. A round of hugging ensued and then Jacob left, reminding them that he would be back after he had 'done a spot of shopping.' Juliette gazed at the mannequin in the window, who had been dressed in the prettiest puffed out wedding gown.

"Isn't that beautiful," Sophie gushed, linking her arm through Juliette's.

"Proper princess," Juliette agreed, "Molly would love it."

As they entered, a bell tinkled overhead and a shop assistant looked up from her magazine and smiled.

"We're looking for prom dresses," Melanie said, taking charge.

"Come this way," the smartly dressed assistant introduced herself as Helen and led them through the bridal section of the shop to a large room full of rails of dresses.

"My word!" Ann exclaimed, "they certainly have plenty of choice."

Helen asked if they would like a drink.

"We brought our own," Melanie lifted up a carrier bag, "is that okay?"

"That's fine," the shop assistant smiled, "I'll leave you to browse, but give me a shout if you need any help or advice." She went back behind the counter and resumed flicking through her magazine.

"How many bottles did you bring?" Evelyn asked Melanie.

"Just four." She opened the bottle of Prosecco and poured the fizzy wine into five plastic cups, "I can have one glass and then I'll go on the pop."

"Evelyn and I brought nuts and crisps," Sophie emptied her bag onto a nearby table.

"And Molly and I made butterfly buns," Juliette opened her tin and they all eyed the cakes hungrily.

"My contribution is sausage rolls and onion bhajis," Ann slapped the ready to eat packets down.

Melanie gave everyone a cup of wine and held hers aloft, "here's to prom dress shopping. Cheers."

"How about this one?" Melanie held a frilly peach dress aloft for Ann's inspection.

"Yes, it would suit you, *Melanie*," Ann smirked and sipped her wine, "I've never drunk this early before. It's not even ten thirty."

"This is a celebration for finishing uni," Melanie reminded her, "you've all worked so hard. You especially, Ann."

The curtain on the changing room swished back and Sophie stepped out. There was silence as they all perused the long white gown with the tight bodice and high leg split.

"No?" She revolved on the spot, "I kinda like it."

"It's okay if you're going to a celebrity wedding I suppose," Ann sniffed.

"Yes, it is a bit over the top," Sophie disappeared back behind the curtain.

"Have you spotted anything you like?" Juliette asked Evelyn.

"Yes," Evelyn tugged a dress off the rail, "isn't this beautiful?" She ran her hands down the periwinkle blue lace.

"That is gorgeous," Juliette replied, "try it on."

"Where's the black section?" Ann asked, shaking her head at a pink monstrosity that Melanie had picked out.

"Black?" Melanie frowned, "how about navy. This." She picked off a bodice covered with sequins and matching silk skirt.

"Come on Ann," they went into the changing room, leaving Juliette alone to rifle through the red section.

"So, we're all sorted," Sophie was sitting cross legged on the floor, munching her way through a bumper bag of Dorito's, "red for Jules, Blue for Evelyn and Ann, purple for Melanie and gold for me."

"Crikey we've been here hours," Ann gawped at her wrist watch, "Sam and Jon will be worried, I should message them."

Juliette hiccupped, "we've drunk all the wine."

"Definitely time to go then."

As they were collecting their belongings together, Sophie addressed the group, "I've decided to ask Andy to accompany me to the prom."

"Andy from work?" Juliette scooped a handful of rubbish into a black plastic bag and tied the handles.

"Yep. Just as a friend," Sophie quickly countered, "I was going to ask Mum, but as you're all bringing men, I thought ..."

"I'm bringing Tasha," Melanie corrected, "remember her? Curly hair, beautiful, my girlfriend."

"What I mean is you're all bringing husbands and erm ..." she looked at Juliette, "partners."

"I think that's a lovely idea," Evelyn rubbed her arm, "and I'm looking forward to meeting your friend."

"So, shall we go home?" Ann wheeled towards the door.

"Back to Chattlesbury," Juliette said, with a smile.

* * *

"Grr I hate wearing ties," Will pulled the offending item of clothing from around his neck and threw it onto the bed.

"Let me," Hema said with a sigh. She stood on tiptoe and wound the tie back around his neck, "there. Perfect."

"In fact I hate wearing suits," Will looked at his reflection and then pulled a face at Hema who was looking also.

"Better get used to it, Mr Journalist," she slapped his derriere playfully then dodged away from his grabbing fingers.

"Are you going to get dressed," Will surveyed her, standing there in her bra and knickers, "or shall we go back to bed?"

"I want to get ready alone," she replied, pushing him towards the door, "go see if our daughter's okay."

With a last furtive stare at Hema, Will left the room, closing the door softly behind him.

Downstairs the kitchen was in carnage, "woah. What's going on in here?" Will gazed in disbelief at his dad, who was covered in flour.

"We're making fairy cakes," Max replied, bouncing a dishevelled looking Esme on his hip.

"Okay, but where's Mum?"

"She's dashed round to Brenda's. We ran out of eggs. You look nice by the way."

"Thanks," Will replied, "I suppose I had to make an effort for my one and only prom."

The door swung open and Flora dashed in, puffing and panting.

"Brenda's entertaining," she explained, "so thankfully I had an excuse not to stay and chat. Here." She placed a box of eggs in Max's free hand and turned to appraise her son, "you look very handsome. Are you ready to go?"

"Hema are you ready?" Will looked at the ceiling and hollered.

They heard the creak of the stairs in response. A moment later, Hema stood in the doorway.

"Wow!" Will's draw dropped towards the floor as he gazed at his glammed-up girlfriend, "you look amazing."

"Thanks," Hema giggled, then spun round so they could see the low cut back on her sparkly dress.

"Let me take photos of you both," Flora was already reaching for her camera and encouraging them to huddle close together. After Flora had finished snapping, they kissed Esme goodbye and then clattered outside into the warm evening sunshine and Flora's freshly valeted car.

* * *

"Jules you look amazing!" Marie was standing on the bed, squirting lacquer into her sister's hair, "Dr Rivers is going to be blown away."

Juliette stared at her reflection. She hadn't been sure about the dress. When she had tried it on in the shop it had seemed too provocative, too clingy, too wanton, too red. But now, with her hair and make-up done, it looked perfect.

"Mum, you look like Ariel," Molly clambered onto the bed and began jumping next to her aunty Marie.

Marie took her hands and they bounced in unison.

"I'll leave you to have fun," Juliette said with a smile, "are you sure it's not too much?"

"It's beautiful. You're beautiful," Marie cried, tears glistening in her eyes, "I should have been a beautician, huh?"

"You certainly have an eye for colour," she blew a kiss at them both and then went in search of Harry.

"You look fit, Mum," came Harry's verdict. Juliette kissed him on top of his head, slid into her silver shoes, picked up her sparkly handbag and then waited for her prince.

The doorbell rang five minutes later.

"I'll go," called Harry. Juliette was standing up, folding washed clothes into the ironing basket when Ben walked in and her breath caught in her throat. He was wearing a black suit, bright white shirt and the most gorgeous satin tie she had ever set her eyes on. His gold cufflinks gleamed, his shoes shone, he smelt divine. They both spoke at once.

"You first," he grinned, and her stomach flipped over.

"You look so handsome," she drifted towards him.

"And you are breath-taking," he whispered, taking her in his arms, "are you really mine?"

Juliette stared into his dark, stormy eyes, "I'm yours."

"I suppose we should go then, but Juliette later ..."
"Later." She promised, holding her hand out for his.

Chapter Thirty

"This is fantastic, isn't it?" Sophie shouted in Andy's ear as the speaker next to them blared pop music. She looked around at the sports hall which had been transformed into a prom palace for the evening. Hundreds of balloons bobbed around the room, disco lights bounced off the polished floor and flashed across the beautifully made up tables.

Andy gave Sophie a big thumbs up, "it's great. The food wasn't bad either."

They had just finished a sumptuous three course dinner and were drinking the table wine which had been liberally distributed.

"I'm getting a pint. A real British ale, want one?" Andy stood up, fumbling for his wallet.

"I'm okay with wine thanks," Sophie gazed up at him.

He went round the table, asking the others if they wanted another drink. Ben went with him to the bar. As soon as they had left, Juliette grinned and spoke into Sophie's ear.

"He's lovely."

Sophie watched his retreating figure, "he's nice," she agreed.

"He's hot," Melanie shouted. "Now why don't us girlies go dance?"

Ann was spinning on the dance floor, making everyone laugh with her crazy arm movements. Evelyn was hugging and bopping with Sophie, and Hema, Melanie and Tasha were jiving in a circle round their handbags. Juliette stood apart from the group, spinning on her own. She waved at Wilomena Smythe and Brian Hodges and at Leon Broome, the Head of the Student Union. *This is it*, she thought, *this is the end of university.*

Melanie shimmied over to her, "what are you gonna do now Uni's over, Jules?" She hollered.

"I've been accepted onto a primary PGCE," she replied, "I start in September."

She was telling Tasha about the course when she felt a tap on her shoulder. Thinking it was Ben she spun around, a huge smile on her face. When she saw who it was, her smile slipped, transformed into a frown.

Helena Mulberry's blonde hair was piled high into a lopsided chignon, her foundation was way too dark for her skin tone and her lipstick was smeared. Juliette looked down at the bottle she was carrying and felt pity for her.

"Hi. Are you okay?"

"I'm drunk," Helena replied, swaying.

"I don't want any trouble tonight," Juliette held her hands up, her eyes scanning the room for Ben.

"No trouble. I just wanted to say s-sorry," Helena hiccupped, "I've been a real bitch to you."

"Okay," Juliette nodded.

"I was wrong about you. What I said about you and Ben. It wasn't true. He's in love with you, any fool can see that. And I don't think he's ever been in love before with anyone, including me."

"I'm sure he's had previous girlfriends," Juliette said, smoothly.

"I mean here at university. You're different, I can see that now and I wanted to apologise for giving you such a hard time." There was a pause, Juliette looked down at the floor, "can you forgive me?"

"Yes. Of course," Juliette smiled, "I hope that you can be happy and I wish you well."

"You're an angel," Helena pulled her into a rough embrace, "thank you."

"Everything alright here?" Ben looked over to Juliette with concern.

"Everything's fine," she replied, hooking her arm around his waist.

"I was just apologising to your lovely *girlfriend*," Helena smiled at them both, "you make a beautiful couple. So I should go, more wine to drink, more people to annoy." She touched Ben's sleeve, "it's good to see you so happy." She turned away, vanishing in the throng of dancing staff and students.

"You sure you're okay?" He stroked Juliette's cheek.

"I'm fine," she replied, "and I'm having the best time. Now you, mister, can stay on the dance floor with me."

An hour later, almost everyone in the room was on the dance floor doing the 'cha cha slide.' Andy had Sophie in hysterics with his fumbled attempts at dancing and then suddenly the music stopped. The lights were snapped back on and people started filtering back to their seats. Leon Broome hopped up onto the stage, microphone in hand.

"Sorry to interrupt your dancing folks," he paced the stage, "I just needed to make an announcement." All eyes were on him. "As you probably know, I'm the head of the Student Union and I have the honour of presenting an award each year. For the past two months, student union members have been voting for their graduate of the year award and we have a clear winner with five thousand one hundred and sixty-six votes." He paused as an impressed gasp resounded around the room, "this year's award goes to a lady who is thoroughly hard-working and super clever. She's managed to bag straight A grades for *all* of her essays." An appreciative murmur chorused throughout the room, "she's also participated fully with university life; involving herself with demonstrations and contributing to the debating team."

Sophie, Juliette, Evelyn and Will grinned at a shocked looking Ann.

"She's an outspoken member of Chattlesbury University, who can at times be controversial, but she's not afraid of standing up for herself and others and she's brave, really brave. This lady is disabled but she doesn't let that stop her from excelling and achieving her goals. Her friends describe her as fun, witty, intelligent, ambitious *and* with a heart of gold. She aspires to be a lecturer herself, hopefully one day here at Chattlesbury university. So, raise your hands ladies and gents and give Ann Stokes a humongous clap for winning Graduate of the Year."

"I can't believe this," gasped Ann, "is this really happening?"

"It's happening," echoed Jon with a proud smile.

"Jon, will you come ..."

"Of course," he stood up and pushed her to the front of the stage. The main light focused on her and momentarily blinded, Ann shielded her eyes. Jon stood back as Leon Broome came bounding over.

"Here she is," he shouted into the microphone, "well done to a very worthy winner. We have here our graduate of the year plaque," he held aloft a wooden shield with Ann's full name etched across the middle and surrounded by silver stars. He bent to kiss Ann on her cheek and handed her the plaque, which she stared down at with wonder.

"We also have high street vouchers to the generous sum of three hundred pounds." The envelope slipped from his perspiring hands, floating onto Ann's lap.

"Thank you," she mumbled.

"Can I give you this?" Leon offered her the microphone.

"Okay," Ann took a deep breath and took it from him. "I'm actually speech-less," she began, "and totally unprepared of course. Firstly, I want to thank whoever put my name forward for the award.

Melanie waved and wolf whistled.

"And a big, big thank you to everyone who voted for me. Leon mentioned that I'm brave, but so is every other student here. So is anyone who tries to better their lives through education. Studying for a degree isn't easy and we should all be applauded for devoting three years of our lives to whatever subject interests us. For me it was books, and I've loved every minute. I've made some great friends who will stay in my heart forever," she glanced over at her table, where the women were dabbing at their eyes. "This is a great university and I've learnt so much, not just about books but also about friendship and loyalty and love and life. I've had a blast. I've literally had a ball. Thank you everyone."

Ann burst into tears and the room exploded into deafening applause. Staff and students pushed back their chairs and rose to give Ann a standing ova-tion. Some of the younger students even hopped up on the tables and began cheering. Ann looked towards her table of friends, and they rushed towards her, enveloping her in warm hugs and tender kisses.

* * *

They were all on the dance floor again, this time to cheesy eighties pop music. Will shook his head at the sight of Ben and Juliette bopping away exuberantly, "you guys are so embarrassing," he mouthed with a slap to his forehead and a skulk off the dancefloor.

Then the lights were dimmed again and the music slowed down in tempo. The dancefloor was heaving, but Juliette was only aware of Ben, as he spun her around and cuddled her close.

"This is perfect," she said dreamily against his shoulder, "the perfect end to three years of study."

Ben pulled back slightly and regarded her flushed face, "are you okay?"

"I'm extremely happy and a little bit tipsy. How are you?" Her hands fluttered over his back, moving in soft circles.

"Sober and feeling rather nervous."

"Why?" She murmured, snuggling against his chest, "what's wrong?"

"This," he clutched her left hand, stroked her fingers, "this is what's wrong."

"What?" She shook her head in bemusement, "what are you talking about?"

Suddenly he dropped down on one knee, took her hands and gazed up at her.

"Ben …" Juliette squeaked, as realisation of what he was about to do hit her.

"Juliette," he said in a serious tone, "from the moment I saw you I've loved you. You've captured my heart Juliette and I wondered … what I'm asking is … damn this is difficult."

"Yes," she spurred, vaguely aware that the music had stopped and people were staring.

"Will you be mine forever, Juliette?" He fumbled in his jacket, took out a small box which opened to reveal the most exquisite solitaire diamond. He grinned, his heart racing, stomach-flipping grin, "will you marry me?"

The question hung in the air, people were gasping and whispering but Juliette stood still and silent, savouring the moment. She stared down at him, this gorgeous man who had turned her world upside down and knew there would only ever be him.

"Yes." She nodded.

"Yes," She hollered. "Ab-so-lutely, yes. Yes. Yes. Yes."

Ben scooped her in his arms, "I want to take care of you for the rest of your life. You don't ever have to be alone again."

Juliette touched his face lovingly, "and I want to take care of you right back."

"Mrs Rivers," he leant his forehead against hers as the crowd cheered and balloons and glitter were released from the ceiling net above them, falling softly to the ground.

August …

Evelyn woke up at four thirty with a burning desire to write. She slid silently out of the warm bed and pulled on her dressing gown, careful not to wake the sleeping form of Jacob lying next to her. Once downstairs she clicked on the kettle and let the dogs out for their early morning reprieve. As the teabag stewed in the hot water, Evelyn fired up her laptop and looked through her notebook. Only two chapters left to write, which she calculated in word length as a couple of thousand. Her publisher had given her Christmas as a deadline. Evelyn was pleased that she would be finished in plenty of time. Time to relax over the festive season and begin a fresh project in the new year. She added milk and sugar to her drink, stirring it until the tea was just the right colour she preferred. Dark brown or commonly known as builder's tea. Evelyn sat down at her table, opened Word and wiggled her fingers in preparation.

She was lost in the valley of Llandriff, with Luella and Byran as they fought their last battle against the mighty dark forces of Ranglan, when the kitchen door creaked open and Sophie wandered into the kitchen, yawning.

"Sorry," Sophie whispered, "I didn't know you were writing. Just let me grab a drink and I'll leave you in peace."

"It's all right," Evelyn replied, saving and closing her document, "I've finished for the day."

"But it's only six thirty," Sophie opened the fridge and poured cold milk into a cup.

"Yes, and I work better first thing in the morning," Evelyn replied, "the afternoons are for editing."

Sophie regarded her friend, "you're amazing. How many followers do you have now on Twitter?"

"Last time I checked it was just under ten thousand," Evelyn snapped her laptop shut, "social media can be very distracting though."

"It's important for you to build a fan base," Sophie said with a smile, "don't be afraid of modern technology. Not everyone on the internet is a baddie, Evelyn."

"And not everyone is my friend either," Evelyn sighed, "you're right of course, I should devote more time to marketing."

"You need to be more pushy," Sophie held her hand up, "that's all I'm saying."

"What are you doing up so early anyway? Couldn't you sleep again?"

"I'm still suffering from jet lag," Sophie plonked down on a vacant seat, "it seems to have bypassed Josh and Jake though."

"Children are resilient," Evelyn passed her the half open packet of chocolate digestives, "was it wonderful?"

"Hong Kong was ... just unbelievable." Sophie nodded vigorously.

"I was worried you wouldn't come back."

"I *was* tempted to stay. Being with Dad and Barry again was lovely but my heart belongs to Britain."

"Good to hear it," Evelyn stretched.

"Why don't you go on back to bed," Sophie suggested.

"Have you forgotten what day it is, Sophie?" Evelyn's eyes were round with excitement.

"Monday? The worst day of the week?"

"It's graduation day Sophie – remember?"

Sophie shot upright, "crikey yes. We passed our degrees and today we get to officially celebrate."

"I'm so nervous my legs are shaking," Sophie said to her friends as they waited backstage for their names to be called. "Meet me outside by the fountain?"

"Yes," replied Ann, "we need to take photos."

Will was the first one up. Following a line of others, he climbed the steps onto the stage, squinting as he perused the audience.

"Will!" Hema's voice caught him unawares and he stumbled over his shoe lace. He looked around, found her in the audience with Esme in her arms and his mum and dad waving frantically. Will grinned, raised his hand and then took the proffered degree certificate from the Dean of the university.

"Very well done," the man in the posh cloak and hat shook his hand and then that was it, he crossed the stage and walked down another flight of steps, back to his graduate seat at the front of the auditorium. He watched his friends: Juliette, Evelyn, Sophie and Ann collect their degrees amongst the many other students who were there to celebrate passing three years of hard study. The Dean made a long speech and then the graduates were led out first, to the sounds of a live orchestra.

"That was amazing," gushed Sophie as her black cloak flapped around her. It was a windy day, they had to hold onto their hats to stop them from blowing off.

"Shall we do photo's?" Jon held up his camera and they took it in turns posing in their fancy degree ceremonial gear, clutching onto their ribbon-tied parchments.

When they had finished with the photographs, the five of them sat on the wall of the fountain, chatting and laughing.

"I guess it's time for the results to be revealed," Will gulped, "good luck everyone."

"You first," Sophie prodded him.

Will stood up, untied his certificate, and stared at it blank-faced.

"Will?" Juliette asked, nerves getting the better of her.

"I don't believe this," he mumbled, "I've only got a 2.1. Yes!" He punched the air. The others whooped with delight.

"I'll go next," Juliette said, "my hands are shaking," she held her trembling fingers out. "I can't untie the ribbon." Will went to help her and she stared down at her results with tears in her eyes. "A 2.1 hallelujah."

The others clapped, exuberantly.

"I'm too scared to look at mine," Sophie said, biting her lip.

"Let's open ours together," Evelyn took her hand and they both stood up and unravelled their parchments.

"Oh my god! Oh my god!" Sophie looked as if she were about to faint, "I've done it. I've been awarded a 2.1"

"Well done!" They all shouted.

Evelyn hugged her tightly then looked down at hers, "oh my word. I have a first."

"Fantastic!" Ann and the others raised their arms towards the sky.

"Just you Ann. Just you."

They waited with bated breath for Ann to unravel hers. She nodded, tears glistening in her eyes, "a first as well."

"We've all passed with flying colours," Sophie cried, jumping up and down with Will and Juliette.

"Here's to passing our degrees," Ann shouted, gleefully, "hat's in the air, everybody?"

"After three," Juliette confirmed with a nod.

They counted down together and then pulled the hats from their heads and threw them upwards. Jon snapped his camera, taking a perfect shot of five unique people celebrating the achievement of passing an English degree, with Chattlesbury University standing majestically lit up, open and welcoming in the background.

* * *

The janitor watched the last students leaving the university.

"That's it then, Gladys, time to turn off the lights."

The cleaner put down her mop and bucket and stared around at the empty refectory.

"This is my favourite time of year," her voice was an echo in the large room.

"Mine too," Bert wiped at his perspiring brow, "anything else that needs doing can wait until the new term starts."

"Amen to that," she agreed, "who'd think that in a month's time this place will be packed full of new students, ready to learn, ready to start a new chapter in their lives and to the ones who've just finished, well Bert, their lives are just beginning, aren't they? For them it's the year of new beginnings."

"I like that Gladys," the janitor slipped an arm around her shoulder, "we could teach them a thing or two about learning, eh?"

"You're right about that, our Bert. Come on let's get off home now." She pulled the double doors closed and Bert inserted a large iron key into the lock. They walked into the warm sunshine together, heading for home, thankful that another year was over at Chattlesbury University.

Epilogue

Eleven months later ...

Juliette awoke at three o'clock in the morning. The air in her bedroom was heavy and cloy. She unfurled herself from her duvet and watched the shadows dancing on the ceiling and the curtains flapping in the breeze from the open window. The past two nights had been uncomfortably hot, not unusual for August but still, it prevented her from sleeping. Juliette turned onto her side and then her stomach. *Please let me sleep* she thought, *I do not want puffy eyes.* But sleep eluded her, replaced instead by a growing excitement, a delicious anticipation of what the day was going to bring. But for now, she needed to lie back in dream land so she pushed all thoughts aside and thought instead of the calming effect of the sea, lulling her to sleep.

Her mind, however, was suddenly occupied by someone else. She shifted onto her back, her arm spread across to the empty pillow beside her and then her legs were itching and her face was covered with perspiration; so, with a resigned sigh, she sat upright, rubbing the last vestiges of sleep from her eyes. Juliette swung her legs off the bed and tiptoed across the floor. In the mirror she caught sight of her reflection. Her pale skin looked luminous in the moonlight, her hair looked wild and unkempt. It tumbled down her back, almost touching her waist. *No wonder she was hot with all this thick hair!* She tied it into a ponytail, picked up a discarded t-shirt of Bens and pulled it over her head. It clung to her skin, outlining her curves, the hem skimming the top of her bare thighs. Across the landing she padded, her feet sinking into the plush carpet. Juliette opened a door, peeped her head inside to see Harry cocooned inside his summer duvet, fast asleep. She went to the next door, carefully opening it without making a noise. Molly was upside down on the bed, pyjama clad legs splayed on her pillow. She too was fast asleep, her chest rising and falling rhythmically.

Satisfied that her children were okay, Juliette went downstairs, into the kitchen, where Heathcliff raised a sleepy head and looked her way with adoring eyes. Her hand was in a tin, offering him a biscuit, which he took greedily. As she crossed the kitchen, he hauled himself out of his bed, following her around as she prepared herself a cup of tea. It seemed wrong that she was alone in Ben's house. While he was spending the night at his friend's Brian Hodges, Juliette had the four-bedroom detached to herself to leisurely prepare for one of the most significant days of her life: her wedding.

She sat at the table, sipping the tea and looking around at the spacious kitchen, so different from the one she had left behind. For three months now she had been living here and she utterly loved it. At first, she had been uncertain, worried how Harry and Molly would adapt, but they had settled in without a murmur and appeared very happy in their new abode. The maisonette which she had lived in for ten years seemed a distant memory. Her old life. Before university had happened. Before Ben. When she thought of marrying him, her stomach dipped and twisted like a rollercoaster, a huge smiled formed on her face and she felt like swinging her arms on the spot and dancing a jig. She was outrageously happy. He was everything and more she could ask for in a partner and today they would be making it officially forever.

Juliette drank the rest of her tea, took the mug to the sink and swilled it underneath the hot tap. It was far too early to be up. She needed to go back to sleep. Up the stairs she went, back underneath the bed covers she slid. She switched on the lamp and picked up her half-read novel. Snuggling beneath the covers, her eyes flickered over the words and slowly she relaxed and was soon fast asleep.

She was woken by Molly, a bundle of excitement which ran into the room, squealing and shaking Juliette's arm.

"Wake up Mum, wake up!"

Juliette looked at her groggily, pulled herself into a sitting position and asked what the time was.

"It's seven o'clock."

"Seven O'clock?" Juliette shot out of the bed, "I should have been up an hour ago."

"Lazybones Mummy slept in," Molly picked up a decanter of expensive perfume and sniffed it, "can I have some of this on today?"

"Yes of course," Juliette pulled on her dressing gown, "but first, we're having breakfast."

She cooked them all poached eggs on toast, with wedges of watermelon on the side.

"Eat it all up now," Juliette shook pepper over her eggs, "we won't be eating until later this afternoon."

"Is the church service long?" Harry asked, with a sigh.

"Not too long. But you must both behave," she warned, "you can't run around in the church."

"We know that," Molly looked affronted, "does the hotel have a nice garden?"

Juliette nodded, "the hotel has a beautiful garden. Very big and colourful and at the bottom there's a lake." Molly squealed with excitement.

"Are you both okay?" She put her knife and fork down, "not too nervous?"

"Nope." Harry wiped the runny egg with a crust of toast, "you look a bit scared, Mum."

"I am," Juliette admitted, "my stomach's full of butterflies."

Harry pushed his chair back and stood next to Juliette, placing his arms around her neck in a warm hug.

"Oh." Tears sprang to her eyes and then Molly clambered on her lap and they were joined together in a group hug.

"Love you both," Juliette sniffed.

"We love you too, Mum," Harry kissed her cheek, "don't you need to make yourself look like a princess?"

"Yes," she nodded, "but first you two can have your showers and then aunty Sophie will be here to do our hair and make-up."

"Yippee," Molly bounced with excitement and followed her brother, who was charging back up the stairs.

Sophie arrived an hour later, pulling a suitcase full of makeup and hair styling gadgets. While Juliette was showering, Sophie played boardgames with Harry and Molly and frisbee in the garden.

"What a glorious day for a wedding," Sophie stared up at the azure blue, cloudless sky.

"I'm ready," Juliette hollered out of the window. Sophie and the children trooped up the stairs.

"Can I go first?" Molly asked, staring at Sophie expectantly.

Sophie lugged her suitcase onto the bed, "you can."

While Sophie was chatting to Molly about make-up colours, Harry skulked off to play his computer and Juliette went downstairs to open a chilled bottle of champagne.

"Here," she thrust a glassful at Sophie.

"hmm thank you. Aren't you having one?"

"I want a clear head," Juliette replied, sitting on the bed.

"I can't wait to see your dress," Sophie squealed.

"Mummy wouldn't show anyone," Molly pouted, "not even me and aunty Maz."

"I wanted it to be a surprise," Juliette leaned over to tickle her.

"And what's your dress like, young lady?" Sophie asked.

"White with lots of ribbons and frills. Oh, and there's sequins on it too!" Molly's eyes were shining with excitement.

"Sounds perfect," Sophie said, dreamily, "close your eyes now, sweetie," she applied some glittery eyeshadow carefully to each lid.

Juliette was just about to grill Sophie about her 'friend' Andy, when the doorbell chimed. She hurried down the stairs and opened the door to a smiling Flora.

"Your flowers," Flora held out a large box.

"Come on in," Juliette said, sweeping Will's Mum down the hallway. Flora placed the box on the table and slowly removed the lid. When Juliette saw the contents she gasped, "they're beautiful."

"Your bouquet consists of white roses and orchids. Isn't it stunning? And your daughter's posy is the same, albeit smaller. There are also carnations for whoever you want to give them out too."

"Take one for yourself and Hema," Juliette urged.

"Thank you," Flora picked two out, "I should go. Are you okay? You look really calm."

Juliette laughed, "I'm scared as hell."

Flora reached forward to hug her, "well, see you at the church then. You carry on with your preparations, I'll see myself out."

"Thank you for doing the flowers, Flora," Juliette watched Will's mum pick up her car keys, "they're perfect."

"It was a pleasure," Flora waved and disappeared back down the hallway, leaving Juliette alone to admire the pretty flowers.

"I wonder if Ben's okay?" She said to Sophie a while later. "Maybe I should text him."

"That's bad luck," Sophie replied, as she fluffed out Molly's hair, "there we go princess, all done."

"Do I look beautiful, Mum?" Molly stared up at Juliette with wide eyes.

"Gorgeous!" She pointed at the mirror, "go see."

Molly slid off the stool and went to inspect herself in the full-length mirror.

"Now while I'm getting ready, can you do something that doesn't involve getting mucky?"

"Colouring?" Molly grinned.

"No! Harry Potter?"

"Yay!" Molly shot out of the room.

"And don't rub your face Molls," Juliette called. She glanced at Sophie, "are you ready for me?"

Sophie slugged back a mouthful of champagne, "sit yourself down, bride-to-be, because *I* am going to weave my magic."

"Wow!" Juliette stared into the hand held mirror.

"Do you like it?" Sophie chewed her lip.

"I love it!" Juliette held the mirror closer, looking over the light make-up with appreciation.

"The lipstick's all day stay, so you shouldn't have to reapply. What do you think of your hair?"

Juliette stood up and went to look in the larger mirror. Sophie had clipped the front and sides up and left the back cascading.

"The flowers make it look wildly romantic."

Juliette nodded, she hadn't been sure about flowers in her hair but after caving in to Sophie's pleas, the tiny flowers looked lovely. Bubbles of excitement fizzed inside Juliette's stomach, "how long until the cars come?"

"An hour," Sophie replied after a glance at her watch, "do you need me to stay and help you into your dress?"

"No it's okay. Mum, Dad and Marie will be here soon and you need to get off home and get ready too."

"Okay," Sophie placed the last remaining items back into the suitcase.

"Thank you, Sophie. For everything." Juliette held out her arms and they embraced.

"Good luck yeah," Sophie's eyes were filling up with tears, "you deserve this, Jules, I've never seen two people so in love as you and Ben. Be happy."

Juliette nodded, feeling too emotional to speak.

"Bye guys," Sophie blew kisses at Harry and Molly and then clattered down the stairs.

She opened the door to Juliette's family, walking up the drive. They exchanged hugs and pleasantries, then Sophie was back in her car, heading for home.

* * *

"It's time," Marie called up the stairs, "we need to go."

Next to her, the photographer and video recorder vied for a space to capture the first appearance of the bride in her dress.

Juliette's Mum, Violet, appeared at the top of the stairs, looking resplendent in a cream dress and feather topped hat.

"Is my daughter ready?" Frank asked.

"She's ready," Violet replied, "come on then, love."

They waited with bated breath for Juliette to appear. Slowly she walked out of her bedroom, across the landing and smiled down at the waiting group of people. Her dress was exquisite; a long ivory tight-fitting crepe dress with a scoop neck and sequined hem and bodice. She heard them gasp as, carefully, she made her way down the steps with her long veil trailing behind her.

"You look ... you're exquisite," Marie's mouth hung open in shock.

"You look like a million dollars," her dad held out his arm, "shall we?"

"Let's do this," she said, beaming at everybody, "where are my children?"

"We're here, Mum," Harry darted out of the living room, looking so handsome in his suit and cravat, it made Juliette's heart swell, "you look ..." he trailed off, his eyes widening as he gazed at her, "like an angel."

"Like a princess," Molly corrected from behind him, "you're a princess, Mummy."

"Who finally found her prince," Marie finished.

* * *

They arrived in Castleford thirty minutes later. Juliette waited a while in the vintage Rolls Royce, taking deep breaths. She could see the guests making their way into the church and wondered if he was already inside and if he was okay. Or was he a bundle of nerves, like her? The driver hopped out and opened the door.

"Are you okay?" Her dad asked, holding out his hand for her to step down.

Juliette nodded, placed her shaking hand in his and stepped onto the tarmac. Her dress swished behind her and Marie, her only adult bridesmaid, rushed to put it straight.

"Are you ready to get married, sis?"

"Try and stop me," Juliette smiled for the photographer, took her dad's arm and walked steadily towards Ben's uncle's church.

His uncle was waiting just inside the church door, dressed in his religious robes. He smiled broadly when he saw her.

"Welcome Juliette," he said warmly, "welcome to the family."

"Thank you," she leant forward to peck him on his cheek. Then she looked behind her at her excited children, "ready kids?"

The music started, the congregation stood and looked round as Juliette floated up the aisle, passing candles and flowers and pews decorated with ribbons. People were murmuring and staring her way, wide-eyed. She caught snippets of what they were saying as she walked past, "Beautiful" "Stunning." Then she saw him, and the whole world dwindled away.

He was standing with his back to her at first, tall and lean, his back ramrod straight. Then he turned and their eyes met and Juliette's face matched his grin as she quickened her pace towards him. He was staring at her as if he'd never seen her before. A look of total shock on his face as his gaze traversed over her. As she neared, she drank in the sight of him; his cleanly shaven face, his carefully combed hair – so different from his usual tousled - just got out of bed - look. Juliette stopped walking, her heart racing as she gazed through her veil into his eyes. The music stopped and the service began.

They listened to the most beautiful speech about love and God and light. Then the congregation stood and sang the hymn For the Beauty of the Earth. Ben stuttered through his vows, she had never seen him so nervous. When it came to her turn, she spoke confidently and clearly.

"Juliette wanted to add a few lines onto her vows," the vicar said with a warm smile.

She cleared her throat, "I choose goodness, I choose light. I choose kindness and love. I choose truth and divinity. I choose Jesus, a million times over. I choose you for eternity Ben Rivers, I choose you." She gazed at him and saw love etched across his face. As the vicar pronounced them to be husband and wife, Ben lifted her veil and kissed her lips tenderly.

"This is forever," she whispered "I love you so much."

* * *

The five of them were sitting on a low wall in the hotel grounds overlooking a serene lake that sparkled in the moonlight. Will, Ann, Sophie, Evelyn and Juliette in the middle.

"This is the most awesome wedding," Will said, leaning back and dripping champagne over his tie.

"I didn't think I'd ever organise it in time," Juliette leant her head on his shoulder, "it's been perfect."

"It's been divine," Ann agreed, which was high praise indeed. "Will we be able to order photo's as a memento?"

Juliette nodded, "yes of course."

"I've had an idea," Sophie declared, standing up, "speaking of mementos, why don't we make our own?"

"Huh?" Will slurred, "what are you on about?"

"I mean," Sophie began with excitement, "why don't we make a video like we did in the first year remember? Our video of who we were and what we wanted to achieve. Why don't we do it again?" She stood up and swept her arms out wide, "we can take it in turns. We can use my phone again."

"I've an even better idea," Juliette called the wedding videographer over and explained what they wanted to do.

"Great idea for a keepsake," he nodded, "who's going to go first?"

"I will," Sophie smoothed down her dress and stared into the camera. "I'm Sophie and I've been on such a journey."

"We all have," shouted Ann.

"First of all, I graduated. I'm the proud owner of an English degree and I'm currently half way through the Hanley and Hanley's graduate management scheme." There was a series of whoops. Sophie waited for them to abate before continuing, "and personally I've done heaps. I've got a divorce," she raised her glass, "I've bought my own house in the same street as my dear friend Evelyn.

I've found my Dad again, after all this time and wait for it ... I'm officially together with Andy from work. And I'm happy, so happy." The others cheered as she sat back down.

Will took his place in front of the camera, "pleased to say I, too, have successfully passed an English degree and I'm a fully qualified journalist." He slugged back more champagne, "I'm Will by the way and I'm moving to London, the big city, to work on a daily newspaper."

"What?" Ann squealed, "way to go, Will!"

"What about personally?" Sophie shouted.

"I'm with the most beautiful girl," he continued, "her name is Hema and she's decided to restart her dreams of becoming a social worker. I have the most perfect daughter. Esme starts nursery next month." There was a chorus of ahh's, "life is pretty perfect at the moment." He sat back down on the wall with a thud.

"My turn," Ann said. The videographer swung to face her. "I'm Ann and I got a first," she yelled, scaring the birds out of the trees above them, "I got a bloody first and I've started my masters. And my home life is ... well let's just say I'm very content. I have a son called Samuel who lights up my world every day and an awesome husband who loves me just the way I am. I'm in the process of adopting a second child – a girl called Ruby and that's about it, folks." The others cheered.

"Your turn, Jules," Sophie pushed her to her feet.

"My names Juliette," she began clearly, "and today I married the man of my dreams. I have two beautiful children," she paused to touch her stomach, "and another one on the way."

"What?" Sophie burst into tears.

"Yes folks, I'm four months pregnant, which is why I haven't been able to drink *all day*," she pulled a face, "this child is going to be so loved, *that* I can guarantee. And professionally I'm an English graduate and a fully qualified teacher. I passed the PGCE course and have my own class in September." There was a thunderous round of applause. Then silence descended.

"What about you Evelyn?" Sophie asked gently, "what are you up to now?"

Evelyn's face shone with happiness, "hello my names Evelyn and I'm a writer. My second book is due out anytime now and I've had numerous short stories published in magazines. I completed an English degree and met the most amazing people," she looked around at their faces, "my dear, dear friends. And basically, I'm very, very happy." She dabbed at her eyes and then the others surrounded her, hugging and kissing each other.

"A toast!" Sophie cried, "to friendship."

"To hope." Evelyn sniffed.

"To happiness." Ann added.

"To success." Will hollered.

"To love." Juliette beamed.

They held their glasses aloft and shouted in unison, "to dreams!"

* * *

Juliette was on the dance floor, in his arms, swaying to the soft beat of Labrinth's 'Beneath Your Beautiful'.

"Are you okay?" Ben's words were muffled against her hair.

"Just perfect," she swooned.

Gently, he touched her stomach, "how's our baby?"

"Sleeping," she hooked her arms around his neck, "have I told you how much I love you?"

"Ditto," he pressed his nose against hers, "I love *you*, Mrs Rivers."

He moved back slightly to call two little people over. Harry and Molly skidded onto the dancefloor. Ben swung Molly into his arms and Harry clutched onto Juliette's dress. They revolved on the spot, while outside, fireworks popped against the backdrop of a silvery sky.

"This is so romantic," Hema slid her arms around Will who was bouncing Esme on his hip.

Will kissed his daughter softly on her forehead.

"Daddy ... princess," she gurgled, pointing to a luminous Juliette.

"Yes, sweetheart," he looked across at his friend, "maybe some fairy tales are real after all."

THE END

Dear reader,

We hope you enjoyed reading *The Year of New Beginnings*. Please take a moment to leave a review, even if it's a short one. Your opinion is important to us.

Discover more books by Julia Sutton at
https://www.nextchapter.pub/authors/julia-sutton

Want to know when one of our books is free or discounted for Kindle? Join the newsletter at http://eepurl.com/bqqB3H

Best regards,

Julia Sutton and the Next Chapter Team

You could also like:

The Lake of Lilies by Julia Sutton

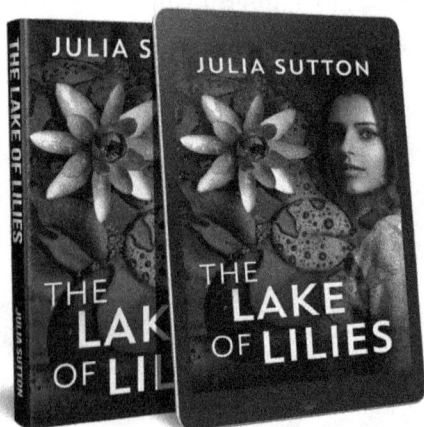

To read the first chapter for free, head to:
https://www.nextchapter.pub/books/the-lake-of-lilies

Note from the Author

Thank you for purchasing The Year of New Beginnings.

I hope that you have enjoyed reading it and all the other books in this series ?

If you have enjoyed this book, I would be very grateful if you would leave me a review on Amazon or Goodreads. Reviews help with exposure and make us authors feel all warm and happy.

So wow, I've finished writing about Will, Sophie, Ann, Evelyn and Juliette. My writing journey has only just begun though. I have lots of ideas for new projects, but for now I just want to say a big thank you to my readers and good-bye, School of Dreams!

About the Author

Julia Sutton was born in Wolverhampton in 1972. Julia loves spending her time writing, reading all sorts of genres, drawing, walking and watching movies.

CPSIA information can be obtained
at www.ICGtesting.com
Printed in the USA
BVHW070946040920
588121BV00001B/114